For Linda and Beverly

Part One
Chapter One

As a teenager Lenny Boles was unremarkable in every way possible in a place where even average implied mediocrity.

At school his teachers gave him barely passing grades for no better reason than getting him gone, getting him out of their classes. And on the field his performance was no better, lacklustre at best, his embarrassed coaches always putting his sorry ass on the bench. He was a failure at all that he tried, an underachiever drifting through his teens when other boys were competing for recognition and scholarships that would ensure a good life and get them forever the hell out of Troupe County.

Where he might have excelled was with the girls, in another more forgiving time and place. He was 5'10" with passable good looks, slim, blessed with curly dark brown hair, liquid brown eyes, a pleasant smile, an easy manner, and they liked him well enough. The thing is, through no fault of his own, Lenny was the unfortunate son of simple folks not as well off as others in town. They had nothing much they could give him, despite doing their very best, what with the little if any wisdom they might impart from their own narrow minds, teaching him right from wrong as best they could. Leastways they tried, they supposed.

Still, when the other boys would sit in class wearing nicer britches and shirts and polished shoes, riding nicer bikes with more money in their pockets for Cokes with their gals after school, Lenny walked the mile to school the days that were dry. Other days, when ceaseless rains poured down, his pa would get him there in the truck. And girls being girls, Lenny spent most of his first three months of high school leading to the Christmas dance alone.

And in a town of ten girls for every eight boys Lenny stayed home in his room that special evening; he was ashamed. He didn't have a girlfriend, or a suit, or extra money for splurging on a burger and fries after the dance, even if he did have a girl he could impress with nice words and smooch with on the porch, which he didn't.

When summer came he stayed at home helping his pa mend broken furniture. That's what folks did in the day; then came grades ten and eleven with unfamiliar awakenings and feelings and Lenny hadn't yet touched a live girl like the pretty ones he conjured up most nights when he was sure his ma and pa wouldn't walk in on him. But by his last year at school all that had changed.

He was eighteen and, even though by then his pa had scraped and saved enough to buy his son a practically new bike that would suit his purposes just fine, Lenny continued walking that mile every day. Except those unwelcome times when he would peddle his way through puddles and along slick roads, shivering under his raincoat with wind and rain splashing against his reddened face when the other boys had flashy new cars. He hadn't driven with his pa in a very long time.

Problem was, in those flashy cars were girls; pretty girls waving and giggling and blowing kisses as they passed him by, making one rainy Friday in Troupe County the defining moment in Lenny Boles miserable existence.

The next day he asked his pa for a few minutes to do his urgent business. When instead he hurried inside and robbed a quarter from his ma's savings jar that she wouldn't likely notice, something he'd been doing for a year with enough saved in his own hidden jar to get himself by bus to the next town and back.

On the Sunday, telling them he was going into town on his bike cause there was a picture show he wanted to see, he went to the bus stop where he leaned the bike no one would want against a pole. An hour later, give or take, he stepped off the bus into a life he could in no way envision. For if he had Lenny might have stayed home that fine day. Maybe.

Instead he was ambling along one sidewalk and down the other, doing what was all-important, following the plan he'd been thinking on for some time with as much precision as he could recall. He was familiar with the place well enough, having been there on occasion with his ma and pa, and he knew mostly in his head what he should do.

Sauntering into the drugstore he walked the aisles, stopping at a rack of sunglasses with his head down and his high school cap tugged on tightly over his forehead, proceeding when he was ready toward the cash not particularly nervous cause he was confident; he'd thought this through night after night since Friday. In a few minutes he would have enough money to buy himself a car, the one he'd seen and wanted badder than a ready dog wants a bitch that was his for 495 dollars.

When the cashier saw the glasses on his head she smiled kindly, folks did back in the day, all polite and friendly, asking for the tag and holding out her hand, taken aback when he passed her a badly scrawled note explaining the gun in his pocket that he wasn't the least fearful of using.

Was he sure? Wasn't too late, boy. That's what she told him. He could put them down and scoot, or pay what was owed. The cost was 12.99 plus tax. Something he might think on before getting his sorry self hauled off to the county jail.

He shook his head. Not talking was part of his plan. No, ma'am. He sure did have the 12.99. But better yet he had himself a plan. So yes, ma'am. He was sure. He surely was.

She shrugged, opening the till, seeming as how that's what he had fixed in his mind.

The town bell hadn't yet chimed the noon hour and what was in her tray wasn't at all worth agitating the boy. She even wrapped the thin stack of bills with a band before stepping back, folding her arms and shaking her head. She'd been a teacher for nigh on thirty years and wasn't about to let herself be intimidated by some smug country boy thinking himself smarter than he was.

When he was gone, headed toward the park, she called the sheriff at the jailhouse before telling her boss who was busy with a customer at the back of the store what had happened.

Hurrying along the sidewalk, headed for where the bus was waiting, and would for another ten minutes, Lenny wasn't thinking he would find the doors of his refuge closed and the driver enjoying his lunch at a picnic table while reading his Sunday paper. Instinctively, using his wits, Lenny chose another table that was shaded from the street by trees where he reversed his school windbreaker inside out, disguising himself, sitting with his head down and counting his money that was, as near as he figured, a disappointing 217 dollars. But he wasn't at all discouraged. He was eager. His plan had worked once and surely would again. There were other stores in other nearby towns and now he had his very own money that would get him wherever he needed to go.

*

One cop came from behind with the pharmacist, another directly toward the thief with the guard on his holster unclipped, a hand on the grip of his revolver and his thumb on the hammer. That the kid was wearing the glasses with the tag dangling against the side of his head didn't mean he didn't have a gun.

"So Lenny, what ya'll bin doin'?" The cop asked more as a matter of introduction. "Might wanna put that there money on the bench, son, and the shades along with it. Ain't no spendin' bein' done here today. Leastways not by ya'll, boy."

Lenny's head jerked up, twisting left and right. Lurching sideways in a futile bid to escape, the cop's gruff hand grabbing at his collar from behind.

"Yer in trouble, boy, real sticky shit. Should've listened to the good lady and gone home."

"I'm sorry. Truly, I am. You can take it back." He gave the first cop the glasses. "I won't do it ever again. I promise, sir."

The cops didn't think so, the pharmacist agreeing.

Instead he was being shuffled through park, down the street toward the station: the town's news event of the week.

Long story short, though not the last sad chapter in Lenny's life, he got eight months in juvie. He lost his year and never returned to school cause he didn't need an education; he had other plans, better plans that made more sense with each passing month given his recently acquainted real-life mentors and their considerable and meaningful influence.

When he got out he was nineteen and there wasn't a single eye in Troupe Country that did not look down on Lenny Boles, not a mouth that did not curve into a smirk when he drove his pa's beat-up truck into town. A situation badly in need of remediation to his way of thinking. He needed out; he had outgrown Troupe County, the folks, his ma and his pa. He needed a real town, a big town where he could get things done the way he wanted.

With that firm resolve embedded in his thinking he made his way to Lafayette, a nothing town forty miles farther west where he found work washing dishes in a 24/7 diner, earning enough money to spend his night off in Birmingham some two hours away, once in every while taking his favourite waitress with him. Other times hooking-up with a mutually needful young woman in his favourite motel bar.

Until his last night in Lafayette months later when again he made his way by bus to the Montgomery motel. He paid upfront for the room like always, put down a few beers while getting himself ready for a connection, and sat by the window killing time by observing the goings-on.

The gal, whoever, wouldn't show until later. The gals never did; neither did he. Gals, the smart ones anyway, they needed options. So did he, all fancied-up in his one suit, white shirt, his tie and running shoes. But what he did see was some guy from somewhere in Georgia park down the way, stumble out of his flashy sports coupe, empty the trunk as fast as he could manage and get himself inside with some middle-aged woman his full bottle of Jack Daniels wouldn't make pretty anytime soon.

And the guy stayed inside, Lenny thinking he was either having a good time or passed out drunk. Not seeing much of a difference either way. What he kept seeing was the white sports coupe gleaming purple under the flickering vacancy sign with the engine running, purring louder the closer he got. Half an hour later he was pulling up in front of a dance bar, the one he'd heard tell was the city's most popular.

An hour after that he was connected with a gal one year younger who was all aflutter at the twenty-something guy from Atlanta inviting her for a few drinks and dinner. He was in town on business and even had a hotel room, which he mentioned in case, which he was certain would come after dinner and a few more drinks since most Alabama gals of an age were agreeably amenable.

He suggested a restaurant he could hardly afford, but she was young and had the looks, a step above, something he wouldn't ever snag back at the motel and the evening was in its infancy. Soon other guys who could actually afford her would flood into the place, real business guys who could put her into a real hotel bed, and he'd be up Shit Creek.

Leaving the lounge for the restaurant Lenny was guessing she was more like eighteen, for what it mattered. Whatever she was, she wasn't any twenty-two.

Helping her into the passenger seat, slamming the door shut, he hurried to the driver's side and slid in beside her. Reaching across, thinking he would kiss her, anxious to taste those rosy pink lips that were smiling at him so invitingly, her sparkling eyes confirming that, oh yeah, she was ready for a real good time, the spell was instantly broken by the flashing electric blue lights behind him practically blinding him through the rearview mirror. The cop swinging his door open, and his partner at the girl's door, were both armed and taking no chances.

"Ya'll must be the god-damnedest stupidest butthole I ever did see, boy. Git yer dumb ass out. And you, missy, ya'll do likewise. Hear?"

"Mister Officer, what've I done? We was just leavin' fer a bite, is all."

"This yer vehicle, boy? You Mister Gus Leblanc? Is that what yer sayin'? Cause ya'll don't look like no six-foot black man, the one whose rightly real pissed with ya'll fer stealin' his pride and his joy."

"No, sir. But he did lend me the keys fer the night, fer me and my gal here. He did, I swear. I didn't steal nothin'."

The cop chuckled, more at the girl's disgusted expression than at the idiot he was patting down, reaching into Lenny's jacket for his wallet, swinging him around, pushing him brusquely onto the gleaming hood and cuffing him. The other cop, speaking with the girl, called to her partner that one Miss Priscilla Knots was seventeen and a juvenile. A few moments later a cop standing by the cruiser blocking the coupe added that she was a Montgomery runaway missing for several days.

Lenny's cop guffawed. "This here is what we might call a life-changin' experience, Lenny boy from Georgia. Looks like ya'll gonna be stayin' in this here Alabama fer a good long while."

"I just met up with her, Mister Officer. Told me she was older. Ain't my fault she lied. She don't look like no seventeen in the least way and we was just goin' fer a quick bite is all."

The other officer left with the girl, crossing the street,

walking through an empty parking spot between two cruisers and into the police station, Lenny Boles realizing exactly how royally he had fucked-up once again.

He spent the night in jail, appearing before a judge the next day wrinkled and mussed, learning he would remain in Alabama four years, doing time at the Elmore Correctional Facility north of Montgomery for grand theft auto. Because an uninterested defence could not prove misdemeanour joyriding and the female judge displayed no patience toward a Georgian dimwit who was intent on causing mischief in her town and inflicting grievous harm upon a young Alabama girl.

Though the years did pass quickly. Elmore was easy time, doing canteen work and eventually earning the privilege of walking and picking up after the warden's dog most fine days. Lenny Boles liked dogs a good bit, but wasn't much interested in books or learning things he didn't have a need to know, books written by rich folks, the words most of which he didn't understand anyhow. He didn't see the point, is all.

What he did like was having friends for the first time he could ever recall, all 1176 of them, most inside for doing something stupid like Lenny albeit several notches smarter than the new boy who, the more he heard and learned, spent his nights on his top bunk creating in his mind a living dream he would one day make real. He would finally be someone important, better than all them folks back home.

And when that glorious day did come, he left Elmore with 1461 dollars in his pockets cause he didn't smoke, play poker or drink on account of booze was a luxury beyond his dollar-a-day income and he had a more important ambition for his considerable earnings.

He hadn't cut his hair in six months, making his first stop a Montgomery barber. His second was outfitting himself in black leather boots and black leather pants, a crisp white shirt that was whiter against his darkly tanned skin, a black leather jacket and racing gloves. Then he boarded a bus headed for

Atlanta, much wiser, equipped with know-how and definitely no longer the dumb-ass country boy of days gone by. He was twenty-three and serious about his future. This time he would do good, he would become someone.

When he arrived in the biggest city he had ever in his life seen, he set himself up in a motel where his friends in Elmore told him. He paid for a week in advance and that first night began work as a confident entrepreneur forging his way into a good life and making his name mean something.

*

He wouldn't borrow anymore cars or steal plastic sunglasses; those days were over. The guys back in Elmore, they were right. They all wanted the very same thing that wasn't smokes or booze. What they wanted, what they all shared an urgent need for, was the sweet scent of a female and in that part of town there were plenty of fellas whose only possibility of inhaling that rousing fragrance was pulling over and paying for the taste of it. That's what they told him at Elmore, that's what he needed. They also told him not to get in anyone's way, to negotiate. "Payin' a reasonable sum was beneficial and a shitload better'n not breathin' bro." Be cool. Talk straight with the man.

He knew what he should do and where he should go. What he wanted was a Priscilla Knots: Young and impressionable, lost and confused, eager for someone to take them in and love them. What he didn't need or want, they told him, was any bagged-out skank surviving on ten-dollar BJs and doing enough of them each night to keep themselves drugged-up and believing till waking in some dump the next day that they weren't just sewers in spiked heels. That's if they weren't just dead. Which didn't mean his girls wouldn't need their minds in a relaxed state, promoting good relations. Uptight girls were not good for business, which was Lenny's first order of business, making that all-important contact.

He hadn't ever done drugs before, his first experience a

goodwill freebie with assurances they could do good business if he didn't mess-up and think to go his own way. He agreed, waking the next morning curled into a ball on a damp bathroom floor, although that much smarter and promising never again.

His second night in Atlanta proved equally successful, this time with a girl from somewhere he didn't care a hoot about. That's what they told him: Never care, never get close. These girls, they weren't like other girls, they were investments. So choose the best and manage them; treat them right till they stop producing.

He bought her a meal and brought her to his room where they spent their first night together, Lenny quickly and agreeably ascertaining that she would do fine for him. She was attractive, young and shapely. More importantly she was amenable; she understood how she could quickly make money in a way that would hurt no one, so that she could move on some day and make a good life for herself. No worse than having a few more boyfriends like the ones she left behind. And better yet, she would never ever have to go home.

On his third night he put her to work and when she came home to sleep alone on the dank sofa she had one-fifty in her purse. By week's end Lenny had earned over a grand, easily paying his associate a third off the top for more product and renting a furnished flat by the month. By the end of her second week she had doubled her earnings and Lenny rented an adjoining flat, eagerly extending his operation. And by the end of his first month in Atlanta Lenny Boles had three girls and nearly six grand in his mattress, kindly buying his street nymphs come-hither outfits for day and night cause he wanted them clean and looking fine. That's what the associate told him: Keep the girls looking prime. Do not mess with your investments.

By the end of Lenny's first year he had several other girls, twelve in all who loved and adored him, who each had an apartment of their own to live and work in. He was on the road to his dream in a shiny black Mercedes sedan with a quarter mil in the bank and an uptown condo.

What he never did again was drugs. What he bought he bought for the girls, rewarding them, giving them well-deserved moments of pleasure. He gave them Sundays off, days when johns were at home with their loving families, and the week between Christmas and New Year's when he treated them to a full week in Vegas. He was treating them right, managing his investment, but increasingly his associate was urging him to do more. A quarter mil was peanuts. He could bring in ten times that much the coming year, do them both some good. What was the point in just supplying his girls to take the edge off? Made no sense at all. The girls, they could do double-duty servicing the clients in a way that would keep them coming back big time.

Which is how Lenny began his second year, by February hiring an accountant who would manage a growing concern and by March he owned a doughnut shop.

By mid-summer life was good and getting better each day. He was in the big league. He had money, respect, and for his clients he had the best women, booze and drugs. He was the one to go to for a good time and the word got out. But near the end of June he made his first personnel change. His third girl was rapidly declining in her abilities, her last few clients telling Lenny she was too pissed or high to be any good, that they weren't paying the big bucks for a limp body and a sloppy mouth.

So he took her one bright and sunny Saturday on a day trip to Savannah where he fell in love with the city at first sight and left her there with a grand in her purse and her entire wardrobe in a designer luggage set. He was taking care of her, assisting with her transition and certain she would do just fine on her own. There wasn't no need for tears, he told her. His partin' with her wasn't nothin' personal. She possessed an abundance of street smarts, her body still greatly appealin' to a needful man's eyes. She just wasn't good for his business no more, is all.

He hated leaving her, he surely did. He liked her and she loved him. But now he had to fill the gap, maintain his revenue stream, something he'd been thinking on for a couple of weeks now, musing on how he would best take care of the girl. Something else that wasn't good for business. He didn't need some out-of-town hooker working her own corner, stealing his potential clientele.

Chapter Two

Kansas City, Missouri wasn't anyone's idea of excitement. Certainly not for a nineteen-year-old girl who had never travelled farther than four hours east to St. Louis where she would spend her long summers with her brother, helping his lethargic wife raise their eight irritating brats.

That wasn't the life she wanted. She didn't want kids or their residual lifelong scars, or for that matter a single man in her life for what would seem like a hundred years of monotony. She wanted adventure and novelty; she wanted to see and do things. So when she reached her majority, the very day she left high school behind with honours, she kissed her mom and dad goodbye and left home with a backpack and all they could afford to give her.

She wanted to travel the country, find somewhere she could settle down and find work. That was one year ago and now she was sitting under a street lamp waiting for a bus in a short plaid skirt, five-inch stilettos and a blouse that would stop traffic. Which, of course, was the entire point since no law existed in Atlanta against waiting for a bus. Despite which she never overstayed her welcome in any one place.

She was doing alright for herself, busy each night of the month save those few days she was decommissioned by virtue a young woman's natural frailty when she would shop to enhance her business wardrobe or clean her one-room apartment.

By day she would work out at the gym, never mixing business with pleasure. By night she regularly earned 50 bucks for thirty minutes in the backseat of their cars, servicing a couple of johns before going home. Or 250 tax-free dollars for a dedicated night of exquisite sex with a better class of customers, which was often the case, which brought her the most pleasure, earning her more in her first year than her work-weary dad who had spent his entire life sweating at the mill.

Her life was good and soon she would have enough saved for a downpayment on a car and, in a few years, a small home. She enjoyed what she did. She got off on the thrill, the arousal of being with different men, of their fascination with her, with her tight and lithe body, always wanting more of her, many of them repeat customers or referrals.

However she would soon increase her fee and stop the backseat specials. They were good enough to jumpstart her career, but now she was established and recognized, too highly skilled in her trade to act like a common whore. She was done with guys bouncing her on their laps, groping her breasts and mauling her bum under her skirt in some dark parking lot. She was better than that. So why not start right then and there? From then on three bills a night and a nice hotel room or don't even bother.

She had a good twenty years ahead of her, if not thirty, and worth every penny earned. She was the best, suddenly jolted from her reverie. Immersed in her own thoughts, she hadn't noticed the guy getting out, leaning against the black sedan's quarter panel with his arms and legs crossed.

"This here bus yer waitin' on could be long in comin', miss. Where ya'll headed?"

"Get lost, buddy. Not interested."

"I ain't no cop. Got no love of 'em either. The name's Lenny Boles, somethin' you should already be aware of, and what yer doin' on this here bench and the others is messin' with my business. Which I'm thinkin' ain't particularly good for either of us, ya'll most of all. So I'm thinkin' we should sit and talk things through like decent folks, speak our minds some."

"You're not a cop?"

He shook his head. "I ain't no cop."

"So you're a pimp."

He shook his head. "I ain't no pimp neither. My ladies are self-employed, free to come'n go. Ain't never touched a single one. But ya'll, uh-uh, one day soon ya'll gonna be all bandaged-up and not lookin' the least bit appealin'. Surprisin' nones beat on ya'll already."

She bowed her head staring into her lap. She probably didn't have much choice. Of course she didn't. Work for him or get the shit kicked out of her so badly no one else would ever want her. She took a deep breath, doing a good job at not being afraid.

She stood, walking toward the car. "Okay. So let's talk."

He nodded, swinging open the passenger door, watching her slide in, suggesting drinks at a quiet nearby lounge, and by the second cocktail she was convinced—partly. She would have a nice place of her own, a place for conducting business, nice clothes and no worries. He would take care of her, protect her, take care of every little thing.

"But I keep my own clients, Lenny, most of them out-of-town business guys. Five-star hotel guys. They won't like me bringing them home to a brothel. That won't work, not for me, not for them. I'll move in, I'm good with that once I see the place. But it's business as usual, my way, and Sundays are a good time for me. I don't need or want girlfriends. If you're good with that, we've got a deal. If not, I'll move on. But know this, that'll be your worst mistake ever."

He agreed, nodding, ordering a third round. "Once ya'll see the place and once I see what exactly I'll be takin' on. Ya'll look fine, but let's both of us see for ourselves the finer details."

She scarcely blinked. More importantly, if she could get herself in tight with him, do something good, what was a little peep show? "No problem. Just one thing. You and I, we're strictly business. No touching, no nothing. I also don't do drugs.

Your other ladies can do what they want, but this girl's staying squeaky clean."

He was good with that, and they shook hands.

Lucy liked the apartment. The place was clean and nicely furnished with a modern decor, a wet bar, sound system and sixty-inch flat screen. Not the usual brothel, but not her home either, more like a place to drop in throughout the week staying current with him and the ladies. That was part of the deal she would keep to herself, understanding what came next, matter-of-factly stripping to her panties and bra and turning a full circle. That was all he was getting. No freebie, no dry run.

*

She moved in the next day with a single suitcase, busying herself making the place her own before dinner and leaving for the bus stop where she didn't wait long. Ten minutes later on queue her first client of the night pulled to the curb, agreeing with her terms and conditions before driving with her to a downtown hotel for the night.

She quickly became Lenny's best decision, his most profitable resource and envy of the other ladies. She was stunning and seductive yet, despite being a lady of the evening, she emanated a natural innocence and purity which contributed to her success in no small way.

Since meeting Lenny she hadn't once paused to remember her simple life back in Missouri, she confessed during a lunch with her co-workers near the end of her first month. Her life was so much richer and wonderful because of him. She was living her dream while bringing in thousands each week, adamant she would not get involved with him and spoil a good thing despite his occasional invitations to dinner at his place. She was with him for the money, the fun and the good times. She did not need getting serious. She was too young and not interested, but she was definitely in tight with him and the ladies who treated her like a kid sister.

The building was the city's least likely brothel, Lenny's

operation mystifying even his most curious competition. The cops had no business in the bedrooms of hard-working women who ostensibly spent their days toiling for an entrepreneurial Mr. Boles in one of his three doughnut shops.

Until one evening several weeks later when she did accept his invitation, when the other eleven ladies were all preoccupied entertaining exceptionally special friends.

"Thank you, Lenny, for inviting me over. This is quite some place you've got." A politesse which fell somewhat short of an understatement. The place had a fourteen-story view of the glittering city, a wraparound patio and eclectic furnishings that were expensive but, sadly, Lenny didn't have an ounce of good taste. Lenny was a hillbilly, was and forever would be. She swirled her wine, smiling. We are what we are, Lenny Boles.

"Knew ya'll would if I kept persistin', sweetheart. But tell ya what, no funny stuff. Just a fine meal as best I can cook, a bottle of this here fine wine and could be a toke later on I'm thinkin'. Ain't like yer with a client this evenin'. Must say though, yer lookin' real fine. Makes a man's heart threaten its limits. That there is fer damn sure."

He had a point. He'd once before seen her practically naked, a spectacular image he hoped would never fade from his mind and the little he couldn't see of her now wasn't difficult to create in his best dreams. Her mauve blouse was loosely buttoned and sheer, the three-quarter mauve bra under it enhancing the swell of her breasts lightly speckled with silver dust. Her purple silk skirt was short, flared and flighty, exposing most of her perfectly shaped legs that were bare and tanned, wrapped at her ankles with the thin straps of her purple stiletto sandals. She was a vision.

She was the essence of female perfection. Long auburn tresses cascading over her shoulders framed clear hazel brown eyes, an aquiline nose and smooth full lips shimmering with clear gloss. She wore no jewellery, she never did. Not even a watch or ring. Those things were personal; they belonged to her other life and were never part of the job.

Dinner was simple. Lenny was a steak and potatoes guy unless he was paying to impress. The filet mignon was okay, undercooked in the middle, and what he sorely pronounced as pomme de terre purée aux carottes was mashed potatoes with mashed carrots, neither one steaming. The dessert was an apple pie, thankfully served with cognac that would kill the taste and moisten her throat.

"That was wonderful, Lenny. Thank you."

"Ain't the best cook, I suppose. But it fills the belly." He stood, taking her hand. "Let's sit ourselves down in the livin' room, sweetheart, after I refill these here glasses and take a moment to relieve my increasin' anxiety."

"Why don't I get the cognac while you're gone. But don't be long. I'm enjoying myself, Lenny."

"Damn straight," and he left her.

When he returned she was slouched on the sofa with her legs crossed, completely relaxed and clearly oblivious to her skirt not being of much use. She was excited about their evening culminating the way she had been hoping for weeks, always wanting to accept, to know more about him, but always hesitant to rush things, pleased with the way the evening was going her way.

Lenny changed the CD to soft and romantic, taking his glass and swallowing a good portion of what was in it before he sat.

Talk about rushing things. "Lenny, I don't dance. I hate dancing. Do you mind?"

He shook his head. "Nope. Can't say I'm any good myself, swingin' and swayin'." He sat beside her, running a cupped hand along her thigh. "I'm thinkin' we're better off sittin' here talkin'. Might take a puff or two later, mind."

She put a hand over his, halting the upward direction. "Good. I might even join you. I am a little curious and I did come expecting I would enjoy myself." She giggled. "Besides, if I don't leave soon I might be imposing myself for the night."

He squeezed her thigh. "Sweetheart, that there would be no imposition at all. Not the least bit. Now ya'll sit here while I add some to this here fine elixir." He stood, taking her glass. "Won't be but a—what the fuck!"

The snifters flew from his hands the very instant Lucy screeched in panic, her body jolting into the air, landing twisted on the sofa, quickly grabbing her skirt that in its current state served no purpose whatsoever.

The condo door was practically smashed off its hinges, six heavily armed and uniformed men rushing into the apartment in all directions screaming at them repeatedly to get down, to spread themselves on the floor and put their hands behind their heads.

Lucy clapped a hand over her mouth. She was terrified, instantly reverting to the little midwest girl wanting and needing her mom, dropping to the floor and pressing her hands tightly over her ears.

Lenny Boles stood his ground, defiant, spewing out curses and threats until one task force agent took the tirade kind of personal and dropped him to the floor, begging his pardon, and not much caring about the weeping hooker stretched out beside her pimp.

The night would be the worst in Lucy Tatum's life. She was dragged to her feet and handcuffed, the team agreeing to a man with smirks that she probably didn't need a pat-down. One of them, the biggest and seemingly the team leader, expressed his sincerest laments. But he supposed they were right. She was the prettiest thing, though, all mouthwatering and put together all sexy like. Damn shame, truth be told. Hmmm-hmmm. Damn shame.

She ignored him, forgetting her fear and snarling "in your dreams, dickhead."

Lenny was next, dragged vertical by two men and cuffed. The door of the condo he would never see again was sealed behind yellow tape and they were taken downtown and booked. Lenny was charged with operating a brothel, money laundering and trafficking, stunned when told that all his other eleven ladies had also been arrested. Seems their special friends that evening were all well-acquainted, all of them members of a six-month task force bent on shutting down Lenny Boles, his primary associate and his fair ladies of the evening.

Lucy Tatum was arrested and taken away separately for questioning about her involvement.

After an extensive debriefing with her captain and team, Detective Trisha Tallum went out with them for an evening of decompressing, celebrating their win over Lenny Boles at their favourite watering hole after first punching the big guy for earlier being less than a gentleman: her partner who would not on his life ever let harm come to her. Though she would see third-time loser Lenny Boles several times from then until their court date for sentencing when the other ladies would appear with him for due justice.

When that day came several weeks later Lenny Boles was given seriously hard time: ten years in maximum security. His associate got twelve, his accountant whimpering pathetically when the judge read aloud that he would serve two years plus a day in a minimum state facility.

The eleven ladies, due in large part to Agent Trisha Tallum's compelling testimony, were given six months of community service and would have a clean slate after a five-year parole.

Chapter Three

Lieutenant Vance Matthews was a teddy bear good cop with a gold badge that would never mean as much to him as the gold band on his finger, despite spending more hours in the week with his drop-dead gorgeous partner than his lovely and loving wife of fifteen years.

What he didn't particularly like however were the ladies' monthly Girls' Night from which he was arbitrarily excluded despite his repeated supplications and offers to pick-up the tab. Jan Jenkins was more than his partner; they were good friends, buds, except on those evenings when he didn't trust either one not to besmirch his good name and character with liquor-induced giggles and exaggerated tales out of school that he was never privy to.

He was forty-five and in excellent shape for a mid-lifer, his wife Marla at home and Sergeant Jenkins on the job equally obsessed co-conspirators in keeping him that way. Creamy doughnuts and enticing French pastries were long forgotten memories. He and Jan were homicide detectives with fifty plus Savannah murders each year ensuring they would be late for dinner most evenings, which made Saturday, October 27th all the more special.

Matthews and Jenkins were shut in several hours at the precinct finishing off paperwork that would appease the DA while Marla was doing chores at home, excited about Jan coming over that evening for dinner—alone, poor thing. She was young and exceptionally attractive, but cops seldom wanted other cops for romance that might last longer than a fortuitous tickle in search of temporary relief that was never mentioned, was soon forgotten, and so much better than doing drugs.

Get in, get out, and go home alone or whatever. But thanks, we both needed that and anything more was bad karma. Quickie affairs were always complicated given the job and most non-cops couldn't handle the male-threat or their girl acting all macho, carrying a ten-millimetre and shooting bad guys while they were at the office licking their emotional wounds and wishing for something ready and willing to assist in repairing their damaged egos.

On the job Matthews and Jenkins took turns behind the wheel of their '97 brown Crown Victoria, a chrome-trimmed tank that screamed Cops! He wore loose-fitting suits, loose-fitting shirts, laced shoes, a fedora, and preferred his outdated . 38 revolver on his belt; she wore tailored pantsuits, expensive blouses, low-heeled pumps, designer glasses, and her compact Smith & Wesson .45 pistol fit snugly on her hip inside any one of several handmade holsters that would complement her handbag du jour. She was a cop, but she was a wealthy one.

Off the job her one true love was a bright yellow mustang SVT Cobra, pulling into the Matthews' driveway Saturday evening in suede boots, dark tights, a short tweed skirt, a raglan sweater and her glasses with a girlie gift for Marla and a bottle of perfectly chilled '86 Chardonnay that would complement dinner. She was a Georgia girl through and through, a Southern belle with poise, Southern manners and a gun she was good with. Proof positive that some guy somewhere was missing the mark.

Karen's one dinner rule however, which she strictly enforced, was simple. Shop talk was verboten and chatter began at once about the women's outfits while Vance attended unnoticed to their cocktails. Then came talk about upcoming vacations and what Jan would do for Thanksgiving and Christmas, Marla making that one very clear; Vance making very clear his views on his partner's sad social status, wondering aloud when the heck Jan would get some sort of boyfriend, anyone, so that he would have something to say to someone who would listen. They looked at him, empathized with him in a way he understood wasn't the least bit sincere, and went on ignoring him.

The music was calming 50's crooning, the ambiance subdued. Marla's misoshiru soup with noodles and a salad from her garden prefacing a braised lamb and homemade sorbet was a four-course epicurean delight leading to the more relaxed ambiance of the living room and digestifs.

The women curled together on a sofa, resisting the urge to loosen a button or two while Vance served his prized Courvoisier XO with a flourish. The dark amber curative was well beyond the average detective's paycheque and palate, an occasional treat he allowed his old self and extra special guests. His old self quietly content to sit back and take in the exceptional view. He loved them gals, Marla as a lover and wife; Jan as a best friend, partner and quasi-kid sister.

He was relishing the rare evening alone with them, one without his and Jan's phones chiming simultaneously that would inevitably precede dead bodies or stand-offs that all too often spoiled Marla's sumptuous dinners. Dead bodies came with the territory. See enough of them and glibness about bullet holes in bloody chests, daggers sticking in backs or the wide-eyed shock of slit throats and blunt force trauma smashing in someone's fragile parietal bones, becomes easy if not a requisite part of the job. Just not in Marla's home anytime.

Savannah needed more good cops, she would always pout, hugging them tightly and kissing them at the door, ordering them to call her as soon as whatever and to keep each other safe from harm. But this evening was all about his ladies and he went to refill their snifters. He wasn't thinking that Sunday he would solve the city's most vicious murder. Or that by crossing paths with one Lenny Boles in a fleeting moment they would together reshape the future and desperate world of the neglected baby girl he and Jan would be useless to help earlier that morning.

Chapter Four

Marshal Baker didn't run in from the cotton or tobacco fields at the sound of his wife's hysterical screams, into a ramshackle shack, his face and brow beaded with sweat, his thin work shirt clinging to a body made hard and lean by tedious labour that oppressive day in mid-July that held such fond memories for him. Nor did he crash through the door to see his wife in much worse condition than himself cradling a newly born daughter tightly bound upon her heaving chest. That isn't quite how his day went.

Instead, once disconnecting the call, he left his ninth-floor law office dressed in Armani and Italian leather. He climbed into his Aston Martin convertible and drove to the upscale clinic where his wife Leanne was achieving her life's ambition while he sat in refined comfort containing his excitement while perusing client files and savouring a chilled Pinot Grigio. As much as he loved and adored Leanne, and he did, he saw no value in storing that particular imagery in his mind for a lifetime.

Not to say he wasn't concerned, far removed from the groaning and straining, Leanne's wide-open eyes and twisted mouth, the urging and the snarled cursing; he was, albeit confident that she was in capable hands and that each high-tech test had predetermined that the emerging girl would be absolutely perfect in every way. In spite of which, Marietta Baker was not coming easily into the world. Her apparent firm resolve to delay the inevitable, to forestall the amazing future her father had planned for her, was in fact ensuring that she would never have a younger sister or brother.

When Marshal was finally brought into the room, his joy was real despite what the doctor had told him. He made no mention of the future. What they were living in the moment, what they were seeing and holding was too special. His daughter was too special. Tears for what might have been one day would come later, if ever. The future was an indefinite space in time, never certain, and crying over such a vast unknown had no real place or purpose in the moment.

And apparently neither did he, Marshal leaving her to sleep, to regain her strength, waiting to speak more in-depth with the doctor. He was pragmatic, accustomed to dealing with sad realities each day, often dismissing a client's dreams and fantasies as being without merit.

The next day the family went home and, from the very first moment held in his arms, Marietta was her daddy's little girl. She was his pride and his joy who could do no wrong, growing very quickly into her first year of private school by which time she was fully accustomed to, and very comfortable with, the polished silver spoon in her mouth without any kind of practical barometer that would indicate how fine and pampered her life actually was. She was also by then a practiced manipulator, precocious and brilliant at getting her way.

She was pretty and would one day be as lovely as her mother with big blue eyes she could make sad in a blink. Her face with its button nose and flawless skin was a picture of purity and innocence framed with a curtain of straight blonde hair she could twist into curls with her delicate fingers as easily as she could her father around them. And that she was popular with the boys from day one, never without a willing escort who would carry her books home or walk with her to church, was the norm taken for granted by everyone.

Through no fault of her own she had learned from her father and her uncle, their friends and their neighbours, that she was a special little girl, that she was adorable and could never do wrong.

Those early years for Marietta were an innocent time of handholding, of sipping lemonade on the patio swing under her mother's watchful eyes, of giggles and furtive pecks on a chosen boy's cheek before sending him home when called in for Sunday afternoon dinner. Until the morning she woke in a panic at seeing the alarming mess she had made in her bed, calling out in a shrill voice to her mom on the verge of discovering with a gentle embrace and tender words that her age of innocence had abruptly terminated. She also quickly understood that with her lost innocence went the effusive attention. She was no longer that adorable little girl; she was simply Miss Marietta Baker.

However with high school in September, in yet another academic enclave for the children of successful fathers and socialite mothers whose main functions were the maintenance of the home, social dinners, looking the part, having a worthwhile cause outside the home and organizing benefits, came a new era that she recognized at once would necessitate upgrading her own social skillset. Ninth grade also came with a fresh influx of students she didn't know taking the place of those who had moved on to other cities or had downgraded to more affordable public schooling.

She no longer held hands; she no longer wore tunics with crests, knee socks and patent leather shoes for school. She wore short pleated skirts she would hike past her mid-thighs once out of sight, crisp cotton blouses and school ties she and the other girls would arrange under crested blazers with the undisguised intention of better stupefying the already numbed minds of the boys whose thoughts and preoccupations were even more singular than her own.

Church socials with parents looking on were passé, replaced by school dances and Saturday nights at the more convenient venue of movie theatres. Though most Saturday afternoons when her chores were done, and Sundays following the preacher's histrionic threats of eternal damnation for those who went astray of God's greater plan, she would spend hours at the lake until dinnertime with the boy she liked most that week or month.

Despite the frequent turnover of boys, those sunny and warm afternoons never varied. Girls would lay under the warm sun, acting older than their years behind designer sunglasses, their bodies greased and glistening, watching the boys acting younger than their years doing backflips off the lake's iconic boulder until hands started waving from the shore and high-pitched whiney voices began calling them to their respective eager bodies and blankets.

For newbie teens the long summer was one of exploring puzzling sensations, experimenting with newfound curiosity and clumsy temptation, Marietta's popularity and reputation surpassing the other girls' by far throughout the entire summer and into another school year.

Curiously though, when she might have felt wonderful given her enviable social status, her place on the pedestal once again secure, she did not. The previous year's ephemeral flirtations, the adolescent touching and probing, began seeming completely juvenile and unremarkable. She would never again lie on a blanket on the grass behind bushes and trees with boys whose idea of tenderness was pushing their anxious hands into her shorts and bikini bottoms from all directions. Or groping one breast while failing at reshaping the delicate contours of her other to the accompaniment of loud sucking sounds. She was adamant, not ever again.

She had wasted the entire summer and first year of junior high waiting for something that never happened, something she had no real notion about but felt a deepening and unquenchable desire to experience. Although despite her disappointment, she was in no hurry. She owed nothing at all to the best of last year's misspent tryouts who followed her into tenth grade. She was done with gawky adolescents; she would do what was right for her. She didn't need a reputation; she didn't want to be the life-long memory of any pimple-faced boy. She wanted a real boyfriend, a man.

Of course she realized her gaggle of summertime aspirants who she quickly set straight early into the year would make up and spread lies about her. She didn't care. Let them. Besides, she had an even more damning repertoire of things she could say about them without lying and there were plenty of other girls they could play games with after school. They simply weren't anywhere near as pretty as Miss Marietta Baker.

She was maturing faster than those other girls, each day more attracted to the school's senior students. One in particular who began noticing her and smiling at her, even calling her name one day as he strode by her locker exuding such confidence. The next day when school was out he found her again, seizing the moment, inviting her to the Halloween dance and tenderly caressing her cheek when she giggled a "yes."

That afternoon and for an entire week Marietta floated home on a cloud, not for the first time reconfiguring the truth so that she might spare her parents from needless worry. Besides, she supposed they were much happier believing she didn't have a boyfriend. So what did a little white lie matter?

Telling them she was meeting her friends at the corner, that she was too old for her father to drive her, the date exceeded her most fanciful dreams: the late-model convertible that wasn't his father's, the illicit bottle of vodka, the ardent kisses and confident pressure of his hands against the warm flesh under her crumpled dress. He was absolutely everything she could wish for in her first real boyfriend and by Christmas she was completely infatuated. She was certain he loved her, certain he would wait for her, the indelicate probing and inept mauling from a forgotten time in her life were now tender and fleeting moments spent together in her bedroom whenever her parents were at dinner with friends or at social obligations requisite to one's social standing.

She was fifteen and more of a woman than any girl in her class. Then one day in June he was gone, abandoning her for college and a future on the West Coast, stunning her into disbelief while tugging on his jeans and tee-shirt. He didn't think he would ever see her again, but he would totally remember her.

She would never forget the blasé shrug and his telling smirk, or watching as he closed her bedroom door without looking back. She was devastated, spending her summer at home alone and despondent. Until early in September, barely into her eleventh year, she blindly collided with another senior in the hallway, a twelfth grader she recognized from church.

Ben Keller, with a captivating glint sparkling in his eyes, smoothly begged her forgiveness while he gathered her books from the floor.

Marietta could not create in her worst nightmare how that brief encounter would forever alter her world and that of so many others she would never know or care about. What she did know instantly, her face suffused with a red-hot flush she couldn't disguise, what she could feel in her pounding heart, was that she and Ben Keller would be together, that he would want her and love her the way she deserved. She was smitten. He could not be more perfect with curly blond hair like hers and eyes that were as clear and blue. He was slim and slightly taller, masculine in his gym shorts and school jersey, glistening with sweat and smiling, holding out her books.

She was not for a moment interested in regressing to a living plaything, some tenth-grader's wet dream or dare. She wanted someone who would love and adore her once again, the memories of her first love still painfully fresh. She wanted him. Oh how she wanted him.

Peering into what she believed was his soul she could practically feel his warm hands caressing her body, feel his lips pressed urgently against hers, his warm breath melding with hers in tender whispers. She wanted him; she wanted others seeing her with him, seeing her with a senior walking her home, not for a second hesitating when he pleaded for her number.

That evening Marietta scurried to her room the moment her phone began chiming, speaking with him for an hour or more, the Bakers guardedly pleased that she did at last have a boyfriend and would finally stop moping. Their daughter was an intelligent and decent girl with proper moral values; he was from an upright Christian and church-going family like their own, a decent boy who would take their daughter to movies and school dances, who they would soon invite to Sunday dinner with his parents.

From then on Marietta and Ben were together most afternoons, Marietta increasingly craving the attention he was giving her in abundance, despite the degree of his affection varying with the degree of their time alone. He clearly cherished her for whom and what she was: a beautiful and alluring young woman emerging from a girl's body who would one day become his loving wife and, soon after, a doting mother. She was a girl, and that's what decent Southern girls did. They married and gave their husbands beautiful children. She could not imagine how beautiful their life and their children would be.

They spent the entire year together into the following summer when Ben Keller graduated at the bottom half of his class, not thinking that she was largely responsible for his sad academic standing. But he did graduate, celebrating the day by first taking Marietta to dinner on his father's card before escorting her to the prom in his father's car. The motel room came after, Ben paying cash upfront for their first real romantic evening alone as lovers that would last about an hour before taking her home. Though even before she was safely in bed, reliving each torrid gasp, Ben was at a local bar with his envious buddies keeping them entertained until closing with exaggerated and vivid particulars of the evening's main event.

Then too quickly for Marietta her glorious evening deteriorated into another long and terrible summer that wasn't at all what she had planned, especially since her mother had taken on another charitable and time-consuming cause and Marietta was spending her days wretchedly unhappy and alone in an empty house.

Whereas Ben, never destined for higher education, began working on the bottom rung of his father's successful camping and gun shop chain where he would presumably earn his way to the top eventually by putting in six-day weeks and proving himself more capable than everyone else. This while leaving Marietta desperate for the precious moments she shared with him each week in her bed while her parents were sitting across from his each Sunday as errant children nodding their heads in unison at the wisdom of the zealous preacher.

She was eager for the distraction of school, her final year, September coming painfully slowly for the love-struck girl, each hour more monotonous than the one before. All that kept her from the grips of utter misery were the hours she spent dreaming of her graduation, of finally being eighteen, of becoming an adult, of being accepted into a nearby business college. She had decided she wouldn't be a socialite mom; she wanted more from life than her mother, her privileged schooling and GPA making her an obvious candidate for any college. Of course she would live at home, near Ben, and one day spearhead her own company. That was her goal, crowning her accomplishments by marrying Ben, building a nice home, and one day beginning a family with him.

In the meantime, once in college, her mom and dad would finally get real. Of course she loved them, but she would at last be an adult and she would behave as one. Despite which she became increasingly lethargic and irritable with each passing day, particularly since Ben seemed oblivious to their time apart, showing more interest in proving himself to his father than he did in her.

She began her final year on a Wednesday, her sombre mood dramatically darker at seeing the other senior girls each day with their boyfriends. On the Friday she woke feeling ill, staying home with a worried mother until the doctor arrived, when, worse than any young female malaise she might have conjured up in her mind, the reality of what he told her froze her body and her thinking. She didn't see her mother jerk violently backward against the wall or hear the woman's pitiful wail. She was paralyzed with fear: fear of her father and Ben, fear of what would soon happen to her nubile and unblemished body. She was barely seventeen.

Mrs. Baker spent what was left of the longest and worst day of her life weeping quietly alone in her room, loathing herself for telling her husband that all was well, that Marietta was fine and that he shouldn't worry. When despite staring at her door, her mind spinning with the most awful images, she could not bring herself to face her daughter. Instead she sat in agony, retracing seventeen years, wondering what as a mother she might have done wrong and when.

She and Marshal had always been loving parents, giving her the best possible education and life. Neither one ever physically punished her, never once administering a mild spanking or an evening alone in her room without dinner for whatever childish misdemeanour. She was always such a perfect and loving daughter, and Ben such a respectful and courteous young man. "Ben," she groaned, pushing herself from the récamier, reaching for her phone with no idea whatsoever what she would say.

*

Nearing the dinner hour Leanne sat waiting for her loving Marshal on the veranda with a pitcher of his favourite ice tea. The sun was blinding, the Georgia air thick with humid heat, steam still rising from the ground soaked with a torrential midday Southern rain.

Since taking on her new charity she missed meeting him at the door at day's end with a chilled glass, kissing and hugging him, anxious to hear about his day; though not this particular evening when all she felt was incredible sadness for him as he stepped from the car, his face beaming with a disarming bright smile. No one seeing him would doubt for a moment that he was a man in love.

She didn't doubt for a moment that he did love her deeply, standing when he waved, fortifying herself as best she could with a long and deep breath. She couldn't smile; she doubted she ever would again. Instead she opened the screen door and took a step back.

At once shaken by her visible distress Marshal reached for her hands, scanning every inch of her, pulling her closer.

"Lea, what is it? What's the matter? Has something happened to Marietta?"

She said, "Your daughter's pregnant, Marshal," managing by some miracle not to falter on the terrible words.

His breathing stopped. He stared at her, speechless, coughing a burst of air as though stifling a laugh, as though wondering why she would say such a ridiculous thing about their daughter. Until she nodded, even a single word too difficult to form, rivulets of tears trickling past her pursed and quivering lips.

The silence was palpable. She might as well have torn into his chest and ripped out his soul, since at that precise instant his safe and predictable world imploded. Still, and above all, he was an adoring and devoted husband. Embracing her, he pressed a cheek to hers, commanding his sense of self not to compound his wife's emotion. He took her hand, guiding her in a daze into the dining room where he drained the first generous whiskey while standing at the bar; the second he swallowed in a single gulp before dropping his dead weight onto a chair.

"There's no doubt?"

"She's pregnant...three months. I called Doc Peters."

He rubbed his face hard. "You should have shared this with me earlier, Lea."

"I couldn't, not that way."

"Where is she now?"

"In her room, beside herself with worry. She's been alone since Doc Peters left. I can't find the words to speak with her. What could I say?" She wrung her hands. "I called the pastor instead, darling. He'll know better than us what should be done. She is our daughter after all and not the first girl who's put herself in harm's way."

Marshal Baker was a Sunday handshaking Christian, beyond which he did not believe in God, think about God, or understand why any intelligent person would. He was a good man with strict values, with no need of guiding lights or a preacher's rehearsed admonishments. He didn't swear, cheat on his wife, or ever raise a hand to her in anger; he didn't fabricate truths or pretend for a moment that his guilty clients were innocent. He believed in Southern gentility and mutual respect in an increasingly self-absorbed and uncivil world.

On the other hand, being seen as an upright Southern Christian was good for his firm's bottom line. If not his personal clients, many of the names in the dossiers of the Baker Law Offices were those of Christians like himself who would pray and sing praises every Sunday to their advantage while temporarily masking the true nature of human kind.

His firm was the busiest in Savannah for a good reason: Not all things in life were bright and beautiful, quite the opposite because most of God's creatures and the preacher's flock, great or small, would eventually or with some regularity commit what was illegal or morally wrong, bad or indifferent. Such was the human condition, the one absolute that a few shallow hallelujahs would never reverse or eradicate.

He snorted derisively. "I doubt that he does, Lea. Truthfully, I doubt he knows anything at all about women, particularly their psyches or their many conditions. He's young and self-righteous, and a bachelor for whatever curious reason that might be. He knows God, Lea, and what he may or may not understand from what he reads in the Scriptures. All that matters now, for us, is what Marietta knows and how she came to know it. I presume the Keller boy did this?"

She nodded. "I called his mother. She was utterly horrified by the news." She glanced at her watch for no particular reason. "They're expecting us this evening, darling."

"I presume along with the righteous pastor."

"He's waiting for us. Should I call Marietta?"

He shook his head. "No. She stays where she is until we're finished with the Kellers. I have no interest in hearing what she's thinking to tell us, which no doubt she's working devilishly hard at. She's lied to us for three months that we know of, so we can't for a moment believe there'll be much truth in whatever flows from her mouth like silk. She's done this freely and wantonly, Lea, so I frankly don't give a good goddamn that she's worried. She should be. She's done more than get herself pregnant. She's ruined her life and destroyed our family."

Marshal raised his empty glass, staring at it as though gazing into a crystal ball. Pushing his weight from the chair he put his arms around her, squeezing comfort into her. He poured a third substantial whiskey and a glass of wine for Leanne while he listened to her recount details of the morning's shocking revelation. She told him everything she knew; Marshal Baker was not one for half-truths. She told him how she had left her daughter in tears, unable to console her.

"What she's done is done, Lea." He put down the empty glass, snorting. "I don't believe there's a bottle anywhere big enough to get me through the evening. Either way, the Keller boy will answer for this. Count on it, Lea. Which in no way means she's innocent; she's far from innocent now, but in law Ben Keller's an adult."

Walking ahead of her into the kitchen he splashed cold water onto his drawn face, rubbing hard with a dishtowel as though believing or hoping he could somehow erase the deep hurt that would endure throughout his lifetime.

Chapter Five

Not entirely mollified by the whisky, Marshal went with Leanne and the pastor to the Keller home without Marietta, without speaking with her, the supercilious preacher's impromptu and unwanted sermon on the virtues of a clear mind falling on deaf ears as they drove. Not that Marshal didn't hear that the calming effect of strong drink might soon wear off and make matters worse. He did, retorting caustically that he had no doubt whatsoever that Keller was imbibing his fair share of ungodly hard drink and that the two men might well have another together.

Instead the fathers spoke amicably and with purpose without Ben in the room, while the women sat quietly feeling humiliated and selfishly cheated. Worse than what their neighbours and the congregation would surely think of their children's incredibly lewd behaviour, each was being cruelly deprived of becoming a loving grandmother to an untainted child brought properly and with love into the world.

For Leanne Baker the thought of her daughter laying naked in her bed with one boy, doing those things intended between a loving man and wife, was beyond horrific. Then hearing without warning that he wasn't the first was more than she could bear. She stood and walked out without speaking a word to the Keller woman; she needed to breathe in the fresher night air, to clear her mind and dry her wet cheeks. She didn't care about social niceties. She was losing her daughter, a girl she no longer recognized as lovely and sweet and could no longer believe in or trust.

As for Mrs. Keller the fact that the prettiest girl at school, a young lady she once thought of as a daughter, had lured her son into such despicable behaviour, ruining his entire life for the sake of a few moments of aberrant carnal pleasure, was suffocating. She listened mournfully until she could not endure another word, hurrying to her room in tears before the men's decision was declared and mutually agreed upon with firm handshakes.

Keller, being a devout and decent Christian man, wanted nothing to do with his son or the girl, agreeing with Marshal that a simple and private wedding would take place at the earliest possible date. The girl would have no father to give her away, nor a mother who would fuss over her.

Neither would Keller stand for the boy; nor would his wife play the groom's proud mother. There would be no gaiety, friends or family, no tea party for the girl or a gentleman's right of passage for the boy. Marietta would have a husband and Ben would not do hard prison time or become some other prisoner's de facto wife. They were in Georgia. That was the reality. With the right judge the Romeo and Juliet clause wouldn't mean much, the very words that set Mrs. Keller fleeing to her room clutching her chest.

Marshal, for his part, would keep the girl in his home and on a short leash until the day, reaching for his billfold to pay the preacher in advance before standing and walking out as Keller reached for his wallet to sponsor the preacher's cab ride home. Neither father had solicited his input, ignoring the few trite words of hope he did put forth. They weren't interested. In fact, contrary to Leanne's best intentions, neither couple would ever again set foot in his elaborate glass house of God. The Kellers would find another congregation with which to praise the Lord, as would the Bakers for more practical purposes.

*

When they were gone a stunned Ben Keller sat listening as his father made clear his immediate future.

Claiming that what happened was all Marietta's fault was absurd, and suggesting that she practically coerced him into her bed made matters that much worse. Keller could accept that his son was not God's brightest creation, but he did expect the boy would stand tall and man-up. Which didn't happen, prompting a disappointed and disgusted father to tell his son precisely what would happen, and when, ordering him to remain in his room until morning.

Closing the door and his ears to the desperate whining of a spoiled child no longer welcome in his home, he returned to the quiet of the living room where his wife was sitting staring up at him with no tears left to cry. With not the last brandy of the evening in his hand, he sat by her side to helplessly make her day worse.

The next morning Keller went early to his son's room with the Saturday Edition, waking him unceremoniously by yanking the pillow from under his head, telling Ben unemotionally exactly how his life had changed, tossing the newspaper onto the bed.

He was excused from his workday without pay. He would leave the house immediately without the luxury of a home-cooked meal and without seeing his mother. Not only would he marry the girl, thereby avoiding a worse penalty, he would find other accommodations or another cheap motel to live in by day's end without the convenience of a car. Either way he would never again step foot in the house. He would no longer work at the chain's flagship store; instead another entry-level job was open to him at one of the smaller stores without the privileges of family or the expectation that he would one day advance himself. Or he could quit without the benefit of references. His choice.

Restricting himself to curt and expedient responses to frantic questions clearly showing that Ben was either too numbed by current events or too incredibly stupid to fully grasp the consequences of his dramatic life change, Keller left taking with him Ben's car and house keys, his computer, phone and his credit cards. He returned thirty minutes later, searching through the boy's closet and drawers, ensuring that all Ben's clothes and worldly goods were packed into a couple of suitcases that he stood by the door. Suitcases Ben would never again use.

Moments later a taxi arrived that would drop him at a coffee shop, motel, or wherever. He was done, evicted from his good life in under an hour, forfeiting his family in a daze as he trudged toward the curb as though from a stranger's house without the slightest fanfare or a father's good wishes, a firm handshake or a mother's loving embrace.

When he was gone, out of sight and mind, Keller went again to comfort his wife who hadn't spoken to her son since the previous afternoon, too traumatized by Leanne Baker's call, whose life had turned upside down and, now, whose misery and sorrow were his greatest concern. They hadn't failed as parents, Ben had miserably failed as a son, and together they sat praying for the healing that would come soon and for a guiding light that would one day brighten their days once more.

*

Several blocks over the Saturday morning Savannah sunshine was bright enough at the Baker home for what Marshal held in store for Marietta. Returning home the night before, while Leanne was in the dining room pouring a glass of wine and a whiskey for her husband, he had called to Marietta from the bottom of the stairway in a voice she couldn't misinterpret that she should not make her day worse by opening her door for any reason. Morning would come soon enough, he promised. After which he joined his wife in the parlour with soft music that made their conversation private.

In fact morning did come quickly for Marietta who sorely regretted the long interval of deep sleep, who showered and dressed in her private ensuite before joining them timidly in the kitchen with nothing to say, her blue eyes glistening with the tears she had dropped into them moments earlier. She believed her father would speak first, that he would be furious and that her mother would hug her and tell her everything would be fine, that she would be fine. She was certain they would believe her, that this horrible thing Ben did to her was over before she could understand what he was doing. Instead what happened was silence. Marshal didn't yell or scream and Leanne remained as she was, standing by her husband's side, Marietta wondering why the table was cleared of dishes, wondering aloud, "Why isn't breakfast ready, mom?"

"Because it's 11:30. Because we have already eaten. Because, Marietta," Leanne continued, "from now on while you remain in this house you will prepare your own breakfasts, make your lunches and cook your suppers." She added, "That you will eat once we are finished."

That wasn't what she was expecting, not what she planned would happen. "That's crazy, mom, really crazy. You know I can't cook."

"You'll learn, sweetheart." The endearment was flat. "You have eleven weeks. That's when you're marrying Ben Keller and leaving us," she amplified her words with a flourish of her hands, "leaving this."

"What! No!" She was horrified, smearing eye-drop tears across her cheeks. "No! Mom, he did this to me. I swear I didn't know what he was doing. I swear."

Marshal broke in. "Let's be clear about this, Marietta. There is no illusion here. You are pregnant, you are having that baby and you are marrying Keller."

"Dad, no. I won't."

"Yes, you will. Or on your eighteenth birthday you'll be an unwed mother as well as homeless and indigent. We've given our consent."

She lurched forward, clutching her stomach. "Mom, this is crazy. Tell him."

Leanne wisely remained quiet. What was coming was

wholly Marshal's domaine.

"Marietta, please stop the lying. Stop the bullshit. He's been in that bed upstairs for a year and the year before someone called Higgins had his time with you. Getting his West Coast number wasn't difficult. I spoke with him this morning. I told him he wasn't in trouble, that I merely needed confirmation that my daughter was a guiltless and compulsive sleep-around." He took a moment, pausing, studying her, wondering who exactly he was seeing. "It was one of those times, Marietta, when one should be careful what one wishes for. Higgins was completely forthcoming, possibly excessively so from a father's perspective. Seems my innocent daughter was as popular at school as she was at the lake in earlier times."

"That is not true, dad. You cannot believe that. I don't even know any Higgins guy. Ben was my first boyfriend, you and mom know that."

"You're telling us honestly you don't know him, that you were never with him? That's what you're saying?"

"I swear, dad."

He shook his head, not certain whether he should laugh or cry. "Marietta, he described your bedroom perfectly, your closet, your ensuite and your posters. Enough said." He put an open palm between them. "What we naïvely believed before meeting with the Kellers were a few months of lies, of poor judgement, this morning became a few years of lewd and morally corrupt behaviour inside what we believed was your safe sanctuary. Worse, you were indifferent toward us. So this is how your next eleven weeks will play out. I want your credit card this morning, before you make your lunch. I want your phone and your computer, which I will return each day for school and emergencies, which I will take back and check each evening while you're preparing your dinner. In short, we do not trust you. In eleven weeks you'll be a wife, in six months a mother to whatever comes out. You will be a woman, an adult for lack of a better word. So become one, and become one quickly." He took Leanne's hand. "We're done here. Get me that card. From here on you'll be paying cash from your savings for whatever you might need. We will house you and we will feed you, which is all you can expect. Welcome to the real world, Mrs. Keller."

*

On the Saturday of Thanksgiving, as promised and with little to be thankful for, Ben Keller was a husband opening the portal of his bride's new world. She was five months pregnant with only her suitcases and her schoolbooks for him to carry over the threshold.

Walking in behind him, Marietta stood gaping, feeling her stomach churn, her throat constrict and her eyes blur with real tears. The entire space was smaller than her bedroom and ensuite. With no one to hear or care, she wanted to scream. She wanted to run home to her mom and her dad, to her room and her nice clothes, but she no longer had a mother or father. Like Ben, she had forfeited them and all they had given her weeks earlier along with all the inherent rights of a daughter.

Earlier that November morning Leanne Baker had stood peering from her bedroom window desensitized and numbed by the past weeks and Marietta's lewd history, lies and deceit, not feeling the least sorrow or lament at the loss of a daughter. The girl her husband was escorting to the waiting cab, and not the limo she had often and dreamily envisioned, had evolved into a stranger too far removed from a mother's dream of an innocent bride in an elegant gown to be recognizable. She was wearing faded jeans with ripped-out knees and a raglan sweater to her wedding. Turning her back, Leanne went into the parlour where she would wait for the one true love of her life.

At the curb Marshal and his daughter scarcely looked at each other with nothing left to say. Over the past weeks as she was learning self-reliance she had come to despise her father, while Marshal had without much difficulty steeled himself for the final fleeting moments he would at once expel from his mind. Despite which she took his 100 dollars before squirming into the backseat and closing the door without so much as a hug or a backward glance as he turned on his heels, returning to the house and a woman he would always love.

*

The bride and groom had not seen or spoken with each other in all those weeks on pain of severer punishments and restrictions. When she did see him, entering the chapel on her own with her belongings in tow, she was horrified. He was slouching alone on a bench by the altar as though waiting his turn at the gallows, dressed in sneakers and baggy jeans, a washed-out tee-shirt and shapeless hoodie. He looked like a homeless person. He looked hopeless.

He was disgusting in every way. He'd put on weight, and lots of it. His face was dirty with patches of sparse beard, made worse by his uncombed hair tied into a ridiculous man-bun with an elastic band. Then, within five minutes of being told where they should stand, they were exchanging outdated pawnshop estate rings and empty words that held no joy or meaning.

The pastor, whose modest fee was no incentive to do more, simply declared them man and wife and sent them on their way into damnation.

Marietta, seeing for the first time where they would live, believed she would perish then and there. The basement flat was a single room whose door was wedged between the laundry room and a stairway leading to three upper floors and much smaller than the comfortable room she would never again sleep or mindlessly fornicate in.

On one side was a pull-out couch, on the other were a small wooden table, a decades-old television and two chairs. What he called a kitchen was a countertop with a stove he had never used and a fridge filled with pizza slices and beer. Behind one cheap louvered door was a closet scarcely wide enough for his clothes, let alone hers; behind the other was a bathroom with a toilet and sink, shower stall and bath that made her instantly ill.

That was her reality that would obliterate her past and ruin her future, made worse by bare walls and a single window affording a close-up view of the building's parking lot and garbage bins, although standing on her toes and craning her neck would allow her a view of the Interstate.

Making use of her newly acquired skills she spent her wedding day cleaning and scrubbing real filth for the first time in her life, resisting the urge to vomit when she should have been at the mall with girlfriends or in her room making a Christmas wish list. Then, feeling too exhausted for a proper dinner, her wedding banquet came from the fridge; the bride later spending her wedding night devoid of romance on the pull-out without champagne or music, without dancing or throwing a bouquet, losing track of time while facedown on her elbows and knees resisting the urge to sob.

Only when her husband pulled away satiated, falling asleep beside her without a single "I love you" or a comforting "we'll get through this" or whatever, did she surrender to her pent-up emotions. She truly wanted to die. This was not what she had planned.

She woke early the next morning, pulling on a tee-shirt and padding to the kitchen, fumbling her way through her second trial as a wife, making coffee as she waited for him to wake. With so many familiar images she couldn't prevent flooding her mind of her mother and father in their kitchen preparing for a festive dinner with friends, she was certain they were thinking of her. She was certain they were teaching her another life lesson. Oh how she wished. Surely they regretted having treated her as heartlessly as they did, teaching her a cruel lesson, surely one day soon they would find her and make things right between them. They would. They had to; she was their daughter and they would always love her deeply.

Then, startled back to reality by a loud and vile smelling

noise she hadn't once heard her father make, it dawned on her that she hadn't once showered with Ben. They had simply dressed each time and gone down to sit on the porch like normal teenagers who hadn't minutes before fornicated with careless if not wild abandon.

She felt no particular need to smile. She didn't know what or how she should feel. She felt miserable, dreading the thought of returning to school on the coming Tuesday as a married woman with no way of avoiding a gauntlet of side glances and disparaging innuendos that would haunt and ridicule her until graduation, if she graduated.

Her father was adamant and cold at the door the previous day insisting that whatever the offspring of her continued bad judgement might be, it would be hers to care for, not theirs. In their minds and in their hearts she was no longer their daughter. She had done that, he told her; she had stolen herself from their hearts.

And while other girls would spend Spring Break on exotic vacations with their parents and boyfriends, she would be in stirrups becoming a mother with no mom of her own who would coo over the baby or help her through the first difficult months until graduation.

Chapter Six

She watched Ben tug into his stained boxers, wondering why he wasn't smiling, wondering what he was thinking as he came toward her.

"This is totally effing weird, Marietta, you and me like this. Married. I mean, this is total shit what they did to us."

"It's what you wanted, me like this…you and me alone. That's what you always told me."

"Yeah, but I never said in a one-room shithole. All this is on you, Marietta. You should have taken better care of things. It's not like you didn't know what's up, especially being the way you were with those other guys."

"Fuck you, Ben, for saying that. I mean, really. Fuck you. You're the reason we're here, not me. We should be at home with our parents." She looked around. "I mean, really. What is this place?"

"No. No way. The blame's all on you. I'm the loser here, taking on a wife and a kid. I mean, shit…why me?"

"Why you?" She pulled the hem of her tee to her waist. "This is why, Ben. Last night is why, when you weren't particularly worried about being a loser."

"I did what I should. I was treating you right."

"No, you didn't. You fucked me on my knees like a whore without saying a word." Her misty blue eyes conveyed what she could not, the unfamiliar emotions of an older woman. Not that he realized or cared. "You hurt me, Ben. I didn't deserve that. I'm your wife now."

He didn't need reminding, taking a step back, understanding she probably wasn't going away till death do they part, that they weren't having a petty quarrel by her school locker. All this was too effing real.

He was sorry. Of course he was, if not for hurting her. He was sorry for himself, for losing his friends, his freedom and his family. His father had made crystal clear that he no longer had family and that marrying her was the least of two evils, reiterating Baker's threat verbatim that he had overheard with his ear pressed against his bedroom door.

They would do better, Ben told her. They would get a better place once she graduated and began bringing home her fair share. They would have an okay life, he promised without the requisite conviction of an adult. The way he once might have promised that he would do better at school, not at all certain how to interpret her exaggerated teenage "whatever" and indifferent shrug as she rummaged through her suitcase for a tuque to help muffle the muted sounds coming from next door. Pulling on her wedding jeans she ignored him, sitting on the floor where she began studying for the first-term exams.

With nothing much to add he flopped onto the pull-out with a gun magazine. Whether she believed him given her current state-of-mind was not his problem. He had other things on his mind, hardly noticing when she finished studying and went into the bathroom alone to shower and dress. When she came out looking every bit the expectant teenage mother, and prettier than she felt wearing one of the few dresses she had bought with her savings and without her mother's help, she wasn't expecting a compliment and she didn't get one.

Standing at the door, Ben showed no interest in her at all. It wasn't as though they were on a date or even a honeymoon; they were going for a dinner he could scarcely afford. Though what was more peculiar for a girl accustomed to appreciative second glances and envious stares, was that she didn't care.

They walked to the corner diner without holding hands, each one in a separate and desperate world. Inside there was no soft music, candlelight or linen tablecloths. The place was devoid of ambiance and impossibly bright, loud with the clatter of dishes, of waitresses yelling instructions at a row of greasy short order cooks, and low-rent families seated for the Thanksgiving turkey special talking over the din as though Marietta might be interested in their sorry lives. She wasn't. She had her own life that was sorrier by the day to worry about.

Everyone's sole purpose was getting in, consuming something that wouldn't make them ill, and getting out. Most of them leaving with scraps in a box for the next day's lunch, which is what she did the moment she finished her club sandwich and tap-water dinner in awkward silence. She stood and walked out, dreading the remainder of her evening alone with him, justifying that, at least in the position that was easier for him given her changing body, she wouldn't see him.

She was heartbroken recalling the past year, understanding that what she mistook for tender romance flamed by ardent love, her boyfriend adoring her, was getting perfunctorily laid by someone different, someone else doing her for the first time. She realized that her single pleasure wasn't pleasure at all, but the ephemeral thrill of someone seeing her completely naked and desirable. She realized she had no idea about tenderness or romance and probably never would because no one had taught her, because she'd been laid by eager boys and never loved by a thoughtful man.

Worse, with no one to blame but herself, she had selfishly sacrificed the one man who did care deeply for her, her mind reeling at how matter-of-factly he had disowned her, scarcely speaking a word to her in weeks. She inhaled deeply, filling her lungs, expelling a muted and melancholy sigh. If he had even once yelled and screamed at her for being stupid, or scolded or berated her for embarrassing her family, she would have exploded into tears and begged his forgiveness, begged him to love her again. But he never did scream, and she never cried, father and daughter growing farther apart each day until, on the last day, one might have believed they were complete strangers.

Now the second evening of their life together was ending with Ben collapsing once again with his back to her without kissing her or whispering the tender words she desperately needed to hear. He didn't think to nestle into her back or stroke her hair, comforting her, because he had no sense whatsoever of what a true and sophisticated lover would do. All he did was use her for a single urgent need, putting her aside until the next time like a child with an exquisite toy he would never appreciate, like that bastard Matt Higgins she would never stop hating.

Neither was he sleeping, his breathing was too irregular. The jerk was laying there, blaming her for what he did, feeling good, feeling like a man for punishing and demeaning her, making her loathe him more than she thought possible, making her loathe her father who she realized would never come for her.

She eased onto her side avoiding touching him, praying that a deep and everlasting sleep would come quickly one night and set her free. If not, she had options. Particularly since she no longer had a family to shame or embarrass. She was a woman, a smart one, at the top of her class at school. He was a part-time clerk in a gun shop when he wasn't sweeping floors or stocking shelves. Who for a moment and in their right minds would believe they were meant to be as one? She sure as hell did not, not then, not ever.

She woke the next morning missing her mother calling her for breakfast, missing her father's wide smile and tight embrace; Ben woke an hour later, inhaling the aroma of over-brewed coffee, correctly believing his life sucked, correctly assuming their lives would never be better. He had stayed up half the night trying to figure things out in his head, despising her more with each failed thought.

With his meagre wage at the shop, especially with her and her kid coming, he wouldn't own a decent car for years, if ever, and the bank had refused him a credit card forcing him to decide between a tablet and a cheap flip phone that came with a pay-per-use plan. Her fault, all her fault. Everything was her fault. And now, when he could have been doing her in a real bed while the Bakers were at church or wherever, if she hadn't been incredibly stupid, he would spend the day doing groceries with her when the few dollars left in his otherwise empty pockets after dinner the previous night would barely get him to the next payday.

He did always want her alone. He did tell her that, but for a long weekend, or at least an entire day, not an entire lifetime. She was a good lay, a good time. That she was crazy in bed, like she could never get enough, wasn't exactly a school secret, Ben hardly believing his good fortune when his turn came from out of the blue, when she put out for him so quickly and keenly. He'd never been with a girl as eager, as though getting royally laid was breathing life into her.

Now he would never get away from her. He had nowhere to go, with hardly enough money left for a six-pack after taking care of her and the kid, when he should have been frequenting bars and meeting people, having fun and going on Spring Break and getting laid with his buds. Not living in a shithole with the school slut he could only do one way without making himself sick. He was barely nineteen. He did not deserve this for having a bit of fun with her. The shit he was living should not be happening; this was all her fault.

When he saw her coming at him in the chapel the day before he thought he would be sick. She came in looking like a runaway, like some other guy's nightmare, not his, not at all the way he remembered her. And she wouldn't get any better anytime soon, if ever.

He couldn't imagine the coming weeks. He couldn't

believe this was his life, or that his parents had let this happen, that they hadn't stood up for him when everything that happened was her fault. All they talked about that night was him doing what was right or doing time in prison, not a single word about giving the thing away or getting rid of it.

He wanted out. He wouldn't survive with her and a screaming brat in one room. Who would? All he could hope and would pray for was that something really bad would happen, that she would die on the table or something equally bad. Things like that happened every day. Then he could walk away and start over.

"What?"

He shrugged. "We'll need that hundred dollars."

*

Tuesday Marietta returned to class after tossing her démodé wedding ring into a trash can. She didn't need the reminder of what her life had become, telling the other girls that she and Ben had decided against such meaningless tokens. They were deeply in love, nothing else mattered.

No one cared. She was no longer the girl they envied or wanted. She was shunned, gossiped about by the same girls who a year earlier had idolized her. For their part, the boys were relieved that Ben got into her first, making certain their current-year girlfriends going forward weren't as careless or as stupid. And by Christmas nothing had changed, with no one applauding or celebrating that her grade point average was the highest in her class.

Christmas morning she woke quietly beside Ben, padding quietly into the bathroom and kitchen, doing her best not to wake him. There was no tree or decorations or presents wrapped with ribbons and bows; her single gift would be the few precious hours each day without him until the second semester. Their Christmas dinner would be whatever was in the fridge, without wine or eggnog or her father's hot toddies. Her parents hadn't called with a warm invitation, Marietta not believing or hoping for a moment that they would. She hadn't spoken with them in over a month and had stopped wondering or worrying whether her mother would forgive her by March and help her through a difficult time. All she wanted and longed for was getting the thing out of her, leaving school and finding a job, making money and moving into a real home.

New Year's they spent alone, not bothering to invent conversation. The champagne evening was for friends and family, and they had neither. They had no money for dining out or clubbing. Or, from Ben's narrow perspective, a way out his private and excruciating hell.

By Valentine's Marietta rarely thought of her parents, increasingly preoccupied with her worsening condition to think of what little gift her father might have bought his precious daughter had he not callously discarded her. The girls at school now completely ignored her, the guys resorting to calling her Miss Preggie. Then too soon for Ben and not soon enough for Marietta, while the other girls were in the Caribbean getting royally pissed and agreeably complaisant by mid-afternoon, she was on her back with her feet in stirrups straining, her cotton gown soaked with sweat, her face and her mouth distorted in agony, screaming her way into motherhood.

She thought she would die, instantly hating the thing, hating the smell and the look of it, hating everyone that was smiling as though she wasn't living her worst fucking day, telling her it was a girl as though she had won the fucking lottery and not completely ruined her body and her life as little Jodie Keller began hers.

She didn't care about her mother's wretched state; she had her own issues. She was terrified and cold, not understanding what was happening to her or that for most of her young life she would regret ever being born and, like her mother, hope that she might die one day soon.

In fact, the tepid bath water and the nurse's warm hands would be the only warmth the girl would feel until her birthday twenty-two years later when, sitting on her corner damp with the oppressive heat of New Orleans, devastated by a stranger's sudden and cruel death, another stranger would come to her and she would at last be reborn.

Chapter Seven

Two days later Marietta was back in the apartment with her daughter and a volunteer home care worker who would watch over the baby each school day through to her finals and graduation.

With no spare money and nowhere to go, she spent what was left of her Spring Break holiday watching the woman teach her about being a mom because she no longer had one of her own.

As for Ben, he decided his first evening as a father that working more hours for the overtime, often till late at night, made more sense than being stuck in a room unable to think, talk or sleep with a wailing brat and a girl whose body had gone to shit and who wanted her life back as much as he did. Despite which, from the moment he stepped through the door that night into their one-room hell, the marriage soured more each day.

The following Monday Marietta was in class, paler and thinner, the centre of attention until she made clear she would not play show and tell, without question establishing the social climate for what remained of the school year when she graduated at the top of her class without attending the ceremony or prom. She had no reason or desire, leaving the building as quickly as possible without girlish hugs or tearful goodbyes, taking her time getting to the apartment where she thanked the volunteer for everything the woman had done, disappointed the woman's mandate had terminated.

Monday she dressed in her best outfit, one she hadn't

worn since leaving home; she put the baby in a stroller and went looking for work. By week's end she had met with the HR of a dozen or more firms, visiting twice as many by her eighteenth birthday, yet no one was returning her calls. Until at the end of her third week, discouraged and depressed, she left the baby in the stroller by the door and fell back exhausted onto the pull-out.

Such was her life, her present and her future, and she understood why. The very life she was living was condemning her to continued misery and privation. The life she once enjoyed with her parents was gone, over. She would never again wear nice clothes, or dine in fancy restaurants, or travel to exciting foreign places. Nothing in her life would ever be exciting again.

No one wanted a teenage wife with a baby. Especially, she supposed, one whose constantly angry husband worked in a gun shop. The mix was predictably bad for business, bad for morale. She understood without being told. How often had her father cautioned her to stay single as long as possible, that young married women were the worst possible ROI for any worthwhile employer?

Now what was he thinking, if he even thought of her at all?

Waking in the dark she lay inert, luxuriating in a rare moment of quiet, one warm tear melding with another, trickling across her cheek onto the pull-out. She wanted her mom and her dad, but that was a dream that would never come true. The best she could hope for was an impossible miracle, creating all manner of fanciful scenarios in her mind.

She went to the kid, feeding it and doing what the volunteer had taught her, gagging, and more than once retching, forcing herself not to make the air in the flat even worse. She had to get out, get away from the smell, from her husband and her life. But how would she do that with a paltry few hundred in her savings account that he wasn't aware of, when he gave her nothing from what was left of his weekly pay?

Get out or lose her mind. So she did. With the baby asleep in its stroller she changed into a tee-shirt, cut-offs and flip-flops, stole a beer from the fridge and went out into the parking lot for air, leaning against the chromed grill of a modified F-250. Something no guy who might own a Southern good ol' boy's macho ride would much appreciate, like the way Clyde Gill didn't much appreciate the girl plunked down on his chrome bumper. What he did like seeing from his third-floor window were the long and wide-open legs keeping her there, legs that were smooth, young, and extremely inviting through his 10X50 range finder.

He'd never seen her before. There was no mistaking she was a nice enough package, out for a cold one on a steamy Georgia evening, and ten minutes later she was still alone, still perched on his bumper. Whatever she was she could easily pass for twenty. He was twenty-seven and worked on a rig. He was also a confirmed and successful bachelor, successful at loving and leaving, most times preferring detached and professional lovers who didn't care about broken hearts. "So let's do this thing," he thought aloud. He damn sure had to try, startling her a few minutes later in a crisp white shirt, designer jeans and dress boots.

"That there's my truck you're usin' for a bench, girl. You shouldn't ought to do that with a man's pride and joy."

She didn't move. He was 5'9", give or take, trim, and didn't look as though he would take shit from anyone. He was good-looking, not handsome, with wavy black hair, his eyes and his voice telling her that he didn't mind at all.

She stood quickly, snarling, "I really don't think I hurt the thing. Besides, I thought I was alone."

He scanned the parking lot. "You were alone, till now." Looking past her, making a show of examining the bumper, he shrugged, a thin smile forming on his lips. "Well, looks fine from what I can tell. Could be a few smudges though. Could need a good buffin' in the mornin'."

She was every bit as easy on the eyes as what he saw from his window, but up close and personal he could see she was dragged down and tired. Which wasn't quite right for a girl her age. She had beautiful eyes, but they were sad eyes. Her Georgia accent was soft and sweet; she was definitely a prep girl, but her voice was woeful and flat, as though she had nothing left in her life to care about.

"I'm supposin' you're new here in the buildin'." She nodded; he waited, extending a hand. "Clyde Gills in 312, pleased to make your acquaintance."

She hesitated, taking his hand, thinking. She didn't know what she was thinking, that compared to Ben Keller he was perfect, a man. "I'm Marietta. I'm sorry for sounding like a bitch."

"Not what I was thinkin'. I was thinkin' I should get myself to town, put down a few while sittin' with a gal who don't mind me talkin' a whole lot. But seein' how you're blockin' my way, I'm thinkin' I should be neighbourly instead. Sort of like neighbourhood watch bein' that it's dark and all."

Or take me with you and buy me a drink. "Don't bother. I'm kind of married. Not that I wouldn't like a real man's company, but he's a bit of an asshole and I'm already in deep shit for taking a beer."

His shock was real. "Seems to me you could've waited a while, instead of rushin' into things. Don't somehow seem right."

"Yeah, well, whatever…" She shrugged. "I'm sorry for smudging your car. Have a good time."

"Whoa! Hold on there now. This asshole, your husband, he beatin' on you, Marietta?"

"He doesn't have to," she glanced at the half-empty bottle, "but then again he doesn't know I took a beer." She forced a smile. "Anyway, shit happens. Right?"

"Yes, ma'am, it sure will if I hear about it. Beatin' on a girl over a beer? Might happen one time, not twice. You remember that. You remember 312, anytime."

Yeah right, male macho bullshit. She began walking away, pausing. Why not? Really, why the fuck not? No way was he going for a few beers. He was on the hunt hoping to get laid, he was definitely hitting on her and Ben wouldn't be home for a couple of hours. Anyway, she didn't give a shit and the kid was strapped into its stroller. She was out and she wanted to stay out, away from Ben, away from his kid if only for an hour.

"Clyde, you wouldn't have another beer up there in 312 by any chance? I'm a gal, we're talking, and I could really use some good company."

"What about this husband of yours?"

"That is precisely right. What about him?"

Bam!

*

Clyde's apartment shocked her, the closest thing to luxury she had seen since being evicted from her childhood home. He had a real kitchen with stainless steel everything, a living room furnished with high-end European designs, a balcony and real doors, a bedroom with a proper closet and a real bed draped in satin sheets and a duvet she would die for. He didn't understand the big deal, shrugging, selecting a perfectly chilled Chardonnay that didn't have a twist cap from his cooler, telling her he didn't know much about such things, that the lady sales clerk patiently helped him figure things out.

They spoke about his work and her job search, about why she married at such a young age, about being pregnant but losing it a few weeks after the wedding she was forced into by parents who wanted nothing to do with her. She told him about Ben, that he was a huge mistake, a high school dropout and loser who couldn't find steady work. She explained how hopelessly trapped she felt without her family or friends, describing how he treated her, the mental abuse, the single room in the basement and how she desperately wanted out, that whenever she could she would run and never look back. She would start over, find a nice man who would forgive her mistakes and for once be happy with her life. She would, talking to herself as much as she was winning over Clyde. She would do whatever was necessary. She had nothing to lose and everything to gain. She already felt like a cheap whore on the pull-out with Ben and no way would she ever find a decent job if she didn't get out. So she asked him straight up, adding that she did not want to hear bullshit.

He answered the same way, unfazed, as though she had asked where he did his groceries and whether he used coupons. He ate, worked and slept twenty straight days on a rig in the middle of the ocean with hard-fisted men who weren't always socially correct. He did not have and did not want a girlfriend. Not for a good while. So what other choice did a guy have?

"Mostly from the phone book, darlin'. Once a week most times, dependin'. No ties, no expectations, and you get what you pay for. Most local gals are labour intensive and a crap shoot. Can't tell what you're gettin' till you unfold 'em. Then good or bad they get 'emselves attached real quick, expectin' breakfast and phone numbers, gettin' abusive at the door. Not what a guy like me needs. Better to pay 'em, kiss 'em goodbye, and you bein' the one callin' back."

"That must get expensive."

He chortled. "Some folks spend more on booze, and a whole lot better than a good time turnin' bad, darlin'. Like what happened with you."

From Marietta to darlin', that was a good thing. "How much, and most times depending on what?"

He thought for a moment. "Five hundred, give or take, not countin' the room. And dependin' on if I like her, a bit more those times when a man needs family. Christmas and the like, even bought one a gift once; took another on vacation one time. Kissed one at the door, kissed the other at the gate and never did see 'em again. On the cheek, mind you. Can't recall ever kissin' one on the mouth. Not a thing you do."

"That's a lot of money for a couple of hours in bed with a stranger, Clyde. Sort of like sleeping in a hotel bed. Clean, but used. And used a lot. So what if you could kiss my mouth? I'm eighteen and that poor excuse of a husband was my first. So why don't we help each other? You pay me the 500 plus the cost of a room and the weeks you're in town I'll keep you company a few times. More than a few, dependin', darlin'. Then we definitely renegotiate. At least till Christmas, maybe a while longer if you like me. Then I'm gone. No ties, no expectations. I can get away and start over. That is a very good deal, Clyde. Me instead of renting a douched whore, but you let me keep some things here for when I'm ready and you do not fuck around on me because I'm clean and I'm staying that way."

Now he was fazed. Bedding a pro didn't come cheap, the local gals did notwithstanding the predictable awkwardness of waking with them the next morning and sending them on their way. Marietta was a good deal, and eighteen to boot. What did he have to lose? If she wasn't a win-win nothing was, for however long she might last. What one might call a no-brainer.

He couldn't tell. "You yankin' my chain, darlin', or what?"

She shook her head once. "No long-term contract, cash on the first of each week, and cancel anytime. Just do not fuck around on me and I will do my best for you not to do that... cancel, that is. So yes, I'm serious. Very serious."

"This thing startin' when, darlin'? Seems to me this is about quittin' time as it is, much as I'm enjoyin' you bein' here."

He was right, not that she cared. She stood, sauntering toward the door, feigning much more confidence than she felt. "Monday afternoon, all afternoon if you like. Don't forget the cash and lunch would also be nice. We should get familiar with each other first." At the door she turned, tugging her tee-shirt over her head and turning a tight circle. "Unless, of course, you change your mind. As for the asshole, I'm done with him."

Holy shit! This he could not believe. His ladies, all of them, were prime. They were top grade and young, some were post-grads paying off loans, some wanted the thrill of novelty, others did it for the money or the variety or both, each one single and drop-dead gorgeous, each one refined and dedicated to mutual fulfillment. A job worth doing..., oh yeah. But this, what he was seeing, would be special: young, perfectly sculpted, practically untouched and eager, if not a little overly eager, which probably brought them together in the first place. Whatever. That wasn't his concern, but seeing the improv preview he was sure he wouldn't be changing his mind anytime soon, despite the incontrovertible truth that all good things, even some miracles, must come to an end.

Strutting into the hallway, disappearing into the stairway without glancing over her shoulder, aware his door had not closed, she was beaming and in no great hurry to regain her modesty, in her mind reinforcing his need, though suddenly realizing she was famished. Then too soon, back in her flat with enough time to warm some leftovers and care for the kid that greeted her with tears and wailing, protesting over her continued neglect, Ben came through the door heading straight for the fridge without a word or the slightest interest in her or the kid.

Slamming the fridge door he glared at her, which she thought was comical. "Where's the other beer? There were two. Where is it Marietta? I mean, goddamn."

"I took it outside. This place was making me sick, that thing's making me sick and so are you. So deal with it, and starting Monday I'm searching for work without that to explain. It'll be good enough here alone for a few hours each day. And I'm also done with you, with your shit. We're done. Once I find work, once I have money saved, I'm getting rid of you legally and forever. This is your life, your future, not mine. That means no more of your doggie bullshit, that means no more anything. Nothing, starting right now because tonight you are on the floor.

66

If not, I swear I'll leave right now without it." She paused for affect, smirking. "And you know I will not have any problem finding a better place to sleep."

"Guess not, because once a slut always a slut." He snickered, guzzling the beer. "Must be really tough, Marietta, not being the main attraction anymore."

"Fuck you. You made me a slut, you and Higgins. That's not what I wanted," she pointed at the stroller, "especially not that. You should be grateful, though. At least with a divorce you won't do the prison time you fucking deserve for what you did to me, for what you're doing." She coughed a laugh. "Not that your life isn't already pure shit."

Chapter Eight

Ben did sleep on the floor that night and Saturday he borrowed the company truck and bought the best mattress he could afford, stopping by a familiar package store for a six-pack where he knew cash receipts were more important than IDs.

Saturday night after a painfully quiet supper, Marietta fed the kid and fell asleep early and alone while Ben laid awake on his foam mat dreaming of his upcoming freedom.

Early Sunday they went for groceries without the kid who was safely strapped into its stroller, Ben spending what remained of the day drinking beer on the floor and reading more about guns, completely oblivious to the reality that he was not getting any smarter. Marietta in the meantime spent her day ironing the outfits she would wear throughout the coming week for job interviews, content with not speaking a word, preoccupied with capricious and wonderful thoughts and plans now that her life was taking a joyous turn. One in particular, whose seed was planted the previous week, which she believed at the time was impossible for lack of money, would be quite possible once paid by Clyde Gill for their first day together.

She had met another young mother in the building who, by chance, was in the laundry room as Marietta was struggling with getting her darling daughter through the door of her first home as a happy bride. The female condition instantly acted upon as one new mother hurried to discover what she could about the other mom and her baby. The result being that each one said too much too quickly, the other woman suggesting a mutually beneficial solution to each other's dilemma: One badly needed freedom to search for work; the other, a single mom, was badly in need of more money than her social assistance cheque was giving her.

She put that god-send solution into effect Monday morning, bringing an excruciating weekend to an end. No sooner had Ben left than she literally bounded up the stairway, banging on the woman's door, explaining that her situation had greatly improved. Not taking long before agreeing on terms and returning to her one-room cell elated, practically giddy, adamant that she would never again be a mother or put herself in such a vulnerable state.

She lingered under a cool shower, humming while she styled her hair and did her makeup, pleased that her body was returning to an alluring pre-maternal state, making certain that what he would see was even more enticing. At noon she put a silk robe from another time over her best panties and bra and carried her worst nightmare to the woman's apartment, promising she wouldn't be later than 9:00 that evening, explaining that the interview might lead into dinner.

Taking her time dressing for the occasion in her shortest silk skirt, satin sandals and silk blouse she could never wear for Ben, would never wear for Ben, making certain she was flawless, she climbed the stairs an hour later to 312 taking with her a designer handbag that was strictly for show.

When Clyde opened his door her eyes flared open in concert with her mouth. She was gaping, something resembling a stifled laugh accentuating her utter amazement. She wasn't seeing a good ol' boy rigger; the handsome guy standing at the door was a young and trendy businessman, a stockbroker or account executive dressed in a blue tailored suit accented with a silk pocket hanky that completely blew her mind, a button-down opened at the neck and tasselled dress loafers. All of which for the briefest moment made her want to explode into tears.

His smile was wide and bright. "Never had a girl come callin', darlin'. Can't say I mind a whole lot." He made a twirling motion with a deeply tanned hand, which she did as though floating on that once familiar cloud. "Damn, if you are not the prettiest thing."

"This," she scrutinized him from his wavy black hair to his tasselled shoes, "what is this?"

"This is me, darlin'. Things aren't always what they seem, I suppose."

"I was not expecting this, you like this. I feel like I'm on a date."

"You said you wanted lunch. So in a way I'm supposin' we are." He took her hand, guiding her in. "You sure about doin' this thing, darlin'? Still time for a change of mind. Won't change us goin' for lunch. Got us a nice table at Bentons."

What! Bentons! "Yes, I'm sure. Are you kidding? Like I told you, like I promised you. He is done. He's sleeping on the floor and if this works for us, for you, he'll be history by Christmas and I'll be Savannah-free." She giggled for the first time since she couldn't remember when, she was happy. "Now seeing you like this, I don't know. I'm thinking I could hold out till March. With no ties, no expectations."

"Thanks. Should tell you though, if we're being completely upfront, I am not a Southern boy or a rigger, not as such. I sort of adopted the speech on the rig, made working with the real riggers easier. Still working on the drawl thing, though. What I actually am is pure Boston. MIT actually, an engineer eager for the company of a charming Southern girl at lunch and learning much more about her. I apologize for the ruse, Marietta. I didn't think you would speak with me otherwise," he grinned, "bein' that some of ya'll Southern gals are a mite particular ayn' all."

"You are shitting me. For real?" He nodded, his green eyes sparkling. "Good, we both lied, sort of. What I told you Friday was all true, except that I have twelve years of prep school, which kind of makes me a spoiled Southern bitch. Or I was, who ain't never bin with a Union boy. Can't rightly say pa would take much of a likin' t'ward ya, if'n I had one, Mista Gill."

He asked whether she preferred another crisp Chardonnay or a lighter Pinot Grigio. The day was too warm for anything red. His choice; she didn't know much about wine. What she did want to know about however was the lady sales clerk who graciously helped a confused hillbilly graduate of MIT furnish his apartment.

He saw no reason for living in a fancy condo when he lived most of the year out of a duffle bag on a rig. The place kept him level, helped him fit in. At the same time providing a constant source of annoyance to his mother who all but lost a lung when hearing he would not be joining the family's Boston firm or marrying the proverbial girl next door. Compounding the issue, hearing that his career choice would be working on a rig practically put her into a coma and his father into a cardiac ward.

Perhaps so, but Marietta was in heaven, putting down her glass near 2:30 as Clyde discreetly slipped an envelope into her handbag. At the stairway he took her arm until reaching the ground floor where he held open the door and took her hand. At the F-250 he helped her onto the running board and into her seat, Marietta commenting that she'd never been in a hillbilly's ride. When he joined her, she continued in her best Southern Belle accent that she liked the Southern boy Clyde as much as she did the MIT Clyde, but that Savannah girls most certainly preferred being seen on the arm of dashing gentlemen handsomely attired in fine suits.

She had dined at Bentons many times before with her parents, Clyde not at all surprised when a waitress who remembered him by name also recognized her. And, once seated, they were in no hurry to rush the day. The meal and the wine were exquisitely paired, the conversation easy and unassuming. They were learning about each other, Marietta thinking all she was missing was soft music and dancing, several times wishing her parents would walk in and see her with a real man.

Leaving the restaurant not far from 5:00, Clyde suggested a stroll along Savannah's famed Riverwalk, famed for romance and lovers most evenings after darkness has fallen. She answered by slipping her arm into his, because not taking his arm would seem silly the way they were dressed, the way they were enthralled with each other, Marietta enquiring coquettishly "Do you often stroll arm in arm with your lady friends, Mr. Gill?"

No. He did not.

They strolled for an hour, not once searching for words. The evening was easily the high point of Marietta's unwanted and tragic life, returning to the building she loathed unquestionably the lowest possible after Ben. Earlier when they were leaving the parking lot she felt as though she was escaping her worst life, anxious for the day she would say goodbye and leave Savannah behind forever. Now, parking mere feet from her solitary window, she would not let any thought of her time with Clyde ending, that day or any other, creep into her mind.

Once inside his apartment she kicked off her sandals, curling onto his sofa while he filled fresh glasses with wine. She wasn't nervous or afraid of what he would think once seeing all of her. He had already seen a significant part of her, her bare breasts visibly whetting his appetite for her, breasts that were younger and better than any whore's.

She was half-hoping at the time that he would take her right then on the sofa or the floor. Anywhere. She didn't care where. The problem was him, he was a gentleman. He would wait. He would never frantically pound or hurt her; he would feverishly love her, he would caress her and adore her with each tender stroke, wanting and needing more of her. That's what she hoped, that's what she wanted. What she was adamant about was that Ben would never again see her naked. Seeing Clyde, thinking how her father and Keller had colluded to ruin her life made her ill. She deserved Clyde, she deserved any man like him.

He was easy company, laid back, sitting by her side, reaching for a remote that brought Dean Martin to life.

"This morning I cleared out a drawer for you, a private drawer for whatever."

"Thank you."

"Nervous, a little?"

"No, what I am is excited. Thank you for lunch, Clyde, and for this. Thank you for making me free." She sipped her wine. "Now I think I should know what you're expecting from me, from all this. I am a little less experienced than your other ladies. I do know that. But if you're a good teacher, I will be an even better student. I promise."

He had already mused on their "thing." He got that she might need a drawer in his bedroom, the girl's go-bag, which was no big deal. That said, they needed guidelines and boundaries set in place. She did. "How does Monday, Wednesday and Friday with 800 each week work for you?"

Eight hundred! Holy shit! "That definitely works for me." She put down her glass, standing, taking his hand without the slightest shame. "Not that I'm rushing things, Clyde, but it is six-thirty."

He held her in place, taking her other hand. "Works for me also as long as we're clear in our minds that this is a special arrangement. Very special and very unusual, although an arrangement nonetheless. This does not mean we're more than good friends with different needs who like each other and share a common solution that is strangely unique. Meaning that I need my time alone, my weekends. I don't have friends here because I don't have time for friends. Weekends aren't weekends for me. More like the time alone I need for getting things done. Something you should understand going forward. You get that, don't you?"

She patted his face, peering into his eyes. "Darlin', all ah truly wants is outta here. I already got me a husband, don't need me another. Not fer a long, long spell. Sides which, you a North'n boy." She brought a thin smile to her lips because he wasn't convinced. "Yes, Clyde, I do. No one, not you, not anyone, can understand alone time more than me. Believe me, all I want is out of here and you are my saviour." She tugged him to his feet. "Okay, so I can't ever love you. I get that, which does not mean I can't really like you, that you can't really like me. So can we get on with this teacher thing? Please."

In the bedroom Marietta didn't pretend she was the sensual or erotic creature he might be accustomed to; she was eighteen and, despite how she yearned to become that creature, thus far her skill in bed was limited to plain getting laid in a race against the parental timeline. So she undressed the way she remembered performing in front of her mirror each evening in her bedroom, when she would caress each curve and contour with scented lotion the way he was now waiting to explore and adore her with gentle caresses.

Her blouse went first, followed quickly by her skirt, pirouetting for him with her arms outstretched and stopping, searching his eyes, her heart pounding more than she thought possible. She did not expect he would pull her in close, or that he would steal her breath with a heated kiss pressed gently to her lips; she did not expect he would expertly unclasp her bra, or intently push her panties past her ankles onto the floor, his warm palms skimming the soft flesh from her hips to her toes.

Matt Higgins had never kissed or fondled or romanced her in bed. He groped and he probed and he prodded. He never once undressed her that way or seemed remotely intrigued by her body while she undressed herself. All he cared about was getting into her, getting off, and getting out; like Ben who hadn't once played the lovestruck boyfriend, who didn't think or care that he should kiss his bride at her wedding or anytime since while her ass was in the air. That's all he ever wanted: her ass in the air. But this was, she didn't know, fucking fantastic, a tiny gasp escaping her lips at his most tender touch of all, looking down as he teasingly trailed warm kisses from her thighs to her labia to her breasts, her shoulders, her neck and her mouth, for a fleeting instant reading in his eyes that he was savouring her like the delicious creature she was, adoring her.

She couldn't be wrong.

Taking her hand he led her to the bed, throwing back the down-filled duvet and sweeping her feet from the floor, laying her between the cool satin sheets. She wanted to shriek or scream, she didn't know which. She was elated, transfixed, watching as he sat on the bed tugging at his socks, then standing, pulling away his shirt, loosening his belt and kicking away his pants, all the while smiling. Not for a moment taking his eyes from her until, deciding she had seen enough, he eased in beside her wearing microfibre straight-backs. A situation he immediately corrected upon hearing a terse "Get them off."

She had no sense of time, moaning when he rolled onto his side. For the first time in her life she lay naked on damp sheets glistening with sweat, his gentle hand gliding across her belly and her breasts every bit as titillating as the first electric shockwave that jolted and twisted their bodies. She smelled of sweat, of her own pungent aroma and his. She lay in a euphoric daze feeling—she didn't know what. She hadn't once felt her vagina throbbing that way, hadn't once felt her lips smeared with gloss pulsating that way. Her pain was the ecstasy she had always sought and had never found. She was entirely enraptured.

She turned her head to kiss him, purring. Until she saw the clock on the wall and sprang from the bed in a flurry of satin and flailing arms, gathering her clothes. Eight-forty! Shit! Two hours! Was he kidding? Ben never lasted more than a couple of minutes and Higgins was no better. In fact there was nothing better about either one of them. High school jerk-offs coming by her home for a fast fuck as though she were a convenient roadside diner.

She had to shower and hadn't yet seen her smudged face. She had to dress, get downstairs for the kid and change. She didn't care a whit about Ben, but she didn't need more shit in her life either.

He chuckled. "I suppose this means class is dismissed."

"Shit Clyde, twenty-minutes. That is not funny."

She scurried into the bathroom, closing the door, letting the water run while she peed. Despite his taking full control of her body, she was raised as a young lady and was not anywhere near ready for sharing that much with him.

When she came out dressed, a little fresher and a little less harried, he was in the living room wearing designer sweats and sipping twelve-year double malt scotch.

"I wouldn't worry about being less experienced, Marietta. You are definitely gifted, if not blessed with natural inclinations. That, in there, was definitely A-plus work. We should start planning a graduation ceremony; I'm thinking dinner at Bentons or a weekend in Miami once your time here is up."

God! "Thank you." She shook her head. "But right now I'll settle for a two-day reprieve. I think you seriously ruined me forever and please do not talk about my time here being up. Being here is all that will get me through to Christmas. Besides, no ties, no expectations. Remember?"

He didn't need reminding, he was adamant. "Wednesday we'll do a dinner here."

She thought maybe not. "That is not a good idea. I don't cook, sorry."

"Not a problem, I'm a fantastic cook. Helps me pass the time on the rig. You'll be my sous-chef. We'll cook something together." He kissed her. "Two o'clock good for you?"

She nodded, hugging him, fairly certain his whores never hugged him. Then she left, walking out as nonchalantly as she could manage and not looking over her shoulder. Leaving him was difficult. Whatever was in his head, she did not want to leave her dream. She did not want to deal with her divorcé-to-be loser husband and sure as hell did not want to deal with his kid that she left by the door tucked into its stroller. She wanted the envelope in her shoulder bag, seconds later counting out 800 in fifties.

She was ecstatic, delirious. Nevertheless, what remained of her evening was tedious without him, wondering what he was doing, what he was thinking.

*

Ben came home at 11:00 after work and a fast meal at a doughnut shop, caustically informed the previous Friday that she would never again cook his supper or do his laundry and that the one sure way out of the shithole, out of his pathetic life, would mean working overtime every night for the rest of that life that she wanted no part of. More importantly she would be gone by Christmas, certain she could not endure her existence till March.

With Clyde's 800, after paying the woman upstairs, by Christmas she would have four grand saved and, by March, six. Which would come at a price she wasn't willing to pay. She fell asleep counting the days until her emancipation, wondering what gifts she and Clyde would buy each other for Christmas, believing and hoping she would spend the entire special day with him, then go clubbing with him at New Year's and not give a good shit about the loser or the kid in the basement.

Tuesday she put the kid upstairs with the woman and went shopping for an inexpensive phone, selecting an outdated model and spending her afternoon in a park with a newspaper jotting names and numbers into a notebook. She had to find work. What Clyde was giving her wasn't enough and, call what they were sharing a quixotic friendship, love in bloom or mutual gain, he was paying for the use of her body. A rose by any other name still made her a whore without a CV.

Tuesday evening Ben came in late again from the same doughnut place where he would become a regular because he couldn't afford anywhere that sold beer, not until he was rid of them. He didn't know about the phone under the pullout, her hair appointment the next day or her Wednesday evening culinary class. Nor would he ever learn of her benefactor in 312, content with spending his nighttime hours flipping through gun magazines.

Wednesday Marietta treated herself with an early lunch on River Street after having her hair styled into a playful updo and shopping for silk panties and bras that Ben would never see and hopefully Clyde would never forget, sexy satin thongs and push-ups her mother would never allow, knocking on his door at precisely at 2:00 PM.

She was eager to pirouette for him, delighting him once her other sets were stored in her drawer. She was even more eager for her mind and her body to soar with his twice more to the heights of rapture between their preparations for dinner that was a cream of broccoli, a simple filet mignon served with oven-baked puréed potatoes, steamed veggies and a requisite full-bodied red. Her dessert was a fruit flan, his was Marietta an hour later and again in his shower.

She left at 9:00, hating that she must, kissing him at the door, her body tingling from their shower when she had wrapped her arms around his neck and her legs tightly around his waist, urging him to do more, for the first time in her life and in her mind making torrid love with her man under a torrent of steaming water and wondering how she would ever survive without him.

In her flat, the terrible thought didn't leave her. She had one more precious day with him before enduring three unbearable weeks without him, thinking that Friday she would suggest five days together from then on without the expectation of anything more. Why not? It's not like she would move in. No way that would ever happen with Ben in the building and, besides, he was obviously crazy about her.

With a real job she would leave Ben immediately. She would find a place of her own, hire a lawyer and tell Clyde he would no longer pay her for loving him. Having a girlfriend, especially one as young and as drop-dead gorgeous, wasn't the worst thing in anyone's world.

Thursday she called the numbers in her notebook, arranging promising appointments for the coming week, throughout the evening wondering how Clyde could be as near as he was without constantly thinking of her, without wanting her. He must. Of course he would, was, unless she meant nothing to him beyond her age and her body.

Living with Ben was impossibly more abysmal each day since meeting Clyde. He was gaining noticeable weight with each passing week, waiting until nothing clean was left in his suitcase before washing his clothes. His hair was creeping past his shoulders and he hadn't once groomed his beard. He looked indigent and would soon be exactly that if he didn't somehow grow a brain. His daddy, father or not, was his top boss and, as much as she despised Keller for what he did, the man was sophisticated and smart.

He would not accept being embarrassed by an indolent employee.

Friday morning she cleaned and fed the kid, making coffee and toast and sitting on the pull-out losing herself in another world until he was gone. At noon she carried it upstairs. Savouring the relative peace and quiet, no longer hearing the drone of washing machines and driers or the dull thuds of garbage bins dropping shut at the end of her hallway, she showered and dressed for Clyde in pumps, flared linen shorts and a loose-fitting sweater before walking in circles for the next couple of hours mumbling to herself. She was rehearsing her lines, feeling a little peeved that she had to wait, feeling as though she had an appointment.

When he opened his door, dressed in boots, blue jeans

and a crisp button-down, he stepped into the hall admiring her. They were going for pizza and to the cineplex where they would sit in the dark and hold hands without talking. That's what he wanted.

What she wanted was more time with him, deciding she wouldn't corner him, deciding she would wait until the restaurant.

"Is this thing we're doing working for you, Clyde? Are we on for your next furlough?"

"Yes, definitely. And yes, we're definitely on. Didn't you think so?"

"I was hoping. But I'm not good with having a schedule. So please listen. I don't feel good with alternate days, like I'm some sort of part-time worker punching a clock. I want five days with you next time, like a trial, which still gives you that much time alone for whatever you do. It's not about more money or the sex. I mean that. It's about me, about me feeling good. I should even have a job by then, which means I wouldn't be hanging around all day being intrusive, being a royal pain in your ass. I don't want that." She went on, reading his eyes, refraining from reaching for his hands. "Clyde you don't have friends because you don't want friends, but at least you have a family. I don't, not anymore. I don't have anyone. They literally condemned me to living in a drab cell with someone too pathetic for words and I haven't had a girlfriend to share girl things with since he got me pregnant. He said he loved me, but he didn't. He said I was lying, that it wasn't his, making everyone at school treat me like a slut."

He took her hand, he understood. He was expecting as much, in some form, particularly since he wanted more of her as well, at least in the short-term. Five nights though…whoa. What she was suggesting was serious shit, real serious. Let's slow down here. He was not getting bogged down with a girl he hardly knew and he certainly was not throwing himself under the bus of her messy divorce. They had a good thing going on, but it was just a thing and she had to realize that would never change.

"This, us, happened from out of the blue, Marietta, something we cannot rush into for the wrong reasons. First off, I am far from being anyone's saviour. I was in the right place at the right time for both of us. Pure and simple. This is not divine intervention by a long shot. If we want more, that will happen; if we need more that's a big problem." He chuckled, kissing her hand, calming her mounting agitation. "Let me finish here, sweetheart. I'm good with testing five days, that works for me, especially since I'm free tomorrow, leaving early Sunday though. Understand that. So I'm sittin' here thinkin' let's you and me do something real special like, darlin'," which earned him a wide and bright smile, a squeal of delight and a smothering kiss he wasn't expecting.

He called all his ladies sweetheart, never giving the reason any thought. Why would he? And he couldn't help wondering as he stood when the emotional shitstorm would happen his way if she was already encroaching on his time. Five days was a big enough problem after three nights, thoughts of what would happen with her at Christmas, when he would spend his ten days in Boston with his parents and their delicate natures, flashing across his mind. No way could she go with him. Despite her fancy prep schools, which would certainly impress them, she was eighteen which would give them each a debilitating stroke if not immediate and catastrophic heart failure.

At the half-empty theatre they held hands without quiet whispers, although neither one was particularly interested in watching millionaires playacting for an audience hardly able to afford their popcorn and Cokes. The male and the female mind were focused on Marietta's five-day strategy from essentially incompatible perspectives, forgoing the 'Coming Soon' feature, wasting no time getting to his apartment and into the bed Marietta would not luxuriate in for another three weeks, his body and mind both grateful for the ardent distraction. Although at 9:00 when he closed the door behind her, sending her back to her husband, he closed his mind to her as well and, slumping depleted against the door, mused aloud, "What the fuck!"

The next day would come soon enough with a picnic lunch in the park, more outstanding sex and a one-sided woeful parting he couldn't imagine not happening. The girl was getting attached, no shit, making more of what they had going than a simple money source for her eventual escape. Not that he didn't like her, he did. He liked her very much, but he wasn't wrong, despite making Saturday everything she could have wished for.

The next morning he prepared a simple lunch with a suitable Italian white, packing a blanket and portable radio. She met him at his truck at noon wearing a short denim skirt, flat sandals and a tank top: Female Psychology 101: Positive Reinforcement. She would not let him go. No way. They were good together, great together, Marietta not surprised when he stood gaping at her.

That's right. That's what she thought, pleased with herself. He wasn't ready either.

They found a private and grassy space under a huge oak draped in Spanish moss and let time pass them by; he took her canoeing, meandering their way between flocks of indifferent ducks and idle swans, neither one spoiling the serenity and silence. Then he took her to his bed where she made love, too enraptured or blind to recognize through his eyes that his mind and his body were discrete and autonomous entities worlds apart despite leaving her weak with zealous ardour.

Then Sunday morning, as was his custom, he took ten days of laundry for cleaning, repacking his duffle bag with the clothes he had dropped off the Friday he first met Marietta in the parking lot, preferring the practice to mixing his clothes in a public tub with God knows what. Then he left his truck at the airport and forgot her. He forgot the picnic and the lake; he forgot her fingers strumming the still water and the distant gaze in her eyes that spoke volumes.

He forgot her slumped shoulders and sad expression at his door, boarding a flight to Miami where he climbed into a corporate helicopter that landed him on a speck in the ocean 200 miles offshore.

Chapter Nine

Marietta woke Sunday feeling dejected, deciding she would spend most of her day at the park with the stroller answering the same stupid questions because she could not stand the thought of being trapped in her hell with Ben. Then, later in the day, when staying a moment longer with him was again not an option, she suggested more as a threat that he go somewhere and not come back anytime soon.

When he happily obliged she made supper, remembering her cooking lesson with Clyde. She prepared her clothes for the morning, for a another round of interviews that week, hoping she would sleep through the night and wake looking and feeling her best, impossible most nights because Ben bluntly refused to touch, clean or feed his kid that for once mercifully decided it would cooperate with mom and stay quiet.

Waking, seeing Ben sprawled dead asleep on his foam bed, she dressed and did her makeup in the bathroom, maintaining her promise. She left before he woke, more likely before he opened his eyes, dropping off his kid that she had no connection with. Most days she could scarcely think of its name, a name she never used, a name suggested by a despicable and insensitive old nurse when Marietta answered that she didn't have one, that she didn't care what the thing was called.

She remembered the nurse turning on her, scathingly. And the others gaping at her, their fake hospital smiles disappearing, scolding Marietta with scowls that she did not deserve such a beautiful little girl with such a pretty name and that she would certainly be a terrible mother.

Bitches. What did they know?

Stepping from the bus in front of her first appointment, she coughed a feeble laugh. The nurse was wrong. She was not a bad mother; she wasn't any kind of mother, period, which didn't make her a bad person. She didn't belong with a going-nowhere slug like Ben, she belonged with a real man like Clyde. She deserved Clyde who was becoming more tender toward her, like a boyfriend slowly learning to love her. Their Saturday in the park could not have been more romantic after almost breaking her heart, or their lovemaking more passionate. She could only imagine their next full week together with so much more time in each other's arms, when she would have a job and no longer be dependent on him for her survival.

At the building she blew a stream of warm air past her lips, studied herself in the glass doors, and went in. She did the same nine times that week, eating a sparse lunch between interviews, until the last HR manager, not sugar coating the way things were, gave her a rude reality check.

No one was hiring high schoolers with no practical experience. She had good manners, good language skills and poise, but none of that was enough. None of that mattered. Reputable firms wanted college grads with outstanding GPAs and summer internships detailed on their résumés, something tangible to offer. And what made matters worse beyond not having any practical work experience, she didn't have a résumé.

The fact was, she was young and inexperienced with nothing whatsoever to offer. And her best chance of not wasting the privileged education she did have, was gaining a higher education that would benefit an employer. Perhaps then they could talk.

And so went her days along with most of her 800 dollars. No one wanted her and returning to school would never happen. She had no money. Nor did she know about money; she knew about daddy always being there for her, always giving her what she needed or wanted. Her life was the purest shit, married to a bum and chained to a five-month-old, destined to serve coffee or flip burgers because of them.

Still, she persisted until the third Friday in August when the interviewer abruptly ended the afternoon appointment within minutes, furious with her for wasting his time. Marietta, shocked that anyone could be that unkind, thinking she would die of embarrassment and praying her legs wouldn't fail her before reaching his door, arrived home with no sense of hope. She was at her wits' end, trapped with no way out, all the more disconsolate at seeing Clyde's truck in the parking lot.

She wanted him badly. Her life had been hell without him, the next two days promising an even worse hell knowing he was so close, frustrated and angry with herself for not having his phone number. At least if she could speak with him, hear his voice.

Making matters worse Ben was losing it, muttering on the floor about his shit job with his dirty face inches from the television. He hadn't done her in weeks, nor had he seen her naked or remotely sexy in all that time. He didn't have money for a whore, or for beers to drink some bimbo blind enough to take him home and he was getting royally pissed about things.

He hadn't cooked a single supper since her privation decree and the kid was not helping matters, leaving them virtually broke at month's end. Not to mention the cost of its daycare she was secretly funding, which in the future would take half of what Clyde would give her. It was getting bigger by the day, eating more, making more of a mess, and the woman wanted an extra fifty each week that would double her fee. That on top of more clothes and a crib bought from the Nearly New Store because it no longer fit into Marietta's spare suitcase lined with a blanket.

When she did see Clyde on the Monday, knocking on his door near noon, they went shopping for groceries, wine and liquor; they relaxed over cocktails, ate dinner, went to bed, showered together, and she left. Not exactly feeling like a hooker, though definitely not feeling like a girlfriend. How could she? She couldn't, first stopping at the woman's for the kid that had spent its day locked in a pen that mom didn't care enough to ask about. What she cared about was staying with Clyde, making him happy, working at becoming his girlfriend and even moving to a nicer building with him because no way would she ever have enough saved by Christmas.

They were happy together through the first part of the week, Clyde begging off until late afternoon Thursday and Friday for service to his truck and a medical exam without feeling the slightest guilt that he was enjoying a few hits in the Hilton lounge one day without her and at the Doubletree the next. He figured she would have a job by then, spending time with him at night like normal adults without entertaining her throughout the entire day.

She was sensational in bed, no doubt, her spectacular body seemingly tighter than what he remembered, but eighteen was not a long-term workable age. She was a teenager, not a young woman, unemployed with no prospects to negotiate or skillset to leverage, Clyde understanding completely when she asked him how she should prepare a résumé. She simply wasn't marketable.

So they designed one together, for the little good she would derive, Clyde not feeling the least bit sorry for her when hearing of her dismal few weeks. She hadn't worked a day in her life. She hadn't earned a single dime she could call her own, hadn't participated in sports or volunteered, which worried him, which made him ponder why a society girl would hookup with a high school dropout when any guy multiple times better would jump at the chance to get her in bed. She was spoiled, was spoiled, until the day she disappointed her well-to-do daddy.

Saturday he was on his own, alone for dinner on the far side of town. Friday she was adamant that she would not be pushy or intrusive. She wouldn't overdo a good thing. She would spend her Saturday focused on finding a job, when in truth the daycare woman had told her without notice that morning that she needed her weekends to herself.

Sunday he left early for the airport with a bag of soiled clothes, forgetting her completely before he entered security. Marietta spent the day doing groceries and cleaning the room, deciding she could work in a restaurant, an elegant one perhaps as a hostess. Determined that in fact she would, she left Ben on the floor and went outside to the parking lot where she at last formulated a workable plan.

Monday she went shopping for an outfit that would ensure her success, and the library where she prepared a CV from Clyde's template detailing her education and the unpaid work she did helping her mother at countless charitable events. More than the few her mother had practically coerced her into, but who would know?

Tuesday she went to her hairdresser for styling, her nails and her makeup all but exhausting her meagre finances, walking confidently into several of the city's finest establishments by day's end. Wednesday she walked through more doors, again without promise, and Thursday was no different, leaving a half-dozen restaurants without the slightest hope, until her phone chimed unexpectedly Thursday evening. The hostess at La Bonne Assiette was no longer an employee. Could Marietta take over those responsibilities the next day, and from then on Wednesday through Sunday between 3:00 and 10:00 PM at seven-fifty a week?

Yes! That was double Ben's paltry wage for sweeping floors, not that he would ever know. Nor did he matter worth a shit. Like it or not he would deal with his miserable life, leave the shop earlier, pick up his kid and be responsible for once. Then, when she was ready, he could just fuck off. Or, better yet, she would.

Chapter Ten

What mattered to Ben was her three-fifty a week and the deal she made with the woman upstairs who would take the kid three days a week, arguing that a hundred bucks was a rip-off, agreeing that Saturdays the kid would be good alone for a few hours. Thinking, yeah, and Sundays.

The following Monday Marietta went to the bank with a letter from her manager, leaving with a credit card that Ben would never hear about. In the afternoon she bought four outfits for greeting her patrons; she bought a tablet that he wouldn't hear about either, a real phone and internet service that would remain her secret since she would always be first at the mailbox each day.

The clothes she had left her parents' house with went into the trash bin in the hallway. She was no longer that girl. La Bonne Assiette was top-end; she needed to fit in and she would. Mostly she wanted to impress Clyde, the last Monday of September not coming nearly fast enough, and not because she needed her drawer or the 800 that would help honour her first credit card statement. Because she wanted him.

When he opened the door to her two hours later than he expected, she could not have been more delighted. He was speechless, mesmerized. The metamorphosis was remarkable. She looked different and she was different, somehow more mature, Marietta pushing her way past him in low-heeled pumps, a linen A-line skirt and the slightest hint of her three-quarter balconette bra showing through her silk blouse, telling him nonchalantly that he should dress for dinner. She was taking him out, and not for a pizza.

While he was changing, his curiosity largely ignored, she filled her drawer with several of her purchases, things Ben had no right to see. En route to the restaurant she was equally tight-lipped, surprising him all the more when she ordered and approved the wine, waiting until the waiter filled their glasses and left.

"I've been working for three weeks, Clyde. I'm the hostess at La Bonne Assiette."

He knew the place, his astonishment not entirely diplomatic. "I'm happy for you, Marietta." He raised his glass, clinking the crystal rim against hers. "That is truly an accomplishment, a real stepping stone."

"No kidding, a stepping stone to a Christmas that is looking really good."

"Needless to say you've told him."

She shrugged. "Why would I? Christmas is all about surprises and I do love surprises."

"The obvious question is: How does this happy revelation affect you and me, what we have?"

She inhaled an invisible deep breath, hoping and praying that her sweet Southern voice was disarming. "That's your call, Clyde. What I mean is, weekends are Mondays and Tuesdays for me unless you want me with you late on Saturdays, like normal people, like we actually mean something to each other. I am not climbing stairs so I can get laid. I never did." She sipped her wine. "I can get laid anywhere, anytime. This is all about whose bed I want to make love in. However, that said, I am way better than any whore you might remember and our agreement remains in effect until Christmas. Then, whatever happens, I'm gone. I will not stay a minute longer in that building."

Clyde sipped his wine, loosening his tie. "The lost and lonely girl becomes a lovely and determined young lady. Good for you, sweetheart." He took her hands from across the intimate setting. "The agreement stands. And something resembling a real weekend would be nice for a change, Saturdays too. That said, I think Saturdays you should stay over. I can't see where he would care. And if he does, I'll take care of that business real quick."

"Sleep over? You mean actually wake up together, like, I don't know, a couple?"

"I mean like making you feel good about yourself until Christmas. In fact, since you are adamant about leaving Savannah, starting over, why not move in. Being down there makes no sense." His smile was captivating. "I'll even give you another drawer for the short-term, Marietta, an ad hoc measure between friends."

He was beginning to love her, missed being with her. Thing is, the timing was all wrong.

"I can't, Clyde. I don't trust him. I don't trust what he might do and it's important for me to ditch him. I'm filing against him. Can you understand that? But your Saturdays, yes. Very yes. Besides, now that he's got my money he'll be out drinking and whoring." She squeezed his hands. "I leave by noon though."

He was good with that: two evenings and two nights, not five difficult days. She was ecstatic; she would wake by his side two Sunday mornings. What more could she expect…in the short-term? Everything. She wanted everything, signalling the waiter for a decadent chocolate fudge sponge topped with chocolate ganache and apricots they would share and her first ever Rémy Martin.

Back at his apartment what she did not want was hurried and functional sex. She wanted the next day and Saturday when she would come to him near the midnight hour to dance with him, make love and fall asleep in his arms for the first time. And for the first time she left feeling good, strangely eager to see Ben since she couldn't remember when.

When he did arrive home, unaware, whether by virtue of

his unfortunate birth or his utter lack of interest, she told him about the man she met at work, a gentleman customer who asked her out, who was taking her to a late dinner Saturday evening.

"That's right, a real gentleman."

He went to the fridge for a beer. "Can't say I'm surprised, Marietta. And what you mean is, this guy's buying you a meal before he takes you somewhere for a good fuck."

"Of course he'll fuck me, somewhere better than a shithole like this and not on my knees. So don't expect me here till Sunday. At least now you have beer money, and do not forget you have a kid here. Clean it or smell it, I don't care, but you will be here for it. Because if you fuck that up, like you do everything else, you'll be in even deeper shit." She snorted, seeing in his dull eyes that he wanted to strike her. "That will be on you, Ben, not me, because her mommy works nights."

*

The next morning she left minutes after Ben, taking a bus to the mall for alone time. Back in her one-room hell she cleaned the kid, fed it, carried it to the woman and climbed to 312 with more to put in her drawer.

Saturday evening she finished her work and hurried home to Clyde, to a fantasy world of dinner and wine, dancing and love-making, reigniting the passion Sunday morning after serving him breakfast in bed wearing the babydoll and G-string she bought earlier in the week. She was excited about her renegotiated relationship with him and that she was making friends at work. She was going for drinks with the girls after work the following Friday. And how cool was that?

Sunday was September 30th. When Clyde left for the airport she went downstairs to her one-room penance she was enduring for the evil she had done to her parents, to a thick smell that made her retch, wondering how she could ever balance the horror of that life with her heavenly times with Clyde.

She didn't believe she could, pondering why she couldn't move in with Clyde? He loved her, or he would one day soon. So why not? She didn't care about Ben, thankful he wasn't with her. He was a non-issue that soon wouldn't exist at all. The kid was the problem, the reason why not. He didn't give a shit about his kid; not that she ever would, but her long-term plan did not include jail time for child neglect or worse. The kid was the one thing keeping her from being whole with the man she loved.

She cleaned it thoroughly in the bath, holding it under the faucet until she was satisfied. Leaving it in the tub to dry she opened the window and got a cold beer that she took to the parking lot where she thought things through and breathed fresh air, realizing that leaving Savannah didn't matter because her parents and Ben didn't matter. What did matter was Clyde, her and Clyde together, though what she couldn't realize was how close she actually was to her freedom day, the day that would soon be the happiest and second worst day of her life.

Leaving for the restaurant, standing at the bus stop, Ben moments later unexpectedly stumbled out from the footwell still hung-over as Marietta stepped in as though passing a vile stranger.

Chapter Eleven

Friday, October 26th, was no different from 364 other days in the mid-Atlantic. The sea was calm, the sky was clear blue, the air was unusually warm and Clyde Gill was doing what he had done hundreds of times before: He was going home. He would land in Savannah near the dinner hour; he would stop for his cleaning, get home, pour a deep scotch and decompress.

He hadn't thought about her since kissing her at the door, an oil rig was not a real good place to fuck-up because of a woman or a thirst. Though he was pleased with their revised arrangement, pleased that Christmas Day was her go-bag day when he would resume his natural state of life as a serious and committed bachelor.

Arriving home he poured a double chilled with ice, showered and tuned into a couple of hours of pay-per-view girlie porn as an effective means of neutralizing three weeks with men, thinking how Marietta's body was definitely right up there with the best.

At midnight he fell asleep, leaving a pizza box and a half-empty wine bottle on the floor. Saturday, October 27th, he woke late. He guzzled a power drink, took a run, called his mom for his weekly admonishments, and prepared dinner for Marietta.

*

Saturday morning Ben woke blurry-eyed, his senses dulled from the several beers the night before, living with his whore wife marginally better since making his own smart choice to get out and live life, especially since he hadn't bagged her in months and she wouldn't be home again that night. He couldn't believe he was ever that stupid to fall for her, but she had a way. She was, he didn't know, magical or something, like a witch or whatever. And what was for sure, what happened was not his fault. Girls, they had a responsibility. Every guy knew what was. Girls, they were the ones getting laid and, if not his mom, which was crazy because she was way old enough to know the facts, at least his dad should have known and stood up for him.

The good thing was, she was getting home late most nights. Yet not so late that she couldn't manage the kid. And now, whenever she'd be out getting laid, he'd be out getting some too. No kid ever died from shit in its pants and he deserved more than his shit life with a whoring wife.

He showered and dressed into the same sneakers, jeans and the company tee-shirt he'd worn since Monday, thinking a tee with a logo made a difference. It didn't.

He disliked working Saturdays the most, feeling angrier each day with his mom and dad for how they royally fucked up his life. Hourlies and minimum-wagers worked weekends, not private school graduates. His dad was punishing him, pure and simple, making him a joke at work, trapping him in a job he couldn't leave because one day his dad would relent and see what was.

What's worse, he was trapped with her. His one hope was her job, that she wasn't bullshitting him about taking off, about getting a divorce, that the guy who'd be nailing her that evening, if he was the same guy, might not see her as a complete slut.

He hadn't eaten a decent meal since his parents threw him out. She'd even stopped making his morning coffee, stopped doing his laundry. She hated the place, so what the fuck? Seeing her asleep on the pull-out fully covered in sweats and socks and looking all pure and innocent he felt like, he didn't know, punching the smug bitch or something. She deserved something like that or worse for being a whore, for ruining his life.

Screw her, she wasn't worth shit. Besides, he knew a great place for girls better than her who were strictly out for a few beers and a good time.

Saturdays were the worst at the shop with many more customers, never knowing who might walk through the doors that he would know to see him opening crates or holding a broom, menial work made painfully more humiliating because they all knew. The friends who left him behind for college all knew and soon they'd be coming home for Thanksgiving. He didn't care about going in earlier or leaving later than the others, mandated by his asshole boss to polish counters and refill empty spaces, turn off the lights and activate the alarm.

He didn't care because all that was better than being with her.

*

Lenny Boles had metamorphosed into a man decent folks might cross the street to avoid. He was now thirty-two, not particularly muscular given his countless days in the yard pumping iron, and no longer particularly good-looking as a result of the hard life the once handsome teenager and failed criminal now wore etched in his face given that he had spent virtually all his adult years incarcerated.

He walked with his fists clenched, with a peculiar bounce in his stride as though ever-ready to pounce or spring on demand. He constantly glanced over his hunched shoulders, regularly turning full circles without missing a step. Though more unnerving in the mind any passerby were his dark brown eyes that were no longer liquid and charming, sunken into dark grey rings on an ashy prison-grey and scarred complexion, making contact with every wary soul he passed.

His dark brown hair was dull and streaked a yellowish-grey, long and slick, and tied in a tail. He had nothing in life but the clothes on his back that he would rummage for in charity bins several times each week for a fresh change that would alter his appearance as part of his strategic plan.

He was a loser cum drifter who for the past several weeks had saved his quarters and dimes panhandled each day while bunking down at a halfway house at night, saving for bus fare that would carry him to his dream because he had not the remotest chance in hell of hitching a ride. And now he was there, on the streets of Savannah, in his promised land. A place that long ago captured his heart.

He could have enjoyed a good life, but the good life and loving family he did have as a teenager abruptly ended the day he relieved a drugstore cashier of her morning's receipts not many months into his eighteenth year. He was always a lazy kid and lacklustre student, but that day he downgraded himself to plain stupid, proving his caseworker right that he was not worthy of remediation in the least way. He would come to no good, which he proved was the case with amazing consistency, particularly the day he met up with the young and lovely Lucy Tatum.

He didn't didn't think much on her, the one who put him away, not for a long while anyhow. But she sure was a pretty thing, and smart. Damn straight. Could've blown his socks clear off, though, the day he saw Trisha Tallum in court with her shiny gold badge and the fancy holster hangin' on her hip. Not in handcuffs cryin' and whimperin'. Didn't seem as though she was gloatin', but she was. That was fer damn sure. Yes, sir. Proud as punch she was for nailin' Lenny Boles.

He got out in seven years ostensibly for keeping his nose on his face and following the rules, when the truth was they needed the space. He was a changed man, at long last boarding a bus Savannah-bound several weeks earlier for a new beginning because this time he was smarter. He truly was.

He had a real plan, a good one, taking his time figuring things out that did not include begging assholes as bad or worse than him for minimum wage jobs. Been there, done that, where he wouldn't last a week. Instead he spent some evenings behind restaurants eating scraps, sometimes getting laid by women not much cleaner or prettier than the rodents scurrying across his legs and chest when he slept against walls or under cardboard blankets, spending other nights at the mission on a cot when he could shower in the morning and feel in some ways human.

The Savings & Loan was small, located at a four-way intersection, with three female tellers and what he supposed was their female boss he'd seen several Sundays while standing at the ATM as though he was actually familiar with using one. The branch opened those days from noon till 5:00, apparently with no or not many customers after 4:30 when traffic was light. Easy, real easy. In and out with at least—a bank that size—fifty K easy, with four possible escape routes.

The gun shop he had come across was a few blocks down and would be even easier any Saturday night with plenty of time for him to get things done. He had a good hiding place for the gun and maybe some cash from the till with plenty of time to get himself there and hunker down for the night. The guy he'd been watching from a safe distance several nights, cleaning up, playing Commando Joe on account of he thought no one was seeing him duck behind counters taking aim at some invisible bad guy, would not be a problem. If anything he would shit himself blind. He was as tall as Boles, which wasn't an issue. He was a kid going nowhere, a beefer, Boles guessing thirty, forty pounds extra on his belt with zero survival skills and way past being a threat.

Glancing at the watch he'd slipped onto his wrist while passing a drugstore display, the cheap face glowed 9:55. And the gun shop guys, they were going home.

He waited twenty minutes or thereabouts, feeling a mounting rush of adrenalin, crossing the parking lot and walking through the unlocked doors.

"We're closed, friend. Come again tomorrow."

"Listen, I got me five hundred cash. The best I can

manage given my depleted circumstances. Give me somethin' used that ain't broke and we're done. That ain't too much to ask."

"No can do. Sorry. Come back tomorrow."

"Five bills, cash, fer somethin' you got layin' around. Help me out here. I'm kinda pressed."

Ben Keller thought for a moment. The guy was half-right, he guessed. His boss almost never checked old inventory and what would a used piece collecting dust matter to anyone? Better still, he could put the money to good use, especially that night.

"Five won't get you much, at best an old police Glock. Nothing fancy. Reliable though. That sound about right?"

Boles nodded. "And rounds. A weapon ain't much use without 'em. Maybe a box?"

Ben nodded. "Done. Give me a minute."

"Thanks, man. Really do appreciate the kindness."

The guy was nineteen, twenty tops, probably living at home with mommy and believing he could actually use the pistol on his hip. And beyond stupid, leaving him alone with handguns everywhere and hundreds of boxes of amo within reach. Glocks were good and the price was right, but they were bulky cop guns with no character and never good enough for the US Marines. He snorted, he didn't have the five-hundred anyway. He didn't have squat. What he did have however was a penchant for the sleek Beretta 92FS with a fifteen-round magazine of game-changing parabellum cartridges, a fond memory from his good ol' days in Atlanta, one he was loading as Ben Keller came back holding a Glock.

"Changed my mind while ya'll were gone. I'm takin' this one here."

"Not with five-hundred you're not. No way that's happening."

Out of the blue Lenny Boles got an instant hate on for the guy, there was something not right about him. "Yeah, about that. I got me enough fer a coffee and sandwich later on. So like I said, I'm takin' this one here."

Shit!

Once he was alone in the shop Ben had again put his favourite Colt Commander on his hip, a serious weapon for serious times, every bit as good as the Beretta and not for pretending he could ever be anyone's hero. But this was his one chance at redemption, to prove himself, to work side by side with his dad at HO and one day take over the family business. No way his father would not be proud of him, or the other guys not finally in awe of him.

He often spent his lunch hours at the range behind the shop, firing off rounds from demo models. He was good, almost always hitting the paper target. And how often had he practiced a quick draw, aiming and firing, almost hitting the outline most times? And this jerk-off was standing close, a few feet away, fucking with the clip, distracted.

He stepped back the way he practiced in the mirror the times he was alone, focused, time standing still. He didn't hear the Beretta's clip snapping in place, or see his own hand wavering. He saw a bright flash that instantly blinded him and mercifully numbed his senses, that blew his forehead apart and killed him.

Lenny Boles whistled a high-pitched stream of air through his lips, skipping backward a few paces, scanning the shop for no reason other than he had royally fucked-up—this time big-time. He'd made a royal mess he was not anticipating. He did not go in expecting he would kill the guy; that just sort of happened as though in that exact instant he somehow knew that he should. In spite of which the night was decidedly not going as planned, which did not mean losing his cool.

He quickly took a handful of fives and tens from Ben Keller's pockets, enough for a better meal at an all-nighter and a breakfast that would fortify him for the coming day. He shut the lights and went into the back, happily surprised, thinking that sometimes things happen for the best.

By the time he was finished, satisfied with his evening. He hadn't fucked-up after all, proud of himself. He'd done good. He was dressed in new boots and clean socks, camo pants and camo tee-shirt, and a warm khaki fleece. He was a man reborn, standing at salvation's door, taking the minor disappointment of an empty cashbox in stride.

He was gone by 10:45 through the back door, leaving Ben Keller in peace, sitting at a table not long after and not far away eating a steak and potato dinner with a beer and key lime pie.

Life was good and would soon get a whole lot better.

Chapter Twelve

Saturday night Marietta hurried directly to Clyde's apartment from work. She was starving, under his strictest orders not to eat more than a light salad for supper. He had spent the entire day making bread rolls and cooking a spicy carrot soup. Cornish hens and puréed potatoes were browning to perfection in his oven, a melody of freshly cut veggies steaming and glistening with butter on the stovetop.

The wine was a delicate French white from the Loire valley; dessert was a frozen sorbet later served with biscuits Suisse and a sweet dessert wine. The fine cognac, requisite to the most sumptuous dining anywhere, he served in his living room as a prelude to lovers entwined on his sofa listening to Dino.

Exhausted from their separate days and dancing to wear off what they could of the exquisite meal, his lips smeared with as much gloss as hers, he laid her in his bed. Crawling in beside her, kissing her, promising he would make the most passionate love with her in the morning, he fell into a deep sleep and woke what seemed like moments later to more soft kisses and sparkling blue eyes.

*

8:00 AM Sunday:
Marietta spent a restless night and early hours drifting in and out of sleep, caressing and loving the man in her arms while she could, dreaming of him when she couldn't.

Rather than waking him, rather than spoiling his serenity

and her dream they would one day share, she slipped from their bed and padded into the kitchen brewing coffee and sitting quietly in their living room creating an idyllic life with him.

*

8:30 AM Sunday:

Jan Jenkins woke late, dreamily, stretching and yawning, hating that she would go for a run. But she would. She seldom enjoyed two days off in a row and no way was she going to the testosterone-dominated precinct gym for a workout in flannel sweats that were her first-line of defence against catcalls and frail egos. The second were her fists and her feet and the fifth Dan hanging in her locker. Her microfibre shorts and crop tops were strictly for her private runs and the rare times she made use of the gym at her upscale address where both male and female neighbours approved with beaming smiles.

So what!

Sauntering into her bathroom she stopped by the full-length mirror, doing a three-sixty. Wow! did not describe her. She was thirty-two, could pass for mid-twenties, everything was in the right place and flawless. Somebody's loss, she mused, convinced she would be a spinster by fifty or a desperate lesbian by forty. And what would her best friend Marla think of that? She gurgled a laugh, fairly certain of what Vance would think.

Squirming into her shorts and top, she shrugged at her reflection. One day. Maybe. But until then she was not about to play lap pogo with her fellow cops, giving them a quick thrill and her an instant reputation. She thought too much of Vance. Dammit.

*

9:00 AM Sunday:

She loved Clyde. She loved everything about him, letting him sleep late in their bed while she sat curled into their sofa musing on how she adored him, how he adored her and how perfect their life together was and would be. And despite being expected at work in six hours she was not about to let Mr.

103

Sleepyhead renege on his promise.

She sauntered into the bedroom, standing gazing at him, carrying a tray with more freshly brewed coffee and decadent French pastries she had brought home from the restaurant, wearing her latest and most intoxicating slip and panty set to-date. She was learning. She was becoming an elegant and sophisticated young lady, the woman she always dreamed of becoming, a woman intent on making him love her and miss her more each day.

Their precious Sunday mornings together would never be for God's word, hand-clapping and joyous hallelujahs, not for the week in review or expert advice on one's financial security. Those few hours were all about them, her jubilation steadily reaching a high-pitched and delirious crescendo.

*

9:40 AM Sunday:

"That girl is an absolute doll. What a splendid evening."

"A super evening with two hot girls to myself. Doesn't get better than that. Uh-uh, no way." Vance Matthews eased his tray from the bed to the floor, staring down at the half-eaten toasted bagel and the empty bowl smeared with yogurt and granola. "She's probably already doing a run, turning heads."

"So should you when I'm gone, my love." Marla chuckled. "Can't be very good for your male ego knowing your petite sergeant can beat you up."

"Jenkins, maybe. Not you, missy." He reached over, pulling her across his legs, tugging at her nightie and turning her sweet Georgie white bum a deep shade of pink with several meaningful slaps. "This day is mine, woman, all mine. Destinations: The fridge for a few cold ones and the hammock."

She scowled, creasing her brow and pursing her lips, pushing away, stripping away the chiffon turn-on with her back to him, accusing him of spousal abuse and ungentlemanly conduct. Though several minutes later she emerged from the bathroom wrapped in a towel and a turban, smiling, tugging a skirt and blouse from her closet, her lingerie and nylons du jour from her dresser before disappearing again into the bathroom.

Reappearing moments before ten, dressed for her short-stick Sunday at the bank, she was still smiling. "I'll be in that hammock with you at six, latest, my love."

He smirked. Of course. "I thought you might."

She leaned over him, kissing him, patting his face. "Love you."

He drew a hand between her legs from her knees to her thighs and squeezing, smirking. "Ditto. Enjoy the day. "

Pushing him away, eventually, she stood, a second later twirling toward his personal phone, whispering a strong and meaningful "Shit, Vance! Really?"

*

10:02 AM Sunday:
Jan Jenkins' run was a good one, garnering countless appreciative smiles and envious glances.

So what!

She arrived home sweating and breathless, checking her pulse, ready for a cool shower alone and an afternoon shopping spree alone, thinking she might just rent a man for Thanksgiving and Christmas with Marla and Vance. And how desperate would that be?

She didn't care; she was pathetic. She wasn't just a single girl with a big gun, she was filthy rich. So the ones who weren't intimidated by the gun or her ability to crush their nuts with her feet, they couldn't deal with her money and the million-dollar condo. Creeps.

Towelling herself dry, humming as she laid out her newest skirt and and blouse, she stopped cold. No! She would not look. She wouldn't. She wasn't there. That was the reason; that was the real reason men ran from her: The fucking phone. Shit!

Seconds later she pressed *End*, disconnecting with a curse. Then she pressed *Send,* hearing that her partner would be there in fifteen.

*

9:45 AM Sunday:

Like clockwork three employees of Keller's Hunting & Gun Supplies drove into the shop's parking lot where they assumed their usual casual stances, leaning between their trucks, their boots braced against the running-boards, enjoying their coffees and the warmth of Georgia's autumn sunshine, talking about their Saturday night hits and misses and their high-performance redneck rides.

The trio scarcely needed to check their watches; Sundays in the South were casual days, a time for decompressing and being with family, dispelling whatever wasn't so great about the past week and getting on with life. They weren't expecting the boss' kid, shaking their heads, not entirely surprised the doors were unlocked, not sure what they should do or say about the incredibly careless oversight. Not that something like that wasn't bound to happen some day or other, bein' the boss' kid was a total fuck-up ayn' all. Pure shit fer brains, truth be told.

Walking in, none of them understanding Keller's reasoning since their hounds were smarter than his kid most days, they stopped dead in their tracks. Fear mixed instantly with horror, an icy chill few men experience coursing through their veins, each mind downloading and processing the bloody atrocity at different rates of speed per second, each one turning in an instant, running like all get out into the parking lot and the trucks for their own weapons.

*

10:03 AM Sunday:

Within moments of the frantic call Savannah uniformed cops began arriving from all directions, sirens blaring, electric blue dome and grill lights flashing, forming a barrier, the last car in barricading the entrance. Though no one was rushing in gung-ho, no one needed a civic funeral making them a hero or someone's wife a widow. They weren't at a bank or anything as simple, this was a weapons utopia for anyone with a wife-gone-bad, a grudge, a hate-on for life, or some righteous anti-government pissed-off activist making things right. No one was going in till the robot inside and the drone peering through windows and over the rooftop confirmed a reasonable expectation of safety.

What they got was that and a whole lot more. What the robot/drone combo showed them up close and personal in HD colour-enhanced imagery made each cop nauseous.

Once inside, what came first into view were the blood splatter and particulate that was much of Ben Keller's face, jaw, and the contents of his head sprayed across a wall rack displaying high-end handguns with one notable exception. On the floor behind the counter lay what remained of nineteen-year-old Ben Keller soaked in blood.

Two of the three Keller employees weren't paid enough. However one man, the oldest and a war vet, did volunteer to verify what was missing. Which didn't mean much. Whoever the guy was, he wanted a gun. Not a big deal in the South. Who didn't want a gun?

*

10:25 AM Sunday:
Matthews and Jenkins arrived at the scene that was already cordoned off, interviewing the three men while waiting for the forensic team who would photograph the crime scene, make the splattered wall their own, bag the victim and take Keller to the lab for further examination to prove he'd been shot.

When they were gone Lieutenant Matthews called Warren Keller.

*

10:40 Sunday:
The sabbath was always a slow news day. This one however had news hounds sniffing at every possible corner for tidbits after gleaning practically nothing from the cops inside the taped-off perimeter, finding the Keller home locked-down moments

before Warren and Peggy would have left for church where the pious and the apparently pious would once again join hands in song and prayer and be one in God's eyes. Others fell upon Marshal and Leanne Baker, while those with the keenest senses quickly unearthed the mother lode: Marietta Keller's once-upon-a-time classmates who had once either envied or hated her.

The city's most popular affiliate was first on-site, first with the probing questions that would increase their ratings at the cost of—well, no one cared. Ratings mattered more than another predictable statistics. It's what they did, they glorified otherwise mundane statistics that most viewers didn't give a shit about. Not until tragedy might one day visit their homes, but that was for another day, another Breaking News event. Savannah was a city and people got killed in cities every day. Ben Keller drew the short straw, luck of the daily draw; his time had arrived, his fifteen minutes of posthumous fame and glory. Or as long as the media could capitalize on him, despite the interviewer's most sincere and practiced empathy.

*

11:05 AM Sunday:
Warren Keller's Lincoln screeched into his parking lot without Peggy who was at home sobbing in the arms of caring and distraught neighbours and friends. He didn't see his son, didn't touch or kiss his son farewell, his three men assuring him that was a good thing. He did not need the memory already vividly etched in their minds and, with nothing else to say or do, they went to their homes to get seriously drunk.

Matthews and Jenkins let that process happen before stepping in, commiserating with a distraught parent before transmuting into impersonal detectives interviewing a business owner. The cold reality being that Ben was gone, a son brutally murdered, the victim of a robbery gone bad; the sad reality being that a father's final and everlasting memory of his child would be a cruel moment at the family's front door one year earlier that he could now never recant and would, throughout the rest of his years, deeply regret.

When they were done the detectives drove Keller to his home, guiding him safely through a throng of relentless news vultures who would soon be speaking with Ben Keller's young wife. That was the easy part, sitting with a disconsolate mother was not, the curious juxtaposition of their humanity and the impassive nature of the job making their day selfishly worse.

*

Twelve Noon, Sunday:

Marietta waited as long as she dared to shower, mildly miffed that Clyde was watching her and not participating, pouting when he steadfastly refused with a wicked grin to join her, claiming he was simply enthralled.

She loved showering with him; she loved the sensation and the smell of foamy lather coating her body, cascading from her shoulders to her belly, to her thighs and her toes. She loved Clyde. She loved how he would lift her into his arms and kiss her, his hands firmly clasping her smooth and perfect bum, her arms tightly wound around his neck, her breasts pressed against his chest. She loved how he adored her.

What she did not love was leaving him, dressing half-heartedly in a tee-shirt and jean shorts from her drawer, carrying her Saturday outfit over her arm and not caring a hoot who might see her.

Leaving him with an ardent kiss at his door was difficult, yet in her mind and in her heart descending step by step into her one-room hell, knowing full-well what to expect, was that much worse. She had to get out and soon; she didn't know how much more she could take of Ben's silent cruelty, his increasingly vulgar habits and his refusal to acknowledge his kid. The once polite teenager who had captivated her with effusive charm and attention had transmuted overnight into a dishevelled and mannerless boor who she loathed beyond words.

Stepping into the colourless flat she slapped a hand to her mouth, all but vomiting from the immediate impact of the suffocating stench. The one saving grace wasn't that the kid was sleeping, not for Marietta. Her relief was in not seeing the cretin she once loved, the derelict she once willingly shared her precious body with without the slightest inhibition. What fool she, her greatest fear being that Clyde and the cretin fascinated with guns would one day cross paths.

What then?

She slammed the door, totally pissed, slumping against the wall. She had minutes earlier stepped from her Heaven three floors above, spiralling into Hell. She wasn't religious; she was not raised as a God-fearing Christian. She was raised to be a good, kind, and decent girl. In spite of which, at that exact moment, she needed that self-righteous pastor's God to do things right and just eradicate the poorest excuse ever for a human. To get him out of her life for good. He was a total loss, absolutely good for nothing.

*

12:35 PM Sunday:

The kid was strapped again into its stroller and Marietta was dressed for her workday, the open window doing nothing to depollute the foul air. She was leaving, she needed out. She would not taint what she had with Clyde with her otherwise miserable existence. Then came three alarming knocks on her door, startling her, that for some reason made her nervous.

She wasn't expecting Ben, and Clyde was acutely aware that part of her life was not his to share unless Ben did something stupid.

Three more determined knocks made her feel trapped, cursing herself for not leaving minutes earlier, a man's deep voice declaring he was a detective with the Savannah PD. Then a woman's equally firm voice assured her they were the police, needing to speak with her on an urgent matter concerning her husband.

Stepping inside the cramped space Vance Matthews felt instantly nauseous, putting a hand to his throat as though choking back the inevitable. Jan Jenkins wasn't as generous. She was a fashion statement in linen slacks, a silk blouse and blazer and what she was seeing made her feel dirty, disgust screaming from her eyes and wry face.

Nothing she saw matched up with the woman staring at her in a slip dress and bolero jacket: the crying baby girl in a hand-me-down stroller, an open laundry basket in the corner, bare walls, a frayed couch, blankets tossed onto a foam mat on the floor and suitcases stacked against a wall. Neither did the civic address when the Kellers and Bakers lived in uptown suburbia.

Given their unpleasant task she might at least have touched or held the baby, but not this one. The poor thing was naked under a soiled and threadbare blanket that wasn't fit for a flea-infested dog to lie on. No wonder she was crying, Jenkins making a mental note that she would contact Child Protection Services the following day. Babies having babies. At least this time she would save one baby from the other. She most certainly would, Matthews correctly anticipating a female tirade en route to the precinct.

Five seconds later: "What do you want? What did he do?"

Matthews answered; Jenkins had other concerns. "Mrs. Keller, a robbery took place at the Keller gun shop last night, during which your husband was fatally wounded. We are terribly sorry for your loss."

Although he wasn't, neither was Jenkins. Sometimes they were, other times they had no reason. Showing compassion was an optional part of the job, but got old real fast, Matthews realizing he needn't waste the energy on her. He was more interested in the wife's eyes. The girl wasn't in shock, she was processing. He might have said that Ben Keller was issued a parking ticket.

"Ma'am," he continued, questioning the obvious, "you weren't concerned when your husband didn't come home last night?" Silence. "Ma'am, Mrs. Keller…"

"You mean he's dead?"

"Yes, ma'am," Jenkins answered. "He is very dead."

Marietta coughed a curt laugh, a curious smile curving her lips into a sneer. "In that case, detective, you have made my day. I could not have hoped for better news. Thank you. And no, I was not concerned. I thought he was out getting drunk or fucking some bimbo. And you're right, about what you're thinking. You are very right. This place is an absolute shithole, one I'm leaving very soon."

Matthews asked, "I take it, ma'am, that not everything was perfect in paradise, or with the family? The Kellers, the Bakers, they live very well."

Marietta turned a half-circle, sweeping the foul air with an outstretched arm. "This paradise is my punishment for the rich man's loser son practically raping me. That, that stack of shit against the wall, that's my reminder of everything rotten in my life because of him. Not only am I relieved he's dead, I could not be happier. This is my freedom day, I finally have my life back. So when you catch the guy, you thank him for me. He did me a huge favour." She looked at Jenkins. "Is there something else, detective, are we done here? I'm working today and need to get the kid upstairs to its sitter. Do I sign papers or something, or what?"

It? Really? "No, ma'am, no papers. We've done our job. You go have yourself a wonderful day."

She turned and strode out disgusted, although her business with Mrs. Keller was far from over, leaving Matthews to tip his fedora and follow.

"That is one cold woman."

"Cold, Vance? Do you think so? I should have slapped that snide bitch. And, believe me, she's going nowhere but court."

At times rank didn't matter. She was right. Of course he felt sorry for the little girl, but more so as a man he felt sorry for the next guy the Keller woman would meet, thinking as he walked out that he would surprise Marla at the Savings & Loan with a romantic dinner down by the river. The day was beautiful and warm and life was too short not to live every moment.

*

No sooner had they gone than Marietta's phone chimed. Her boss was calling. He was watching the Sunday News at Noon. He was shocked and dismayed by how she had blatantly lied. She lied about being single and unattached. She lied about her age and about her one-year working abroad. Even more despicable was that she lied by not telling him she had a seven-month-old baby.

She was no longer a part of his restaurant family. She was fired.

*

1:05 PM Sunday:
Clyde Gill sat in his living room stunned. He could not believe what was ravaging his mind. Ben Keller was dead, murdered in his father's gun shop for what the cops believed was a failed robbery, leaving behind a teenage wife and a baby girl. A baby girl whose teenage mother left him an hour earlier, who'd been with him the entire night, who was downstairs with the girl and doing what exactly? She never lost a baby. She was downstairs with it, getting ready for work. Crazy.

He relived their times together. The math didn't work. She said Keller was a low-wage earner working two jobs to make half-decent money, not the son of a successful Georgia businessman who had nothing to say about his son's murder. Or her parents, whose apparent indifference to their daughter being a teenage widow was difficult to fathom. Or was, until the media sniffed out her former classmates eagerly describing her popularity and her last two years at school: Miss Congeniality.

Her being eighteen was issue enough, one he could live

113

with—for a while. Could have, not now. He was done. Hearing her described that way, as a teenager, at once made their intimacy perverse and, notwithstanding her aptitude and voracity, she was a persistent and pathological liar.

Pushing his weight from the sofa he went into the bedroom, dressing before filling a plastic garbage bag with her clothes, minutes later knocking on her door, the girl he had already evicted from his mind, his week and his very immediate future.

Her face was wet and drawn, her eyes weary and red, gasping when she saw the bag. Her life was falling apart.

Stepping past her, showing no surprise, he dropped the bag. "What's her name?"

"Jodie. Her name's Jodie." She wiped her face. "Clyde, sweetheart, I can explain this."

"No, you cannot. The way I see things, Jodie's been alone here since this time yesterday."

"No, she wasn't. I swear. I would never do that. There's a woman who takes her, upstairs."

"Most times, not this time. The place smells like a public shitbox, Marietta. Think I'll be taking another shower sometime soon. It's a miracle this little thing can even breathe in here. I know I'm on the verge of puking."

"Sweetheart…"

"No, no sweetheart. No anything, we're done."

"Do not do this, Clyde. We mean too much to each other. We'll get through this. This is not my fault." She went to touch him, pushing him farther away. "I lost my job. They fired me."

"Things catch up with us, Marietta. Nice home your parents have. I can't say they seemed entirely pleased with the media people trampling their manicured front yard. I've been trying to figure out what you did that was so bad that you put yourself here—in this shitbox with him and little Jodie. Something very appalling in the mind of a parent, something more than getting laid behind some bleachers."

She should have been horrified, but she wasn't. "Whatever they said are lies. They never liked me."

He retreated into the hallway for distance and cleaner air. "Like I said, we're done. I'm leaving, Marietta. The building, I mean. I need a complete disconnect from this…from you. Suppose now I will get that fancy condo downtown, make my mother halfway happy. We had some good times together, Marietta, fun times. But this," he pointed at the baby whose bright green eyes he imagined were desperately imploring him, "this isn't right. Give her to someone who wants her. Keller being killed, that's a good thing for you and for her. Start over, let the girl start over. Give her a chance to be better than you."

He closed the door behind him, Marietta watching from her window as he climbed into his truck and drove off. Half an hour later she was back from Ben's once favourite package store with a quart of vodka. A few hours after that she was passed out on the foam mat as Lenny Boles sauntered into the bank and a brighter era feeling relaxed and self-assured, his face masked with a billed camo cap and sunglasses, Detective Vance Matthews recognizing at first sight that his day had gone irreversibly to shit.

*

4:35 PM Sunday

Lenny Boles went in confident that he would succeed, that a fresh beginning was moments away. He'd seen the same three female tellers and their lady boss arrivin' for work at noon, their last customer walkin' in some minutes earlier, takin' his time, some middle-aged guy in a fancy suit and fedora who'd more'n likely embarrass himself the moment things got busy.

He was good to go. The streets were virtually clear of traffic, good, and by the time sirens started piercin' the still air, all hell breakin' loose, he'd be long gone and set for life.

The young teller watching him come closer greeted him with a warm Southern smile as real as a two-dollar bill. The man a few steps away was leaning on the counter smiling and talking smalltalk with his teller about whatever as though they might be familiar with each other. He wasn't an issue.

"Mornin', miss. Seems I'm in need of some cash to git me through the week." No one else was payin' him any mind, not until he brought out the 92FS, evokin' loud gasps from both women that brought a contented smile to his face. "Whatever that pretty little thing sittin' in the glass cage behind ya'll has conveniently nearby would be much appreciated. And let's git that boss lady over here so we can all of us git home fer dinner this evenin'." He faced the man. "Friend, I'd surely be much obliged if ya'll would kindly step back aways. I ain't plannin' on stayin' long. So let's not ya'll and me git complicated."

He waved the gun, watchin' till the guy had calmly back-stepped several feet, too preoccupied to notice the man wasn't the least bit agitated. Then four-thirty-five became 4:40 as though mere seconds had passed, the central teller scurrying over with a large canvas bag. All the trembling girl could manage was "sixty thousand."

He took her at her word, given the circumstances and his pressin' schedule. Reachin' for the bag he thanked her kindly, orderin' the four facedown onto the floor and askin' fer their fullest cooperation, likewise askin' the well-dressed gent for his very kind consideration.

Lenny's escape route was indelibly etched in his mind. He'd practiced and practiced till he got things right. He knew in which direction he would run, where he would hide the money and himself after first losing the gun, the hat and the glasses blocks apart. He hadn't been stupid in a long while. Those days were gone for good. He had at last redeemed himself and this time there wasn't no Trisha Tallum to mess him up.

Turning, fleeing toward the doors, keeping his head down, mere seconds from disappearing onto the street and into the city's alleyways, a glass panel shattered in front of him in sync with the startling and deafening explosion from the cop's service weapon. He lurched forward, stumbling and dropping the bag, feeling numb, feeling nothing, reaching out with his free hand for the doorframe, not defeated once again but very dead.

He was not goin' back, he couldn't. What was the point? Waitin' ayn' all, trapped in a cell, the fear of his pendin' execution festerin' more with each passin' day. This guy didn't know who he was or that he had killed Ben Keller. He wasn't facin' no fifteen minimum for armed robbery and bein' a repeat offender. Georgia favoured the death penalty and he was an unrepentant three-time loser. He was truly and sorely fucked on account of his bein' stupid and nothin' the cop was sayin' made sense.

There was no way they would make this easy, there was nothin' they would work out. What bullshit was that? He fucked-up, is all. He should have somehow been smarter, but he wasn't. Never was and never would be, he supposed. His time had come, was the simple truth. His time had most surely come. He slowly turned and faced the man, the Beretta by his side. The tellers and the boss lady were out of sight, strongly advised in a strangely calm voice to stay down, that things would work out and be alright.

Matthews' weapon was ready, held in steady hands.

"Things are lookin' like I might've misjudged ya'll, friend. Not that ya'll bein' a man of the law makes much difference given our current situation. The name's Lenny Boles, thinkin' I can save ya'll some trouble. Was me killin' that Ben Keller fellah last night."

"I do know that, Mr. Boles."

Boles took a second, snorting, figurin' things out in his mind.

"Wasn't my intention, wasn't in the plans. Just kinda happened, is all, somehow feelin' deep inside like I was supposed to, like I was somehow doin' somethin' good fer once. Strange to say, not that I'm justifyin'." He glanced at the

Beretta. "Sorry about his family ayn' all. That's the truth. Guess, though, this is where things end. Sorry about that fer both our sakes. Things in a man's life just sometimes git outta control, when there ain't no goin' back no how. Now ya'll tell those lovely ladies when this is done that I am truly sorry fer makin' their day unpleasant. Yers as well. Needed some money for start fresh, is all."

Vance Matthews' gun hadn't moved a millimetre. He was focused, and he was tense. In all his years of service he had never shot a man, let alone kill one. Now he would because this would end badly with his wife crying on her knees behind her counter. Fuck!

"Do not do this, Mr. Boles. Killing Keller, that's second degree. That's time, not the needle. Do not do this to yourself, or these fine ladies here. They do not deserve this."

No defence could ever prove second degree. Not a chance, not in Georgia. Even so, he'd be near sixty or worse gettin' out, incarcerated most of his life, caged most of his life. So what was the point? Do somethin' right for once.

He moistened his lips. His mind was fully made up, figurin' a second more of breathin' didn't much matter. Smilin' as best he could, inhalin' his last deep breath, the gaze in his clear eyes was distant. Raisin' the Beretta in a flash, doin' things right fer once, all fingers tightly on the grip, his body jolted violently backward through the shattered door, crashing Lenny Boles onto a carpet of splintered glass.

Matthews' shot was a good one, clean and quick: suicide by a good-hearted teddy bear cop. Boles was dead, his final thought obliterated with a single .38 round impacting his forehead. Although a relieved Matthews would not fully understand until later that Sunday that Boles was in fact better off dead, that he hadn't once done anything decent, good or worthwhile in his entire life and likely never would have. He was just plain bad.

Matthews did what was right, no question. He would

eventually get over the righteous kill, forgetting Lenny Boles completely, yet forever believe that he was meant to be there for his wife and the other ladies. However what neither he nor Jenkins would ever discover or ever envision is how Lenny Boles coming fatefully together with Ben Keller would one day turn desperation into hope for a young woman who never knew of her real father or the luckless ex-con who murdered him for the better good.

Lost and forlorn years into her future, yet paradoxically free from the little she knows of her life, sitting helplessly on her corner watching a man end his life, she wonders why she isn't the one with courage enough to stand facing the speeding bus with her hands outstretched as though expecting deliverance into a better existence: a life she knows she will never see.

However what Jodie Carter does not know that day many years into her future, what she cannot see from her stool, is that her saviour is peering down at her, pondering the compelling girl he sees each day now sitting impassively amidst the panic and mayhem, worried by the envy in her sad eyes, wondering if she's worth his trouble. Or will she simply disappoint him the way they did?

Chapter Thirteen

Monday Marietta woke late, not moving from the floor, staring blankly at the empty glass and near-empty bottle. Not discounting the nausea of a major hangover, she felt sick to her stomach.

She groaned a guttural scream, angry that she had no one who would care or comfort her, angry with Clyde for using and discarding her. She hated him. She hated Ben for getting her pregnant before he had a chance to throw her away. She hated her parents for not calling, for not caring, knowing that her husband was murdered, that she was completely alone and afraid.

She hated the Kellers for not coming when she most needed the comfort of family. They knew where she lived, how she lived in squalor. They did that to her, to their dead son. So he was dead, so what? She snorted at the irony. Ben was dead, murdered at work, killed by his father who put him there.

She jerked forward, sitting straight. She was feeling sorry for herself. She was pitiful; she had to get real and she would. She would survive. Her husband was killed at work, doing his job. He was brutally murdered because of a father's hatred and indifference. How cool was that? How good was that for her and her little baby girl?

She clambered to her feet. Killed in his father's gun shop with no way of protecting himself. He was defenceless, cut down in his teens. That was surely worth something, an insurance policy or something. They owed her something for taking away her devoted husband, the man she loved, the man who gave her a beautiful baby girl.

She brewed coffee she couldn't finish, made toast she left in the toaster after once again holding the kid under the tub's faucet. She fed it pabulum and for a few minutes let the milk she'd drawn into a plastic eyedropper drip into its mouth.

When she finished, when the kid began crying, she left it and went to shower. She put on her best dress and several minutes later drugstore makeup transformed her from a wretched drunk into a mournful and grieving widow.

Leaving the building she felt revitalized, energized with renewed determination, not remotely suspecting that Detective Jan Jenkins of Homicide was walking into the over-burdened Child Protection Services where she opened a case file regarding the probable neglect of one Jodie Keller.

Fuelled by her new sense of hope, Marietta went by bus to the Keller home, assuming he would be there. When Peggy Keller opened the door the women stared at each other mutely until Warren Keller came to see who the visitor was. He didn't waste his time or his breath, not doubting for a moment why the girl was on his doorstep, not surprised that she wasn't wasting time either.

"What is it you want, Marietta? With Ben gone from us, you are no longer family."

"I wasn't family when he was living, Mr. Keller. Neither was he. I'm not here for family, I don't need family. I've learned that from both of you and the ones a few blocks over. I'm here for my husband who was killed, murdered in your shop while working for you. You put him there, you made him work there. And I'm here for my daughter who no longer has a father, who will never know her selfish and cruel grandparents. I'm giving you one chance to make things right, Mr. Keller, because I'm an unemployed teenage widow living in poverty with my fatherless baby. I'm not sure, I'm not, but I sort of think there's a lawyer somewhere in this city who might take me on pro bono."

She stood her ground. In a single year the few friends she did have had turned on her and her loving mother and father had disowned her; she suffered alone through a terrible childbirth, living in a basement in poverty and squalor with a husband who sank into depression and needed beer more than a wife who loved him deeply. No, she was not finished with them, not by a long shot, and they deserved every harsh word. If he believed he was intimidating her, turning his pre-funeral sallow face purple, leaning over her, believing he was threatening her, then think again.

"The fact is, Mr. Keller, you put him there for getting me pregnant. Shame on you for killing him, for putting him where he did not belong. That is on you. You killed my husband, your only son, out of pure spite."

Mrs. Keller gasped, staggering backward, completely mortified. She pressed her hands together as though in prayer, bringing them to her trembling lips and looking to her husband for solace.

Instead he ignored her.

"What a vicious little tramp you are, Marietta. First destroying our family, coming here now in the hope of profiting from our suffering."

"Whatever he was, Mr. Keller, which wasn't much, he was my husband. And you were his employer. So do we talk dollars or do I find a lawyer who will screw you over and put you on the six o'clock news?"

Keller stood silent for several seconds. The girl was right. She was despicable and amoral, but entirely correct. Any decent lawyer would set her up for life at his expense, taking him for the full value of the insurance policy and then some as his punishment for punishing her. A settlement she neither deserved nor would ever see.

"If in your evil and adolescent mind I did as you say, Ms. Baker, you were my extremely willing accomplice... working with such fervour as you did from the very first day to dull his senses with your licentious favours. He was a good and decent boy until you soiled his mind."

A mocking burst of laughter gurgled from her throat. "Mr. Keller, I was the last of many. That fancy school, the one all you parents brag about, it's a veritable whorehouse. Fucking 101: Sort of a human relations study course that your good-boy Ben excelled in." She faced Mrs. Keller, smirking. "It's really surprising those girls even wear panties. He simply pushed his way into me once too often, Mrs. Keller, when he should have moved on to the next girl the way he planned, the way he always did. I guess what he wanted was a special one, a really good one before dumping me. Which is peculiar, Mrs. Keller, because he was lousy."

She turned to Mr. Keller. "So?"

"Ten thousand. An adequate amount given the circumstances."

She was elated. "Really! That much. Wow." Her change of expression was rapid and sinister. "No. I'm not good with that. Fifty-thousand sounds much better, deposited into my account today or I get a lawyer and tell the entire city how terribly you mistreated him…your loving son, how he was working late again that night earning a few extra dollars because he couldn't provide for his teenage wife and little baby girl."

Mrs. Keller squeezed her husband's arm. "Give her the fifty, Warren, for the baby. Then get her away from my home." She went inside disgusted, without another word.

Keller pursed his lips, glancing at his watch. "Fifty thousand, Ms. Baker. I'll be at your bank in an hour."

*

An hour later fifty-thousand was deposited into her account and she was standing on the curb facing Keller, leaving him stunned and speechless. She wasn't through with him. She would not attend the Tuesday funeral. In fact she would have divorced Ben before the year was out. He was an abuser, hateful toward his kid and couldn't think without a beer in his hand. He would never have been better than he was. That he was killed was her best day, and probably his as well.

Then she turned on her heels and left, waiting at a bus stop several blocks down and planning her immediate future. Boarding the bus she remained standing, stepping off not many minutes later in front of the local BMW dealer, soon after driving to her bank with the salesman in a pristine pre-owned convertible.

She closed out her account against their advice, shocking them when she dropped the several bundles of cash into her handbag. From there she went to a lawyer where she removed all traces of Keller before returning to what was no longer her hell where she did the very minimum as a mother before she went shopping for more fine clothes, requisite suitcases, an outfit for the kid, and celebrating her victory day alone with a fine meal and a glass of Merlot.

Back in her room, for as long as she would stay, her car parked beside the F-250, she spent the night packing her wardrobe, too exhilarated for sleep, drinking what was left of the vodka in moderation, hoping a few drops on the kid's lips might induce a few hours of peace and quiet. Morning could not come soon enough, when she would look and be her finest for her last day in Savannah, for her liberation day, thankful the kid was at last sleeping like a baby, all the more surprised when she woke near 8:00 Tuesday morning.

She wasn't wasting time, putting the kid in the tub, cleaning and drying it, dressing it in a new bodysuit, knit booties and a sweater with a bunny hood. She dressed herself in a lacy thong and short pleated skirt, a silk blouse and stilettos; she carried her three suitcases that was all she owned to her car and went for the kid that she lay on the backseat wrapped in a clean woollen blanket.

She was gone by 9:00, leaving behind her life, her memories of Ben, and Clyde who she was certain would one day regret throwing her away for no reason.

Twenty minutes later she was at the Kellers' stately home, pulling in behind a black limousine. Her timing was perfect. Mrs. Keller was standing on the porch waiting while her husband was locking the door, waiting to bury her son, clamping a hand over her mouth when she realized who was coming closer.

"Don't worry, Mrs. Keller. I'm not staying long. I believe I made that abundantly clear with Mr. Keller yesterday. I'm leaving Savannah." She pulled back the blanket. "I just wanted to introduce your little granddaughter before I go. Pretty, isn't she? Her name is Jodie. Miss Jodie Baker because this world does not need another Keller." She turned, walking away, pausing and dropping a key on the ground. "That's in case you're interested in seeing what you really did to Ben and me. And I do hope, Mrs. Keller, that you are enjoying your day as much as I am. Thank you again for making that happen, Mr. Keller. Goodbye."

She smiled at the chauffeur who tipped his cap. A short drive later she was at the Baker home.
The couple was not expected at the funeral, nor did they for a moment consider attending. They were content with their replacement congregation and fresh network of friends, Mrs. Baker coming to the door first.

"Hi, Lea. I figure I can call you Lea since you're no longer my mom. How's that working for you, by the way? It's been a year."

"Don't be disrespectful, Marietta. Why are you here?"

Marshal stepped past his wife onto the porch. "What happened to young Keller was tragic, of course. However you're the one who chose premature adulthood, Marietta, ruining your youth completely against the values we engrained in you. Although clearly not deeply enough, something you must live with. We cannot, nor do we wish to take you in with an ill-conceived child simply because tragedy has visited you.

We have a different and better life without you and because of you. We're starting over. This past year for us was one of difficult and painful healing, but we did heal. Now you coming here, although not entirely unexpected, has reignited our pain."

"Gees. Take a breath, Marshal. I'm not here hoping you'll take me in, ruining your cozy life. In fact I'm leaving Savannah. But I thought you should see your granddaughter for the first and last time before I go. I want to give you and Lea here something to remember since you obviously don't remember being a cruel and heartless bastard." She pulled back the blanket. "She's adorable, isn't she? Her name is Jodie, Jodie Baker. I'd let you and Lea hold her, except she hates the cold. And you're about as frigid as it gets." Her smile transmuted into a sneer, her tone caustic. "You think you lived through a year of pain and suffering, Marshal. You don't know shit. This thing I'm holding didn't need to happen, except you wanted to be the big-time lawyer, be the big man for your friends while I lived in a 300-square foot cell with an abusive drunk and this screaming bundle of shit and colic. Saturday was the second best day of my life, him being killed. And today is the absolute best, seeing your faces, because you do not get to hold your adorable little granddaughter."

She turned her back on them without another word, content that she was leaving them as devastated as she once felt, striding confidently to the car, laying Jodie on the backseat and disappearing from parents who would never see or think of her again.

Chapter Fourteen

Pausing on the soft shoulder at the Savannah city limits, studying the skyline in her rearview mirror, Marietta Baker had not the slightest notion that officers from Child Protection Services were pounding on her door. Or that Homicide Detective Jan Jenkins was with them, interceding with a more threatening tone. She wouldn't for a moment tolerate some undeserving teenage bitch getting away with neglecting and abusing an innocent and helpless little baby. No way would she let that happen, demanding that Marietta cooperate or find her ass in lock-up, shocked when a defeated and perplexed Warren Keller opened the door and retreated.

The plan was New York, an impossible 800 miles she would interrupt with a five-star midway. She deserved. She was intent on making up for time lost, for the year-long privation forced upon her, waiting until she crossed South Carolina's state line before detouring from the I-95 onto a dusty backroad that several miles later led her to Dufresne's Gas, Tire & Food to Go.

The place was pure hillbilly with shingles missing on the roofs, a façade that hadn't seen fresh paint in years, worn and creaking steps leading into the store, twin dull and rusting gas pumps and a wide-open garage she wouldn't dare step foot into. Certainly nowhere anyone except a toothless bumpkin would think to go. Which is precisely what she wanted and needed: a down-home hillbilly in coveralls and a dirty singlet with a corn pipe stuck in its mouth. Or at least someone nowhere near the mainstream and the man lumbering toward her was about as far from the mainstream as she could have hoped for.

*

Charlie Dufresne had not done as well in life as he might have, had things been a mite different. Not that he often dwelled on his many mistakes in life, and not that he didn't have many more years left for making certain corrections or improvements that might improve his current and lamentable condition should an opportunity somehow present itself.

He was a tenth-year dropout working a few years for a local cartage company at minimum wage till his mother passed on and his father took up with another woman who made clear at the get go that she wasn't taking on someone else's deadweight, causing Charlie to at once find himself in a sorry state of homelessness. Soon after tiring of his cot at the mission and his days of fruitless hard labour, finally understanding of necessity that he had sorely underestimated his potential, he decided he would make something of himself. So he joined the army because he was big, he had once even played football at school, and he knew a little something about guns.

He wanted to see places and the pay was good, his Uncle Sam readily adopting him into the fold days after his twentieth birthday. They trained him; they gave him confidence, a uniform, and put him in the middle of Afghanistan with his own rifle and side-arm where he would become a hero, where not many months later he was shot in the hip and sent home on long-term disability.

He found a place on the outskirts of Charleston, the only city he ever knew, and bought a car that wasn't the worst on the lot. He found a job standing at a drive-through window taking orders from midnight till eight the next morning when he wasn't washing or stacking dishes. Till the night Doris Weller came to work with him, watching and listening as he guided her through the complexities of working in a coffee shop.

She was a good bit younger than Charlie, recently out of

school, working days at the grocery mart, figuring that working two jobs and having her own place was better than what she left behind.

Throughout their first week together he enthralled her with vivid accounts of the Afghan battle that got him sent home before his tour was over, of the virtual massacre and how he and his men held their position despite overwhelming and frightening odds. More than being wounded, barely escaping death day after day, bullets exploding the earth around him, hundreds of others hissing past his head, he hated leaving his men behind, like he was deserting them or something.

He was fascinating, much more than the boys from school she left behind, and into their second week she was thrilled when he invited her to a Sunday matinee. She wasn't attractive, but neither was she homely and she could plainly see that he was smitten with her. She hoped as much anyway, not that she ever once in her life got a second invite. The boys she was familiar with, the ones she liked better than others, well they got the best they could of her before going on their merry way happier'n a hound lickin' its parts.

By Christmas that year Charlie was promoted to night manager, mostly responsible for Doris. He got a new name tag and ten dollars more each week, spending twice that much on her gift and inviting her to a New Year's dinner to celebrate the windfall.

She was smaller than Charlie by several inches and half his weight. She was slight, what some might call boney, with a flat belly and tits that were big enough for the rest of her, nice enough tits he was hoping he might see one day soon along with whatever was waiting for him under the short skirt he suggested she should wear to encourage better tips. Her face was plain with a nose like the tip of a thumb and a tiny mouth that seemed like a bright red smudge when her lips were closed tight. The back of her though, he could easily conjure up in his needful mind by the way she sashayed around the tables, bending and reaching when cleaning them, raising her skirt along her taut bare legs to indecent heights, was her primary feature. One that kept him awake most days till noon thinking on them.

When the year's most special evening finally did arrive he met her at her door, not hardly believing how pretty she was in her little red dress, red shoes and stockings, her neck adorned with the gold necklace he'd given her on Christmas Eve before closing the shop.

They went for an all-you-can-eat dinner and a carafe of red house wine, Charlie waiting till he was standing at her door before confessing that he had a burning urge to kiss her, confessing that he had a bottle of whiskey in his car if she believed it proper to invite him in. He wouldn't stay long, but he would like more time with her being that she looked so lovely ayn' all.

In fact he stayed through the night and the next day, driving first to his place before the coffee shop where they went together twice into the men's room without her underpants when the place was empty. And many more passionate pre-dawns thereafter.

That summer some ten years earlier they joined together as man and wife. They honeymooned by the shore for a week, making all manner of plans for their future before returning home and discovering they were unemployed. The coffee shop could no longer sustain a night shift, which did not discourage Doris in the least way. She had a husband and together they would have a nice life and a wonderful family.

Besides, she didn't particularly like Charleston and she had come across a notice in the paper sometime back about a garage and roadside stop for sale. The price was good, within their limited budget, and with some restraint they could get by with his disability cheque till they got the place fixed up the way they wanted.

They drove the next day a good distance westward into the green Carolina countryside. Doris loved the place immediately, envisioning all manner of possibilities. Charlie was good with his hands and knew his way around cars, while she would work in the kitchen making baked goods, sandwiches and coffee.

The place was surrounded by woods and not far from the main road. The place was perfect, or could be with a little work, a quaint place for gas and lunch in a tranquil setting with picnic tables and brightly coloured umbrellas—that never quite worked out. Seems people weren't interested in quaint or in Doris' dreams, the time and work they did invest pretty much wasted.

The locals dropped by once in a blue moon, not given to driving much, except into Charleston on occasion for whatever reason, stopping by first for the cheaper prices. The kids on their bikes, they came by most favourable summer days for ice cream and candy bars, the school bus driver in the winter months for a whiz and some talking. In spite of which, their mainstay was his disability cheque that thinned more each year what with rising costs, the garage scarcely bringing in enough to quench their nightly thirsts.

Over time man and wife declined into man and woman, then to silent partners in a failed business, with nods in the morning and nothing much worth saying in their bed at night. Part of Doris' dream was raising a family, that's what she told him ten years and some months earlier at New Year's when she was gaily stripping off her pretty red party dress and cotton underpants. Turns out, though, the only live rounds Charlie could ever shoot were in Afghanistan where he was accidentally shot in the hip by an unsure female recruit while cleaning her weapon.

Adding insults to injured feelings and lost dreams, Doris had aged badly, hadn't taken care of herself. She wasn't partway handsome anymore, or young. She was twenty-nine and sad, looking like a much older woman and never smiling. She had no reason for smiling. She had no proper clothes for special times or just plain looking like a woman, and no proper furniture for inviting folks in or just plain sitting on.

He never took her anywhere, never to the movies or dinner. Her eyes were dull from being weary with life, her once enchanting tits were sagging and her once attractive backside seemed flatter and less purposeful with each passing year. Her teeth, stained a dark yellow from strong coffee and stronger whisky, would never again be bright white; her face and her arms ravaged by a harsh Carolina sun were no longer clear and smooth.

And Charlie, apart from shooting ineffective marital blanks and eventually giving up, had put on serious weight. He had lost a goodly amount of his once thick hair and seldom shaved. He wore the same clothes most days, except when driving into town for supplies or waiting on his suppliers for fresh product that would restock the store. His limp had worsened over the years as well, what with his spending more time sitting than standing.

Truth was, for as long as he might live, he was purely buggered. Stuck with a woman he couldn't hardly look at, let alone satisfying her nightly urgencies, burdened with a business he could never unload because no one passing by was ever as stupid as the current owner whose smile was less welcoming each time someone leaned on the horn. Truth be told, he'd be better off dead and buried. Should've been killed years earlier by the dumb twat that practically took out his hip instead.

But the one at the pumps, the snooty one giving him the once over, thinking for sure he was a dumb-ass hillbilly, now she was the finest he'd set eyes on in a very long while.

*

Charlie Dufresne ambled out from the store, thinkin' on servin' his customer, wonderin' what in tarnation a Georgia girl, a pretty one at that, was doin' such a long ways from anywheres. Lost, was his natural conclusion, with not enough smarts to leave wherever she came from with a full tank. Then he saw her climb out; he saw her wondrous legs and her shapely tits pushin' at her flimsy shirt. Then he understood well and good, musin' on how they were nicely shaped, bigger and prouder'n the wife's sloppy sacks. Whew! And them legs, long and lovely, leadin' fer sure to a fine and tasty treat layin' behind them swayin' pleats that he couldn't hardly imagine the glory of.

That was thirty-five-year-old Charlie Dufresne in work boots, coveralls, a plaid shirt and baseball cap, happy as could be for the diversion.

"Afternoon, miss. Lost yer way, did ya?"

"No, I didn't. I need gas. You do have gas, don't you?"

He nodded, fillin' his lungs with the perfumed air between them. "Coffee's freshly brewed inside, miss, if yer thinkin' ya might rest a bit and have a bite."

She didn't think so. What she wanted was the I-95 and getting on with her life.

Reachin' fer the nozzle, slidin' it into the car's funnel, Charlie couldn't help thinkin' the girl would be a better'n regular quick poke, makin' some boy somewheres some bit happier'n him. Better'n Doris leastways, who sometime back took to assuagin' those nightly urgencies in her privacy. The wife was a good woman once upon a time, obedient and respectful most days and fair enough in her looks, gettin' careless though over the years in her declinin' appearance and her hateful ways.

He shook his head, inhalin' the sweet air. Wasn't the least doubt about it. She'd be a fine thing, a wondrous thing to poke good and hard for a minute or two in his bed that night. Though with a hapless shrug Charlie made do with watchin' the girl's skirt flutter against her thighs while she went into her purse for money, suckin' in air when she stooped to retrieve a coin she dropped, inadvertently givin' Charlie a lot less glory to imagine and much more to remember.

She didn't want him seeing into her backseat, seeing the kid covered with a blanket on the floor between the seats. When he finished pumping and gawking, she walked directly toward him, keeping her distance. He was creepy, unkempt and dirty and smelled of booze. Paying him, telling him to keep the change, not wanting anything from his hands touching her, she asked where the washrooms were.

They were inside, which wasn't good, which in fact didn't matter. She was fine where she was. She thanked him, changing her mind. She believed she would go in for a coffee after making a phone call.

His smile was real, leavin' the girl to her privacy. Nothin' that delightful to the eye had ever once gone into his place fer coffee. However when Charlie Dufresne went inside feelin' gleeful, Marietta reached behind the driver's seat for the kid, adjusting the blanket and placing it quickly between Leaded and Unleaded, glistening its lips with a few drops of the vodka she had saved that would keep it quiet until she had put an appreciable distance between them. The simple note tucked into the blanket read: *It's name is Jodie, March 31st. Whatever.*

Twenty minutes later Marietta Baker merged onto the northbound I-95 humming and singing, heading toward the life she was meant to live. She was no longer a mother, a wife or daughter. Nor would she be ever again. She was eighteen, single, and she was free; she was smart and stunningly beautiful, alluring and charismatic, and not the least bit uncertain or afraid.

She felt exhilarated, leaving behind the faux-charm and piety of the South, eager for what lay ahead. She was determined. She would become that expensive and exotic creature laying in other Clyde Gills' hotel beds. She would be the best because that's who she was. She would.

Chapter Fifteen

Jodie Baker slept peacefully under the bright and warm South Carolina sun throughout the afternoon. Until sunset when the late October air began cooling, when Charlie Dufresne came out from the store to see what all the godawful wailin' and caterwaulin' was about and shutdown the pumps since no one had come since the girl.

What he saw as he came closer he couldn't hardly believe, circlin' the pumps like they might at any moment explode, inchin' his way closer, usin' the Lord's name in several richly coloured expressions of astonishment. He hadn't ever in his life, not once touched a child. Didn't know what he should do with it except call after the wife who likely didn't know much better'n him.

"Like I told ya, Doris. She was prettier'n all get out, like somethin' from one of them sexy magazines. Musta bin her. None other's come by since. What're ya thinkin' should be done with it?"

She knew exactly. "We're keeping her, Charlie. That's what we're doing. This girl is heaven-sent, making up for you lacking the goods to make me full and whole as a woman and all the times of trying for no good reason. We're keeping her, that's what."

He reflected a long moment on how the wife would look with his hands squeezin' hard as could be at her neck, her leather-brown face turnin' purple, her wide dead eyes poppin' from their black sockets. Damn if he wouldn't truly and dearly relish deliverin' the horrid woman far from his wretched life into some dark netherworld where she best and rightfully belonged.

"The thing's not ours fer keepin', Doris. Ain't in no ways legal. Ain't no papers neither. That'll be shit on our boots somewheres down the road. I'm tellin' ya, we can't keep it. We ain't got the food fer it or the know-how to keep it livin'."

She didn't much care, lifting Jodie from the concrete base and wincing. She didn't care about that either. She had a baby. That's what mattered, leaving Charlie to lock the pumps and the garage.

Inside their home above the store Charlie left Doris to her improvised ministrations. When she was finished he insisted the girl was not spending the night in his bedroom, ranting on as she warmed some milk that she dribbled as best she could into the baby's mouth, barking at him that he should shut his pie hole and begin scribbling what she was telling him he should buy the next day in town. Things her child was in need of.

"Yeah, Doris, but what she ain't clear as day in need of is a mother needin' a book of instructions. That ain't right by anyone's thinkin'. Mine in particular, bein' it's me who'll be carryin' the burden. Ya ain't thinkin' straight."

"You being dry as dirt isn't right either, people forever looking at me sideways because of you."

"Yer about as dried out as I am, Doris. How'd ya think folks round here'll be lookin' at ya now. Yer crinkled hair's black as pitch, mine too what's left of it. This one here'll be as yella as that allurin' young thing flauntin' her invitin' parts at the pumps, likely as fetchin' as well. What then, eh?"

She ignored him and went to cook supper, leaving him to follow if he felt inclined, leaving Jodie on the bedroom floor on a pillow in a washbasin covered with her blanket.

"You will drive into town tomorrow for what's needed, Charlie Dufresne. I want that baby girl raised as our own and that's my final word. Everything will fall into place when need be. She's not the first child left on a doorstep."

He didn't think so, keepin' his mouth shut, writin' what he was told, makin' her happy and his evenin' as peaceful as most. But she was the woman, the wife, to his way of thinkin' takin' on the appearance of a man more each day what with her short hair and leathery hide, her coveralls and her worn-out runnin' shoes. Hadn't dressed like a proper female in years, hadn't acted like one neither.

"Still, thinkin' yer a man don't make ya one," he mused in a low mumble, takin' his blanket to the livin' room couch when dinner was done, leavin' Doris with her newfound joy in the bedroom where she hadn't been joyful with Charlie since he couldn't remember when.

He studied the list, wonderin' at the cost of it all. Sure as can be she wasn't thinkin' clearly, confused in her female mind. "Heaven-sent," he mumbled. "Ain't nothin' heaven-sent in this sorry life, leastways nothin' but misery and woe. Better off dead. Leastways better off alone. Ain't no real purpose in havin' a woman who ain't fully a woman, miserable all the day long, blamin' me with them dead eyes from mornin' till dark. Better off in the ground." He stretched out, tuggin' the blanket to his shoulders. "Ain't right what yer doin', Doris," he called out. "Just ain't right, is all."

She didn't answer.

*

October 31st began with a clear sky and and a balmy sixty-nine degrees, the temperature inside somewhat chillier.

Charlie Dufresne woke with a kink in his neck to loud wailin' and a flustered wife naggin' and proddin' at him to get his lazy ass up.

She was not having a good time and he was being his usual useless self, useless as teats on a bull is what she said. The playful baby Jodie of the previous evening had somehow transmuted overnight into a hideous and unpleasant creature, Doris clearly at a loss as to what she must do.

He waved her away, controllin' his temper, askin' what in tarnation she expected he might do, ploddin' his way half-asleep to the bathroom to pass his water deep in thought.

She possessed not the least understandin' of the infant mind, if there was such a thing, no experience to guide her. And the closest neighbour who herself had produced a litter of seven, who had a mouth worse'n them megaphones at the fair and would certainly make the entire world aware of Doris' recent adoption, was a mile or more down the road. That's what he told her, addin' that, despite her ill-tempered curses, he wanted no part of it.

He splashed his stubbled face and armpits with cold water, rubbin' briskly with a towel before diggin' into his boxers to freshen his privates. He passed by her again, shakin' his head and mutterin', dressin' in what he wore the day before, beginnin' his day with an extra swig of whisky fer the purpose of calmin' his anxiety, leavin' with his mind aswirl with fanciful notions of how he might best put an end to his dilemma.

Wasn't right what Doris was doin', he mused on his way into the city, makin' him pay fer another's jubilation gone wrong. Musta been a good time, though, fer the lucky gent pokin' that girl good and hard. Put himself into a sleep thinkin' back on her, he did, reflectin' on her careless stoopin' at the pumps. Fact is, he'd be thinkin' on that wondrous enticement a good long while. Damn straight.

In the meantime the perplexity she laid at his door needed resolvin' as much as the wife's mental debilitation in the matter needin' urgent fixin'. The thing wasn't yet a year old, the cost of feedin' and carin' fer it impossible to figure, not to mention the dirt and the constant disruptions. No way round it as far as he could fathom. The thing belonged somewheres else, and the quicker the better, with folks best suited to rearin' before the wife got herself overly affixed—and him in trouble with the law.

The possibilities were endless. He could leave it

somewheres like a hospital, a hotel lobby or the train station; or he could deliver it to the law and tell all he could about the much inspirin' Georgian girl. Either way, there'd be no escapin' Doris' tormented mind or her mordacious accusations, throwin' himself into Shit Creek after puttin' himself through all that needless vexation. He needed a better way.

He did hear tell years back of needful womenfolk sellin' off their unwanted spawn for whatever reason best alleviated their trepidations. Done all the time, legal and bindin', leavin' both sides jubilant. He thought on that. Could be the solution to his mournful existence. Could be the thing left at the pumps was heaven-sent after all. Could be the girl was an angel at last deliverin' him into a much improved existence. Or not.

He didn't believe in the Lord, nor had he ever passed through the doors of a church. Never crossed his mind. He never once prayed, never thought he should, never wastin' his time askin' for the good things in life that never came his way. Seems the Lord, if there ever was one, was always tendin' to his preoccupations somewheres else. He couldn't see neither that the Lord or his sincere appeals would be much help in pullin' him from Shit Creek once he was drowned.

Arriving in Charleston, Charlie went into the first coffee shop he came across. The good and genteel folks inside were accustomed to the homeless loitering on street corners and panhandling, they were accustomed to hillbillies from parts west wandering lost and bewildered on their busy sidewalks. They were not, however, familiar with Charlie Dufresne sitting among them in baggy coveralls and a stained singlet with his arms bare to the shoulders, allowing that what was stuck on his boots might possibly be mud.

He took a local paper from the rack at the door, turnin' to the classifieds. He remembered the city from his pre-war years, his pre-marital years when he came and went as freely as he pleased. He remembered the streets, he remembered what he should look fer and where he should go.

He tore small squares from the newsprint, garnerin' stares, meetin' their grimaces eye to eye with smug grins. He knew what he was. He wasn't city folk no more. Never would be again, he supposed, except if things fer once began goin' his way.

In his car, the same one he drove Doris to a New Year's dinner in those many years ago, he called several numbers, dropping all but one square from his window. An hour later he was sitting in Jack Right's law office breathless. The four-story building was old, of no particular value, in no way contributing to the history of the celebrated city. The interior was dark and musty, smelling of its age and in need of repair, lacking the conveniences of an elevator and air-conditioning, the absence of those modern amenities forcing Charlie to rest a moment and wipe his dripping brow with his favourite hanky on each landing.

The man had invited Charlie to meet with him, eager to hear his story, stopping short of assuring his potential client they could most certainly be of mutual benefit to one another. First and foremost however was examining the baby. Determining its condition and appearance was paramount, ascertaining its marketability and potential value before determining a suitable demographic: a simple protocol ensuring the greatest success and highest return. In fact, with what he was hearing, he believed he had an ideal couple in mind, young marrieds anxious for a baby matching Jodie's description.

That being the case, and he was entirely hopeful, Charlie and his wife could expect twenty K in cash less his ten percent finder's fee.

The brief meetin' ended with Charlie agreein' that he would return with the kid the next mornin'. He was elated, stoppin' at a drugstore fer Doris' supplies, stoppin' at a package store fer a pint of whisky that was empty when he left the mickey on a park bench by a stream midway through the afternoon, delayin' his return to Doris fer as long as he dared.

Unfortunately, by the time he arrived home, Doris' mood was far from improved. The kid's single set of clothes was hanging on the line, she had pumped gas three times, brought out three coffees, sold a couple of cakes and cared for the baby, griping that he'd taken his good old time running his simple errands. Until she caught a whiff of his breath, snatching the bags from his hands and cursing, snarling at him that for once in her miserable life he should take her into town for drinks and dinner. Charlie thinkin' then and there on a few places she might go.

*

He woke early on the couch the last day of the month, hurryin' to the bathroom, relievin' the resultant pressures of his previous night's several shots of whisky, when he had thoughtfully served Doris two for his one and plunked her into bed early. She deserved, was all he could think, what with the baby ayn' all. What with her constant bitchin' ayn' all, spendin' what remained of his evenin' gloatin' over his achievement and promised windfall, slouchin' into the couch and callin' to mind the best of the Georgia girl until he lost consciousness, driftin' into another dimension with a smile on his lips and a beefy mitt clenchin' his privates.

He cleaned himself strategically in his usual weekday fashion, always savin' his more intense cleansin' for his Saturday night soak. He dressed quick as could be in the bedroom into his Sunday shoes and trousers, selectin' a shapeless white shirt he might have previously slept in, pleased she was dead to the world as he lifted the kid from its basin.

Makin' his way into the bathroom on tip toes, he thought on what he should do and how. Fillin' the tub with warm water, thinkin' not to shock it into a frantic state, he dropped its shit-filled diaper on the floor fer the wife to worry over before dunkin' it several times with its legs apart, doin' his best to ignore the spittle and the giggles like the thing might be enjoyin' itself.

Leavin' the tub as it was, not intendin' fer a moment to sink his clean hands and arms into the fetid water, thinkin' with a smirk on Doris' eventual fury, he dried it with a towel and took it in a hurry outside wrapped in a blanket where he snatched its one tiny piece of clothin' from the line as he hurried to the car. Then he was gone, leavin' the folks livin' nearby needful of gas to fill their own tanks and put the money inside the store. Leastways till the wife would get herself cured of her previous night's bountiful libations.

In Jack Right's office, Charlie's breathing laboured from his exacting climb, the excited counsellor swept Jodie into an adjoining room where his secretary would conduct the exam. Moments later the woman came out beaming, the baby girl was exactly what their young clients were hoping for. She was adorable, perfect in every way. She would call them immediately, reappearing within minutes with the most wonderful news.

The couple were delighted, the man promising they would arrive to view the baby before noon, the lawyer suggesting that Charlie should go somewhere for lunch and come back after 1:00. Not a moment before, hear? So he went fer a beer, doin' well at containin' his excitation without givin' the wife a moment's thought, certain she was by then livid with hateful emotions.

He was ignorant regardin' all aspects of children. He had no interest in them and not because he shot blanks, never comprehendin' the curious female compulsion. Or any man with half a brain fer that matter when none could ever know fer sure what was comin' out: Good, bad or ugly, crippled or blind, or simply not right in the head. Not good odds, leastways not to his way of thinkin'.

What he did know fer sure, what he was hopeful of, was that these Carter folks, they wouldn't ever find a better one to take home. That's what the lawyer's lady said.

*

Amy and Will Carter arrived at a quarter to the hour. Amy was delirious, all atwitter, anxious to see her baby, eager to take little Jodie home and be her mother. Will was more pragmatic. He had little choice since he'd be the one dishing out the forty grand. The farm was successful, showing a good profit three years running since his dad passed on when Will took over the operation a few years after graduating with a Master's in business and landing a lucrative position in an investment firm where he met the love of his life.

However despite understanding how pleasing his wife was preferable, given their young age, to waiting for a boy they might come across later, or not, forty grand was a significant number and he had to be certain; he needed to see Amy's eyes sparkling and her face glowing. Which happened the moment she saw her baby, the moment she held little Jodie in her arms and fell in love. Jodie was *her* baby, no one else's, practically ordering Will with happy tears welling in her eyes over to the bank for Mr. Right's money. She was not letting go of her baby for a moment until she was home.

They were gone several minutes before 1:00 with documents signed and witnessed proving that Jodie Carter was theirs, Amy kissing and cooing over her precious little baby all the way to the truck. From Will's perspective, he was happy the wife was happy. Still and all, forty grand was a mite steep, particularly for a girl.

From Jodie's perspective, she didn't know better. She couldn't. She couldn't run or hide or scream for help. Instead her big green eyes sparkled as brightly as Amy's, her tiny lips glistened with spittle and she reached out with her tiny hands and arms to love her mommy.

*

Charlie Dufresne clambered his way up the 112 well-worn steps clutchin' the mahogany handrail with moist hands from the midway point, half-believin' he'd expire before layin' hands on his money. Walkin' through the door deeply flushed and pantin' he had one question, not the least familiar with social niceties and polite preamble: "Did them folks take away the kid?"

They most certainly did, with nothing for Charlie to do, sign or say, other than taking his eighteen grand in cash and going home. Doing business with him was a real pleasure, the lawyer thanking him kindly, pleased the transaction concluded expeditiously and to his complete satisfaction. They thanked him again, Right and his secretary standing mutely with arms crossed, Charlie gradually realizing he should get out.

He sat in his car countin' the money and when he finished he started over. The last time he held that much cash in his hands he was buyin' the store, handin' over his life's savin's, handin' over his life.

He didn't hardly know what he should do first, thinkin' on buyin' something fer himself, then somethin' fer the wife fer the purpose of appeasin' her natural meanness, fer the purpose of diminishin' the intensity of the hellacious fury he'd soon be drivin' into once turnin' off the backroad. He had no doubt she'd be there waitin' on him, standin' on the porch with a fiery hatred in them dark eyes, her little mouth squeezed tight and ready to spit out spiteful words.

Anyway, wasn't like he was goin' anywheres anytime soon without her. He wasn't a city boy no more. Over the years he'd let himself mortify into a true hillbilly, movin' to the wrong place fer the wrong reason, givin' in to her spontaneous wishes without much thinkin' on the matter and leavin' behind all them gloriful nights in the men's room when she was passably handsome and not given to cantankerous fits. Cost him a whack of money and a frightful existence leavin' behind them long ago fanciful nights.

When he did get home later than planned, he pulled himself from the car in tasselled loafers and Dockers, a crisp denim shirt and a fitted sports coat, dressed the way he'd seen them men in the city, the ones lookin' all high'n mighty when he passed them by. He was clean-shaven and his thinnin' hair was neatly trimmed. What made him most proud was the gold and ruby ring on his finger, like he was a proper gentleman of means.

Walkin' toward her, walkin' straight into the nasty maelstrom he had vividly and rightly envisioned several hours earlier, he put on his face what he thought was a smile—not intendin' to worsen the ragin' storm.

She jabbed a finger into the air. "Where's my baby, Charlie? What in the hell have you done, you damn fool? What do you mean coming home dressed like a dumb-ass clown? Could you possibly look any more ridiculous? Where is my baby! What the hell have you gone and done."

"The thing wasn't yers to keep, Doris. Situations like that, they catch up with ya. Ya weren't thinkin' straight. I took it to the city, got rid of it all legal and proper."

"What!"

"I sold the thing…made a tidy profit to boot. I was thinkin' ya'd be pleased. Besides, nothin' but a whole whack of cash is gonna improve our sorrowful condition. Ya know that's the truth." He held out the bags he was holdin'. "Bought ya a dress, Doris, and shoes and some under things. Got ya the ring ya always said ya wanted, a gold one fer replacin' the one ya got on yer finger. Got myself one."

"How much you, you brainless fool? How much?"

"Eighteen grand, minus the shoppin' expenses. With what's left, yer half is better'n seven grand. We ain't had that much money in our needful hands in years."

He could practically feel the heat radiating from Doris' purple face. She didn't care about the money, or the dresses she would never wear, or a ring that would forever remind her that she had married a lethargic dimwit. He'd stolen her one chance at happiness, her one chance at making her dreary life more colourful, more worth living, thinking how easily in that very moment and space she could kill him.

Her life was over anyway, finished, trapped on a

backroad that was as neglected and run down as she was. She wasn't homely, not in a way that couldn't be fixed. She was neglected, without a need to care. He made her that way. With any other man, a good man, taking care of herself the way the city ladies did, she could be attractive again. She could. She had her grade twelve and could find work, find a man who would love her and care for her better than the hillbilly she was glaring at.

She was furious beyond words. Twirling on her heels she stomped inside and slammed the door. As bad as her life was she was not about to be euthanized like a mournful dog for killing the village idiot. Neither could she look at him without that real temptation overwhelming her.

She stayed alone in their bedroom, ignoring his calls for dinner. She had no nice clothes; she had no life and no future. She hadn't been inside a restaurant since leaving Charleston, had never taken a vacation since her honeymoon at the sea. And she likely never would. That was not a life, that was her prison. That was worse than prison, though she needed a better solution than the state of South Carolina putting her down for making a point, letting him see and understand once and for all what she truly and honestly thought of him.

She had no appetite for supper, her head still pounding from the night before, from what he did to her so that he could steal her daughter. She pressed her palms against her flushed face, stomping into the bathroom to cool the heat with cold water.

Peering into the mirror, studying her face for long minutes, studying her body, she locked the door before stripping and stepping into the shower. Towelling herself, she spent an hour putting on what little makeup she owned and styling her hair the way she remembered, wishing she had body lotion that would make her skin smooth again, promising she would. She put on her Sunday dress and shoes and stood back appraising the results, resisting the urge to burst into tears.

She was better than that, better than him. She was.

She would never turn heads the way that Georgia girl would, the snooty one she had watched from the store window, making sure the breeze took her little skirt the way she wanted, but she wasn't ugly. She liked what she was seeing, pausing a moment, leaning closer to the mirror as though not believing what she was seeing, filling her lungs with air. She was years younger than an hour ago, nowhere near as plain and she was smiling. She was smiling, something she hadn't done in such a long time. She was twenty-nine again in her mind and, more importantly, what utterly shocked her, at that precise moment she began liking herself.

When she went out from the bedroom to the living room, curious, she found Charlie slouched on the couch halfway between where he was sitting and oblivion. He thoroughly disgusted her, in large part because she was disgusted with herself for ever being his wife, for taking his name and self-destructing. A troll in fancy clothes would still and forever be a troll. Worse, what made her seethe, was that he didn't say a word about how lovely she was. Not that she expected much, anything, surprised by how vehemently she despised him. He scarcely realized she was in the room, or he didn't care.

Then she saw the glass fall from his hand onto the floor. She watched it explode into shards and his head tilt sideways. He was gone, snoring, lost in another place till morning that she hoped and prayed was filled with his darkest demons.

She filled her own glass with whisky, swearing as she did that it would be her last. He did that to her, dragging her into his mire. She leaned against the kitchen counter studying him, loathing, him, puzzled by the shopping bags he'd put by the door.

She wasn't impressed. Not with the dresses or the shoes or the ring. What she did like now that he was oblivious to the world was the bank envelope on the table, counting upwards of fifteen thousand dollars. Not a fortune, but sure as hell food for thought. She snorted, thinking Food to Go. Good food anywhere but there. So why wouldn't she? Their bank account was practically empty, always was, always would be. So how would the village idiot explain a sudden fifteen grand? He wouldn't, he couldn't, and he was blind drunk. She would never have a better chance. Not ever.

She hurried into the bedroom for her vinyl purse, leaving behind everything she owned that was worthless. She took his car keys, the dresses he bought her and the gold ring she would hawk. She tossed the ring from her finger between his wide-open legs as a final good-riddance and went with a purpose to the car she would abandon in the city, swearing she would kill him if he somehow came alive and tried to stop her, and without a single glance over her shoulder she got in and drove toward Charleston where she would begin a promising and sober life worth living.

However not until the next morning, waking in luxury to a bright and glorious day she would begin at the hotel spa before meeting with a divorce lawyer that afternoon, noticing her plain purse laying by the bed, did Doris fully comprehend with tears welling in her eyes the true purpose that had brought little Jodie into her life.

Chapter Sixteen

Amy and Will Carter didn't get a call from Jack Right's secretary that morning. They weren't from Charleston. In fact Amy had never previously been to the city. Their home was in Jasper, Georgia, population 3400, sixty miles north of Atlanta, driving six hours the night before as soon as Amy heard from Right himself that she would not be disappointed. He had been working diligently on their behalf and had found their perfect child—theirs until the end-of-business the next day, he made clear, and Amy Carter was not taking any chances, not risking the slightest possibility that someone else would take her baby.

They checked out from the hotel early, sitting in a coffee shop across the street where Amy hadn't stopped peering anxiously through the window for over an hour.

Right had suggested they arrive punctually at 11:45, but Amy needed to see for herself who was bringing her baby, terribly confused when all she was seeing were business people coming and going and a poorly dressed man carrying a lined cardboard box carefully into the building moments before the specified time when Right quickly and effectively assuaged her fears.

"I have never set eyes upon any such gentleman, Miss Amy. And a cardboard box of all things?" He chuckled. "I can't imagine. No, no, Miss Amy. Most assuredly not. The baby was brought here near nine this morning by the child's grandfather, held warmly and lovingly in the gentleman's arms. The young parents, despite doing what was right for their baby they could no longer care for properly, were too distraught with emotion in their final moments together. They said their goodbyes at home surrounded by family and friends as the girl's father gently pried the baby from his tearful daughter's arms. The grandfather described the emotion, grateful he could tell his daughter and future son-in-law how you, Miss Amy, and Will here, would make such caring and loving parents. The kids, he assured me again, were good people whose single mistake was bad timing. That's all. And time, he was sure, would heal their emotional wounds."

"I wanted to see him, to see the parents," Amy sighed.

"To what end, young lady? You are now the parents. Nothing is more important for the little girl. I met with them, of course, a while ago, interviewing them to make certain they were fully aware, fully in agreement. They are good students, good kids, bright, attractive and healthy. As is your baby. They are now beginning their lives anew and together in a positive direction without the burden of student loans because of you and Will. As will little Jodie with you, living a life she deserves, free from the penalties of her parents' innocent mistake."

When Will returned from the bank with the forty-thousand in cash they left Jack Right and his secretary within minutes, closing two dark chapters in Jodie's life. Then came Charlie Dufresne who, not long before sunrise the next day, would stumble hungover and confused into his darkest.

*

Unlike Charlie and Doris, Will and Amy were educated, successful, and deeply in love. They had degrees from the Faculties of Business at the University of Georgia hanging on their office walls.

He was twenty-nine, 5' 9" in his socks and fit. She was a year younger, petite and curvy, coming to his chin in her stocking feet. He was blond with hazel eyes, tanned by their weekends in the sun; she was fair and blonde with green eyes that perfectly matched their new baby's.

They had taken over the 200-acre sweet potato farm left to Will by his widowed father three years earlier and although they weren't wealthy by any stretch, not yet, their ledgers each month were tallied in black. They lived in dad's two-storey ranch home, renovating the interior over time, making it Amy's as much as Will's. They had an in-ground pool, a mid-range made-in-America truck and SUV, his and her closets filled with city clothes and travelled twice each year to wherever they wouldn't sweat.

They were living a good life, farmers in name only and never pretending otherwise, paying seasonal workers more suited to the backbreaking task to work the fields, while spending their days negotiating, selling and trading. They were privileged compared to many, though never put on airs, Will paying the men a good wage while Amy made certain on the most oppressive of Georgia days that her sweet lemonade never ran out.

Amy's single and recurring dream was raising a family with Will, bearing him a strong and handsome son before or after giving him a beautiful daughter, which wasn't happening for whatever reason.

Will, for his part, wasn't opposed to family, although neither was he remotely disappointed or concerned when month after month the results never changed. He had Amy. So rather than each one enduring a barrage of tests and prodding doctors who couldn't care less, and incredibly expensive bills merely to prove a moot point, they decided together on adoption, researching various venues until they came across one Jack Right, Attorney at Law. The only real issue was boy versus girl, the couple deciding that whichever one came first was fine with time and Amy winning out over male ego and Will.

The Carters never thought about Right again, or that little Jodie was bought and paid for in full. She was their daughter and at forty K the likelihood of a boy coming their way was between nil and never since Amy wanted an infant boy and Will wanted no more of the same invasive state bureaucracy than he was putting up with at the farm each day.

The following Saturday their weekend guests arrived separately near noon from Atlanta. They had no choice despite mixing fire with water for the first time since their wedding. Amy's parents were successful Atlanta realtors, partners in the city's premier firm. Will's older sister Karen was a third-year college dropout, a party girl working as a travel agent and her live-in convenience, Jake Monroe, was the manager of the produce department at a food mart.

Will was the executor of his father's estate since he was the son with an advanced degree going somewhere; whereas his sister was capricious and irresponsible, living for the moment, who for some inexplicable reason had taken up with an amoral underachiever whose idea of marriage was attending someone else's wedding to party.

The farm was a contentious issue, despite Will graciously giving his sister a lump sum equalling half the then current value of their childhood home in addition to the fifty K bequeathed to the disappointing daughter who wasn't married. Not the 100 K left to Will and the daughter-in-law who good old dad adored and cherished as much as old man Maters.

The Maters came dressed in sophisticated casual wear and spent the afternoon cooing over their new grandchild; Karen and Jake arrived dressed for an evening of clubbing, Mrs. Maters quietly shocked at the shortness of Karen's dress and that she could clearly see the young woman's scanty brassiere under her blouse.

At dinner the conversation turned to business. Amy's folks were early sixties which required no further explanation. Will's sister was half their age and, despite being flighty, she was family. Not that either in-law was pleased or happy with the decision. They simply had no choice.

The previous day Will and Amy had seen a lawyer, drawing up a testament of their final wishes. They wanted

Karen as their child's godmother who, in the event of whatever unlikely tragedy might befall them, would care and provide for their Jodie. As for Jake, Will and Amy were hopeful that one day, sooner than later, his sister would get real about her lifestyle and meet someone who could actually maintain a conversation.

"Godmother? Seriously, people?"

"Seriously," Amy answered. "You're family, Karen. It's what we want for Jodie. We told mom and dad earlier. They understand why we chose you and not them. However, they will always enjoy irrevocable privileges should something ever happen to Will and me. Particularly since you all live nearby."

Karen wasn't sure. She wasn't expecting the life-threatening bombshell. She never wanted kids. She didn't need all the bullshit in her life, the pain, the aggravation above and beyond the cost and all the unknowns. "And Jake?" she asked her brother. "Where's he in all this?"

Hopefully somewhere else far away. The man's a shallow asshole. "One guardian is all that's required, Karen. Simply put, you're Jodie's aunt and now, we hope, her godmother and possible future guardian. Jake is Jake and, by virtue of his common law status here, not Jodie's uncle." He faced Jake with a smirk. "Unless, of course..." He waited, acknowledging the man's blasé shrug before continuing with his sister. "You would be the sole trustee of the property, if there is a property. As for the will, we've made provisions for her education and financial security until she's twenty-one when either the sale of the farm and this place, or the farm's profits, are shared equally with you. If not sooner. Personally, I don't see either you or Jodie working a farm. So I'm thinking quick sale in the event of whatever."

"Will I have a copy of the will, since I am the executor?"

Amy replied, "There isn't much to read, Karen, and the bank will act as executor. However you, mom and dad, are all well provided for."

"We also expect that as guardian you will oversee the proper use of Jodie's inheritance, investments, that sort of thing," Will added.

Amy's father cut in. "It's what we call a no-brainer, girl. Just go ahead and do it. You're family; it's what families do." He sipped his scotch when he felt more like draining the glass and throwing it at her. He despised those who merely drifted through life waiting for winning tickets and free rides. "This is not a life sentence we're discussing and not as though these two will leave us anytime soon. That's not the natural order of things. So please nod your pretty little head in the affirmative, do what you know is right, and let's all get on with dinner. Shall we?"

Karen had no use for the old fart or his superior wife. He was obnoxious and self-important, believing he was better than everyone else when what he truly was was an arrogant shithead.

"Dad's not wrong, Karen. Family is family, and we do intend being here for Jodie a good while longer. What we're suggesting is a formality, nothing more. And the most we'll ever ask is for you to babysit your niece once in a while."

"Okay." Karen nodded her pretty little head, not bothering with Jake. "I'll do it." Just don't you screw me over again Will."

*

The next time Jodie would see her aunt was at Christmas and again in March at her first birthday party on the thirty-first, that's what the lawyer told them, which meant nothing at all to the girl apart from grandad bouncing her on his knee and playing with her on the floor. The day was no different in her mind from any other when she would see him or the nice woman with him.

New Year's for Karen and Jake was not a time for family. Not a chance in hell could she ever fake a good time with old man Maters, making merry with the old coot and his staid wife, let alone the countdown and midnight. Her New

Year's Eve was all about partying and dancing, being noticed and envied in something sheer, short and sexy; Jake's was all about hers and anyone else's sheer, short and sexy that was worthy of his attention.

Then came Spring Break, Karen's first working vacation each year that she went on without Monroe since she had five weeks while he waited each summer for his two. She delighted in her time without him, always at Adults Only resorts. She relished her freedom to flirt and mingle, her freedom to explore alternative opportunities he would never be part of. That was her secret life, her treasured memories of fantasies lived without complications, calling him each night before dinner, recounting her workday of guided tours and endless meals, endless meetings and the effusive attention of the resort's management doing their utmost to woo her into making their property her clients' first choice.

She liked Jake, he was safe and easily managed. She wasn't interested in love or marriage or long term anything, and neither was he. He liked parties and good times. What else mattered in the short-term as long as she got away three times a year on "business" that was none of his? He was good-looking, good to be seen with and eagerly responsive to her romantic proclivities when she needed romance, which did not mean she wanted a lifetime of yesterdays.

If she ever did fall into love's abysmal depths, however that might happen, she would not be clinging to Jake Monroe on the way down. Of that she was certain. And kids? That wouldn't happen either, having taken care of that particular female curse years earlier.

Arriving home in Atlanta, tanned and weary from an arduous seven days, Jake waited until she had finished ranting about her exhausting week before reminding Karen about Jodie's upcoming first birthday celebration and that the Easter Bunny was expecting them again in April. No excuses: RSVP. Oh goodie! Another let-loose party with mommy and daddy, gramps and granny.

The kid would get fifty bucks each time. Not a chance would Karen Carter ever once consider challenging the pure hell of a toy store, let alone surviving the in-your-dreams experience, a mommy's nightmare that wasn't hers, telling Jake she could think of much better things to do on her knees than hunt for chocolate eggs. She was tired, but not that tired.

Chapter Seventeen

Old gramps was his usual jerky self acting as though he was the one-year-old and granny was as straight-laced as ever with her polished silver stick up her ass. Amy hadn't yet come down from that proverbial cloud and daddy spent the entire afternoon freezing hundreds of Kodak moments he would later file into another cloud, choose one he would print for the refrigerator door, and forget the rest until he was as old and childish as gramps. How brilliant was that? And Easter? Oh yeah, can't wait for that happy day.

*

In fact as terrible as she believed Easter might be—she wasn't wrong. Not about daddy with his Nikon or gramp's regression into his own long-lost infancy. Although as painful as the day was, the afternoon went mercifully quickly along with Aunt Karen out the door after she and mom put her niece to bed and her brother-silly daddy soon after ended the adult portion of the evening with the abrupt disappearance of liquor bottles. He wanted everyone driving safely.

He was so kind and so pure, forever preoccupied with everyone else's well-being. That was her younger brother, her daddy's brightly shining star, the brother she could never bring herself to love, the one who was always her daddy's favourite when she always tried her hardest for her daddy to love her as much. She knew why, she always did. Because he was a boy and she was a constant disappointment.

The real contention wasn't being a girl striving for love

and attention. Throughout her school years and during her several solitary getaways from Monroe she never lacked either one. She was attractive and sensual, eager to please and be pleased.

The farm was the issue, why she could never love her brother like a devoted sister, never understanding why anyone with a cushy job in the city would give that up to spend his days on a potato farm when they could have shared the several millions from its sale. What her father wanted didn't matter, he was dead and she was stuck in a condo in Atlanta when she would have owned a villa in the Caribbean, Italy or France.

Then, with two more escapes she would fondly cherish, Karen's year was practically over. She empathized with her brother some weeks earlier when hearing how Santa Claus had scared the girl at the mall and needed her daddy to calm her. However, despite the trauma, Aunt Karen lamented how she and Jake would not be sharing the joy of her niece's second Christmas. They would be visiting with friends in Savannah over the holidays, sadly, of course, while enjoying the day alone at home with their phones on mute.

She wasn't big on explaining herself, Will not bothering with an invitation for New Year's. He knew better, keeping from Amy what he actually thought about Aunt Karen taking charge of Jodie in the event—expunging that rarest of possibilities from his mind. Even more unlikely was sis ever becoming a mom. Even though, giving the woman some deserved credit, she did, after some coaxing, agree she would babysit her niece in February when he was taking Amy on a surprise Valentine's weekend in Vail for romance and skiing. At the same time promising she would be there for Jodie's second birthday, grateful she would first have a full week alone in Aruba to fortify herself.

Will spent most of January working with his foreman planning the spring crop, while Mr. Maters spent the entire month and into February maintaining that he and his wife were the logical choice as his granddaughter's weekend guardians. They were perfectly capable of caring for Jodie, more so in any case than a single woman who enjoyed her drinks, was neither interested in marriage or children, and would undoubtedly serve as a poor example for the sweet little cherub.

What was he thinking?

Nevertheless Will was adamant. He had his reasons, reminding the older man during dinner on the seventh, moments after stunning a wide-eyed Amy, that Jodie had quite a few years ahead of her before joining the bar scene. Cased closed.

Mr. Maters accepted defeat graciously with a sigh, providing he could put his granddaughter to bed, and when the evening was over the men shook hands. He wished his daughter a happy and memorable Valentine's, hugging her tightly, while Mrs. Maters scolded Will for dangling her so tightly in his arms. They would see each other soon.

The week that followed flew by for an excited Amy, planning her wardrobe, waxing and polishing their skis, telling Jodie a hundred times about what she and her daddy would do. They hadn't taken a vacation since bringing Jodie home, hadn't shared very much alone time or done right by each other, diapers and colic usurping candlelight evenings and romance.

She would make her special weekend the very best ever, she told the happy little girl who giggled as though she might have understood.

They left home at 10:00 AM on the Thursday, leaving Karen with a list of dos and don'ts, names and phone numbers. They were good to go, Karen assuring them that Jake was busy enough at the condo. She and Jodie would be perfectly fine, which Amy knew in her heart was true, despite calling first from Atlanta before boarding and in Vail four hours later at Baggage Claim when Will grabbed the phone he would return Sunday evening, said goodbye to his sister, and went to Car Rentals. Until then, unless the world would somehow abruptly end, they were on vacation.

Arriving at the lodge they had time for a couple of runs before luxuriating in a deep tub of scented foams and dressing for dinner at a table with candles and fine linen. Something else they hadn't done since bringing home Jodie, Will firmly refusing with an irritating smirk to return her lifeline.

The four-course meal was sumptuous, the twelve-year Paulliac divine. The quiet and dimly lit ambiance that followed in the lounge was romantic, soon evoking thoughts of dessert, something sweet, delicious, and low-cal: Amy, who an hour later left a depleted Will begging for seconds.

Saturday they spent the entire day on the slopes, Will either racing past Amy or circling her, Amy claiming each time that she was letting him. That was a male thing, a male deficiency thing. She had nothing to prove, gliding past him with her nose in the air the time he ungraciously landed on his male ego.

When darkness began falling, however, Amy did not mind at all when Will reignited the male deficiency in their suite before lingering in the tub's steamy froth, cooling their heated bodies with perfectly chilled champagne, whetting Amy's appetite for another low-cal dessert he would serve soon after dinner. Her second dessert; the first was a blue velvet box that would come as a marvellous surprise. Inside was a gold family ring dotted with his sapphire and her emerald stones framing their daughter's aquamarine.

The next day was all about Amy, whatever she wanted that would make her day the most special except for her phone, which was spending her morning in bed admiring her beautiful gift she would treasure forever and loving him.

"I love you."

"Of course you do. What's not to love? Hello."

She punched him, straddling his legs. "Do you think Jodie's alright?"

"She's fine. Besides, I gave Karen the number for 9-1-1."

"I'm being serious here."

"Then get dressed. You're too naked for serious." He cupped her breasts. "Nice. And no, you're not getting your phone, not until the airport." He glanced at his watch. "Six hours. Deal with it."

She scrunched her face. "I lied. I don't think I love you anymore. You're very cruel and very heartless."

He shrugged. "Not worried. You did see the ladies staring me down on the slopes, didn't you?"

"No, I didn't. And for your information they were not staring you down, they were feeling sorry for me. They were wondering how this," she palmed her body teasingly from her breasts to her belly to her thighs, "all this, could possibly be with," she waved those same open palms over him, not touching him, "you know…this, whatever. Yes, darling, they were feeling sorry for me."

For that remark, for taunting him, the corporal punishment came swiftly, evoking a girlish squeal. Two hours later, not many minutes before check-out, she admitted breathlessly that she might have been hasty in her judgement. Maybe she did love him after all.

*

The day was biting cold, bright and clear, the bluish white snow blinding, crunching under their boots as they ran toward the car. Moments after the resort disappeared behind them, they were turning onto the I-70 thirty minutes from the Eagle County Regional.

"Dad was really disappointed."

"I did him a huge favour. He's obviously forgotten the diaper phase, all the fun he once had dealing with you."

"So you're thinking what, that Karen's into diapers? Really?"

"I'm sure she's had a few special moments, but women adapt easily to these situations. It's in your genes, like a natural instinct."

She ignored him, holding out a hand and snapping her fingers. "Let's see if she survived. My phone, please."

"She's fine. Besides, her doing this is sort of a litmus test vis-à-vis the will. If she has survived we'll know we did the right thing for Jodie."

"We had no choice, darling. Not that we don't love her."

She took the phone, scrolling to their landline.

"Love is a foreign concept to my sister. That Monroe guy is a perfect example. Why she keeps him around is a complete mystery. The guy's a fool." He snorted. "She's been doing those getting laid vacations of hers for years, though I can't say I blame her, especially now. She's not hard on the eyes and, besides, she's probably a much more pleasant woman when she's on her back."

"What a terrible thing to say. She's your sister."

He shrugged. "Three times a year and he hasn't clued-in. Good for her."

She put up her hand. "Karen, it's me. Hi."

"We're fine, Amy. We're alive and well."

"No issues?"

"Not a thing." A pause. "Well, nothing after the initial bouts of nausea. The air got pretty thick at times."

Amy giggled, covering the phone. "You were right, darling. She's had some special moments." Then: "We're headed for the airport, Karen. We'll be home for her bedtime," she patted Will's arm, "and you are staying for pizza and a Will!!"

The last word Karen heard was her brother's name screamed into the phone. The last sound she heard was the carnage of a crowded van carrying several teenagers slamming head-on into their rental, killing them outright; the kid driving the van and the girl beside him, hurled through their windshield, coming face-to-face with their victims on the rental's crumpled hood. Then nothing, an eerie quiet.

Karen froze where she stood, calling Amy's name

repeatedly, frustration mutating into anger that Amy wasn't answering. Swearing into the air, she dropped the receiver. She ran for her purse, for her cell, calling 9-1-1, telling the annoyingly calm voice the little she could, the man assuring her that he would get back with her as soon as possible.

When that call did come, when she heard the chilling words, Karen Carter dropped onto a sofa paralyzed with dread. Her brother was dead. How could that be? She had just heard his strong laughter, then he was dead.

She went to the dining room filling an old-fashioned three fingers deep with scotch. She had to think, to compose herself and think. Putting down the glass she went into her brother's office, searching through papers and files until she found the will and dropped into his chair. In the event—she was to decide whether to sell or keep the farm, entitled to half the sale price. Gramps and granny were getting a hundred thousand, everything else would be held in trust, managed and disbursed on Jodie's behalf however her legal guardian judged appropriate until her twenty-first birthday.

The Maters! Shit! She reached for the phone. As much as she despised the old coot and his supercilious wife, she was minutes from destroying their perfectly idyllic world. Then pausing a moment before pressing *Send*, pressing a palm to her cheek, she realized she hadn't shed a single tear.

When Amy's father answered, Karen simply said, "Mr. Maters, Amy and Will are dead. They were killed an hour ago while driving to the airport." A very long silence. "Mr. Maters, hello?"

Monday morning Jake Monroe brought all Karen's clothes to the house while she spent the day boxing Amy's and Will's wardrobes that she would drop off the next day at a grateful mission. He always did like the place, eager to move in with her.

Tuesday she met with her brother's lawyer at the bank, putting into effect the terms of the will and having his and

Amy's financial portfolios transferred to hers. She quit her job and met with a realtor at her condo, calling Jake and making him aware that he was homeless, on the street. He wasn't moving in, she was moving on—without him.

Wednesday morning she met with Will's foreman and in the afternoon put the farm and the ranch house on the market much to the disgust of the Maters. Thursday Amy and Will were brought home, met by her father who, on Friday, received a cheque from the bank that he neither needed nor wanted. What he wanted was his granddaughter, what he needed was his daughter and Will back in his life.

The following Monday, eight days after the fatal crash, her disconsolate and grieving parents laid Amy and their son-in-law to rest following a simple service in the chapel, their granddaughter napping peacefully in her aunt's arms: a wholly despicable woman who hadn't expressed a single word of condolence. Instead she handed Mrs. Maters a small box of Amy's jewellery without enquiring about the matching gold bands and family ring Mr. Maters had earlier accepted from the coroner.

What's worse, Karen Carter made very clear they would never have Jodie alone in their Atlanta home. She would honour her brother's wishes, naturally, but by appointment. No cold calls, no showing up at the door unannounced. However in the same few breaths she did invite them for Jodie's second birthday at the end of March for a social afternoon. Unfortunately, she wasn't as good in the kitchen as Amy. Sorry.

What she didn't say was that she was taking their granddaughter on a beach vacation in Aruba, to a resort where she had arranged for a full-time nanny. A fact they discovered when arriving on-time at a house that was no longer a home without a single colourful balloon or streamer, silly hats or a cake. Just a different lady of the house with a rich suntan and their choice of vodka, scotch or wine.

*

The condo sold above asking in a matter of weeks, the farm and her childhood home near the end of July at the peak of summer and the growing season for eight million, Karen agreeing with the foreman that he could speak with the buyer on behalf of his crew. She wasn't getting involved.

The difficult part for the Maters, still tormented with grief, was hearing she would have them over for an afternoon the first Sunday in August—and why. She was moving north with Jodie to Vermont. She was done with oppressive 100 degree summers. She wanted out. With Will gone she had no family, no reason to stay. She wanted a new beginning with his daughter, her niece.

However she did understand their need to visit occasionally.

Leaving Jodie behind that Sunday was the second cruellest day in the Maters' lives, reliving the horror of their daughter's and Will's horrific deaths. Their one consolation was what she had done with Monroe.

Chapter Eighteen

The following Friday Karen sold her car. Saturday she left the furnished house and Georgia behind and arrived in Vermont through JFK with her niece without allowing the Maters the courtesy of one last call.

Wasting no time she hired a realtor and architect on the Monday, purchasing a thirty-acre forested and lakefront property a half-hour drive from the state capital, an easy one-hour flight to New York and an easier couple of hours by car to Montréal's French-flavoured nightlife she was eager to taste and savour.

All that together was one dream, the second was opening her own travel agency and finding a nearby daycare where she could drop the kid until Jodie was ready for school.

She did admit the eight million was a reasonable enough tradeoff, rarely thinking of her brother or his wife. She was too busy with building her dream home while creating her agency specializing in sophisticated adult getaways and vacations better suited to the topless and thong crowd than the modesty panel and underwire camp.

By Thanksgiving The Carter Agency was open for business with a hire her age who definitely fit the thong demographic and by Christmas Jodie Carter was playing by herself on the polished floors of the home she didn't care was the envy of locals, more fascinated by the cold frost on the garden doors. She had already learned about snow, Karen's penchant for walking in it, and the cold on her face that she didn't like while she was dragged behind on a sled.

The Maters arrived on the 23rd, surprised by how their granddaughter had grown, albeit nowhere near as staggered as they were at seeing the candy apple red Hummer in the driveway of the luxurious three-storey home overlooking a private lake. They left on the 26th, not invited for a New Year's that Karen would celebrate in Montréal. The old folks' March incursion into her life would come soon enough.

*

Which it did for the next three years, Karen first packing thongs and not much else each spring for her requisite vacation prefacing Jodie's dreaded birthday visits. Arriving that third year however the Maters were greeted by a smiling Mark Hampton in sweat pants and a tan, someone they judged at once as a single pay grade higher than Jake Monroe.

Still those fast-paced years alone were good for Karen, not once suffering from the pangs of loneliness. The agency was successful and her several vacations each year interspersed with spa and club weekends in Montréal and New York got her through nicely. Until she met Mark who fully met her criteria for moving in, realizing she was ready again for in-house convenience. A fact that didn't sit well with the Maters.

He was handsome, fit and muscular, athletic in bed and five years younger, an account executive from a nearby sleepy town in Maine who she met in Cozumel. They were each other's instant success. She saw a man she could live with as lovers without debilitating emotions and leave on occasion as a way of maintaining her independence as well as her compulsion for sharing her remarkable body and fantasies with like-minded strangers.

What Mark Hampton saw in her was a woman who lived the good life. She was stop-traffic gorgeous, her body tight and willing, her mind completely wanton if not wholly debauched. She never said no, never demurred. Moving in for as long as she lasted was a no-brainer, which he did mere days after departing Mexico with her.

But the Maters didn't like him. There was something smug and low-end about him. He wasn't anyone's account executive, at best he was a peddler. His shirts and suits were a size too small, his bright orange Mustang convertible screaming showy if not plain juvenile, Mr. Maters seriously doubting he'd ever read a book that didn't capitalize on blatant sex or a magazine that didn't present a naked female splayed out midway through the trashy articles.

Until Jodie would begin school that September, eager for her first day, her granddad promising he would call to wish her well, she hadn't learned much about anything beyond playtime. Karen never sat reading bedtime stories with her or watching kiddie time television; that only happened when the Maters put her to bed, spending too few precious days telling Jodie stories about her real mom and dad, showing her the same photographs and videos during each visit, making certain she would never forget them the way Karen clearly did. She didn't see the need for stories or fables or dwelling in the past, nor did she have the time, always preoccupied with her agency, sandy beaches and being a very popular tourist attraction.

Jodie's sixth birthday was the last time she saw her gramps and grammy, never again speaking with him every Friday evening before bed, never questioning why because she was a child with countless other important things flooding her mind, Karen deciding she wouldn't tell the kid the old man was dead or that his wife, never recovering from her daughter's death, had aged several years overnight and that her failing health had made air travel impossible.

Despite caring deeply for her granddaughter, despite knowing Jodie was lost and alone, she was helpless to intervene other than naming the neglected child as her sole beneficiary.

With the recent sale of her real-estate agency, her husband's insurance payout and hers that she hoped would come one day soon, Jodie would inherit well over ten million dollars held in trust for her by the Southern Colonial Bank until one day after her twenty-first birthday. That along with her family history that would include photographs and videos, Christmas and birthday cards, and notes for each year lost to them until the day she could no longer bear living without her husband, her daughter and Will.

That royal bitch Karen Carter could burn in hell, is what she would pray for, and take that horrible man with her. Jodie would one day become a fine and successful young lady. She would make her mommy and daddy proud and never forget them.

*

Jodie did however forget Amy and Will, her gramps and grammy years before the old lady died, peacefully reuniting with her devoted husband and loving children who Karen never spoke about beyond telling Jodie they were killed in a crash when she was a baby. And as she grew into her teens Jodie saw no point in being curious.

She was quiet throughout most of her formative years that followed without much choice in the matter, becoming prettier each year until leaving grade eight with high marks and not many friends because Karen was forever strict about whom she brought home. She had no boyfriend, worried at first that she would stand out entering high school without one, spending most evenings studying alone in her room after finishing the dinner dishes, singing the lyrics of her favourite hits into her hairbrush the Saturdays when Karen and Mark would go to town for dinner and clubbing.

She didn't mind Mark. Neither did she love him as a friend or even like him very much. He was just there, a fixture, a guy living in the house the way her Aunt Karen was just there. She never went out with them unless shopping with Karen for au courant outfits each season and she never went to dinner with them. Nor did they ever dine out with friends because they had no friends and had recently begun taking her on vacations to

Caribbean resorts except when Karen travelled alone for her business, when Jodie would stay at home alone with him.

When she was six she didn't know enough to care or worry about his hugs and the playful pats on her bum, the hugs becoming gradually tighter each year, the pats evolving into tender squeezes. She didn't mind that either, not really. It was the only attention she ever expected, increasingly aware as she was turning twelve of how he began seeing her differently, sitting closer to her while watching movies the weeks Karen was gone.

Once during one of those weeks, a year later, he walked in on her while she was showering. Of course he apologized, after pausing for several moments spellbound, when she went to bed too mortified to face him until morning. Not that he hadn't seen her all summer at the pool in her bikini that wasn't much bigger than Karen's thong.

More recently, and much more telling, spending her last summer weekend sunning by the pool, he had wrapped his arms around her from behind as she was reaching for her coverup, cupping her breasts through flimsy triangles, squeezing gently before telling her he was sorry, that he only wanted to toss her playfully one last time into the pool. But that time she didn't believe him because he and Karen were both laughing and her aunt never laughed or smiled.

She was fourteen, days from entering high school and to say she was pretty in no way adequately described her. Without makeup she was attractive, tall for her age, blessed with natural poise and the fashion sense of a European model. Adding lipgloss and mascara to the mix, those times on vacation with them, she was alluring beyond her innocence which was increasingly difficult for Mark Hampton to ignore.

Deeming the moment propitious one month later, he turned his recurring fantasy into partial reality the last Saturday of September while Karen was thousands of miles away acting out her own current fantasies.

Jodie was in her room putting away her school books, changing from jeans and a sweater into her pyjamas for another evening of movies with Mark. Not going down, staying in her room, was pointless. He would come for her, insisting that she join him. Besides, the only screens in the house were in the kitchen and cinema room and she was increasingly regarding her room as a cell without a lock, the house as her prison without any possibility of escape or parole, eager for the day she would leave for college and actually make friends she could be with.

So the sharp knock at her door came as no big surprise on cue, Jodie thinking, yeah, sweats and a muscle tee, smirking when she opened the door. She had the guy down pat. There were always movie nights with him the weeks Karen was gone, which weren't particularly special times for Jodie. Something to do, unlike other Saturdays when she would stay home alone with her hairbrush and be herself while they were out partying with strangers and having a good time without her.

"Hi, I've got something for you…sort of a present." He came into the room, putting the box into her hands. "Hope you like it, Jodie. You deserve."

They never bought her gifts except at Christmas and her birthday. Mildly curious about why and what she tore at the wrapping, pausing, even more curious, not realizing she was instinctively wary at seeing the embossed *Seductive Selections*. She was familiar with the store from shopping with Karen, the silk and satin fashions Karen always insisted she wasn't yet old enough to wear. So why now?

"What is it, Mark?"

"Open it. You'll be totally surprised."

She did, slowly. "A babydoll!" Her wide-open eyes and gasp were sincere. "Does Karen know about this? I mean, does she?"

He nodded. "She sure does, of course she does. I convinced her you're way too old and mature for pyjamas or shorts and tee-shirts, and she agreed. So these are from both of us."

Jodie pulled the set from the tissue paper, not sure what she should think, say or do. Karen never had a problem walking around the house in her panties and bras, her teddies and slips. Or going topless at their pool, the lake, or on vacation.

"Thanks, Mark. I guess. But this is kind of weird. Am I supposed to wear this tonight, downstairs?"

"Yeah, sure. Why not? In a few years you'll be a beautiful young woman, in fact you are now. You should begin acting like one and what better place than your own home? You see how great Karen is in her lingerie and bikinis." He chuckled. "You'll be like sisters, a couple of hotties."

She thought for a moment, unsure. "Okay, I will. I'll be downstairs in a few minutes."

"Great." He turned to leave, stopping at the door. "Oh, a quick FYI because I'm not sure you would know, sweetheart, that is the complete outfit. Anyway the fire's roaring, we have cozy blankets, and you also have a glass of wine waiting. It's about time you learn about things like drinking before you leave home. Just a small glass though. Let's not get in knee-deep shit with Karen."

She closed the door when he left. She had to admit she was excited, anxious to see herself in the mirror. She did like wearing her bikinis over the short-lived summer, but this was big-time different, ranking in her mind as highly as her dreams of leaving the house behind with him and Karen when she really would be a woman.

She undressed quickly, first slipping into chartreuse panties that were flounced and high-rise and covered nowhere near as much as her snug bikini bottoms, absolutely shocked. Then into the matching babydoll that was décolleté and split at the sides, her breasts covered with delicate lace. Shit! Really! She had to think this one through, twirling, bending and stretching, studying each pose and what she was seeing was fantastic. She was fantastic. She had curves that made the other girls in her class envious. She had breasts that could actually fill her bikini tops and give the boys at school something to wish for and, yeah, a phenomenally cute ass the guys had never seen because no one had ever invited her to the beach.

And she was seeing all of it in the mirror, not at all certain whether she felt embarrassed or sexy. She would do it, she would. Besides, how many times had Mark seen her in a bikini, or that time in the shower when she was naked, or the time he groped her breasts and Karen didn't care? So why not? If Karen could act younger than she was, why couldn't she act older? She would do it, pausing for one last glimpse, skipping to her door and the stairway before she could change her mind.

In the cinema room the movie was set to play, as was Mark Hampton stretched out on a love-seat and ottoman sipping wine.

"Wow. That is incredible. You look super great, Jodie."

"This is absolutely too weird, Mark. I feel like I'm someone else."

"You are someone else, a spectacular someone else. Now do a little turn for me. Let's see the whole picture." She did, twirling, feeling absolutely exposed and strangely titillated. "You are sensational, Jodie, totally sensational." He patted the cushion beside him. "Come on, sit with me. Let's get into the movie."

She sat, pulling her ottoman closer, stretching out inches from him and telling herself "So what?" She was doing what she always wanted, looking the way she always wanted, not ever thinking she would be with him. What did it matter, what did he matter? He was Mark, the fixture. No big deal.

He passed her a goblet filled with a rich Bordeaux, clinking the crystal rims together. "To a long-awaited era of sophistication, silk and satin at the Carter residence. Karen will not believe this new you. What's the word, feminine, mature? I don't know." He began the movie. "Whatever the word, the transformation is remarkable. We should send her a picture. She'd be delighted."

Which didn't happen. What did happen halfway through the pay-per-view was Mark Hampton refilling their glasses before brushing some imaginary thing from her bare thigh and lounging beside her. Near the end of the film he took her empty glass from her hands, reaching between her legs, placing one over his and easing his free arm around her shoulders. Cradling her head against his chest he whispered that she should sleep, that he would cover her, keep her warm and wake her in the morning.

Then he let her sleep peacefully—an hour later laying her on the sofa, caressing her body once more with tender strokes she would not remember, waking her the following morning near noon with gentle urges pressing into her back.

Chapter Nineteen

As Jodie Carter was making her way through her sixth year, as yet ignorant of worldly affairs, caring more about her doll yet eager to commence her formal education in the coming days, James Castle, his girlfriend Louise Laplante, and his longtime bud Cedric Deacon were days from their freshman year at university.

They were seventeen and best friends, an inseparable trio throughout high school. Now they were in the big league. James was sophisticated and polished, captain of the debating team, the son of a successful downtown developer, entering psychology because he had big plans. Though not wealthy, the family was certainly well-off and liberal, giving their son free rein and four years to create and be responsible for his destiny.

Louise was a spoiled daddy's girl, entering architecture because she didn't like anything else and, once married, could one day design her own home. Mr. and Mrs. Laplante, extremely pious in their beliefs, whose richesse was more affected for the sake of neighbours and friends than real, whose firmly shared doctrine was one man one wife, raised their daughter as the decent and good girl that she was.

Cedric was captain of the high school football team. That was his father's empty dream: his son in pro ball. Though Cedric chose finance instead, realizing he was better than fantasies, than living on the wrong side of town. He possessed a rare aptitude, his career counsellor convincing him the big bucks were in high finance, investment and trading, not in any way pro ball.

As much as Louise liked Cedric, and she did dearly, James was the one with a car, always with more money in his pockets, always buying her flowers and candies. Deacon couldn't do that. In addition to which, Mr. Laplante saw no value in his daughter having a friend from that other side of town. What good would come of a childhood friendship that would not possibly stand the test of time, when eventually they would part company as well they should?

They were all good students with impressive grades, always at the top of their class. And as in high school they remained inseparable, always together until their final year when graduating with honours was all-important, more crucial to their futures than frat parties, chugging beer and getting laid. Early into that fourth year James and Louise saw each other mostly on weekends, Deacon and Louise whenever and wherever they could steal a few precious moments of intimacy.

They were twenty-one, months apart and seated together, each elated grad watching the other's crowning cap and gown moment on stage with the dean, their caps flying high into the air amidst a flurry of hundreds more and a chorus of raucous cheers when the ceremony concluded.

Drinks and the evening's good times were on James Castle, his deserved penalty for achieving the highest academic standing.

When the celebration was over Deacon went home to mom and dad, James and Louise went to a hotel for urgent sex. When they were done, their bodies satiated and moist with sweat, their chests heaving from the strain of youthful vigour not yet evolved into titillating lovemaking, they collapsed onto dampened sheets, James suggesting a shower might be in order before driving her home.

On her veranda they sat on the swing kissing and holding hands, when out of the blue he invited her to dinner the next evening, without Deacon, appearing quite excited, his eyes glassy with emotion. There was a matter of considerable importance he wished to discuss with her. And she accepted, of course, as he was certain she would. They had been secret lovers since high school, at first timorous, giving vent to their deep feelings, exploring a new dimension that was their unfolding and burgeoning love for one another that was bound to endure till death do they part. Or so James hoped.

He would call on her at seven, suggesting with a sly grin that she might dress in a fashion appropriate for Chez Antoine.

The next evening James arrived on time with a box of sugared fruits for Mrs. Laplante, assuring Mr. Laplante, as one gentleman to another, that he would indeed deliver his lovely and precious daughter safely home no later than the stroke of midnight.

At the restaurant, one of the city's most elegant, the reserved and intimate setting was tucked in a dimly lit corner, a single candle flickering shadows on the wall.

Once seated the gentleman ordered for the lady, as was proper, beginning with a delicately spiced consommé au xérès accompanied by a light Pinto Grigio served by the glass. The entrée was saumon grillé served with steaming legumes glistening with a glaze of butter, for which he confidently selected a medium-bodied Sancerre which the sommelier had previously and kindly recommended over the phone.

He was nervous, anxious one moment that the meal would soon end, hoping the next that it would never. Which wasn't the case, waiting until the waiter had refilled their glasses.

"What a wonderful evening, James. Thank you. I must tell mother how nicely you're treating me. You are always such the attentive gentleman."

"I enjoyed immensely, Louise. What do I not enjoy whenever we're together? Last night in my bed, all I could do was think of you, dream of you and me together before leaving you on your doorstep broke my heart."

She blushed. "Father did not like me coming home at such a late hour. He was quite flustered."

"I wouldn't worry. Your father and I, we're on the best of terms. We spoke, Louise."

Louise patted the corners of her mouth, leaning closer. "You spoke, James, with father? About what?"

"About you, Louise. About us, me and you."

Young Castle reached into a jacket pocket, extricating a tiny cube wrapped in pink foil that was further secured with pink ribbon. He placed the thing in front of her, with hands not as steady as when he'd practiced in his room.

Louise sat gazing at her gift, gazing at her first-ever lover. "James, whatever...?"

"Please open it, Louise. Or must I sit here at the precipice of my premature and very undeserved expiry?"

She did, teasingly, tugging at the ribbons, smiling coquettishly, delicately unfolding one lip of foil before another. The tiny leather box was red and smooth, Louise glancing at him one last time.

"Oh, James, is this...really?" She raised the tiny lid. Inside, set in white velvet, was a simple sterling silver cushion cut solitaire with a diamond speck the jeweller assured him was genuine, and that James was certain he could pay down in twelve monthly instalments. "James, can this be real? Am I dreaming?"

"Louise, I desperately want you as my wife, to stand by your side forever, to love and protect you always. Will you please be my wife? Will you please be mine throughout that briefest of eternities?"

The excited young woman practically leaped from her seat, hugging and kissing him, too beside herself with glee to notice the hum of polite applause and reserved smiles appropriate for the occasion. Chez Antoine catered to a more refined and privileged clientele.

"Yes, James. Yes, yes. I will."

"You have made me the happiest man alive. I promise, Louise, that I will love you forever."

Later at the Laplante home Louise was visibly taken aback when she saw Mr. and Mrs. Castle sitting with her parents. Hugs and handshakes, kisses and tears ensued along with the soon-to-be father of the bride's best champagne that was recently bought and perfectly chilled. He toasted his daughter and adopted son, Mr. Castle doing likewise, complimenting his son's exquisite taste in young women. And of course the women had much to discuss that was of particularly little interest to the men who left their ladies to their initial plans. Particularly since Laplante had a bottle of twelve-year single malt in his study that hadn't yet been opened.

*

Sunday Louise woke in a dream state, hugging her pillow. She had graduated with a Bachelor of Architecture and was getting married. She would tell Deacon at once, her way, whether or not he was already aware, because despite how deeply she loved him for what he was, for the way he was, a dear and loving friend, she wanted the prestige of being Mrs. Louise Castle that much more.

James was going somewhere, he would become someone important. Besides, how often had Cedric scoffed at marriage, the institution, the need, the obsession with submitting oneself to the pressures popular public opinion? And children? No way, not in a world already over burdened with too many hungry mouths.

Then there was her father who would never have approved the union, often voicing his opinion of Cedric as being different, not like them, borne of uninspired stock and would likely amount to nothing.

She called him from her bed, where throughout the past year she often lay beneath him sharing stolen and fleeting moments of zealous and hurried passion.

*

Cedric Deacon answered with a simple and despondent, "I heard. Congratulations. He asked me to stand for him."

"And?"

"And what? I said yes. He's my best friend."

"Cedric, you know why. You understand why, don't you?"

"Because your father thinks I'm shit, the slum kid who couldn't make the pros."

"That's not true. You did what was right for you."

"So what happens now with us, with James?"

"Nothing happens. Why would anything happen? I love him and I love you. So what? We'll be careful. It's not like we'll be working together, the three of us. We'll find our way through this. We will be together, we will. I promise you. I'm marrying the guy, not joining him at hip. Besides Cedric, that could have been you last night in the restaurant. That is on you. You like me enough in bed, just not at the altar."

"That's not who I am. That will never be me."

"No, but this is who I am and I am telling you nothing will change. This is a good thing for us, Cedric, the best of both worlds. James wants me in his life, you want me in your bed. That's a win-win for all of us." She paused, waiting. "I love you, Cedric. I will always love you. You know that's true."

"I do know that. That's why you're taking the lead on this. Your call. We're too good together to let this get between us. So we'll be smart about this, no stupid mistakes, no cutesy anything whenever he's around…whenever anyone's around."

"Anyway, we have a full year. Until then I don't owe him anything. Do I?"

"Or me."

"I never did, Deac. But I will never put him before us, that I do promise." She giggled. "For ever and ever."

Deacon wasn't in a laughing mood. "He says he wants some sort of meeting tomorrow, says he's got some sort of plan. Something he's kept secret until he got things worked out.

Something good for both of us. You know anything about that?"

"No, I don't. What I do know is that my parents will not be here this afternoon. James took me to a hotel Friday night after we dropped you. What he did with me was awesome and, being fair, you deserve the very same or better. Or I do. Meaning you be here at two. And, Cedric, I am expecting something much better than awesome."

*

Monday in the PM James met his friend for wings and beers. James did have a plan, a good plan, and he wanted Cedric in on the bottom floor.

"Congrats, man. Louise is the best. You guys will be the best together. Hell, you are the best ever." The guys clashed their steins together, ignoring the hectic splash. "No shit, man. You're getting married, and to Louise. I mean, wow, that is unreal." Another splash. "And, Jamie, thanks again for asking. I will not let you down."

"You're the man, Deac. I mean, shit, we're practically brothers. You think I wouldn't? Not a chance."

"Yeah, well...you treat that girl right. Or I'll be on your sorry ass. Now, what're we doing here? What's this amazing plan of yours?"

"I want a store, but not just a store. And I want you in on it. A store like none other anywhere. A dollar store but not a dollar store with strictly high-end knock-offs at low-end prices. I'm talking really low-end prices. I've done the study, the figures. We can make this thing work, Deac, and my father's in one hundred percent. He's fronting the startup costs, money he wants returned over time sans interest. He's excited for us. He says, done right, this can be really big."

"A store, that's your big plan? Are you shitting me? I didn't bust my balls working my way through university to work in a freaking store."

"Not a store, a chain of stores. I'm thinking C & D something or other. Whatever. And much more than a store, I'm talking something much bigger. With ours degrees in psych and finance we can do this, Deac. We'll be unstoppable. I'll do the people thing, you do the money." James downed his beer, exhilarated. "Deac, it's a no-brainer. I'm talking partners here, you and me, fifty-fifty. Also, if we fuck up, if we somehow go shit for sugar, dad let's us off the hook. Something he never does. That's how confident he is in us, you and me." He recognized the look, signalling the waitress. "Deac, what?"

"I don't do charity. You know I don't. This is total bullshit."

"No, it isn't. You not jumping at this is bullshit. This is not charity, Deac. This is you and me, a team." James Castle held out his hand. "Deac, a team, you and me. Let's do this thing. We'll be freaking millionaires in no time. I swear we will."

*

That evening Louise Laplante lay in her bed in shock, once she stopped sobbing.

A month later, after lawyers and deeds and negotiations with cautious suppliers, the first Ten'll Get U Change opened its door in New Orleans under the corporate umbrella of C & D Enterprises, the contract binding the men together written without the slightest legal ambiguity and in good faith because they were best friends and kindred spirits.

As stipulated, they would work as equal partners with equal pay for as long as each man remained with the firm. Their weekly remuneration would never exceed that of their future and highest paid employee; their year-end bonuses, whenever that ambition might come to fruition, derived from ten percent of the year's revenues, they would share equally. However, in the event that either partner, and for whatever reason, should at anytime quit the firm, that partner would do so with the clear understanding that he would forfeit, thereby conferring upon the remaining sole partner, forty percent of the firm's accrued assets. Additionally, which his father suggested would keep things from souring at some point in the years that would follow, should opinions differ greatly or should either partner act grievously against the other, be it from greed or spite or envy, or any malicious intent or action, the same forty percent forfeiture would apply in favour of the offended party.

Jamie and Deac chuckled at the thought of such a ludicrous thing ever happening, striking the clause from the contract before Mr. James Castle and Mr. Cedric Deacon co-signed their future and shook hands as brothers and partners forever. They found a liveable apartment with separate bedrooms which they designated as private spaces, alternating their Saturday and Sunday afternoons for well-deserved time off. They survived each other's trials and errors in the kitchen when they weren't eating what mom prepared, or Louise the weekends she would spend one afternoon with James and occasionally being there with Cedric by the time her fiancé arrived after his tiring afternoon alone at the store.

James took Louise as his lawfully wedded wife on the last day of C & D Enterprises' first year. The evening before, once the bachelor party was over, celebrating more than his marriage, the groom and best man went to separate rooms at the DoubleTree for much needed rest before the wedding in the hotel's main salon. Not many minutes later Cedric Deacon made his way to another room on another floor where the bride-to-be was laying irresistibly naked in bed.

By the end of that first year the partners had paid off their student loans with sufficient funds in the corporate account to negotiate their second store, hire staff, and move into separate living quarters better suited to up and coming executives. They stepped up from their secondhand Ford and Chevy, leasing current models, and James took his blushing bride on the best day of her life on a seven-day Caribbean cruise of lovemaking and luxury.

The couple had decided together that their careers were more important than family. From one perspective James realized the unfairness of never being home to raise a family; from another, Cedric Deacon could not abide them and Louise realized the unfairness of being pregnant with another man's child.

Over the next seven years C & D opened twenty stores and early into their eighth year the corporation purchased a plane and hired a part-time pilot because frequent travels on airline schedules was becoming increasingly inconvenient. Both men moved into their own homes designed by Louise, they were driving European luxury models and wearing thousand-dollar suits. They were millionaires and not looking back, limiting themselves to three weeks of exclusive vacations each year, although never together.

James complemented his travel agenda several times each year by attending conferences that would continue ensuring their mutual success, endlessly amazed and grateful that Louise never once complained about his frequent absences, that she was wholly committed to her husband's success. He was equally surprised that his partner, a catch by any woman's standard, had never married. Although Deacon did date occasionally, he had never kept a woman in his massive home longer than a weekend, as committed to his bon vivant lifestyle and freedom as he was to the corporation, a curiosity James never thought to question.

By year seventeen they owned fifty stores, half of them franchises, boasting very near a billion in assets and yearly revenues in excess of 100 million. Life could not in any way be better, until he returned home unexpectedly from a conference that summer when, from his bedroom, while changing into his swimsuit for a refreshing dip on a steamy June day, he stood watching his best friend and partner frantically fucking his wife like an excited teenager in the shallow end of his pool.

*

That was nine months and eight days ago, when he must have stood at his glass wall for an hour, watching in a daze as though fabricating a compelling and sick fantasy in his debauched mind.

He might have strode onto the deck and confronted them, coughing a laugh at the imagery of Louise jerking with fright, snapping off Deacon's dick. Which he might have done were he a regular person, but he hadn't been any such person in years. Nor did he intend becoming anyone less than the James Castle he was. He was a multimillionaire, not living a dream but building on one that he would not compromise, for the first time in his life regretting he did not carry a phone.

Instead he left with his suitcase. He called her from the Sheraton leaving a message that he would be home the next day well past the dinner hour, that the plane was scheduled to land at eight and that she should go out for dinner. He loved her and would see her soon.

Then he went to the bar, downed a double Johnnie Walker Blue and went for a walk. He needed time to think and space to breathe. That's when he saw the girl on the corner with her easel and stool from across the street. From what he could see of her she was lovely with legs to her neck and long blonde hair hanging in a straight curtain that draped over her tanned and bare shoulders. She was indeed a divine and flawless creation.

He remembered leaning against a building studying her, curious about her, above all thankful for the respite from the haunting imagery of Louise and Deacon in the pool. The girl was saving him from the insanity he was urging his heart and his mind to suppress, that would indeed threaten all he had worked to achieve.

He had innumerable questions, but no answers, recalling all the times he had been away from home on business. However, he would do nothing in the short-term. He had not succeeded in business and in life by acting rashly. He would bide his time, collect data, be prepared and come out on top as was his way.

The most difficult part was maintaining the ruse, sleeping with her, filling the void she must indeed feel when not with Deacon. They weren't simply fucking that day, some impetuous desire erupting from excessive drinks or loneliness. They were making the most of their time together, not knowing when next they might be together to fornicate and cheat.

How did the love affair begin? How could Deacon face him each day, or had the affair become so natural that he was deemed the intruder? How could she sleep with him each night he was at home in their bed? What were they thinking whenever they were with him alone or together, mocking him? And what were they saying when they were alone?

He remembered wondering what the girl was thinking as she watched the world pass her by, seldom noticing her, the way he had never noticed her.

He remembered filling his lungs with humid air and holding his breath. Arriving home he was eager to see her, to dine with her and tell her about the conference, about how well his address was received and applauded by the retail association, realizing as he fled from his own home that Sally was not in the house. The young woman working her way through college by cooking their meals and cleaning their home because Louise had sometime ago forgotten how, or lost interest, or, he supposed while fixated on the young artist, decided that such chores were below her station.

He remembered pushing his weight from the brick wall, glancing up at his private office windows a few blocks away, abruptly turning on his heels and staring at her. He had previously noticed the girl, as an insignificant speck by the gaudy and flashing window of Earnie Lebeau's lounge. An establishment he hadn't once thought to step foot in. He had noticed her. So why had he never once thought about her, or thought to commission a work of art?

He enjoyed a few JW Blue before dining that evening many months ago at the hotel and again in his suite, spending the entire night until dawn determining what he should do. He hadn't once cheated on her, or thought that he should or would for the thrill or the memory. They were each other's first love from the last year of high school through their college years to their wedding night. So when did the proverbial shit hit the fan without him being aware? When did she fall out of love or was Deacon a flight of fancy, a one-time thing? No, he wasn't. He most assuredly was not.

The next morning he hired a private investigator. He gave the man three things: One month to complete a comprehensive dossier, full authority to spy on his wife and Cedric Deacon 24/7 with his best team, and a key. He had no desire to see Deacon's bare ass between the whore's spread legs, but he did want to hear whatever they might say about him, about each other and when they first plunged the knife into his back, the private detective suggesting the bedroom, dining and guest rooms as the most likely places.

With the meeting concluded they shook hands and would meet again in thirty days.

Arriving home that second night, greeting her with a reasonable facsimile of a smile, Louise acted perfectly natural as though she hadn't been caught starring in a homemade porn flick. As did Deacon at the office throughout the week that followed and one other, James leaving home on two week-long business trips, rightfully assuming there was no point in hiring a private eye if his loving wife and lifetime loyal friend weren't afforded ample opportunity to snare themselves. Though the weeks he was at home the sex he did manage with his wife was perfunctory, since he wasn't much interested in bedding whores. That was until the day he met with the private cop over lunch, hearing and reading irrefutable evidence that he was in fact already fucking a whore. Later in the day, in the privacy of a suite at the Sheraton, discovering the exact extent.

He spent the entire afternoon and into the evening listening to them reminisce. He learned about her compulsive cheating in high school and college, how when he and Deacon first shared an apartment she was in one bed as often as the other. Though when he heard her giggle, recounting the eve of their wedding, Castle hurled the crystal old-fashioned against the wall and poured JW Blue three-fingers deep into another. He listened to them talking about the weeks of planning and construction of Deacon's home, hours of sickening audio embellished with sounds and words consistent with urgent and passionate fornicating.

He remembered staying late and leaving a 100-dollar tip for the young housekeeper as an apology for his ill-temper causing her more work. He remembered not feeling anger or hate or even disappointment; he felt like an idiot, cursing himself for disregarding his father's forward thinking years earlier, when in his hands he held proof positive that he was indeed an aggrieved partner and spouse who otherwise would now own one hundred percent of C & D and not fifty. He felt betrayed and ridiculed, though not by a cheating wife, rather by his partner and duplicitous lifelong friend who seventeen years earlier understood perfectly the meaning of malicious intent and action.

He wasn't certain, though the fact that one day his father would discover the unpleasant and damaging truth was unquestionably his primary reason for not divorcing both of them, more than the loss of the 400 million he would forfeit to the bastard who was fucking his wife. Nor would Deacon likely ever show himself man enough to resign or go one better and throw himself under a bus.

Divorcing Louise was an insignificant concern, Deacon was not. They were equal partners with a billion dollars in assets, neither man with the authority to terminate the other.

The one bright and comforting light was that Deacon's whore wouldn't get a cent, or the mansion, or any part of C & D if and when he divorced her.

*

On the first Tuesday following his secret meeting, Castle sat sidesaddle on his desk gazing down at the intersection of Canal and Royal, at the specs of bright red and blue crowned with what he imagined was her lustrous blonde hair. But he couldn't see her, couldn't see the details of her lovely face and or the contours of her youthful body.

The next morning, making himself uncharacteristically late for the office, forewarning his secretary, he purchased a sixty-power Bausch & Lomb telescope and tripod at a camera store, eager for four o'clock when the girl would again sit on her corner and wait patiently to draw.

He understood then and now that what he was doing was immoral and insensitive, spying on the girl, studying her, somehow completely unable to resist the increasingly deep sadness etched onto her lovely face or the dire hopelessness each day making her deep and compelling green eyes all the more sad, incongruously dressing in colourful and sensual fashions each day. His favourite being the dark tights and sweater ensemble made all the more alluring with her French beret.

Alluring indeed, Castle believing that such a lovely young woman could not possibly be alone in life. The idea was preposterous.

She was compelling and through to that very day, the last day of March that was muggy and oppressive, he watched her when he could, missing her when he could not. Not that he was in any way obsessed, for that would never happen, all the same wishing he was twenty years younger. She had become his diversion, his escape, envying her simple and uncomplicated life. For how could anyone that young not see hope in the future?

However that particular day he was for some reason more interested in her client, a man who had gone directly to her with a purpose. He hadn't walked toward her casually, or slothfully under the sun's insufferable heat. He clearly had an objective.

Castle never subscribed to the amateur psychology of body language, of folded arms and crossed legs. Pure nonsense. Eyes were the thing, the single most important barometer of lies and deceit, of love and devotion, spontaneously screaming out the best and the worst of the human condition for anyone who cared to see through them or give a damn. And that man's eyes were screaming out dejection and despair. He'd seen the look many times before on Friday afternoons when things weren't working out, though not one of them would have imagined immortalizing their inner grief in caricature.

He zoomed in inches closer. They were shaking their heads. Then the man put something else in her hands that wasn't money and stood, checking the time on his wrist and twirling in a blur.

A second later James Castle stood dumbstruck, his flesh rough with cold.

Chapter Twenty

With summer over and Karen Carter planning no major trips until her Thanksgiving excursion with Mark and her niece, Jodie discovered that what she once regarded in primary as a bunch of childish playmates had transmuted into cliques of self-important and marauding teenagers in high school.

They were the in-girls, eager for opportunities to sneer and be cruel for no better reason than peer pressure. Except that Jodie was taller, lovelier in a mature way, and more confident— virtually impossible to insult and belittle. She was smarter, achieving the best grades in her class, and independent, firmly decided by the end of her first month that she didn't need them. Or the jocks in senior grades, a different one each week asking her out in the hopes of being the first one in.

She didn't need them either, content with studying and spending her weekends in her own company. She didn't need the bullshit or the history, and what was another four years? She wanted college and a degree, when she might get serious with someone or at least see what all the fuss was about with someone making the grade.

She also discovered that, in fact, Karen did not mind her occasionally wearing more mature lingerie around the house. And in November on the heated white beaches of Martinique she wore her first thong, by week's end thinking nothing of it, and secretly enjoying the attention. From then on cotton tees and fleecy pyjamas were a thing of the past, replaced at Christmas with an evening wardrobe of silk and satin robes, slips and chemises and rompers for the coming summer.

At school she wore microfibre tank tops and shorts for phys ed when the other girls wore loose-fitting pedestrian polyester shorts and floppy tees. In the locker room she slipped privately into silk camisoles and tap pants before stepping out to casually finish dressing in short designer skirts and blouses as the other girls were changing into six-to-a box cotton underpants, brassieres and their habiliments ordinaires.

At Valentine's she stayed home from school and the Saturday dance, no longer worried about not having a boyfriend when most other girls had gone through theirs like a swap meet. It was like a swapping game, like getting it right before summer when having a guy who would pay your way in exchange for letting him do you was crucial to any popular girl's reputation and pride.

Then in March when Karen made her first hedonistic sortie of the year into the intrigue of novelty and strangers, Jodie stayed home once again for Spring Break with Mark Hampton.

Karen never did find out about the wine a year earlier. Nor did she call from her sunshine adult retreat on Jodie's birthday the evening Mark took her to dinner and brought her home, sharing a bottle of robust red and, what the hell. Why not, she was ready enough. A little sip of cognac wouldn't kill her.

"I'm sure Karen's thinking of you...probably a time difference thing, sweetheart."

"Yeah, I'm sure you're right. Thanks for dinner, by the way. That was very exclusive."

"You deserve. You've grown into quite the lady this past year, smart and more stunning each day. You're going places, Jodie. Anyway, I have some gifts for you. This one," he passed her a sleek velvet box, "is from Karen."

She tore at the paper, raising the lid without emotion, expecting a bracelet or a chain, mildly taken aback at seeing a gold chain and pendant of her name written in script. She wanted to show delight, elation, something, but it was a thing, like her phone and her tablet, bought without much thought when what she wanted was a cake with a candle.

"It's very nice, Mark. Thanks. Thank Karen when you speak with her." She turned, holding the delicate ends at the nape of her neck. "Can you please help me?"

He did, turning her by her shoulders, holding her in place. "A beautiful bauble for an even more beautiful girl, a young woman fast becoming a lady." He led her to the sofa, refilling her wine. "And this one's from me. I hope you like my choice. Karen agreed with me that we exchange two gifts each time, so why shouldn't you from now on? And I figured since you do like the boutique, why not stick with a good thing?"

Seductive Selections, which didn't particularly shock her. What did take her breath away were the plain midnight blue chiffon robe and the matching lace thong and bra. And, let her guess, she should wear it for their movie night.

"Mark, this is too much. Thank you. I suppose Karen knows about this?"

"Of course she does. She let me do my thing and wasn't much help."

Yeah, no shit. "I love it, Mark. Would you like me to wear it this evening?"

"Sure. Why don't you change while I get the movie set up?" He passed her the crystal wine goblet. "Take this with you. There's more. And take your time, enjoy the moment."

She didn't have to be told, leaving him. In her room each evening, changing for bed after her studies, or on weekends spending a few hours alone while they were gone, or occasionally when they were home, was a special time for Jodie. She enjoyed studying her changing body; most of all she enjoyed witnessing the changes in her mind and in the mirror that would make her the person she would one day become, certain that person would be of her doing and no one else's, mentally counting down the days to her long-awaited emancipation.

The ensemble was over-the-top gorgeous. The robe wasn't a robe at all, but a flimsy and sheer shirt barely reaching the top of her thighs, the panties and bra her most delicate ever that the other girls wouldn't wear or afford for years, if ever.

She was abundantly aware without being told that in body and mind she was older than fifteen, but in that moment, in that outfit, she was seriously into her twenties and very alluring. Which she believed was a good thing. What girl didn't want to be gorgeous and older? And if Karen didn't care or see a problem, why should she?

Twirling once more in front of the mirror, cupping her hips and her breasts, her grin was practically devious. She liked what she was seeing, wondering how she would look in ten or fifteen years. That he would like what she was seeing was a no-brainer, that he wanted to was obvious. So what was the big deal? More importantly, she would model the ensemble for Karen on her first night back. That would speak volumes, woman to woman. In the meantime he had seen as much of her during their last vacation, albeit not draped in chiffon.

*

Downstairs in the cinema room Mark had the movie on pause. Already dressed in silk pyjamas he was tending bar, pouring cognac into crystal snifters which she didn't mind or think strange. She had no friends, and the girls who might have been her friends were out drinking in backseats anyway. So what the hell.

"Jodie, wow. That is incredibly elegant. You are stunning. Do you know that? I mean, wow.

She giggled. "Thanks, Mark. And Karen's been a very good role model for me. I feel nice dressing this way; strange and spoiled, but nice. Much better than cotton and fleece. Thank you."

He passed her a snifter. "Not spoiled, sweetheart... deserving. And super sexy, no kidding." By which Jodie, at that very moment, understood that he meant something more meaningful. "One day soon you'll be breaking hearts."

Yeah, just not yours. "Maybe not, but thanks. I can't wait to model this for Karen."

"She'll love it as much as I do. Now come and sit beside me. This one's an epic, three hours."

They stretched out inches apart, Jodie holding her digestif in her lap, Mark holding his cognac with one hand on the arm of the sofa while the other rested on his thigh closest to her bare legs.

By early into the second hour and partway into their topped-off snifters, Jodie was feeling a strange euphoria, struggling to keep her eyes open. By the end of the second hour she was purring softly, curled onto the sofa and cradled in his arms, Mark maintaining the volume level until he was certain she was sleeping soundly.

Easing their bodies apart he lay her down gently, leaving her, hurrying for his Nikon. And for the next hour he photographed his lover's fully compliant and insensate niece, framing her smooth and slender body with white chiffon, capturing their special and intimate evening together for his eternity. Then, kneeling by her side he spent long moments tenderly living his year-long fantasy, fearing he would wake her. He caressed her and kissed her, reluctantly retracing his steps, restoring her scant modesty before laying by her side.

He woke alone Sunday morning, finding her in the kitchen, exchanging a warm smile, acting as though nothing had happened between them, as though he hadn't discovered much more of her, nonchalantly apologizing for falling asleep and not carrying her to her room.

She shrugged off the faux-regret. Waking with him did feel peculiar though, seeing his face that close and feeling his breath was strangely disturbing. Seeing her chiffon robe pushed up past her belly and feeling his hand resting on her bare hip she wondered where else he had touched her, wedged between him and the sofa until she crawled over his dead weight, padding her way softly upstairs where she showered behind a door that she locked.

She couldn't help being curious about the evening, about the liquor, about falling asleep and making herself vulnerable, about how she woke, deciding as she dressed that anything he might say would be a smooth lie. She decided as well that she wouldn't care, that he must have done something unless he was a eunuch or had somehow metamorphosed into a gentleman while she was sleeping.

Though neither attribute was particularly applicable to Mark Hampton. He was handsome enough and fit, but he was no gentleman and he certainly was not dead. If anything he was morally bankrupt, if not corrupt. And, anyway, how would she even ask?

She decided that she wouldn't, that wondering about what he did in fact do would make her crazy. So she didn't; she buried her fifteenth birthday where she wouldn't think of it again and spent the day in the solarium studying as her dopiness gradually wore off.

*

Throughout the coming week Jodie spent her days alone, staying dressed until she was in her room ready for bed.

The following Saturday evening when Karen arrived home tanned and tired from a week of being cajoled and bribed each day by the resort's management, making time for playful antics with friends she would never see again toward day's end and into the evenings, she was completely awestruck when Jodie greeted her at the door in sheer chiffon. Not that Jodie was surprised by the gleeful reaction; her aunt was as debauched as Mark. She was beautiful and she did exude a natural sensuality; she just wasn't as morally retarded.

In June, to no one's surprise and everyone's envy, Jodie left grade nine with the highest marks in the entire grade. She left school early that last day, snubbing the afternoon assembly and her award. She wasn't interested, which earned her the title of "stuck up bitch" and a summer alone, which she could not have cared less about. She knew who and what she was, where she was going and what she would do with her life. That's when she would meet people and make real friends, that's when she would begin enjoying her life.

She spent her summer days alone by the pool in her thong, topless until hearing the groan of Mark's Corvette speeding along the driveway when she would quickly change into a bikini. She never once felt lonely, though; she was, in her own innocent way, being supercilious. Her home, her aunt's house, was the finest and most envied in the area and none of her classmates had ever visited or stayed over. Their problem, not hers.

She wasn't interested in being an in-girl, getting laid in the back of some car or behind some bush or degrading into a Karen; she was going somewhere, leaving them behind with her aunt and Mark Hampton.

Chapter Twenty-One

In November Jodie was once again excused from class; she and Karen were leaving Mark behind for ten days in Aruba where the aunt would attend a tourism symposium most days and Jodie would lay on a beach lounger daydreaming into a glittering sea or at poolside sipping spritzers and delighting every male with a beating heart.

The week coincided with a corporate meeting in Vegas that Mark Hampton was mandated to attend. He would miss them, but on a positive note he would have a few days for getting things done around the house, though Karen forgot him before boarding the plane and Jodie never thought of him.

The trip was Jodie's first experience at ordering wine with her dinner. However when Karen spent her early evenings at the casino where Jodie was considered insufficiently adult and until early morning at the resort's dance club, Jodie was left to aimlessly roam the expansive property on her own and later sit quietly on their private patio dreaming of everything she wanted from her life, though never pondering with whom.

Throughout the ten days aunt and niece scarcely saw each other except at breakfast and dinner. More peculiar was that, by the time they were packing to leave, one tanned and exhausted from a hectic schedule of daily forums and evening seductions, the other tanned and lethargic from doing nothing because she had no interest in iguanas, zip lines or dangling from a parachute 200 feet over a spec in the ocean doing thirty knots, neither had captured a single memory in a photograph.

Returning home in time for Thanksgiving they found nothing different, Karen not surprised that Mark had changed his mind about doing even the simplest house maintenance. He was getting too comfortable with her lifestyle and her money, Karen doubting that he had ever once in his life held a paint brush or hammer.

Nor did anything change for Jodie through to her sweet sixteen and seventeenth birthdays, not that she was aware of. She went twice to the Bahamas those Christmases and spent two more Spring Breaks watching movies with Mark Hampton while Karen did her hedonistic thing, although she no longer mixed her wine with cognac or drifted into a deep sleep that might put her at risk. Not that she thought or believed Mark was a predator or even a mild threat, but he was as intrigued with her as ever and, since that first time waking with him, she didn't trust what she couldn't see.

He was forever filling his Nikon's memory card with her at the pool in her bikini or on vacation at the beach with Karen in their thongs, being a nuisance as though he'd never seen ass before; Karen never particularly caring, never seeming jealous or showing concern for how her niece might feel being smothered by the constant and effusive attention. Her single reprieve from him were the nights they went partying, when she would sing and dance through the house and, into her seventeenth year and grade twelve, gradually began seducing her secret lover who she alone could see reaching out to her from inside her mirror.

She didn't care about not having an outdated and overrated sweet sixteen party. She didn't think of herself as particularly sweet and practically all the girls in her class had lost their sweetness in grade eight. Then by seventeen she was looking more like twenty with a fleeting year remaining before finally being her own person, when she could stay home and do her thing, never again vacationing with them but leaving them behind for a better and freer existence at college.

What she wanted for her sixteenth was driver ed and her permit; she got both. What she wanted a year later at seventeen was a shopping spree weekend in New York City with Karen where she had never been, and she got that along with 1000 dollars. Mark Hampton stayed home contentedly putting down a few while watching home videos from his private and prized collection.

A few days later Karen left for a week of social frolicking in Saint Martin, leaving Jodie to spend her last ever Spring Break evenings with Mark. That was the deal since Jodie's first teen year when Karen judged her sufficiently mature to spend her days alone in exchange for exotic trips in November and at Christmas, since Santa Claus hadn't been by in a few years and the festive spirit had never become part of Karen's temperament. She put sufficient effort into being an aunt, into having a baby, then a girl, then a young woman constantly at her side—constantly in her way.

When she was a little girl, that was fine. They put her on Santa's knee, gave her a gift and left her to play, which hadn't been the case in years. Christmas of necessity, Karen's necessity, had evolved into week-long sunny and warm getaways without joy to the world, pretence or gifts as Jodie evolved into her teens.

*

On her eighteenth birthday Jodie woke from a deep sleep, rubbing her face and sweeping her legs from the warm bed onto the floor, padding to her mirror anxious to see how she looked as an adult, legal everywhere except America's bars. Instead she saw a weary teenager.

She showered and dressed, went downstairs to the kitchen where Mark was doing Saturday breakfast and Karen was watching the morning news on her tablet.

"Morning, sweetheart. Happy eighteen. Wow, is that special or what?"

"Good morning, Jodie." Karen closed her iPad. "You

never did decide what you wanted, so we're giving you a week by yourself in Tampa as soon as school is finished. A five-star, of course, with a mid-size rental for getting around and a little spending money. I believe a grand will do nicely."

The new adult was stunned. "What! Are you serious?"

"Yes, I am. But it is more like a working vacation, finding a place to live for your first semester at U of T." Karen held out a weighty manila envelope. "Your acceptance papers came last week. We thought today would be the perfect time to tell you that your first-year tuition has been paid in full. Congratulations, Jodie."

"Yeah, congrats, sweetheart. This is really big news and dinner's on me this evening, ladies."

Jodie tore at the envelope not believing what she was reading, her acceptance into the Graphic Design Programme: her ticket to her dream. She went to her aunt and hugged her, displaying rare emotion, and to Mark which was an even rarer event and entirely theatrical.

Too excited for breakfast she hurried to her room where she spent most of the day in a daze. She was finally leaving, getting out, on the verge of living her life her way. And Tampa in June—alone—was only the beginning.

*

Saturday evening Mark Hampton took his ladies out for dinner. The following Friday Karen left for a week in the Caymans, jump-starting her tan and satiating her social appetite.

Saturday Jodie undressed in her room after dinner, taking her time, deciding what she would or should wear. The evening was practically a celebration of her last movie night with him, Jodie pondering how often she would actually see them once she left, hoping never once she stepped into the real world with an honours degree.

She showered, luxuriating, her mind drifting between familiar fantasies and longed-for sensations as the heated water caressed and teased the contours of her body. Patting herself dry with a warm towel she pampered her body with lightly scented cream, curling her straight golden- blonde hair into soft curls at her vanity before highlighting her deep green eyes with liner, mascara and eyeshadow, enchanting herself, lost in a strange new world and not thinking what she was doing.

She dressed by the mirror, twirling with her arms outstretched when she was satisfied, stopping to examine what she was seeing, a curious smile forming on her lips. She was pleased, mesmerized by her own body. Yeah, to-die-for. She was lovely and elegant, transformed into a woman beyond her years draped in silk when other girls her age were at home or in the backseats of cars wearing buy-for-less jeans and sweaters.

Scarcely believing the transition, delighted with her work, she joined Mark in the cinema room not far from nine o'clock. When she came into the dimly lit room he stood in a tee and sweats, visibly in awe, complimenting her full-length violet charmeuse gown and the robe she was tying at her waist.

"No question that you are a heart stopper, sweetheart. Absolutely stunning." He passed her a crystal goblet, half-filled with a deep red Bordeaux. "This is an '89 Chateau Haut Rion, an excellent red and one of Karen's best. I also picked something different for the evening, something I'm sure you'll enjoy, something a tad more adult than monotonous comedies and that homey stuff."

While he was alone waiting he had rationalized that since she was now an adult and had previously been exposed to adult vacations, he would select a movie rated on the questionable side of 18+ romantic. He didn't see a problem, certain Karen would agree; she always agreed. They were cut from the same faded and threadbare moral fabric. She wouldn't mind at all.

Jodie took the glass, putting her nose to the rim, inhaling the rich aroma before her first sip the way Karen had taught her, thinking the least he could have done is dress a little less casually for the evening.

"Thanks, Mark. It's delicious. What's the movie."

He sat, reaching for the remote. "It's about a girl who leaves home to begin the life she wants, sound familiar? But, in her case, she doesn't have much going for her. She can't find work and she ends up making friends with a couple of bad dudes who take her in." He patted the cushion beside him. "There is a little T and A, but all mild stuff and nothing you haven't seen up close and personal on the beaches. Or here for that matter. I previewed a few random scenes when you guys were in NYC. Didn't want to spoil the ending for tonight."

He pressed P*lay,* beginning Jodie's introductory journey into mild porn, the opening scene showing a naked young woman stepping from a rooftop pool onto their wide-screen, taking a towel from a much older man who was owed money by the bad dudes.

She made it through the first ninety minutes and two glasses of wine before the sedatives in her wine put her into la-la land, a never-never-land where life was innocent and pure, where she would wander happier and safer cloaked in innocence and well beyond his reach and probing touches. But her mind wasn't what Hampton had patiently waited years to fully appreciate since first seeing her body beaded and glistening in the shower. He wanted his dream coming true. He wanted his fantasy becoming reality, not merely closing his eyes and putting her face on Karen's warm and responsive body, biding his time, savouring his wine and adoring her while waiting for the film's credits before dimming the lights and finally achieving the desired mood and effect.

*

Hampton carried Jodie to her bed near 1:30 AM , laying her in her panties between satin sheets that would require no explanation in the morning, laying her gown and robe across her bedside armchair. He knew that most nights the girl went to bed that way, always keeping her robes close at hand.

So no big deal. And if she did feel anything in the

morning, he would simply reply that she drank more than she realized, which probably brought on her sudden cramps. His fault. She had wanted a third glass, insisting on seeing the movie's ending and, to his utter disgrace, he demonstrated poor judgement by giving in to her. When the movie did end he gave her something that would ease her discomfort, helped her to her bedroom door and left her, apologizing for not being a better role model. That's all. Sorry, sweetheart.

Which is what he did after lifting the top sheet for a final glance and darkening the room, returning to the cinema room where he put things in order, cleaned the slight mess she had made on the sofa, and turned over the cushions. Satisfied, he poured a three-finger scotch he couldn't afford on his own dime and dropped onto the same sofa blowing a stream of warm air past his lips.

She was fantastic, soft and warm, better than any fantasy or dream, and not experiencing her a third time demanded the most extreme willpower, surrendering to reason more from the fear of her waking than what she might feel when first stirring in the morning.

Not kissing and caressing her more ardently was difficult, not squeezing her harder or digging his fingers into her flawless and perfectly shaped buttocks demanded incredible restraint; her breasts, the most perfect he had ever touched or kissed were soft and warm and firm, while the moist warmth inside her, gripping him, caused his arms to strain and threaten to weaken when what he most wanted was to ease his body against hers and, for a moment, picture her arms tightly embracing him. Instead he eased away from her, massaging his arms while he stood over her adoring her. Not adoring her from then on, not treasuring their evening together, would be impossible

Gently cleaning her, removing his scent from her with a soft cloth and soapy warm water and drying her, was no less arousing. Then removing as much as he could of what he had put in her, he dressed her in her panties and raised her gently in his arms from the sofa. Not that he hadn't seen her that way hundreds of times since her week in Aruba with Karen. He had, but feeling her weight, hearing her purr and seeing her naked in his arms was exceptional.

Anyway, now that she was able to stay at home on her own, he had planned a week of out-of-town sales meetings and would be leaving her by late morning.

*

Jodie woke near one o'clock Sunday afternoon, realizing instantly she felt like shit, enduring several minutes of misery and discomfort curled into her pillow before making her way to the bathroom hunched over and pressing her hands hard against her belly.

Sitting on the toilet she noticed a pink stain in her panties, furrowing her brow, pushing them to her ankles and onto the floor where she left them, padding to the mirror where she stood frozen in shock. The beautiful girl with the killer bod from the evening before had transmuted into a hideous creature. Her eyes were blurred and red, her lustrous blonde hair hanging in matted strands. Her makeup had streaked and smeared into a grotesque mask, her smeared lipgloss distorted her mouth and whatever was happening inside her was causing her vagina to pulsate.

What had she done? What had she let happen? Shit! She hadn't once in her life felt as horrible and, if she felt like shit, which she did, the dumbstruck girl leering at her from inside the mirror looked that much worse. She could never have imagined herself being that repulsive. Yet she was, because she was stupid, acting older than she was. And what was multiple times worse, she broke a promise to herself. Something she would never in her life do again.

She went to her bath, pouring water as heated as she could withstand. She added salts and oil, sliding in to her shoulders, searching her mind as calmly as she could for answers, and how she got into bed wasn't the most troublesome question. Mark was. She wasn't sixteen anymore, she was not a kid anymore.

Stepping from the tub oiled and fragrant, towelling herself dry, she felt much better which did nothing to console her. But the nausea was gone and the curious throbbing was at least subsiding, replaced by serious hunger pangs. She hadn't eaten in over eighteen hours and was as famished as she was determined, combing her hair into a damp tail and dressing into jeans, a thick woollen sweater and suede boots. She wasn't nervous, she was adamant that she would confront him, adamant that he would tell her everything she couldn't remember.

Their bedroom door wasn't closed and the bed was made, Jodie assuming he was downstairs. But he wasn't. Nor did she find him anywhere on the main floor. What she found instead was a printed note in the kitchen taped to the fridge door.

*

Jodie, hi,
Guess you had a bad night, or should I say morning? Sorry.
Really glad you had a good time. I hope. Isn't that what counts?
Got you safely to your room, though. To your door anyway.
Guess you got into bed alright, since I didn't hear any crashes.
Anyway, FYI: You were very lovely and excellent company.
Thank you for being you. Don't ever change, sweetheart.
Will call this PM and see you sometime late Friday.
Ciao, Mark.

*

She shrugged, crumpling the note. She was starving, that was more important. She made a fast lunch and went out onto the deck with a store-bought pizza and a twenty-ounce soda to enjoy the quiet and unseasonal warmth of early spring.

Ciao, Mark. One of those stupid things he said, like sweetheart, like they were sweethearts, like that would ever happen, and baby girl when speaking with Karen who hadn't been a baby or a girl in decades. Stupid. And he hadn't mentioned a word about leaving town for a week, which she did not mind at all, which was complete bullshit. He was avoiding her. He fucked-up big-time getting her drunk and thought that leaving her alone for a week would somehow make things right.

She chuckled. A week alone and the weather guy was promising sunny and hot the entire time. So, yeah. Ciao, Markie. Asshole.

*

Jodie spent what remained of her afternoon on the deck regaining her well-being, absorbing the sun's warm rays, elated by the fact she would have a full week of complete freedom months before her much-awaited sojourn in Tampa.

Later she made a light dinner of baked beans and ham that she ate with a tall glass of milk, swearing off wine and booze for the rest of her life, hoping he would call soon so she could get him over with. Being honest, they had both fucked-up. Him as an adult and her teetering in an unfamiliar present between a past that was for years scripted daily to accommodate her and her future that was as yet somewhat ambiguous.

So what? Karen would never know, so let's get on with life. Besides, three months after first seeing Tampa she would leave Vermont behind forever. She had better plans formulating in her mind, good plans that did not include marrying a Jethro and popping out his hillbilly spawn that would completely destroy her life and her body. She would be somebody one day, do something good, and be the best at whatever she might become because being the best was who she was, an inherent part of her that came long before Karen.

And suddenly she felt sad, hugging herself. She couldn't remember the last time she thought of them or tried to remember their faces from what seemed like very ancient times. Why was that? Why did Karen never talk about the past, about her mom and dad? She didn't remember her grandparents either, their faces and her memories of them stolen from a child's mind by time and wonder.

She would ask Karen, tell Karen she wanted to know. She deserved to know exactly who she was, not simply Karen's perception of whom and what she should be. She would, she was through being a child, that thought instantly erased from Jodie's mind by her phone's chime.

Chapter Twenty-Two

In his New Haven motel room, since Karen steadfastly refused to supplement his workweek, Mark Hampton cleared the desk and poured an inch deep of the pedestrian bar scotch his company allowed him each travel week that in no way compared with the booze she financed at home. He sat with his legs stretched out on the narrow mattress, slouched against flat pillows with his laptop by his side, remembering every inch of her, the taste of her lips and the warmth of her breasts, the smooth contours of her naked body that filled the computer's screen, and the weight of her in his arms so few hours ago.

He could not believe they'd been together as ardent lovers, thankful he had no meetings until the next morning. His memory of her, of them, what he was seeing, was overpowering, all-consuming. He couldn't get her out of his mind. Just knowing he would be speaking with her, hearing her sweet voice in moments was exciting. He pressed *Send.*

*

"Hello, Mark."

"Hey, sweetheart. Listen, I'm sorry for leaving you like that. You know, since you weren't feeling good. Things got a little relaxed last night, I guess. But what the hell. We were enjoying, right?. Thing is, some unexpected business thing came up. Anyway, I'll be home Friday. Then you can tell me about your week over a glass of wine. One glass, sweetheart, not four."

"What?"

He pressed P*lay*. "Yeah, that's right. That third little sip you wanted turned into four full glasses. Not real smart of me, letting the evening get the best of us. Next thing I knew you were gone, purring like a baby. So I let you sleep awhile, later thinking you'd be better off in your bed, especially this morning. That's when I helped you stumble to your room. I waited in the hall till I saw the light go out. You were pretty drowsy. That's about it."

"I was pissed, Mark. Absolutely and totally pissed. I woke up feeling like shit. Thanks for that."

"I take it you don't remember the movie?" And now you're being undressed, sweetheart, very very slowly, very tenderly. "She kills them, by the way."

"Good for her. What I remember is being pissed. I'm surprised I didn't puke my lunch."

"I'm glad you're feeling better because you complained on the stairs that your stomach was aching. You were groaning a little. You are feeling better, aren't you? Was that a female thing, perhaps because of the wine?" And now you're naked, Jodie. Very naked, very sexy, and all mine.

"Yeah, a girl thing. No big deal."

"Good, I'm glad. I was worried about you." He brought her in closer, watching himself lean over her, tracing a tender path from her thighs to her belly to her breasts. "God, you are so fantastic."

"What?"

He jerked, slamming the lid closed. "No, sweetheart. Not you…Karen. She's my desktop, with me wherever I go. I can't get enough of that woman. But definitely, no question, you are both lovely ladies." And I can practically smell you.

Bullshit. She didn't believe a word he was saying and, what's worse, she couldn't do a thing about it. No way did he leave her at the door. That was total bullshit. He stripped her and put her in bed before whatever else drooled into his sick mind. That's what she believed; that's what was true. That was

Mark Hampton: a total pig. And believing that he would have seen her and touched her that way made her ill. "I should go, Mark. I'm tired."

"I understand. I'm a little beat myself. And Jodie, when I speak with Karen later, I'll tell her about our evening. Just not the four glasses. That would definitely set her off."

"Whatever. And, Mark, no more wine and no more movie nights. I'm done with that shit."

He saw that one coming, sighing for affect. "Once bitten, twice shy. I get that, as long as you're okay."

"Yeah, I'm good." She pressed *End*.

He snickered, tossing his phone on the bed. "Yeah, you bet you're good. Sweet dreams, sweetheart. Ciao."

Jodie went to her room angry, studying until she fell asleep; Mark Hampton remained on the bed with his open laptop, spending the next ninety minutes watching himself loving and caring for Jodie.

*

The next morning her mood was no less foul, certain Hampton had done something sick to her, happy she had a full week without him or Karen. She needed the time for getting her emotions under control. Three months was a long time to pretend she didn't mind living with a creep.

She didn't mind the movie nights and she did like dressing in silks and satins, being a woman, but she knew Hampton crossed the line Saturday evening in a big way, deciding that from then on she would stay dressed in streetwear until securely locked in her room for the night. As for the pool the coming summer evenings and weekends, those would be strictly full bikinis and no bullshit.

Tampa could not come soon enough and the best summer days would be the ones spent alone since Karen's deal eliminated the need for a summer job, making her even more of a bitch to gossip about at school.

That she was accepted to the U of T surrounded by white

sandy beaches was bad enough, that she was travelling there alone in June to find her own apartment was even worse. When the other girls should have envied her, they resented and hated her because they weren't her. Would never be her.

Because while they would be out desperately searching and competing for menial summer work, Jodie would spend her pre-college days maintaining the pool alone in her thong, doing housework and preparing evening meals that would earn her 400 dollars each week. This up from 200 the previous year and seriously complementing her usual 100-dollar weekly allowance, although Karen would no longer support her wardrobe or give her money for gifts. That was part of the deal, which was a non-issue for Jodie with not far from fifteen K in the bank.

She went to her window where she opened the blinds, squirming onto the sill, bringing up her knees and staring into the green countryside and rolling hills to plan her week that would absolutely begin and end with a maximal tan and minimal lines. The weather guy was promising high temps, lots of sun, and the day was already warm and bright.

Easing from the ledge she was smiling, thinking of the other girls out on Spring Break hunting for work when she would be on her private deck lounging topless, tanning and sipping lemonade while she studied and formulated plans for Tampa. They were the real bitches.

Then a silver glint caught her eye from inside the fresh air vent mounted near the ceiling, the sparkle disappearing when she stood along with her curiosity and she went to the kitchen.

She spent the morning cleaning the deck loungers and chairs, polishing the barbecue and getting a jumpstart on her summer. After a lunch of grilled hot dogs and Coke she lounged and read until the sun's warmth gradually gave way to an early evening chill. She went inside for a quick shower and made supper, spending her evening fast-forwarding through documentaries, going to bed early and locking her door.

Tuesday morning she woke in microfibre shorts and a tee, gazing blankly at the gown and robe she hadn't yet hung in her closet, deciding she would do her laundry and the two pieces as well since she was certain—anyway, he'd touched them and that was reason enough.

Rolling onto her back, yawning and stretching, the glint from the day before caught her eye again, Jodie wondering why until she realized she hadn't closed her blinds. She had no reason, they had no neighbours. Twisting onto her side, she scanned her room from the window to the silver sparkle, puzzled. The moulded cover wasn't gleaming, or the screws, so why would something inside the vent glisten?

Curious, she swung her feet from the bed, padded to the wall and stared up, uncertain, her subconscious mind at once paralyzed with fright, her entire body gripped by a deep chill that made her shiver and squeal in horror. What she was thinking, seeing, could not be real. No way! He could not be that psychotic, that warped and depraved.

In fact he was—sick and perverse. Her robe and gown proved that and she hurried to dress, frantic yet resolute that she would not panic, running downstairs for a ladder and screwdriver from the workshop. Back in her room she wasted no time climbing to the vent, working at the screws until the cover fell to the floor.

She wanted to die. She didn't know what to think, but she absolutely wanted to die. What she felt in her heart and in her mind was true. Too stunned to cry or scream she stood on the rung for a moment thinking, staring into the lens, wondering if at that very moment he was watching her, laughing at her. Or was he worried? Or pissed that she had proof positive that he was completely amoral and loathsome, spying on a girl whose safety and well-being should have been his and Karen's top priority?

She all but bounded down the stairs to the workshop,

searching for a hammer, minutes later glaring into the lens and telling him to "fuck off" an instant before she smashed the thing from its mount. In the vent it looked ominous, on the floor useless junk, Jodie sitting awhile on her bed dispelling her confusion and anger and eventually thinking rationally.

She carried the ladder and her tools into her ensuite bathroom, feeling even more violated and vulnerable at discovering a second lens capturing her from behind a fan casing near the floor, ripping it out within minutes and wondering where else she would find him tracking and violating her. The obvious answer was their bedroom and their office, memories of Karen's giggles and indifference to Hampton's unwanted poolside antics, all his hugging and squeezing at once more meaningful than she ever would have imagined or could have believed.

And that's what she did. She ran to their bedroom which, for some reason, they never saw fit to close. Possibly assuming she wasn't as malicious as them, which was true two days earlier. Though not now, not ever again.

Karen's bedroom was three times bigger than Jodie's with garden doors, a wraparound deck and private Jacuzzi she was never invited onto overlooking the lower deck and pool. The walk-in was filled with his and her designer fashions, his side boasting an array of tailored suits and shirts, ties and Italian-made shoes mostly paid for by Karen, their ensuite resembling a Roman spa more than a bathroom.

Hampton wasn't merely a voyeur, a predator and creep; he was kept, and for some bizarre reason kept around and dangled. The puzzling question was, why? Karen was rich; she was successful and attractive. She didn't need him, so what could the attraction possibly be? Unless she was as despicable as him and Jodie had somehow been blind or blinded to a truth she couldn't bring herself to believe. That thought obliterated once she stepped onto the deck and within seconds found what she wanted: a lens fitted to the side of a control panel, spying on the pool—spying on her. Not hidden, just there, that she smashed from its mount.

There was no point in not smashing it. If he was watching her, he would already know. And unless he called her or cancelled his week she had three days before their face-off. Though now her planned week of lounging topless in a thong by the empty pool was abruptly at an end. That she found three didn't mean there weren't more, and what was not over was her search.

By mid-afternoon she had searched through every inch of their walk-in, her dresser and his highboy, the cinema room, every CD in the library and every closet in the house. She went through their office meticulously, finding nothing she could use to accuse him or resolve her Karen dilemma.

She put her bathroom and bedroom in order and the lenses in the garbage for Thursday's pick-up. She returned the ladder and tools to the workshop, then walking by the wine cellar she paused, tempted to take a break with one of Karen's most select vintages. Why not? She deserved. What better way to assuage her torment? She could not imagine the mental anguish she would endure over the coming three months, forcing that certainty from her mind, determined that from then on she would be a recluse in a house she would never again call her home.

She forgot the wine, scolding herself. That was the one life lesson she would never forget and never forgive. Instead she swung, staring at the workshop door, the one space she hadn't thought to explore, the one room she and Karen never went into. Neither had a reason or cared. Besides which Hampton was protective of his ridiculous man-space, forever inventing excuses for spending his Saturdays doing whatever while she and Karen drove into town.

She went back, scanning the room before checking behind each door, probing each shelf and toolbox, leaving his multi-drawer steel cabinet till the end for no particular reason, not wasting time wondering why he would lock the bottom drawer. She knew exactly why.

She coughed a snide laugh, spitting a harsh "well, fuck you," marching to where he kept a perfectly suitable steel bar and within a minute, sitting on the floor with her feet braced against the cabinet, her hands and arms jerking and straining, she tore away the lock and handle.

Tossing the bar and mangled combo aside, she sat there not certain whether she was afraid or relishing the moment until slowly leaning forward, reaching for the twisted frame, a guttural moan instantly escaping her throat. She didn't wonder for a moment what was in the DVDs, she was.

She counted several dozen, all dated and stored by *Bedroom*, *Bathroom* and *Pool*.

Barely able to stand and too stunned to cry, she made her way in a daze to the kitchen for a bag, then the cinema room where she sat in a worsening and disconnected state, determined that she would view every moment of what he saw of her most personal and intimate moments over the past couple of years. Until at last she drifted into a deep and merciful sleep numbed by shame and weary from conflict: The young girl in her mortified, her sensibilities crushed; the young woman in her consumed with rage and a deepening desire to kill Mark Hampton.

Wednesday morning she woke curled into herself on the sofa, famished from not eating the day before, heating a frozen pizza before sitting through the several DVDs remaining, deciding what she would do, deciding that Hampton was no longer an issue and that she would get past him.

She would not involve the police. She didn't need or want her name and face plastered across the media and she didn't care about doing the right thing, about exposing him as a sexual predator because doing that would cause even more finger pointing at school, side glances and caustic remarks wherever she might go. She needed and she wanted a better fix.

She wanted him gone for good, out of her life; she would go to Karen.

Chapter Twenty-Three

Friday evening Mark strode through the door, smiling as he passed her as though nothing had happened and went to his room to unpack. Sometime later, refreshed after a day of meetings and travel, he poured a scotch, sat with her in the living room and asked about her week. She told him casually that he was "one sick fuck", that she wasn't interested in his bullshit and left him without either one mentioning the cameras.

Nor did he mention his destroyed cabinet Saturday morning while Jodie was in the kitchen making a breakfast she would eat alone in her room. There was no need, the hatred painted on his deepening complexion spoke volumes, the burning question glaring in his eyes as obvious as the guilt.

He wouldn't ask because she wouldn't tell him, thanking his lucky stars he hadn't yet put the most memorable scenes to-date on CD. Those were still in his camera. He was certain they were, otherwise he would already be in custody, hurrying to his bedroom to ensure that would never happen.

The kid seeing that would have caused an unimaginable shitstorm. As it was she would mope around the house for a few days ignoring him until realizing that what he did was no big deal. Then in a few months she'd be too busy getting herself laid in Tampa and eventually forget the entire episode.

Saturday evening he left her to her dark mood. Speaking with her, reasoning with her was pointless. He went to town for dinner and a few drinks, leaving the bar near midnight with a recently liberated and pissed-off thirty-something divorcée, leaving her in bed mid-morning with a passionate kiss and promising he would call to set up a date night. She liked him, they liked each other, and she was wasn't ready for a relationship. She was making up for time lost, having some fun and experiencing something entirely different, very excited about meeting the three-dimensional Karen.

When he arrived home Jodie was in her room. An hour later Karen drove into the garage, Hampton making very certain he got there first.

*

Karen showered and changed into a lacy silk teddy, recounting her week while he sat watching. Taking her wine, stretching out on her front beside him on the bed, she asked about his time with Jodie, surprised that he went out of town leaving her alone.

"Something came up." He shrugged. "Anyway, she'll be on her own in Tampa soon enough and this is no big deal, except that she is righteously pissed, Karen. She found the cameras; then she went looking for the CDs." He shrugged. "And she found them."

"Shit, Mark. How?"

"I don't see that it matters. She called me a sick fuck and hasn't spoken a single word since." He sipped his scotch. "Although on a brighter note, I found us a new and eager friend. She's thirty-five, alone and lonely and very nice. Very nice and very you. You'll like her, a lot. We're all doing dinner next week."

She chuckled. "So when exactly did you like her?"

"Last night, all night. There was a synergy happening. She's making up for lost time in a big way. I left her place this morning. She does alright for herself." He reached for his phone, dropping it between them. "That's her, Maureen. Like I said…very nice and very playful. She saw you the same way."

"Oooh, I like her. Lucky you. But shit, Mark, this thing with Jodie. That is not good."

"She's eighteen and legal."

"But she wasn't eighteen when all this started. Shit."

"Talk with her. Tell her I didn't mean any harm, that we have them in every room strictly for security. I can install them tomorrow when she's at school."

"No. She already knows there aren't more. That girl is not stupid. She found the CDs, didn't she? And you can bet she's been through every inch of this place. Christ, she was here by herself the entire week." She eased onto her side, passing him the wine. "You stay here."

Pushing herself from the bed, wrapping herself in a matching robe, she closed the door behind her. At Jodie's door she knocked softly, telling the girl in a firm voice she needed a few minutes of down-to-earth girl-talk. Moments later she heard the click and opened the door herself.

Standing face to face with Jodie evoked a strange sensation she wasn't expecting. Jodie was taller than Karen by a few inches and although she seldom smiled, in that space and time, she somehow seemed cold, stoic without the slightest glimmer of a young woman's mixed emotions.

"Let's get this settled and put away, Jodie. He told me what happened, what he did."

"Did you know, Karen? All this time, did you know?"

"No, Jodie. I did not know. Am I surprised and shocked? Yes, I am. But is what he did worth ruining a family? No, it is not."

"He is not my family, you are. He's nothing. He never was and what do you see in him anyway?"

"He's good-looking and good in bed, which is all I want or need from him. Everything else is too much effort and I'm simply not interested."

"Like kids." The statement was matter-of-fact, the undertone was seething.

"Yes, especially kids."

"Like me."

"No, Jodie, not like you. Not at all. You're different, you

always were. You look years older than you are and you think the same way. And as for what Mark did, get over it. He was wrong, he's sorry, and he's in deep shit with me. That said, what happened is history. It's finished. Now, where are the CDs?"

"Really, Karen? Are you fucking serious? They are gone. Why would I keep anything that depraved and disgusting? He is one sick fuck, Karen. You really need to get rid of him, get him out of here."

"He is not sick. He's a man and he's pissed that he isn't thirty anymore while you strut around here most nights untouchable in lingerie that screams out come and get me."

"Yeah, because I had a good teacher."

"Yes you did. Never believing for a moment you would become a sultry tease. That is on you."

"Bullshit. I don't tease and I don't strut anywhere. But that, whatever I did, is history also and let's be honest. You liked him seeing me. What was that, Karen, some demented turn-on? Does he ever talk about me, fantasize about me when he's doing you? Does he?"

Karen's eyes flared open, the impact of her palms snapping back Jodie's head, in that very instant determining and establishing a new set of rules and limitations: Jodie's.

"Good. Thank you for that, Karen. At least now I know."

"What you should know, Jodie, is to be very careful. One year at university on my dime does not guarantee graduation. You're eighteen and not my problem anymore. I'm your guardian, was your guardian, not your parent. Your living here now is a privilege, not a right. So like I said, deal with it and stay out of our room."

Jodie was completely unmoved. She was resolved, bringing a week of endless questions to an end, not expecting the gurgle that erupted in her throat or the tight smirk pursed on her lips.

"You know what's really curious Karen, what I really do not get? For two years that sick fuck has watched me in the bathroom; he's watched me taking showers and baths and naked at the pool getting a burn on when I believed you were gone, even in my room doing whatever whenever he needed help getting himself off. But last Saturday he didn't just get me drunk watching porn, he undressed me. I know he did because I would never leave my clothes where he did. So where is that video showing whatever else he did to me? And shame on me for not checking his camera because, if I had, he'd be in jail now. So why don't we girls, since we're having this talk, do that now? Could be he forgot, because he's not that bright. Or maybe he's in there right now jerking off." Jodie quickly stepped in closer. "Don't even think of slapping me again because you will not like what happens next. And what you should know is that I will graduate in four years. I'm not the only one here who should be very careful."

"Okay, listen. You were drunk, a little, for the first time in your life. That's hard to handle, but he did no such thing to you. As for the porn, I did not know he was doing that. But really, what's your problem? Once you're in Tampa, if you're not watching porn, you'll probably be starring in it one way or another. So do not pretend you're perfect and pure. You're not." She turned toward the door, halting. "This is over, Jodie. Finished. You spend as much time in here as you want, I'm okay with that. But you get your ass downstairs for dinner this evening and do not be a bitch."

Karen slammed the door behind her, making a final point.

*

"That girl has a huge hate on for you that is not going away until she does, Mark. So until she does, until she's gone, you keep your distance from her and your mouth shut. Do we understand each other?"

He nodded. "What did she say?"

Karen blew a stream of warm air past her lips, reaching for her wine. "That you got her piss-drunk watching porn, that you stripped her and played with her a little."

"What!"

Her eyes asked the question first. "You didn't, Mark, did you? Could you possibly be that depraved or desperate?"

"Hell, no. No way would I ever do that. She's eighteen for Christ's sake. Shit, Karen. You know me. Getting off on watching her in the shower or skinny dipping and catching some nudie rays at the pool is one thing. All innocent fun. But that, stripping her, doing things to her? Uh-uh. No way. I would never."

"Well, what you did or didn't do doesn't matter. That's hearsay. What does matter are the CDs and the fact she's got you royally by the balls."

He dropped onto the bed, expelling a long breath. "You don't think she got rid of them?"

"That's what she said, but I don't believe her. Would you?" She glanced across to Hampton's camcorder mounted on a tripod by the doors. "Either way, good luck finding them in thirty acres. Like that will ever happen."

"So what now?"

"You stay away from her, that's what. And when you can't, you don't do anything that will set her off. You keep her happy. We both do." She sauntered to the tripod, aware she would either prove Mark was a liar and a fool or the victim of a blurred and hateful teenage mind. Glancing back at him the raw guilt she saw in his eyes shocked her. Flipping open the empty memory card slot she whirled to face him, her eyes burning.

"Mark, what did you do?"

Chapter Twenty-Four

Of course Hampton maintained the lie, admitting that, while he would never dream of undressing the girl, he did lay her in bed. He did stay with her awhile and he did more or less caress her with gentle strokes that might have been overly affectionate, nothing more. He was a man for Christ's sake. In spite of which, he swore too theatrically, nothing inappropriate happened, nothing. He had no idea how she got herself undressed; neither did she. She was totally wasted. No wonder she couldn't remember, and Karen knew as well as he did how the girl crawled into her bed each night.

That the evening dinner was a quiet and quick function was expected, Jodie locking herself in her room after doing the dishes when she and Karen continued their girl-talk.

"Whatever he said is bullshit."

"I'm not interested in he-said-she-said. Moreover, Jodie, this is how things will play out. So listen up. First off, our current deal stands. You're leaving for Tampa in June, you will find a suitable place and when you return for the summer you will get your weekly and the four-hundred. That said, once you're at the U of T, Tampa is where you will stay. You will no longer share birthdays or Christmas or anything else. In fact, once you leave for college, you will no longer be welcomed in this house. Being very clear, you will no longer have a room or a place to call home, if you ever did. Vacations with us are a thing of the past, your future summers will be better spent interning or working wherever someone gives you a job. More precisely, the silver spoon and your easy living are gone, Jodie."

Jodie listened dispassionately, not believing for moment given the palpable tension at dinner that the day's drama was over. "I think you're forgetting something, Karen. Don't you?"

"I'm not forgetting anything. What he did, as juvenile as he was, was no worse than the few years of frat parties coming your way. We have an agreement, one that is definitely tied to any future mood swing you might be inclined to pursue. Sort of like fuck-me-fuck-you, meaning that as long as you stay balanced and don't get stupid you will graduate. I owe your father that much. We both do."

"Sounds like I'm already fucked, when I didn't do anything. He did."

"Get real, Jodie. You both did, getting to the exact same place from different directions. We're talking here about a new dynamic, one that fits the need. What we had, whatever we had, is gone. I am not interested in more pretence, anymore of your bullshit, or Mark's for that matter; the very way you are not remotely interested in being here with me or with him. So let's not pretend otherwise. This is my home, not yours, not his, and I am cutting you loose."

"Me, not him."

"No, not him. Not yet. And you have nothing to worry about so stop the pouting. You'll do
fine and you will be fine."

Jodie's "I don't pout" could not have sounded more distant. Wherever her mind had travelled, that part of her was lightyears from Karen's designer kitchen.

Karen put up a hand, she was done. She was not debating with a churlish child, particularly a teenage ingrate who had never become her daughter yet was cared for and raised to enjoy the very best of everything.

"This is for the best, Jodie, and for you. You'll receive adequate monthly bank transfers for food and comfortable lodgings, a one-time furnishing allowance and your four years of tuition will be paid in full. The parties, the booze, and whatever you want or think you need are on you. As for the coming summer, keep things clean and modest. No topless and no thongs, whether he's here or a thousand miles away. Then you're gone and you are not coming back for whatever reason. My time with you is over."

Jodie wasn't the least fazed. "Gosh, thanks, mom. And yeah, like I would actually do that, help him get off."

"Yeah, like you actually did do that. Just remember those CDs you've hidden somewhere will reveal as much about you as they would about Mark." She paused for a moment reaching for a wine bottle. "Actually, from what Mark told me, there isn't very much of you that isn't revealed. And while we're talking theatre here, let's be very clear, the mystery video you're convinced you starred in does not exist. That work of fiction is purely yours, not his. You got wasted wearing silky and sexy lingerie that would arouse any man, particularly the one you were snuggled up to watching porn of all things. What were you thinking?" She chortled, filling her wine. "Quite frankly, Jodie, if Mark had done something, tried something, who would blame him after being teased by a little sexpot? But he did not."

*

The following Saturday Hampton and Karen had such a good time before and after dinner with their new friend, they made playtime with Maureen a weekly event. The women hit it off in a big way, leaving Hampton behind near the end of May for an island vacation that was as fulfilling for Karen as it was one of self-discovery and awakening for Maureen. Although what Karen did insist upon was that Hampton would spend as much time out of town on business as he could manage through to September, that week in particular, business and pleasure combined giving Jodie maximal freedom from him.

Jodie breezed through what remained of her final year, leaving on the third Thursday in June with the highest marks in the school, telling her homeroom teacher without the slightest emotion to mail her the diploma. She would not be attending Friday's graduation ceremony or the Saturday dance. Then she walked pensively along country roads to Karen's luxurious home that truly was never hers, finally realizing she was the fixture, the one who was always just there.

Hampton would not be home until the following evening, Jodie changing her flight to Tampa from the Saturday to Friday when Karen would get her to the airport by noon. She would board at 2:00, landing in the Sunshine State three hours later. She would rent a car and check-in to a hotel alone for the first time in her life, thinking she might extend her stay by a few days for a little beach time: Her graduation gift to herself since Karen had made very clear that a week in a Tampa five-star and a free education were gifts enough.

There was not the least effort at pretence over previous three months, although the atmosphere was chilly and frequently icy. There was no last-night celebration dinner at a fancy restaurant or at the house, Karen was ostensibly working late and Jodie finalized her packing while demolishing an all-dressed with a Coke. There was no sadness brought on by her leaving, or elation for what lay ahead. She simply closed her bedroom door when she heard the garage door rumble open and remained in her room until morning.

Friday Karen stayed in her home office until 10:00, musing on her dinner and evening with Maureen, catching glimpses of her niece as Jodie put her suitcases in the car, had breakfast and got herself ready.

Neither woman spoke except when the aunt put her computer in the safe and got her niece's attention with a terse "time's up, let's go," wondering why she hadn't simply given her niece a lump-sum payment for her summer schedule and gotten rid of her that much sooner. Having her in the house was awkward. The girl was cold and withdrawn, never speaking, never smiling. The one message Karen did understand, however, was the glare her niece reserved for Hampton when she believed Karen wouldn't notice, if she even cared. That she would be gone even for a week was the greatest relief.

Even living with him was becoming awkward, something she would never have thought possible, Karen never quite convinced he was as innocent as he claimed about that night, that he merely strayed from a few endearing caresses.

That he was travelling more frequently gave her more time with Maureen who she dearly wanted in her home and in her bed, but couldn't until now. The women were good together, becoming very good friends and frequent lovers.

Maureen was successful in business as a consultant; she owned a gorgeous home and earned much more than him with more perks that included several more weeks vacation she could share with Karen. She was a lady, engaging and charming, and she dressed the part with youthful flair. Whereas with Mark, clothes would never make the man because she paid for most of what he wore. He would never in his life afford his made-to-measure wardrobe on his own dime even at half the cost. He was good in bed, sure, but at what cost and for how much longer?

As for Hampton, her second week alone with Maureen became a festering thorn in his side, and no less irritating for Karen, calling her every morning and night for updates and details like a horny teenager begging for selfies of his best friend's naked girlfriend. He was jealous, feeling left out and endangered, which was appropriate given Karen's feelings. Because he was very much endangered, on the verge of extinction, Karen increasingly aware that she loved a woman but was supporting a man, more certain each day that she would begin a more fulfilling life without him the very day she would get rid of her niece for good. If not sooner.

Chapter Twenty-Five

Jodie arrived in Tampa on time, admitting that, yeah, she was absolutely excited.

Arriving at the Crowne Plaza she followed the bellhop to her executive guest room, following him out a moment later with a ten in her hand, foregoing the tour. She had her afternoon planned—by the pool. Her first stop, though, was the nearby shopping plaza a short drive away for a bikini better suited to Florida than the puritan Vermont she would soon exorcise from her mind.

She had every intention of embracing Tampa, of living the student life without getting crazy, of finally meeting people she could like and making friends.

Friday evening, slightly pink from the soothing Florida sun, she dressed for dinner in the dining room feeling as mature as what she saw in the mirror, though not in the eyes of the waiter who, sadly, could not serve her a glass of wine despite her coquettish frown.

She spent the rest of her evening in her deluxe room with a city map laid out on the bed, circling rental ads in newspapers, connecting unfamiliar streets to the U of T campus with a felt pen and making notes, searching for something safe, comfortable, and nearby for fifteen-hundred monthly or less.

Saturday she phoned them from the almost deserted pool, making several appointments for the coming week. Her future was on track, pleased with herself, driving to the campus after lunch where she explored what would become the centre of her universe until graduation, surprised by how easily she was smiling and waving at other wanderers who were waving and smiling at her.

Dining at the hotel Saturday evening, half-believing her young waiter was falling in love, she was beginning to seriously regret that after her short time on campus she hadn't planned for a summer in Tampa and told Karen that 400 dollars wasn't worth spending one more day anywhere near her pet pig. That she despised him each moment of her life, and would, that knowing whatever ill she could wish for would never come true was torment enough.

Sunday she woke feeling slightly nauseous, blaming the lobster, the cream sauce and the complimentary second wedge of key lime pie at dinner. She did her makeup and glossed her lips, dressing in a simple cardigan, a modestly short cotton skirt and low-heeled pumps before sweeping her hair close to her skull and shaping the light golden tresses into a severe Spanish-styled bun. She was picture-perfect, a young and serious lady prepared to negotiate terms with a letter from Karen's bank and her chequebook, returning to her room mid-afternoon from her interviews feeling despondent and queasy.

She hadn't liked a single one, conscious that her malaise might be the reason since she more often felt like shit than positive living in Vermont, cloaking herself in a protective melancholy that would make her days tolerable. But that's how she was, not who she was, and that, always feeling like shit, would stop at once. She was at last living her dream, lounging at the pool sipping lemonade while standing at the precipice of her freedom.

While at dinner her favourite waiter, who she discovered was working his way through his final year at the U of T and living alone, suggested where Jodie should go. The neighbourhood was quiet and safe, not very close to campus but close to the best beaches and, hey, they would be neighbours. Sort of.

She thanked him with a wide smile, adding a moment before a warm blush washed across her cheeks that she believed she would like having him as a neighbour. But she would not be having desert, Jodie wondering as she strode into the lobby whether he would ask her on a date sometime before the weekend, leaving him to ponder whether she would say yes.

Monday morning she woke feeling worse, scurrying to the bathroom seconds before dropping to her knees and vomiting for no reason she could fathom. Nerves. Waiting, clutching her chest and gasping until she felt she could safely stand, she stepped into a steaming shower, weak and shivering, slowly regaining her warmth and her colour. She had phoned the number the waiter had given her the night before, fearing she would miss out, and now she needed to look her best for the interview. The man had described his upper flat with affection and, if everything he said was true, Jodie would gladly pay the extra 200 a month herself.

She ordered a carafe of hot chocolate with dry toast to her room, feeling almost human by 10:00. She went to the pool where she lay in the sun for an hour, leaving the hotel once she improved on the healthier glow the sun had put on her face, arriving at the man's two-storey home several minutes early where she leaned against the rental and convinced herself the place was a steal at seventeen-hundred. She might even have a good friend or boyfriend to boot. A real boyfriend, how great would that be?

The gentleman and his wife were late fifties and charming, warmly inviting her in for ice tea and pleasantries before giving her a tour that Jodie believed would end in negotiations.

They did not want kids or pets, loud music or loud parties, drugs or mischievous behaviour. In return they offered a place for her car or bike and the use of the pool, the hot tub and their barbecue whenever she wished. Inside the place was expansive and modern with a huge balcony looking onto the tree-lined avenue and another more private space overlooking the backyard. Way too big for a girl alone and absolutely perfect, Jodie certain she would spend every penny of her furnishing allowance—and that she would. However she believed the rent was a little on the high side, raising her concern with confidence the way she had rehearsed during her hour of recovery at the pool.

They agreed. The price was a little steep, of course, leaving Jodie to sign her first-ever lease and write a deposit cheque dated the same day for 1700 dollars, visibly taken aback when the lady invited her for dinner. She thanked them. She was delighted and would absolutely love being their tenant. Unfortunately she was not feeling well, probably overwhelmed by the excitement of her past few days, asking with real hope in her eyes if she could perhaps take a rain cheque.

And yes, she most certainly could. They looked forward to seeing her on the first of September, the gentleman suggesting a backyard barbecue with the neighbours and possibly with the young fellow at the hotel who kindly recommended their home. If, of course, she believed that would be appropriate. Jodie replying that she hoped with all her heart that it would be absolutely appropriate.

*

Monday evening Jodie sauntered into the dining room dressed to kill in a way that wouldn't actually kill him, giving him hope instead, dressed in a way that made her look and feel better than she did. Her lustrous hair bounced at her shoulders in wide curls. Her silk blouse was unbuttoned to allure, not entice; her knee-length A-line skirt was sophisticated, not old, her perfectly shaped legs shimmering with the hotel's rich cream reaching to her open-toed sandals and painted nails that highlighted her delicate and perfectly shaped toes.

With no other gentleman to escort Jodie to her table, her eager waiter happily guided her to a quiet nook, pulling out her seat as he recommended the evening's special. When he brought her water, he stated what was clearly obvious to anyone as though reciting a poem he'd penned: She was very lovely. Then when he brought her dinner he commented on her piercing green eyes, trusting that she would enjoy her meal, passing by not long after to ask the customary question and smiling at the customary reply.

When she was finished he enquired about coffee. She said no. So instead he cleared the table and brought her the evening's pecan pie à la mode that she didn't order, smiling, pausing a moment before confessing his dilemma which he believed required a young and lovely lady's opinion on the somewhat personal matter.

Finally. Yes! She clasped her hands in her lap, furrowing her brow and pursing her lips in keeping with the seriousness of the dilemma. She had no experience with boys, had never been on a date, but she was thinking this would be good. He was definitely nervous, digging his hands into his pockets and rounding his shoulders, leaning discreetly forward as though making a recommendation.

"A personal matter, Brandon. Hmmm, like what exactly?"

"Well, there's this girl I want to invite on a dinner date. Nothing fancy because I'm kind of living in poverty until I graduate. She's drop-dead gorgeous, Jodie, new in town and seems very nice. My problem is she's a hotel guest. Fraternizing is cause for dismissal and I really need this job."

"Wow, that is a problem, Brandon." Jodie paused a moment, giving his quandary due consideration. "Has this very nice girl given you any indication that she would accept, or that she even likes you?"

"No, but I hope she likes me."

Jodie took another thoughtful moment, tasting her pecan pie. Looking up, she was beaming. "Oh, Brandon, I signed the lease. The place is absolutely to-die-for and, yeah, we'll be neighbours. How cool is that?"

"That is great, Jodie, really great."

"Yeah. And if this date girl works out you can bring her for dinner sometime. I've got pool and barbecue privileges."

"Yeah, that'll be great. I'm very happy for you."

She didn't believe him. "Well, you don't seem very happy." She rolled her eyes, cupping her face in her hands. "Oh, the girl thing. Sorry, Brandon. Tell me though, this hotel guest, does she have blonde hair and, I'm guessing here, piercing green eyes?"

"Yes, she does. Really green."

"Is she here now, in the dining room?"

He nodded. "Yes. She's very close."

Jodie turned in her seat, scanning the tables, facing him with wide-open eyes and a palm pressed to her chest. "Brandon, oh my! Do you mean me?"

"Okay, now you're teasing me. Yes, I mean you, if you're good with pizza or Chinese. Like I said, I'm kind of impoverished."

"I was teasing, I'm sorry. And yes, I will...have pizza with you. Thank you, I absolutely love pizza. I'm also staying here three more days. Just so you know."

*

Jodie went to her room thrilled, telling herself repeatedly that she had a date because she had no one else she could tell. She was going on a date with a man she hardly knew, didn't know, in a town she didn't know. How exciting was that! He was dreamy with deep blue eyes; he was tall and athletic from South Carolina with the most charming accent ever. He was polite and bright, a fourth-year marine biology student with much more to tell her and much more he wanted to hear.

Tuesday would be a pool morning and shopping afternoon, Jodie deciding she would wear something nice and new for her best ever pizza and, she guessed, Coke even though Brandon was legal and not restricted to children's beverages. No big deal, because she was going on a date, laying in bed too excited for sleep, surprised when she woke late Tuesday to the brilliant Florida sunshine flooding her suite and feeling like crap.

She groaned a miserable "fuck," waking for the third day with an urgent need to vomit.
Whipping away the duvet her feet scarcely touched the carpet, her moist hands barely raising the seat in time. When she was done, bursting into pitiful sobs, afraid of what was happening with her body, she forced herself into the shower and stood quivering from dread under a steaming torrent.

Her morning was shot. She wouldn't be sunning or shopping for retro shorts or a flighty tie top that would keep him thinking of her until September when something good would finally happen in her life. Instead she dressed without the usual approval of her reflection, noted the address of the nearest medical centre and left.

At the clinic she asked for a female doctor who, upon seeing Jodie, took her in at once. The exam lasted very few minutes, the lab test another hour before the physician sat facing her with a neutral expression that was completely unreadable.

"So what's happening to me?"

"Nothing, Jodie. You're perfectly fine. Except that you told me you weren't sexually active, which is peculiar because, simply put, you're pregnant. Thirteen weeks, give or take."

"What!" Jodie practically jerked from her seat. "No. That's not possible. I told you the truth."

"And I'm telling you the truth. You're pregnant. And speaking very bluntly, Jodie, at your age and particularly entering university, not taking some form of precaution is manifestly stupid."

"I did take precautions, it's called not having sex…not ever. I mean, fuck, this cannot be real. Are you certain?"

The doctor nodded. "I am. The question is, if you are, what are we talking about here? Doing drugs or getting drunk, a date rape? What?"

"No, none of that. I don't do drugs and I don't date. I don't drink either and I think I would know if I was …." Jodie didn't finish the thought, her already paling tan fading to a sickly white. Gulping air, leaning forward hugging herself, she wailed a ghastly "aaagh."

The doctor remained stoic. "Then we are talking rape, which normally implies violence, drugs, drinking or intimidation. So which was it?"

She looked wretched, her cheeks washed with glistening tears. "I don't know, I really don't."

"You're lying. So now it's a question of whom. A boyfriend, a close relative…maybe the postman or a Spring Break one-nighter?"

Yeah, that's exactly right. Jodie sat straight, wiping her face, inhaling a calming breath. "I want an abortion, Doctor. Can I do that? I have money, I do, and I don't need anyone's permission. Whatever happened to me, I do not want this. Not now, not ever."

"We can do that, yes. After you come back tomorrow and tell me you are very, very certain"

"I'm telling you now. I did not do this and I do not want this. I mean, shit, I'm only eighteen. Whatever happened to me, that's my business, but I am telling you now I do not want this and I will not change my mind."

"You should talk with someone, be very sure."

"I'm talking with you, but you are not listening to me."

"Parents, a friend?"

"No. My parents are dead and I have no friends. At least not until last night and I would die before telling him. I'm talking with you, Doctor. I'm telling you I absolutely want an abortion."

The doctor reached into a drawer, sliding a pamphlet across her desk. "Then it's Thursday at 1:00 PM. Come by bus or taxi. Do not drive. Call me in the meantime with any questions or doubts." She scribbled meaningless hieroglyphics onto a notepad. "This will help ease the bad mornings."

*

At the Crowne Plaza Jodie packed her suitcases before writing a note to Brandon explaining the family emergency that called her back to Vermont, that she felt terrible about cancelling their date, that she liked him and definitely wanted pizza with him in September—in her home if he remembered the address and was still interested.

She went to the lobby and checked-out, leaving an envelope for Brandon with the dining room waiter, explaining she wanted to show her appreciation for his excellent service. Then she drove to the closest pharmacy before checking into a luxury suite at the Marriott where she made a spa reservation for the next day and changed into a bikini for an afternoon by the pool. If she was going to feel like shit until Thursday, not expecting Friday would be any better, the least she could do was pamper herself, which did not mean she wasn't seething at the thought of Mark Hampton raping her.

The four glasses of wine was bullshit. He drugged her. Then he fucked her like some inert rag doll, getting himself off and laughing at her every night since in whatever sleazy motel room he could afford.

Chapter Twenty-Six

The afternoon was beautiful with a cloudless blue sky, above seasonal temps soothing her body and her mind.

Stretched out on a padded lounger, studying her contours, she would never have guessed she was three months pregnant, which was a good thing because the thought of Hampton being that vile and despicable with her sickened her, deciding she would simply not think of everything he might have done or for how long. She wasn't like other girls that way. She did not want kids; she did not want her body scarred or damaged, thankful she discovered the truth in time.

She didn't get the female compulsion to dote over babies, cooing and rocking them, staring at them like they were some unique and precious thing, let alone teenage girls eager for their last day of school and their schooling so they could marry their latest boyfriend, start a family, and forever ruin their lives. Or much worse, surviving four years of college then consciously jeopardizing a career with the constant distraction of motherhood.

That would not happen to her; she was better than that, she deserved better, eager for Saturday when she would arrive at Karen's home unannounced instead of going on a date with Brandon, eager for the expression on her stunned aunt's face when learning that the man she sleeps with is a predator, a rapist and pathological liar.

She reached for the pamphlet. For eighteen years she had kept herself pristine and untouched. Now because of

Hampton she would lie naked on a table with her legs spread wide in stirrups while some cold-hearted bitch doctor she didn't know painfully cleaned and vacuumed her vagina and cervix like she was some sort of contaminated receptacle—and painfully. Wonderful, as though she wasn't already suffering. Just fucking wonderful.

She would also experience cramps and feel like puking, she would sweat and possibly pass out. Great. Until then she had no idea what a cervix was, or if she even had one. Why would she? She was a virgin intending to remain that way until she was ready, never thinking she'd be raped where she lived.

She wiggled her way from the lounger, tossing the pamphlet into a trash can. Glancing at her watch she thought of Brandon. She liked him, hoping with all her heart he was disappointed, that he would wait for her because in her heart she was also still a virgin. If not one day soon for Brandon, for someone else she was not in a hurry to meet. That she was drugged, humiliated and raped and about to be hosed before they sucked Hampton's shit from her body didn't matter. She was Jodie Carter; she was a good girl and she was a virgin.

*

She had dinner served in her suite and fell asleep early, waking Wednesday feeling better but not fantastic, hovering somewhere between mildly curious and mildly nervous. She had no idea what her day held for her. She had never done the spa thing. With all Karen's money and love of self, Jodie hadn't once had a Girl's Day with her aunt. Despite which, she was ready. Besides, she paid the 750-dollar charge upfront without regret, beginning her day at 8:00 with a breakfast of one poached egg, a fruit salad, a concoction of yoghurt and granola, and mineral water. Yummy.

Her treatments began promptly at 9:00 with a massage and hot basalt stones strategically placed on her body before she was laced with warm mud and cocooned in linen for a facial and foot therapy before drifting into nirvana for thirty minutes.

At 11:00 she went for aqua therapy, her already young body rejuvenated with pure oils that would somehow bring her the inner calm she particularly needed following a thorough exfoliation of her body and a soothing Vichy shower. This before they patted her dry, assisted her into a warm and fleecy robe, and walked her to the private dining room where she asked for a table alone. She would not spoil her day sitting with spoiled middle-aged housewives who probably had children her age and would not stop with the questions.

They came for her at 1:00 after her luncheon of pan-seared trout served with sour apple mint, a quinoa and kale salad she would never in her life eat again, and mineral water. She was reserved for an hour of Reiki that would bring her balance and harmony through light touching that no one had explained would include her breasts, her bum, and the uppermost delicate flesh of her thighs while promising to infuse her with a positive and radiant energy.

At 2:00 she was escorted to a deprivation chamber where she would lay suspended, naked and alone in heavily salted water and total blackness, the technician assuring her that even a whisper of doubt would cause the chamber door to fly open at once. Though once inside, once entirely deprived of sight and sound and sensation, floating with her arms outstretched away from her body, Jodie was perfectly relaxed, musing that, for a girl who had always changed privately after phys ed class, she was adjusting very well to spending most of her day completely naked with strangers.

An hour later might have been a day later, or a minute. She was completely lost in time, in her reverie.

They gently laid her on a bathing table in the dimly lit room, rinsing her with streams of warm water, patting her dry before helping her ease onto the floor where she let four caring hands expertly moisturize her body with scented cream from her drooping shoulders to her feet before cloaking her in the soft robe.

They guided her to the hair salon for styling and nail treatments that would conclude her day, Jodie walking into her suite moments after 5:00 depleted from self-indulgence, wearing her robe and carrying a complementary spa bag filled with her clothes and goodies.

What she did first was hurry to the bathroom for the mirrors, twirling and posing this way and that, examining herself, believing she had never in her young life looked as alluring. She even smelled alluring, proud of what she was seeing and that she would never be anything less than what she was seeing and feeling at that very moment.

Dropping onto the bed, staring at the ceiling, planning what she would wear for dinner, she fell asleep where she lay, waking a few hours later and deciding on jeans, boots, a cardigan, and definitely the dining room. She did not spend all that money for an hour in a burger joint or some franchise with Billy Bob and Betty Heehaw who wouldn't know designer jeans or a French-styled updo from Betty's coveralls and ball cap. She wasn't being aristocratic, she was being real. The Billy Bobs and Bettys of the world wouldn't get her anywhere in life.

Her five days in Tampa were life-altering, her impromptu spa day making her time there the most meaningful. That's what she wanted, that life of luxury she could share with someone who one day would love her deeply and forever.

She came to see the U of T and find a nice place to live, accomplishing both while meeting Brandon and deciding of her own volition that she would endure the discomfort of an abortion before returning to Vermont with a single objective which did not include working as her aunt's live-in maid and pool girl. She was no longer a girl, her day at the spa made that abundantly clear, what she saw in her suite's bathroom mirrors proved that. Best of all she was more than good to go; that's what floating in tepid water, deprived of feeling and light, proved to her. She was a woman, no longer a child. And, yeah, she was very good to go, somehow finding a spark of humour in the moment that made her chuckle at her aunt's snide fuck-me-fuck-you while she tugged on her jeans.

Her aunt had no idea of the raging shitstorm coming her way, and definitely not Hampton.

She would not stay another night in the woman's house, not that her aunt would want her around over the summer. Not now, not once hearing the vile truth. Nor would Jodie forfeit the deposit on her home, her living allowance or her four years of higher education paid for by her father's loving sister. Not now thanks to Hampton's aberrant libido. Besides, the aunt emphatically said she was to fuck-off and never come back, which is precisely what she would do three months earlier than planned and with their deal fully intact.

*

Striding into the dining room the night before Jodie had made good use of an attractive female's unique sense of self and that species' highly developed peripheral vision, interpreting stares and envy, smiles and appreciation while ignoring them as the hostess led her to a table where she could sit quietly watching them watch her.

Yeah. Slim fitting jeans and a nicely contoured sweater would do that: induce jealousy in some, desire and fantasy in others. Mission accomplished, her day and evening taking their toll as she lay propped against her pillows pondering the months ahead, sleeping peacefully until Thursday's brilliant sun woke her to what she believed was the first day of a new and delightful epoch of freedom and self-discovery. She simply could not foresee to what incredible extent that was true as she twisted in the satin sheets, stretching and groaning, laying with her arms trapped by her side, relishing the inner calm infusing her and the radiance she could feel emanating from her entire body and soul.

She was determined that she would not allow the day's macabre agenda ruin her bright mood. She was doing a good thing; she was doing what was right and decent. Nothing good would ever come from creating another amoral and degenerate Mark Hampton.

Untwisting herself, she showered and dressed. She went for a light breakfast, spending what remained of the morning sitting at the escritoire planning a delightful and eventful Friday and rebooking her original Saturday morning flight to Burlington that would get her in at noon and out again. This time forever by four.

At a quarter to the hour she left for the clinic. She paid her 450 upfront, greeted mechanically by the doctor precisely at 1:00 and got straight to it with an equally chilly detachment.

"So this is over is ten, fifteen minutes. Right?"

The doctor nodded. "Fifteen. After you tell me again that you are sure about this? What you're doing might not seem life-altering today, but sometime in the future…"

"I want this thing out of me, Doctor. Believe me, I am doing the world a huge favour. Enough said."

The lady doctor didn't care. Blah, blah. Another pregnant teen. She asked the question and got the answer, sliding a document across her desk. Whatever she might say would not be heard and would not matter.

"This is an authorization stating that you consciously chose and requested this procedure for reasons of non-consensual sex, that you are of legal age, that you were at the time of the event, and that you have been made aware by me of the options available to you. Do you understand?"

"I do." Jodie didn't bother reading. Scrawling her name, returning the document along its path, she stood with an air of complete confidence and strode toward the door. "I'm ready when you are."

The small and unimpressive room they went into was littered with stainless steel cabinets and sinks, an array of stainless steel instruments, tubes and machines she didn't want to think about, and a single paper-lined table with stirrups.

The attending nurse acknowledged her without a

greeting, pointing at a space behind a privacy curtain where she would undress completely and change into a cotton gown. A few minutes later Jodie was wiggling onto the table and swallowing an antibiotic, planting her feet into the cold stirrups and easing backward onto the cold against her bare back.

She thought she would focus on the glaring light above her and count down from 900, hoping the thing would be out of her well before zero with little interest in seeing or watching the two women preparing to work on her. Instead her eyes opened wide at seeing the gleaming tool she could never have imagined.

"Okay, Jodie. Here we go. This threatening thing is a speculum that let's me get inside there and make you squeaky clean before injecting the anesthetic into your cervix, numbing things up a bit before we start. You might feel a slight pinch or a sting, nothing more than a visit to the dentist and from there the rest gets easy."

Jodie nodded, pursing her lips at feeling the instrument slide into her. She was completely mortified, her entire body stiffening at the foreign cold and unfamiliar pressure inside her. A deep heat washed over her face at the flushing sound and the sensation of liquid dribbling out between her thighs and her buttocks, Jodie waiting for the worst pain ever that was instead so mild she scarcely flinched, relaxing her body and expelling a long breath she only then realized she had been holding.

"That's it?"

"That's the ultimate douche, the best you'll ever get. And what I'm doing now is getting a grip on the cervix with a thing called a tenaculum which keeps the uterus where I need it to be, sort of a cross between scissors and tweezers with hooks at the end. Essentially it's a surgical grappling hook." A slight pause. "Done."

"Doctor, thanks. I know what you're doing, but I really don't need the details. Just do it."

"Yes, you do. Because I do not want you in here again."

Moments of quiet and medical mystery followed that Jodie was not privy to. "This instrument, Jodie, is a canula." She waved the gleaming thing between Jodie's knees. "Nasty looking but sleek and very effective. Think of it as a surgical Hoover for cleaning house as it were, getting into your cervical canal and cleaning out your uterus as we speak. This part takes a few minutes and is where the cramps come into play."

Jodie spasmed, gasping a meaningful "fuck."

"Yes, like that, but they won't last long. They'll diminish as soon as we're done here." A brief pause. "And, Miss Jodie Carter, we are done. You are as good as new. Just from now on be smart about it. You're eighteen and female. However this happened, you did not have to be here like this. So let's you and me not see each other again."

The doctor turned on her heels and left, snapping off her gloves, leaving the nurse to assist the patient from the stirrups onto the floor, the older woman waiting impassively while Jodie dressed. Then she took her patient in a wheelchair to a private recovery room where Jodie sat enduring post-op care and birth control counselling, the more understanding nurse advising that, if she was that adamant, a permanent fix was the one sure alternative.

Jodie said all the right things that would get her out of there, into a taxi and at the hotel pool where she could put the entire experience behind her, sternly cautioned by the nurse not to swim or wade unless she wanted another and less pleasant visit with her favourite physician.

The nurse nodded. She didn't believe so either.

Chapter Twenty-Seven

At poolside Jodie lay stretched out envying the older women sipping adult drinks. She could vote and kill people in a war, but not order a drink in public for another three years. How absolutely stupid was that? Taking some solace in that she felt fine and that those women in their reinforced one-pieces and floral cover-ups were even more envious of her for being young and sexy and very shapely in her skimpiest bikini that would leave their men who would come later no small detail to wonder at and fantasize over.

Although by the time they were gone and, Jodie assumed, gossiping about the young tease making a spectacle of herself, the sun was sinking reluctantly into the bay and the air was cooling.

She ate dinner in her suite and fell asleep flipping through fashion magazines, planning her Friday that was all about her Saturday when she would make a point, when she would shock them with her entrance several hours early, before telling her aunt the truth and her rapist to fuck-off.

Best of all, what she would absolutely relish would be leaving them to their sick lives with written assurances signed by her aunt that she would receive a monthly allowance of 1000 dollars, effective immediately, plus her rent and tuition for the coming four years and one year thereafter until she was settled in a career. Or do time in prison, their choice. Because, yeah, those videos weren't going anywhere except the county prosecutor.

*

Friday Jodie woke feeling better than she had in days, if not—
she didn't know. Maybe forever.

She threw back the covers, squirmed into a bikini and
romper and hurried to the pool where she ordered a breakfast on
her aunt's tab. "And not for the last time," that private whisper
erupting a prolonged gurgle of giggles. Oh, yeah. The next day
could not come soon enough. She may have left her aunt's
house as a victimized and damaged teenager, her innocence
stolen, but that girl no longer existed. She was returning as an
older and wiser young woman with a thoroughly thought-out
objective.

Again in her suite she called her landlord asking if
moving in Monday would be a problem, delighted with his
reply. She called the Crowne Plaza, booking two nights,
deciding she would surprise Brandon early Saturday evening in
the dining room and begin the better life she longed for. Then
she went out on a mission.

For Friday evening she bought a playful white wrap
dress that was silky and short, backless and sexy and deepened
her tan the instant she peered into the mirror, bringing her 5'11"
to an eye-catching six-foot-two with satin sandals.

For Saturday, from breakfast to the Burlington, Vermont
airport, she would make a definite statement. She also needed
her mindset and determination not to falter. She went first with
an olive-coloured blazer with draped lapels and a single brass
button, a white bustier with a single blue ribbon that would
draw attention to the swell of her breasts, and flared navy shorts
with cuffs that fell to the hem of her blazer. That disarming
elegance she completed with low-heeled suede boots in a dark
tan that would in no small way highlight her long and smooth
legs.

Which was for her to adore, and for everyone who
would see her that day until arriving at the airport. Not for her
aunt and certainly not for Hampton. She had a more

sophisticated creation planned for them, something more in keeping with their sick minds: A white microfibre thong body suit and daringly short taupe skirt she would pair with shimmering stay-ups and four-inch taupe pumps. Definitely no longer a Vermont school girl and, at 6'3", several inches taller than Hampton.

The spree was finished by late afternoon. Too tired for the pool, yet too excited about her wardrobe, she modelled each one in her suite, deciding on loose curls for the white wrap at dinner, a Spanish-styled bun for the plane, and a simple ponytail that would offset the fifteen-inch skirt and show-all top she would not spoil with a jacket or coat.

At dinner she was the main attraction, deciding she liked the attention, deciding she would replace her entire wardrobe and eradicate the down-home Vermont affect. However she didn't stay long. She had to pack for an early flight, requesting a 6:00 AM wake-up call before laying out Saturday's morning ensemble, showering and styling her hair for the occasion and waiting an eternity for sleep to engulf her, her flailing legs and arms thrashing away the duvet what seemed like mere minutes later.

*

The first day of July could not have been more perfect, nor would the day be one Jodie Carter would ever forget.

Not a single wisp of cloud marred a deep blue sky. The early morning air was warm and still and the girl sauntering through the lobby was young and drop-dead gorgeous. She wasn't the least bit surprised that her outfit was an instant hit with the admiring night staff and smiling shuttle driver. Or by the millennial geeks all dressed-up in skinny-leg jeans, rainbow sneakers and oversized pastel shirts; the jerks who by virtue of the stupefied male condition of their age and epoch would travel through life devoid of gallantry and propriety, sitting plugged into their iPhones with their heads down believing she wouldn't notice their undivided devotion to her legs.

None of which were the reasons. She was happy, very happy, and she was eager. She was living a defining moment in her life, creating that moment. She was taking control without realizing the great extent to which that would soon become true.

At the airport she strode through the concourse to the gate exuding the essence of youthful beauty and poise, turning heads and evoking smiles, savouring every moment until pre-boarding into her First-Class seat when the young female attendant didn't bother asking her age. Instead she commented on Jodie's to-die-for outfit while serving her a mimosa and by their final approach into Burlington both women were delighted they would be staying that night in the same hotel.

Disembarking at 12:10, eager for the evening and dinner, Jodie went straight to the closest ladies' room where she squirmed and twisted from one outfit into another. Exiting the stall, greeted with wide-eyed gapes and shocked expressions, she ignored them while restyling her hair and left, making her way to the first in a line of limos.

Driving along the last several hundred feet of Karen's private road, smirking as she passed the monitors hidden in the trees, she was calm and collected. She was ready, waiting until the chauffeur had put her luggage by the front door and left, all the while staring up at her aunt, each step to the third-floor sanctum infusing her with more resolve until stepping onto the deck when she burst into a fit of laughter at her aunt's perfect reaction.

"I took an earlier flight, Karen, knowing how much you missed me."

"That's quite the look, Jodie. What is that exactly, teenage tramp, college call girl?"

"Perhaps both. Either way, it's expensive. You taught me very well."

"How was Tampa?"

"I found a place. I also discovered a lot about the U of T and, more importantly, myself."

"How nice for you, an epiphany."

"Sort of, I guess. Like being told I was pregnant because your ever precious and charming Mark Hampton drugged me and raped me three months ago. So I don't know, Karen. Is that an epiphany, or what?"

"Excuse me!"

"Yeah, you heard me. Pregnant. You do remember my porno night, don't you? My silky and sexy lingerie, snuggling up to a rapist and all those videos I found." She took a few steps closer. "I had an abortion a couple of days ago."

"You're lying."

"No, I'm not." Jodie reached into her handbag, holding the unfolded document inches from her aunt's face. "Yeah, he did. He raped me."

"He did no such thing. He would never. But you dressing like this, like some slut, I can see that someone would."

"Actually I dressed this way for him, thinking I would feed his sick mind…and yours, Karen. You must have known about those videos. I know you did, both of you getting off on watching me." She chuckled. "Imagine though, for these past three months while he's been fucking you, which I guess, like you, must be getting a little old, he's been thinking of me, fantasizing in his sick head about me. Unless you have those videos stashed somewhere and how sick would that be?"

Karen's stinging slap snapped Jodie's head sideways. "Get out!"

Jodie hesitated, smirking, raising a palm theatrically to her cheek. "I told you once not to do that again."

"Get out!"

"Oh, I am getting out. No shit. I simply came to say goodbye forever and make a point. You see I'm not bothering with the police. That would be counterproductive. Instead, dear Aunt Karen, sustaining my life without you over the next five years will require 1000 dollars monthly, plus an additional 200 for rent, plus my tuition. And I want that in writing and signed or this piece of paper and those videos will put your rapist pig in prison and you with him."

"You're not getting shit from me, Jodie. Not a penny, or rent, or more tuition because you are clearly deluded and I am done with you. Seeing you like this, though, I have no doubt you will do exceedingly well for yourself. I mean, think about it," she snickered, tilting her head, eyeing Jodie from head to toe, "what guy would not put out for the thrill of fucking that?"

Karen Carter grabbed for the paper, missing. Her body was tense, her dark eyes glaring with hatred, her other hand instinctively sweeping upward in a wide arc, loathing turning to disbelief the instant her head whipped violently backward, the intensity of the impact propelling her body down the steep stairway to the second landing.

Jodie stood staring defiantly at the woman laying crumpled and defeated, waiting for her aunt to move, defiance soon transmuting to shock and anxiety. Moments later, standing over the body, lost in time, a sickly groan escaped her constricted throat. She stumbled backward onto the steps, sitting clutching her chest, staring at the dead aunt, her mind paralyzed not by what she had done but rather what she should do next. She had never seen or touched a dead person, let alone deal with one she actually killed. Though of one thing she was certain, the death was an accident no one would ever believe.

The aunt's arms and shoulders were already showing signs of bruising, the abrasion on her jaw from Jodie's rings turning a dark pink. What she did know was that she shouldn't panic and fuck up. That was key, though her biggest problem was Mark Hampton. Or her best solution, or not, thinking of everything that could and would go wrong with that fleeting inspiration.

She sat where she was, pondering and debating. Yeah, she was innocent and she would call the police. She would explain how her aunt and Hampton were sick predators and hand over the videos as proof. She would tell them about the rape and her abortion; she would tell them how her aunt laughed and ridiculed her when she came home to confront and report Hampton and how there must be videos of the rape somewhere in the house because he would do that and her aunt was no better. She would explain that her aunt went wild, attacking her when she threatened to involve the police, and how she struggled to defend herself until her aunt lost her balance and stumbled down the stairs.

That's what she would do, and Hampton didn't matter. Or he wouldn't once they arrested him.

She stood, determined, noting the time: 1:12 PM. Then came a moment's reprieve thinking of Brandon and the flight attendant, wishing she had remained in Tampa with him and disappointed she would not be dipping into the hotel pool for a late-night swim with a very cute girl who might have become a girlfriend.

Turning to climb the stairs for her handbag and cell, she was seconds too late. Mark Hampton was very quickly closing the distance between them.

"What have you done, Jodie? I mean, what the fuck have you done!"

"I didn't do shit, asshole. She fell. That's all."

Hampton brushed past her, pushing her against the railing. Kneeling by the warm body he shuddered from a cold chill. Checking for a pulse was pointless. Instead he straightened her and closed her eyes, placing her arms by her sides. "This is not fucking real. You killed her."

Jodie didn't trust what he would do. She wanted open space on the top deck; she wanted her phone and the cops, retreating up three steps.

"No, I did not. Or I wouldn't be calling the police. Would I? And just not for her, asshole, for you. Because that night, when you raped me, you got me pregnant. I aborted, but guess what?" His expression spoke priceless volumes. "Yeah, that's right, a shitload of DNA and let's not forget those videos.

So you have a real good time in prison, asshole. Too bad now that bitch won't be going with you."

Hampton bolted toward her with such nimbleness and speed that Jodie stood frozen with no chance of reacting before his fist slammed into her stomach, buckling her, a single loud gasp emptying her lungs. He grabbed at the bodysuit, yanking it to her waist, jerking the top of her skirt to her knees, trapping her, dazing her with a vicious slap and flinging her wildly to the deck where she landed sprawled and afraid by her aunt.

Twisting, all she could see was Mark Hampton coming closer, sneering.

"You're the bitch, Jodie. You always were. And forget the cops, that won't happen. Because whatever did happen here will just be another missing woman on the six o'clock news. Now you and me, that's another matter. You got drunk and we had some fun together. That is no big deal. Believe me, you had a good time." He was staring transfixed at her breasts and silk thong bright white against her tan. "I must admit, I haven't thought about much else since that night. And right now, since you're partway ready, I'm thinking we should be kissing and making nice, putting all this behind us. Karen's not going anywhere and what's done is done. We'll figure out something later."

"You're sick." She eased onto her hands and knees, grimacing. "Go fuck yourself, Hampton."

"No, sweetheart. I don't think so. We are going to seriously fuck each other, you and me." He chuckled. "Our first time was incredible, Jodie. Have to say memorable, both times. But this will be even more incredible, more meaningful. Now get your very sweet ass inside." He pushed her over with a foot against her ribs, ripping away her skirt before grabbing a handful of blonde hair and pulling her to her feet. "And, Jodie, play nice. Another body on this deck won't make my day any worse. But yours? Very definitely. And I don't much care about alive or dead. Just warm and inviting sweetheart. So get your ass in there."

She had no choice; she could scarcely breathe and her head was reeling. She began making her way toward the garden doors, albeit not quickly enough for his liking, lurching forward when he pushed her and mocked her with a guttural and sinister laugh, Jodie praying for strength and swearing silently that she would rather die.

Slowing her pace, she lurched again, urging her mind and her body to unite as one. She could do it. She would do it; she had no choice, the third time not stumbling but reaching for the iron poker laying against the fire pit. Skipping a few steps forward, a burst of energy igniting hope and purpose, she swirled in a tight circle, facing him with prune-coloured lips curled into a contemptuous sneer before driving the poker's claw into his temple, the blunt force of the impact for an instant throwing her off balance.

Retreating beyond his reach, absolutely gloating over her victory, she covered her breasts, staring down at him. "I sort of think your day just got absolutely worse, Hampton." She coughed a wicked laugh, his wide-eyed disbelief for a final instant turning to pure fear as she waved goodbye and said "Ciao, asshole."

Chapter Twenty-Eight

The next instant Mark Hampton lay dead on the deck.

Jodie Carter stood over him, drained and forlorn at 1:23. She was exhausted as much from the double killings in eleven minutes as she was by the happiest of conclusions. Yet, as amazed and proud of herself as she was for surviving, she needed not to panic; she needed to think rationally and she would. She had time. Being in the centre of thirty acres she had no need to hurry or do something stupid because no one would be coming over anytime soon. No one ever did.

She left the couple as they were: Karen Carter seeming peacefully asleep, Hampton somewhat less peaceful with an iron rod protruding from his head haloed in a widening pool of blood.

In her bathroom she dropped her ruined outfit into the tub, cursing, realizing then she was splattered with his blood.

She stood under a heavy torrent of steaming water cleansing her body as much as her mind until one began to prickle and the other began clearing, styling a plush towel into a turban and stepping onto her balcony to dry under the warm sun and gaze across the distant rolling hills.

She would not surrender herself to the police and ruin her life. She would not. She had no reason because she felt no guilt. Instead she had a forty-hour window before another workweek would complicate her life, which gave her precious time, the first and absolute priority being the bodies.

Not a chance anyone would believe her. She knew

enough about the law from watching documentaries and movies. They would put the blame on her, claiming she should have gone straight to the authorities with her evidence. Her rape was no defence, not a justifiable reason for committing premeditated murders months after the fact. She should have known, which she knew was true. And now they would never believe that her aunt attacked her or that Hampton, obsessed with her and incensed, was intent on abusing her a second time.

She needed to think things through; she needed to be smart and composed, devise a workable solution which she could not do until first cleaning the mess she had left on the deck.

She added her towel to the tub, slipped into a thong and went to the main floor for her rain boots and into the garage for a hose and something that would help her drag dead weight.

On the deck Hampton's wound had coagulated, though his discoloured blood was dripping over the edge onto the patio below. She pressed a foot against the head, yanking with both hands, gagging at the sight of fresh blood and bone fragments spraying across her boots and thighs. She lay the polyester band of a ratchet tie-down across Hampton's chest, rolling the body onto its back and securing the band under the arms before bringing the ends together in a tight knot. Then stepping into the loop she dragged and pulled the make-shift litter to the patio level below and into the garage in under five minutes, wrapping the head several times with duct tape before sealing it in a plastic bag as an added precaution. She did not need more blood.

She did the same with the much lighter aunt, minutes later hosing the patio's composite floor and furniture until satisfied the deck was pristine, thoroughly hosing her boots, her body and poker before climbing to the top-floor private deck bare-footed where she opened the hot tub's valve and stood watching the several hundred gallons cascade over the edge.

Inside she added her thong to her tub. Towelling herself

dry as she stepped onto her balcony she pondered what she should do next, concluding she couldn't do anything properly without a formal list, thankful she had almost two full days.

Dressing into a loose-fitting romper and her favourite suede boots, not losing focus, she went to her aunt's office figuring that was the best place to start, first opening an '86 Aloxe-Corton Premier Cru she'd taken from the wine cellar. Not because she was an aficionado of the Côte de Beaune region of France, because she deserved the very best for what she had done. Besides, who was with her to say no?

The safe that was open because her aunt hadn't expected her until later that evening was the obvious first choice, Jodie shocked at discovering that her aunt's financial portfolio totalled over twenty-two million and that her travel business was nothing more than a shelter, a convenient tax write-off serving her prurient nature. She was even more shocked when she discovered twenty-thousand dollars in crisp 100-dollar bills.

She learned about the home she once lived in as a baby, the farm and her parents' last testament she was never told about. She learned she was being cheated by her aunt who was supposed to care for her, who instead was giving her nothing when her father and mother had bequeathed a full fifty percent of the estate to their daughter and that she was owed at least four million plus monies derived from investments: Eleven million dollars she would never see, snorting at the irony that neither would her deserving aunt.

Closing and locking the empty safe she took her glass into Hampton's office, first searching through his drawers and his briefcase. She went through his papers and agenda, including his first appointment late Monday afternoon in Nowhere, New York which gave her a timeframe before someone might starting calling. Although she was more intrigued by the small keys she was jiggling in her hand, while not remotely interested in knowing more about the vile miscreant than she already did.

One drawer was no different from another, each one crammed with dog-eared files, chronicles of a failed and meaningless career until she opened the second to last where she discovered the absolute mother lode. The CDs came as no big surprise. The man was pure vermin, though what she did not expect was the Walther PPK and several boxes of amo.

She put the pistol aside, scooping the several CDs into her hands and hurrying to the cinema room where she began with the one labelled 'Sweetheart', believing her heart would stop beating after the first minute.

Compelled and sickened, she leaned into the screen watching Hampton grope and fondle her while she slept. She watched him ease away from her, easing her into his arms and laying her on the futon before leaving her to adjust the lens that minutes later captured him naked, leaning over her, patiently and expertly undressing her until she lay vulnerable and naked.

Jodie gulped her wine against the bitter taste of bile rising in her throat, watching him kiss and caress her, fondle and explore her, defenceless to help herself. She didn't want to die; as though peering through a stranger's window she wanted to kill. He was hovering over someone else, not her, worming his way between someone else's legs, penetrating and kissing someone else with strained precision that showed on his face and his arms, Jodie emitting a miserable groan each time he shuddered and left her to refill his glass.

Twice before he stood over her, hesitating, grotesquely working at himself a third time before he cleaned her, caressing and kissing her contours from her ankles to her mouth when he was finished, gently lifting her into his arms and disappearing, returning five minutes later for her robe and her slip, her panties and his wine before the screen went black.

The several other videos featured some Maureen together with Karen, the same Maureen with Hampton, Karen with Hampton, merry threesomes and toys and drinking, Jodie fast-forwarding through what she didn't have to see or hear, ejecting the last CD before rushing to the bathroom to vomit. She had lived her entire life with debauched freaks who stole from her, lied and cheated her and used her in the most despicable way.

She would have killed them again. Instead she went to the garage where Hampton was laying at attention, ramming a foot several times into the side of his encased head, ignoring the initial crack; the same foot not resting until Jodie was absolutely certain that several of the aunt's ribs were broken.

Back in the office she put the videos into a suitcase with her parents' testament and her aunt's portfolios, which included the farm's deed of sale, putting everything by the front door beside the one she brought inside that she hadn't yet unpacked. And wouldn't.

She knew Hampton didn't like his job, that he was a loser who hated travelling each week, that he could never afford the clothes he wore or the booze he drank. He was an absolute loser, which always made her wonder what was wrong with her aunt. She was wealthy, she didn't need him. So what was the real attraction? And now she knew.

She had also discovered Maureen who was on both speed-dials, who she hoped would not be coming by for dinner. Which she believed was unlikely since those videos were filmed in hotels or where the Maureen woman seemed completely at home.

*

A reasonable plan was taking shape in her mind, seeming much more doable on paper with several hours of daylight remaining.

She drove to the closest mall dressed the way Karen Carter would dress with a wide-brimmed hat and dark glasses, aptly showing her body more than concealing it, à la Aunt Karen, making herself appear smaller with flat shoes and rounding her shoulders. She bought extra large blue and black garbage bags and dozens of cardboard boxes with her aunt's credit card, filling the Hummer's tank with the same currency and hurrying back.

In the house she emptied Hampton's entire wardrobe from his socks to his cufflinks and laundry into the black bags, not taking much notice, ensuring that nothing at all remained. She did the same with her aunt's intimate apparel and soiled clothing, putting what was decent in blue bags for the mission.

She ordered in pizza, once again letting her aunt pay. With a second glass of wine she passed the evening shredding every document in their offices, stuffing several blue bags with confetti before fitting their empty briefcases, wallets and handbags into black bags for pick-up. So that by 10:00 PM whatever might identify, personify or cloak Karen Carter and Mark Hampton was either in the Hummer awaiting distribution or in the garbage box at the end of a very long and private road.

On a high, unable to sleep with corpses downstairs and understandably haunted by the videos, she went from room to room, floor by floor, leaving boxes at each door labelled as personal items and jewellery, cutlery and décor accessories, making certain she left only furniture behind each closed door.

An hour after a warm and misty sunrise the jewellery she would pawn was in the Lexus; their stereos, their music collections and everything else Jodie didn't care about were in black bags and her aunt's gold-plated cutlery lay at the bottom of the private lake that Jodie dived into from the rowboat when she was finished for an invigorating swim she badly needed. In fact the early morning was so pleasant that Jodie didn't bother towelling and by 7:00 her aunt's prized dish and stemware collections became sunken treasures as well, along with every shiny tool and gadget Hampton had never used.

By 8:00 Sunday morning Jodie was fully energized, driving through town filling bins with high-end fashions and accessories worth tens of thousands, making her second destination the travel agency that now seemed very back-alley.

She knew what she would look for, what mattered and what did not, discovering her aunt would owe nine current clients refunds on their deposits unless Jodie wanted a potential problem. Which she did not, reversing each transaction from her aunt's account before leaving an envelope on the desk containing a six-month rental penalty that would avoid an even greater problem, loading the Hummer with office equipment she would leave at a charity store and client files that would no longer exist by noon.

By 9:30, hyper and on a mission to succeed, she changed vehicles, leaving the pawnshop with three thousand and a gleeful smile. If that wasn't royally fucking her debauched aunt, she mused, apart from killing the despicable bitch, what was?

Overnight the house had become a shell strewn with a jumble of eclectic furnishings. Nothing personal of any value or interest remained. However the best was yet to come because her list was far from complete. She was on a mission she would see through to the end with a timeframe that left her twenty-four hours—give or take as Jodie sat at her aunt's desk reaching for the dead woman's phone after researching the information she needed on the computer.

Karen Carter then called the power company requesting that the power be shut off until further notice; she was leaving town for an extended period. She called her nine current customers explaining the refunds, that she was closing shop and moving to Texas as the result of a family tragedy. This before shredding and bagging those and other files, before endorsing a termination cheque for the agency's employee who wouldn't care a whit about the impersonal regret and goodbye once seeing the exaggerated amount.

She called the company in Houston she believed would best manage her urgent situation, paying upfront in good faith. Pleased, she called a local interstate cartage company she hoped was reliable, asking for an assessment visit that very afternoon. She was moving to Houston and needed to vacate her recently sold home the next day. The guy came by at 2:00, screwing her over with a straight face for nineteen grand, an amount Karen Carter considered reasonable given the extremely short notice. Thank you, kind sir. Thank you very much.

The truck would arrive promptly the next morning at 8:00, would probably be gone by ten, and her furniture would arrive safely in Texas one week later. Thank you, Ms. Carter. Thank you very much.

She gave him the address of the Houston storage facility, signed the contract, paid upfront with her credit card and forgot the asshole the moment she closed the door behind him.

She called the Burlington Hilton, booking rooms for Monday and Tuesday for herself, Mr. Mark Hampton, and her niece Jodie. Then she left, arriving thirty minutes later at Marine & Tackle where she bought her live-in boyfriend a sixteen-foot motorized runabout complete with fore and aft anchors as a surprise gift for her boyfriend on condition the delivery would be made the next day between 11:00 and noon, gassed and ready for launching. They agreed, salesman and customer smiling for the same and very different reasons, a very famished Karen Carter stopping at a restaurant for an early dinner.

Yeah, she was on track.

*

At the house Jodie went to her room, arranging her wardrobe and possessions, discarding into black bags what she no longer wanted or needed along with all she was wearing and had tossed into her tub. By the time she finished the room was empty, the tub was pristine and her entire life was compacted into three suitcases and four bags standing ready by the front door.

With nothing left to do she dressed into what she would wear the next day and went to the wine cellar. She selected a full-bodied '92 Margaux she knew nothing about other than she was thirsty and would seriously piss off her aunt, realizing with a girlishly vindictive giggle that there were no glasses in the house. She woke a few hours later at the pool, purring, leaving behind an enchanting dream she couldn't remember. Which didn't matter. She didn't care about anything other than her plan was succeeding and that she felt good, proud of what she had accomplished in so little time. She felt good about absolutely everything she had done.

She stood, stretching, reaching for the stars before reaching for the bottle that was half-full. The night air was calm and warm; the heated water was still, sparkling with moonlight, beckoning her. So yeah, she would. She put the bottle to her mouth and gulped, celebrating the last evening of her captivity with her warden's elitist wine.

Naked and exhilarated, feeling wholly liberated for the first time in her young life, she dived into what would be her last swim under a starlit sky for a very long time. Until the evening she would surface into the arms of a stranger who at that very moment lay in bed light years away wondering with a saddened heart whether she ever would be.

*

Jodie woke again by the pool early Monday morning caressed by a warm summer breeze, shielding her eyes against a glaring sun that was promising a perfectly glorious day.

She wasn't interested in the floating bottle or the mild residual affects of the wine that would in a few minutes dissipate with a hearty breakfast. Let the thing bob and break, she didn't care. She was not going into the water. She had much to do, much to accomplish by midday and she would not allow anything to interfere with her freedom day.

She gathered her clothes, dressed, and went inside to rediscover an empty fridge and pantry, scrunching her face and thinking she may have acted somewhat obsessively, deciding she would combat a teenager's proverbial need for food by securing the garage, jamming the slider rails of the bay doors as an extra precaution and locking the interior entry before hauling the previous night's garbage to the end of the road for collection later that morning.

Then she went back for Hampton's computer because he

was quitting his job.

*

Fred, good morning,

Here's the thing, buddy. I'm leaving today with Karen for Houston, taking a couple of weeks to camp and see the countryside beginning the moment I press S*end*, meaning this is my formal resignation.

Sorry for the short notice, not really. Because you're a self-infatuated dickhead piece of shit.

The decision was a no-brainer. Being a GM there at twice the bucks versus never being a manager with you and working my ass off for shit. Send the deposit in the usual timeframe.

Ciao, Mark Hampton.

*

The cartage company arrived on time, four young guys tripping over their tongues whenever Ms. Carter came into view wearing her white and whimsical lace romper, white gladiator sandals, a wide-brimmed white Panama and mirrored glasses. The day was hot, she was definitely hotter, and they were gone by 10:30 damp with sweat. Her prized Lexus was the last item loaded, secured with tie-downs and chocks behind everything else she held dear, the lady thanking each of them for their timely service with 100-dollar tips.

An hour later the runabout arrived on its trailer which the driver attached to the Hummer for the very lovely lady who watched closely, who was absolutely certain her boyfriend would adore his gift. He left with a C-note as well, wishing her a wonderful day and happy boating, happier still that he was the one making the delivery.

When he was gone she backed the Hummer to the garage doors, detaching the boat. The property's lake was out of the question. At its centre the depth was a mere thirty feet, good for swimming and diving but not for making her day even more marvellous. She needed serious depth and the deepest nearby water was Wellsby Pond that was not a pond by any description.

She was also on the verge of passing out from starvation and absolutely needed food. She needed the strength—and she needed assurances the pond was a safe and secure location. She had come too far, done too much to risk failure.

She drove to a burger joint, leaving the drive-through with a duo of red hots and bottled water, well-fed and feeling more alert by the time she arrived at the pond that was completely deserted along its entire perimeter the way she had hoped. The lake was a favourite for weekend anglers, too far off the beaten path for tourists and city people. The very deep and very cold water was framed with half-mile craggy shorelines on either side that made swimming and sunning unappealing for the girls and diving impossible for the boys, particularly when the entire area was dotted with smaller, warmer and sandy swimming holes.

Very deep meant guaranteed obscurity and Jodie understood that very cold also meant the bodies would not expand with gasses and float, exposing themselves and her to some hillbilly's hook that would cause the hillbilly to become puzzled and scratch his hillbilly head. She was good to go. In fact she was better than good. This was her moment, her life's finest hour. This was her payback for all the shit in her life.

Back at the garage she dragged the dead couple to the bay doors, pausing to catch her breath, her mind commanding its insolent counterpart to pace itself, which was not about to happen. Intoxicated with adrenalin her body wasn't listening, disregarding the logic, hoisting the lighter corpse first into the boat, not easily and not delicately. But, yeah, she got things done in what she told herself was record time.

Hampton was another matter, much worse than she anticipated. Despite her greatest exertions he was not cooperating, as though somehow he foresaw his bleak eternity and was telling her "no fucking way," Jodie skipping back several times to avoid being trapped under the dead weight of a corpse experiencing the initial stages of putrefaction.

She was agitated and frustrated, increasingly losing touch, suppressing the urge to kill him again. Until she understood, until she retreated a few steps on her own, recalling the concept of leverage from her eleventh grade science class, chiding herself for not being smart and wasting precious minutes.

A few moments later she was propping a portable worktable against the boat at an angle she judged workable, tying Hampton's feet together with the boat's half-inch dock lines, attaching the other ends to the Hummer, et voilà. In a heartbeat Hampton lay sprawled indifferently over the apathetic and greying love of his life and Jodie was gaily working at reattaching the Hummer.

Wellsby was absolutely the best choice, a place she could access without worry within a half- hour drive from the house along dirt roads free of scrutiny, curiosity and the cops. And once she was there she could not have felt happier, more prepared, or more at peace with herself as she threw back the tarp.

She had never been in a powerboat, let alone pilot one. Despite which she got the thing in the water and got it floating, got the Hummer and trailer off the ramp, and stood mildly perplexed.

The boat was floating, which was fine, but it was floating away and she was standing knee-deep in cold water wearing designer elegance.

Chapter Twenty-Nine

Her dilemma was short-lived; her imported thong and bra were as good as any bikini. No kidding, but no way. Not a chance and within a minute the Hummer's shiny yellow hood was a display rack of bright white and seductive silks and satins, and Jodie was prancing and splashing her way toward the transom's ladder alone and naked in the wilderness, holding the compact nine-round PPK high over her head.

Onboard she got to it, starting the engine and making cautious headway until the depth sounder indicated one-eighty at four minutes past the hour. Drifting in neutral she worked with a single purpose. She secured an anchor with ten feet of chain to Hampton's waist with a shackle, tossing the anchor overboard an instant before she gave the body an urgent tug using the chain for leverage and he was gone, bid farewell with another remorseless "Ciao, asshole."

The aunt went the same way, unceremoniously and quickly, the niece lamenting aloud that the bitch wasn't alive and kicking to better appreciate their mutually defining moment, Jodie tossing in her rings as though leaving her signature for anonymous credit seconds after the aunt disappeared with scarcely a splash.

She glanced at her watch: 2:09. Yes! Setting yet another amateur record she could never boast about.

Scanning the shorelines she felt confident, not the least vulnerable. Although as much as staying a while longer for the heat and the sun was tempting she was on a timeline, putting the boat again in neutral at the ramp, hurling herself into the air and waist-deep water elated and scurrying to the Hummer. So what if anyone saw her? She was young and she was incredibly beautiful. Good for them, good for her; she felt absolutely alive for the first time ever, not simply believing she was—and she had a gun she was very certain she could use.

She manoeuvred the boat onto the trailer like a pro, exiting the water and allowing herself until 3:00 to dry. She felt incredibly light-hearted and free, smirking at the imagery of the aunt and the boyfriend resting peacefully on the bottom before erasing them from her conscious mind forever.

Dressing into her French intimates she arrived at the house at 3:30 sharp with her stop-and-stare white ensemble neatly placed on the passenger seat where it would remain until she was ready.

In the kitchen she opened Hampton's computer with a giggle, pressing *Send* with the tip of a slender finger that she presumed would leave old Fred royally pissed and alone, on the verge of a cerebral haemorrhage somewhere in Nowhere, New York and probably relieved the asshole was gone. Either way, not her concern. Shit happened.

The lid snapped shut, Karen Carter reaching for her phone. She called her service provider cancelling her bundle effective immediately. She didn't want bullshit; she wanted the account closed. Then she went to the rowboat, got herself to the middle of the lake, threw their phones and computers along with hers over the side and sat pondering.

The day was too beautiful to pass up. Yeah, her list wasn't yet complete, but what she had left to accomplish off-site she could put in motion the next day. In fact, she justified, waiting another day would lend credence to her plan.

She concurred with herself. She deserved; she'd done well. Yet by the same token she had not forgotten, nor would she neglect her final and crushing blow to her supercilious aunt's smug face. She would not deprive herself of joyfully adding the worst insult to her aunt's worst injury, spending the next ninety minutes merrily emptying a few hundred of France's and Italy's finest creations into the pool, saving five of the nicest labels for herself before converting the twenty plus cases into a half-dozen boxes of broken glass.

Completely self-satisfied she focused on updating her plan and her tan, absorbing the sun's late-day warmth and twelve percent alcohol from a 1988 Château de Bourdines Côtes du Rhône, once in a while glancing at the pool's glimmering rosé water.

By 7:00 her pale tan lines were perfectly blended. The bottle was floating aimlessly in the pool, Karen Carter was once again dressed to kill in white-on-white and doing a final inspection of her completely vacant house. She locked the front door, loaded her Hummer with three suitcases and drove to the Hilton in time for dinner with Mark Hampton.

At the bottom of the driveway, though, without the slightest interest in seeing her past grow smaller and disappear from the rearview mirror, Jodie touched the brake. She put the vehicle in *Park* and screamed, tousling her hair and stamping her feet. She was eighteen feeling, she didn't know, like thirty, accomplishing the impossible that set her free. They were gone, somewhere, Jodie absolutely certain no one would care. More importantly she was gone, and absolutely no one would care.

*

At the hotel Karen Carter explained that Hampton would arrive later and that her niece, Jodie Carter, would not be joining them. Accepting the no-show penalty with a smile she took the two keys and went to her room where she uncorked a wine and watched a pay-per-view. A couple of hours later she surprised an older couple in the dining room by paying their entire bill, explaining how she had won the lottery and was simply sharing her joy with others. Then she went out for pizza and paid cash.

Tuesday morning Karen Carter went to the dining room for a Danish and coffee, leaving with the same on a tray for

Hampton. She was excited, though not overconfident. She was also inwardly melancholy. She missed Brandon. Strange that she did, because she didn't know him at all. Still, she missed him, fully aware and accepting that she could never return to Tampa or the U of T, and whether he might miss her or not no longer mattered.

The university wasn't a concern, neither was the tuition. Whether she attended or not, they wouldn't care. Higher education was entirely self-motivated, one's own responsibility. Study or not, graduate or not. Whatever. No one cared. Her preoccupation was the man who expected his new tenant that very afternoon. She was not an accomplished liar, hating the thought of cheating the nice couple. But she would with little choice, calling to explain that she was sorry, that she was moving for personal reasons to another state and that she understood losing her deposit. She was absolutely sorry for the inconvenience.

Near ten o'clock, in no particular hurry, she left the trailer in the hotel parking lot and drove to a camping supply store where Karen Carter purchased a tent, three folding chairs, sleeping bags and backpacks, lamps and utensils, a barbecue, a radio and bug spray. All of which she dropped off at yet another charity store before lunch and a pleasant afternoon at the hotel pool. Not that she was finished. She was not; nor did she have any intention of sleeping in a bag on the ground. She was being smart, thinking ahead, planning for a dark day she hoped would never come.

*

Of course she was an immediate hit at the pool with gawky adolescent boys, the envy of their sisters clad in mid-west one-pieces, and a peripheral hit with their paunchy dads dripping in threadbare tee-shirts whose goodness-gracious wives could scarcely believe their puritan eyes.

She didn't care. She loved the attention, ignoring them while discreetly toying with her strings to heighten the male experience, particularly when she shimmied into flimsy harem pants when she stood to leave.

Tuesday's dinner was the reverse of Monday's. Karen Carter ordered two meals and the most expensive wine on the menu to her room. Then on a whim after dinner, most likely brought on by a half-bottle of wine, she sauntered to the pool in heels for an evening dip wearing a high-rise microfibre Rio and triangles under a silk robe that left no doubt in her mind they would all miss her the next day.

Spending what remained of the night in bed flipping channels and sipping wine, she woke very early the next morning. She showered and left for her bank dressed in jeans and a tee, taking a single suitcase with her, first stopping for a much needed breakfast at a 24/7.

She rented a midsize safety deposit box for a ten-year term, paid the current balance on her credit card, asked for a printed statement, and withdrew an even thirteen thousand from her account. She thanked the manager for his concern, asking with her next breath for hundreds. She realized the previous day that travelling with three pieces of luggage was impossible, particularly dragging one containing her condemning evidence against Karen Carter and Mark Hampton that was not only invaluable and potentially lifesaving, but heavy and difficult to manage.

She transferred each item neatly into the box, each one previously numbered, detailed and listed on a spreadsheet safely stored in her purse with a Walther PPK and thirty-six-thousand dollars in crisp hundreds. The additional 800 from her aunt's purse and the paltry one-forty from Hampton's wallet, which spoke volumes, would get her wherever she would feel good about starting over without a paper trail. However, wherever her journey might lead her, that place was not in the direction she was heading. What was certain in her mind was the complete absence of snow and down-homers. She wanted warmth and sunshine and someone like Brandon. Whatever else she might need or want would come eventually. Or not.

Before leaving she dropped the printout into the box, shredded her access card and cancelled her credit card that she also made useless. She went again to the camping supply store, paid cash for another backpack, discarded the suitcase in the parking lot and returned to the hotel where she attached the trailer to the Hummer and gave herself half an hour before checking-out as her aunt.

In her room she organized her clothes into Needs, Wants and Trash, stuffing what she no longer wanted or needed into a suitcase she would leave by the side of a mission box, more carefully folding and placing what she could not live without into the other and the backpack.

Then, with no reason to stay longer, she scanned the room and left.

Minutes later she was trailering the runabout on the southbound I-89, not stopping until five hours later when Karen Carter left the boat and trailer at a campground on the outskirts of Syracuse, New York and paid for a night. Although, being that tents and burgers on a grill, noisy kids and nosey one-night neighbours were not her thing, she finished her day at the Holiday Inn's poolside, sipping her own delicate '89 Chablis before an evening of flipping channels, an all-dressed, Cokes and a map that would guide her farther west the next day.

Thursday she woke and left early. She reclaimed what was left of her cash deposit from the night clerk, was hooking the trailer to the Hummer before most campers were awake and heading west into a thirteen-hour journey that ended in Springfield, Illinois where an exhausted Karen Carter secured another campsite on her credit card before driving to a Super 8 and again paying in cash upfront. She ordered-in pizza and Cokes, falling asleep in her jeans and top, anxious for Friday's short six hours that would put her in Lincoln, Nebraska where on the Saturday Karen Carter and Mark Hampton would disappear and never be seen again.

Presumably, Jodie mused with a smirk, for fear of being caught—in the unlikely event she ever was.

Friday afternoon and night were predictable repeats of the previous two. The aunt stopped at the first campground promising everything she cared nothing about and Jodie checked into the Hampton Inn, paying cash for the relative comfort, the pool, and ordering in passable Chinese. Except that while savouring her second-to-last bottle of exquisite French wine she would not taste again for a very long time she was not flipping channels; Jodie was scribbling a final list of where she should make a new beginning for herself. Pros winning over cons in favour of New Orleans, Louisiana.

Saturday she woke lazily, thinking back over every minute and mile of her life-altering and miraculous seven days while she waited for her breakfast. She had no particular timeframe because she had no particular destination except the mall and the bus station, having decided she would board the first bus to anywhere warm and sunny.

She was gone by 11:00, Karen Carter settling her bill at the campsite and disappearing an hour later with directions to the city's busiest shopping plaza where she left the trailer and boat in the parking lot without its papers but with a note reading: Deevorced. Dont need this thing no mor.

Minutes later, not at all surprised the bus station was in a slummier part of town, she took the Hummer's insurance and registration, left the keys in the ignition with the engine running and the windows down and strode away under her Panama and mirrored glasses without a second thought.

At the station Jodie destroyed and discarded Karen Carter's final proof of existence in the ladies' room trash can, declaring herself liberated and alone. However as much as distance between her past and her present was a good thing, a requisite thing, as certain as she could be that no one was forming a Jodie Carter task force, she believed that something she possessed in abundance was equally crucial: Time.

Chapter Thirty

She was certain New Orleans might be the right place, her genesis, the best place for starting over. Certainty tinged with doubt because she knew of Tulane and Mardi Gras, the French Quarter and the peculiar obsession of female tourists to bare their breasts in public any night of the year because they could. And not much else.

Or Miami. Absolutely everyone loved Miami, the sandy and sexy beaches, the sexy in-people and the Latin gaiety of Little Havana. No matter which, boarding a Denver-bound Greyhound bus that first night was a good first step toward somewhere better than Hayseed, Nebraska and Hillbilly, Vermont.

Sunday she was headed to Phoenix, on Monday choosing San Diego's sandy beaches over Tucson's dry desert heat, waking Tuesday in a DoubleTree because she deserved a night of luxury after three days of arduous travel and, discounting a mild headache brought on by what was the night before an '83 Saint-Émilion Grand Cru, she was pleased with herself. She didn't care that she was 925 dollars poorer. She had a solution to her destination dilemma. She would take a month before deciding whether she liked the place. If not she would move on, west to east, never staying longer than a month on a strict budget and being smart until finding somewhere she would fit in. Being smart meaning no more wine and no more fancy hotels, particularly since living without her credit card was fast becoming a major annoyance.

She rented a one-room flat for the month, one mile from the beach. She put her cash and the gun in a safety deposit box, bought a prepaid phone without a whole lot of fuss she didn't need or want and went shopping for groceries, shocked by that reality. Though by the end of the month she struck California from her list. The city was all she could ask for, but she couldn't deal with the asshole surfer mentality, the fake smiles and the hundred guys who wanted a free pass into her panties because they were boxed-blonds, tanned and chiselled.

She didn't think so. Not to mention that no one would give her a job.

August 01st she flew into Corpus Christi, Texas, justifying the 600 dollars and the risk because she could not spend another night in a cheap hotel or another day on a bus with strangers who would either hit on her, gawk at her, or invade her space with their grotesquely obese bodies, their man-spread or both. Money that she discovered was not well-spent. The city was by the Gulf and beautiful beaches, which was a good thing. The downside was Texan paranoia and the guns. Everyone had a gun and the more she learned about the state, the crime and her chances of survival being a woman, the more she wanted out. Worse yet, which was becoming an issue, no one was returning her calls.

She left the Lone Star State on the first of September boarding an eight-hour excursion that would put her in New Orleans, admitting that, yeah, she was a little worried that nobody wanted her. She was from up north, okay, she got that. She also got that they were smug Californian assholes and big Texan dickheads. She hadn't earned a dime on her own in her life; she had no work experience and her fancy schooling was very nice, little lady, however they wanted college students or graduates with proven initiative. Even coffee shops wanted college students. Really?

Their loss. All of them assholes. One day she would attend college and graduate with honours. She absolutely would. Just not by serving expensive coffee to millennial assholes and cleaning their shit for seven dollars an hour and sharing pennies from a tip jar. No way would she do that. She would get there by being Jodie Carter.

They no longer mattered. Those wasted days were behind her, forgotten. Her life would get better because no way could her life be any worse. When she should have been at the U of T forging a career in graphic design, making friends and dating Brandon, she was stepping from a bus in a crappy corner of the Big Easy shocked by the suffocating blast of humid heat that right away stole her breath, dampened her clothes and fogged her glasses.

Hailing a cab she told the driver she wanted a nice hotel and that something under a hundred would be even nicer. The man chuckled with real Louisiana charm and warmth, suggesting the Maison Dupuy for under one-fifty because she could do a whole lot worse, but never and nowhere any better. And the doorman was a good friend who could help a young lady find her way. Which he did soon after with a litany of fatherly dos and don'ts.

She moved into her cramped eight-hundred-a-month apartment the next day after securing thirty K and change with the gun at a nearby bank. On day two she went shopping at an art store on Royal Street.

She was two months into her plan, giving herself and the city a real chance starting with Bourbon Street that second evening with two stools, an art pad and an array of coloured pencils.

All she ever wanted was to become the best graphic designer, once spending hours alone each evening in her room creating amazing affects on her computer, though somehow never placing the slightest worth on her genius for creating remarkable lifelike caricatures, turning sadness into brightness, ordinary faces into spectacular portraits. A rare gift metamorphosing into a timely survival technique despite not earning a dime that night. Nor did she on her third night, returning to a colourless bachelor dejected and pensive. All she had accomplished was sitting and watching the indifferent world pass her by.

She had to get real, be smart and do things right. She might not have that darling Louisiana accent, but what she did have was a 5'11" and absolutely to-die-for body that she would make work for her the following evening as much as she would her talent.

*

The next morning she bought white ballerina slippers jewelled with sequins, a bright white denim skirt barely long enough to cover her bum that perfectly complemented a backless and décolleté white tank top that screamed "Stop!"

She spent the afternoon drawing herself so precisely that the finished product might have been a photograph, creating a sign promoting *J. C.'s Unique PencilArt for 25$. Capture the Moment.*

That evening she captured two moments which fostered another idea, albeit a costly one. For three nights she had seen the same faces, that night many of them slowing to study her works in progress. So what if they saw their own faces? And why was she wasting her afternoons in a dark room waiting for nighttime failure?

The next morning she bought a Nikon that the guy promised was ideal for her. She believed him because the SLR was the least expensive in the store and he gave her a free memory card.

She spent her afternoon practicing on *Auto,* that evening capturing three special moments on paper and several dozen through a 50mm lens, realizing that three caricatures was the most she could manage in an evening, though what came as a delightful and unexpected bonus on her fifth night was that she sold several of her afternoon miniatures. A success she repeated through to the end of September with an extra three grand in the bank, giving herself Sundays to explore the city and The Quarter where she believed she had found her niche in life. She felt at home. Or she believed she did, despite not signing for another month.

She would continue her eastward journey, making Miami her final destination. Otherwise, how could she be certain? She had time. At worst she would return tanned and certain in January, first arriving in Biloxi, Mississippi at noon on October 01st, realizing within days that she'd be moving on.

Her first day and night drained a whopping 500 dollars from her resources, her one-room furnished flat the next day consuming another twelve-fifty. She could barely afford food throughout the month and the casino hotels were not interested in her taking up space in their lobbies. Worse, in a casino town, she wasn't given a single interview. The entire month was a dismal write-off, putting an X on the state the first of November as she boarded another bus for Mobile, Alabama because she wasn't interested in the hillbillies and rednecks further north.

Another huge mistake. No one wanted a wandering gypsy in search of herself. She'd been out of school four months with nothing to her credit except a few sketches, one gentlemen suggesting she get herself back to New Orleans PDQ. An even more candid lady interviewer recommending that she might consider presenting herself in a way that focused on her intelligence and potential, not her more disarming attributes. Neither individual seeing much of anything she could accomplish in Mobile given her current fanciful state.

She told the man he should pull the stick out of his ass PDQ and get real, informing the woman in a scathing snarl that perhaps if she weren't such a Southern Baptist puritan bitch and maybe dressed more like a female and bought some drugstore makeup she wouldn't still have a Miss stuck on her name at fifty.

Worse, she went through another two grand without a penny of income because people weren't interested. They had no time, too busy being assholes, rushing in and out of buildings attached to phones and tablets, scarcely noticing her when in New Orleans even women would stop her and comment on how lovely she was. Despite which she persevered, staying with her plan.

Or she did until believing she would lose her mind if she didn't do something positive, taking a cab to the bus station frustrated and weary and wisely getting out of Dodge three days early.

She was Jodie Carter and she would become someone, convinced that Miami would either be the best decision of her life—or her second best. Either way, she would make her last month a win-win.

Changing buses in Tallahassee she did the 700 miles in twelve hours and an even 350 dollars. Although arriving in the dark she began seriously doubting herself, believing she might be more stubborn than smart, that maybe she needed a reality check and that she should have stayed in New Orleans and been several thousand dollars richer.

The hotel the first night brought the day's tally to six hundred, her first-floor furnished flat equipped with a stunning view of the building's parking lot the next day adding another nine and she hadn't yet bought food for the week.

The 16th Street apartment was an easy walk to the beach, Jodie having decided on the last day of November that she would set up on the Lincoln Road Mall during the afternoons, protected from the harsh sun, and by the most expensive restaurants dotting the South Beach boardwalk at night where she would be protected by the police and private security.

The plan was a good one. Over her first six nights she did eight special moments and sold a couple of dozen miniatures at half the price, spending her Sunday laying back on a rented beach bed on South Beach in a thong and triangles, until flipping over and sunning her buns when she couldn't take another oiled asshole in boardshorts squatting beside her.

More importantly, she was calculating, doing survival math. Things were not adding up the way she had anticipated.

What she was earning would total a grand less than New Orleans by month's end, or worse, barely covering her expenses and working too hard for too little gain. So much for a very merry Christmas. Her rent was higher, food was crazy expensive, she hadn't bought clothes or had fun in months and by year's end she would be down by a full third of her meagre wealth in a little over six months with just an expensive tan to show for her hard work.

So she would cut her losses. Miami was not working out because she was not standing out. She wasn't exceptional enough or unique. There were too many other girls with long legs in short skirts in a town where bikini triangles were more common than blouses. The only way she would have the happier and more lucrative New Year she deserved was by greeting the first of January in a town where she could thrive once again.

Part Two
Chapter Thirty-One

Jodie Carter spent the rest of December getting a burn on, deepening her tan and letting herself be happy. She bought several daring thongs and triangles and scarcely moved from her beach bed each day except for lunches of hamburgers and hot dogs, fries and Cokes, splashing and peeing in the ocean when the midday sun became atrociously hot. And she would often dine out, spending as much time away from her dismal four-walled flat as possible, those special evenings shopping for her winter, spring and summer ensembles with a Miami flair that would make her exceptional, make her unique in New Orleans.

She wasn't vacationing. She was being positive. She was regrouping, focusing on what she had done right and, more importantly, on the many things she had done wrong. She was ready for better times, for getting serious and for university in the fall toward a Fine Arts degree.

She loved what she was doing, the drawing and the candid photos, just not the subsistence she was enduring. She needed a name; she needed to be different and be noticed, understanding that following what she had previously believed was her dream into a graphic design would simply transmute her into an internet clone.

Christmas came and went along with Jodie who finally left behind everything negative in her life along with the 3500 dollars she tried to ignore, departing Miami on the festive day for a week in a Panama City Beach spa resort because she would not be sunning on white sands or dipping her feet into a blue ocean again anytime soon. Better yet, the bellhop was twenty-one, a sucker for either an over-the-top gorgeous girl in strings or his fifty-dollar tip-cum-bribe. Whatever. She didn't care about him or the fifty. If she was old enough to murder a couple of social misfits, run from the law and survive on her own, what was the big deal about having wine with her in-room dinners and falling asleep each night in her deluxe suite feeling good about herself?

*

Rejuvenated and ready she departed on the thirty-first, arriving at Maison Dupuy late in the day, greeted by an amiable doorman who remembered her, who promised he would most definitely sit for her in his uniform that coming Saturday on the corner of Canal and Royal, keeping his word to an excited girl three years and three months ago.

March 31st was an unusually warm spring day, the premature and heavy humidity imitating any of a hundred miserable and oppressive summer days in a town the locals called The Swamp.

She was twenty-two, a year older than when she fell asleep in her bed wondering when the night would come that she would sleep forever, and she didn't care. She didn't care about much anymore. The day would be a monotonous repeat of countless others with no one in her life to make her birthday meaningful or make her feel special.

In fact she had no life at all, often regretting she hadn't called the police that fateful day instead of making things worse. She was innocent; the aunt was a deserved accident, an accident nonetheless, and Hampton was justifiably put down. She could have been wealthy and educated, taking what was rightfully hers. Not living in one room, working six-day weeks and barely getting by.

Day after day nothing changed except the weather, feeling cramped between her four walls on the worst of the rainy days when she would work from her photographs turning faces frozen in time into elaborate pencil art, throwing out more each week than she sold.

She did make an effort soon after arriving, doubling her prices with a more appealing poster suggesting that they *Do Something Special for Someone Special,* which failed miserably, resulting in a wasted week without a single sitting, discovering the hard way that the harried masses don't stop to read or take notice. And that despite changing her looks from sexy to sultry, to demure and sophisticated, from very short shorts and flimsy tops to flighty décolleté dresses to sequinned maxi gowns and shawls she would wear on cooler winter days, she was not being seen.

Mondays were too terrible to think about, which she understood. Most private worlds behind sombre faces were dark and dismal places and, like her, the most desperate of them yearned for somewhere else or someone else. Something better than what they had, like her dream of a Fine Arts degree that hadn't happened because the financial and physical toll of her freshman year had drained her resources and her energy.

For as long as she could remember she had clung to the hope that with university her life would be wonderful, angry with herself for being so wrong. The year was a chaotic and punishing hell. Attending classes, studying and working became impossible. The more she studied the less she earned, eating each month into her dwindling resources until facing a harsh and simple reality.

Without an income she would never afford three more years so she left in favour of surviving, taking with her an enviable GPA and her professors sincere laments, no longer bothering with fanciful dreams or empty promises of the future.

That was two years earlier and nothing had changed. Her spring and summer weekends were relatively her best when the more reserved locals melded with revelling tourists, doing the same or less over the weekdays on her corner between 4:00 and seven.

She hadn't worn a bikini since leaving Florida, hadn't taken a vacation, spending the week between Christmas and New Year's each year in her apartment watching videos borrowed from the library and blocking out the muffled sounds of everyone else's merriment filtering through her walls. She didn't have a boyfriend or girlfriend because she wanted a Brandon and everyone around her was either deficient or excessive in some way or already with an unsuitable someone else. The same way no one worthwhile, the lawyers and doctors, the businessmen and women she saw each day wanted nothing to do with a wretched girl sitting on a stool wasting her life.

She spent her day in her panties, glowing, drawing faces and showering several times under cool water, in no big hurry to drag her portable studio halfway across town, setting up to sit watching the human flood pass her by. The month ending on a Friday, payday, wasn't particularly meaningful since people would more likely go in search of an air-conditioned bar than sit on her stool damp with sweat.

In the mirror she didn't look any different than when she was twenty-one, conceding as she dressed that, yeah, she was still very beautiful. In fact she was more than beautiful; she was undeniably drop-dead gorgeous. She was stunning, she would tell herself because no one else ever would. Everything was in the right place, in the right proportions, perky, smooth and tight. So what wasn't to love and adore?

"Apparently everything," she sighed, commiserating with her despondent reflection.

She shrugged, blowing a long stream of warm air from between her lips. Her life was shit. Her life would always be shit and she was not glowing, she was sweating because her shithole apartment didn't have air-conditioning.

She left at 3:30 wearing fresh panties, sandals and a

strapless wrap dress with her hair tied into a tail. She was set up by 4:00, shaded by the awning of Earnie Lebeau's lounge feeling trapped in a continuum of the present day she would never escape, envisioning a pathetic old woman one of those days tumbling from her stool and laying dead on the sidewalk without anyone caring.

She didn't see the man coming toward her, nor the one studying her closely from his sixteenth-floor executive office a block away; nor did she suspect how very soon the two men would break the continuum, drawing her into a world that Jodie Carter would never have dared to imagine.

Chapter Thirty-Two

His even voice jolted Jodie from her melancholy mood. "I apologize for startling you, J.C. I am truly sorry."

"No. I'm sorry. I let myself go somewhere else for a moment."

"Aren't we all at times, somewhere else? Isn't that a good thing, letting our minds wander where we cannot?"

She put him at early forties, a smartly attired professional at something. He was handsome and fit and, she thought, familiar with the good life without a care in the world. That's what she saw, yet his eyes told a very different story.

"I asked if I might sit with you, for a portrait."

"You want me to draw you?"

"Yes I do, very much. I would also like to sit here a while and look at a very lovely girl."

Wow! "Thank you. I would love to draw you." She swept the air between them, inviting him to sit. "As an office portrait? Something official and proper?"

"No." He nodded toward her placard. "Nothing so self-important. What I would like is a very special memory for someone very special to me. What I need is a statement that will never fade with time. Can you do that for me, J.C.?"

"Please call me Jodie, and yes I can. Just maybe not in a fancy suit and tie when it's a hundred degrees. I mean, how can you even look that cool? Anyway, we can do better. Maybe dress things down a little? You know, lose the tie, open the collar? Maybe lose the jacket and ruffle the hair a bit? You know, thinking out loud."

He did, with a chuckle, dropping his jacket to the sidewalk as though it wasn't tailored-made, adding his hundred-dollar tie to the heap and tousling his fifty-dollar hairstyle. The transformation was instant from strait-laced businessman to dashing and cavalier. A definite ten on the dating scale. Yeah, dream on.

"Better?"

"Yeah, much." She began drawing. "I need an hour though."

He glanced at his watch with a simple, "I'm good."

"I suppose this is for your wife, your girlfriend?"

"Yes, in shades of grey and black. And please add 'Five PM Friday For Sammy' in script at the bottom. That's short for Samatha, in case you're wondering."

"Lucky lady, your Sammy. Some special occasion happening tonight?"

"I suppose you could say that. As I must say that you are very lovely, Jodie. And your outfit is enchanting. I'm Parker, by the way."

Shit! The guy was a Brandon. "Thank you, Parker."

They sat talking a few minutes shy of an hour as Jodie worked her magic, all the while quietly envying the Sammy in Parker's life. He was interesting, interested in her, her life and her work. The guy was absolutely a gentleman. Then she was done, somehow sad that she was.

"And we are done." She signed her J.C. at the bottom edge, peeling her work from the pad. "I hope your special Sammy approves, Parker. I believe she is one very lucky lady."

"Jodie, this is amazing, you are amazing." He reached for his jacket and wallet. "And definitely undervalued. You should do something about that. You should put a much higher value on your incredible work and on yourself." He put 300 dollars in fifties into her hand. "No arguments. I insist. In fact, Jodie, in another time and place I believe I would be asking you to dinner this evening. You are completely captivating and I truly wish I had time left to learn more about you. Sadly, however, I do not." He passed her a folded piece of paper. "This is my wife's address. Please see that she gets this." He stood, glancing at his watch. "And Jodie, I am truly sorry. Please forgive me."

She had no time to answer or react, watching in horror as he leaped from the curb into the path of an oncoming transit bus, killed precisely at 5:00 PM Friday, laying sprawled and unabashedly snarling traffic amidst a cacophony of blaring horns, frantic shrieks and screams.

Jodie sprang from her stool, clamping a hand hard against her mouth, pressing the crumpled drawing to her chest.

The body lay twisted and bleeding, the terror of his final moment etched onto a distorted mouth, his eyes wide-open with fright. Alive one moment with her, then dead. No! She studied the drawing, staring at the eyes she made less sad, at the smile she had drawn more disarming and real. He was not doing something special for whomever the Sammy was, he was blaming her, he was giving her guilt that would endure a lifetime.

Minutes later she was giving a statement, giving the cops his wallet and the six fifties, his tie and his jacket. Then she sat on her stool in shock, depleted, watching them take Parker away, sickened by the mindless rush-hour throng lining the opposite sidewalk and shamelessly capturing a man's worst hour and hers for their few minutes of morbid glory on social media.

*

Most weekdays James Castle stood pensively at a wall of windows atop his billion dollar empire gazing out over the bustling Quarter, the rippling air and meandering Mississippi, making decisions. He would often peer through his sixty-power Bausch & Lomb wondering about the young woman sitting on a stool at the corner sixteen stories below. She had become his delightful diversion, his primary focus, forever curious about her though never acting on his curiosity.

He wondered where and how she lived, rightfully assuming not very well from the small number of sketches she drew each week. Yet she would always come well-dressed and groomed in fashions appropriate to her youth, his particular favourite were the boots and tights she completed on cooler days with a belted sweater and beret. He wondered whether she was any good, not once thinking he should stroll by her easel or sit with her for an hour and discover her talent for himself. She did seem pleasant enough, though he never once saw her lips curve into a smile or her eyes come alive with joy. Which he understood, still wondering why.

He hadn't smiled since discovering his wife's life-long love affair with Cedric Deacon, keeping the shrew's portrait on his desk because he hadn't yet decided what he should do with her, what her deserved punishment should be for routinely fucking his partner of eighteen years and once upon a time best friend since high school.

He believed he could actually enjoy killing them. Not for what they did and were doing behind his back, rather for their deceit and duplicity, for making him the village idiot in his own eyes and mind. Except that he was a self-confessed coward who preferred thousand-dollar suits and exotic vacations to grey denim and steel bars. In truth, had they been honest with him, he wouldn't have given a shit. He would have divorced her and survived, then, a time that was very long ago and long gone.

He remembered the day, the hour, the portrait was taken years earlier, now his constant and haunting reminder of a sham marriage with no need to wonder at the then sparkle in her eyes or which man was the source of those happy eyes. He wasn't certain who he should despise most, the conniving harlot sleeping with two men, or the bastard who stole her. Both being the frequent and obvious answer, often envisioning them plaintively together before him on their knees, if Deacon would ever have the courage. In the meantime content with fucking his dearest Louise without the slightest passion, simply as a matter of perfunctory relief and the single reprisal available to him until he could figure things out.

Which he believed was the basis for his growing compulsion with the unsmiling girl. Why did she not smile? What was wrong with her life? She was exceptionally attractive and too young to worry or care about cheating boyfriends and, he supposed, she must be a passable artist. Each one of the few he witnessed leaving her were beaming with pride. Even the guy lying dead in the street left her with a broad smile before rushing to end his life.

What kind of guts did that take, being slammed so violently into Heaven or Hell? And why? Yet what most drew him to the girl after countless months of spying on her, of actually missing her on Mondays and weekends, was the fright in her eyes and the deep sorrow that visibly gripped her.

He stood for a moment checking himself, his thought process, judging what he was about to do, what he felt he should need to do for some reason not entirely clear in his mind: The need to help someone vulnerable and alone, he supposed, his own hurt feelings aside, possibly making himself a better man than Deacon. He didn't know, concluding that satiating his longstanding curiosity was sufficient enough reason.

The office was closed, Deacon was gone, and soon the girl would be gone as well. He had to shit or get off the proverbial pot, man-up. She never stayed past seven, always pushing herself from her stool as though thoroughly disillusioned with her day, as though nothing in her young life mattered. Like the guy facing-off with the city bus, whose eyes opened wide with horror and dread an inescapable instant before the bus slammed into him, in that same instant realizing that, whatever his reasons, remorse and self-pity, he died a violent death for no good reason at all.

What mattered was that he was dead and by morning

would be yesterday's news and forgotten.

Castle peered once more through the lens, certain the girl would be gone well before seven. He stood straight, reached for his jacket and strode from his office telling his secretary with unusual firmness in his voice that she should go home and enjoy her weekend, instructing her to take her husband out for dinner on her expense account and not be cheap about it. Do the man right. He deserved at least that much for tolerating her outrageous hours all these many years.

Then he hurried out, walking into a cityscape he saw every day but that was very foreign to him nonetheless at ground level. His timing was alarmingly perfect; she was folding her easel.

"One moment, miss. Please." Was all he managed.

"I'm sorry, sir. I'm not drawing anymore today. There was a really bad accident a few minutes ago. I can't."

"I am well aware of the suicide, miss. I viewed the entire tragic scene from there," he pointed to the steel and glass high-rise glistening under a brilliant sun, "as I was watching you, wondering about you, about your state of mind. What the gentleman did to you was much worse than what he did to himself. I saw your face, your shock and distress. I was worried that you might need a metaphorical shoulder to cry on, a friendly ear as it were."

"Do I look like I need a shoulder to cry on, mister?"

He didn't hesitate. "That would be a very definite yes. Indeed. You are clearly devastated and disconsolate. And understandably so. I must also assume you've lost a day's earnings." Castle sat on the stool facing her. "Tell me, how much did the unfortunate gentleman pay you, that in turn the police for some reason saw the need to confiscate?"

Her brow furrowed. She absolutely did not like the man. "Three-hundred, if that's somehow your business. I'm guessing he didn't need it. Is that okay with you?"

"Yes, indeed." Castle reached inside his jacket for his

pocketbook, handing her three crisp bills. "My name is James Castle. I am a reputable businessman, a member of the local board and many others throughout the South, as well as a close friend of the mayor and at the moment neither do I need what will better serve you."

"I told you, I can't draw you."

"Understandable, of course, in view of your trauma. Nor can I see any real value in possessing a portrait of myself sitting on a sidewalk when any number of mirrors and doors in my home and place of business provide the same imagery, albeit three dimensional and regrettably much more critical."

"Good for you. You don't like looking at yourself. Most people do. And what I do makes them feel happy. So if you don't mind, I'm leaving." She dropped the bills into his lap. "Thanks, but I don't need your charity."

"Not charity, a gift. And I beg to differ. I have studied you over the past many months." He glanced at her self-portrait. "Suffice it to say, I would pay you four times what you ask were I that self-indulgent. Your work is excellent. So allow me to fulfill what the other gentleman intended. Otherwise what value is there in the work he commissioned? He must have had a single purpose in mind."

"He did. His wife was the purpose."

"And he thought that you might locate her on his behalf?"

Jodie shook her head. "I will locate her. I promised."

"What's your name?"

"Why?"

He didn't miss a beat. "Well, Miss Why, what I propose, if you can for a single moment be civil, is dinner. I have something to suggest that you will either find completely intriguing or simply decline. Either way, I believe we can each benefit from the other's company and a good meal after what we witnessed." He held out the bills. "Providing you accept my gift and agree that later I will escort you safely home."

"Yeah, right. Dinner and my home, then what?"

"Then I leave you to your evening, either to meet with you occasionally in the coming days or never see you again. A decision I will leave entirely up to you." He grinned. "Scout's honour. First, however, here is the truth, Miss Why. I saw his eyes as he stepped from this life. They were eyes without hope, yet a second later I cringed at the terror in those very eyes when he too late saw death. He did not want to die. In that very instant he saw hope. More to the point, the hopelessness I first saw in his, I also perceived in yours."

"I'm not killing myself."

"No, you won't, because I won't let you. Now take the money you earned. Please tell me your name and can we please attend to a less combative and more beneficial evening?"

"Why were you spying on me all this time? That is absolutely weird."

"Spying, no; intrigued, yes. Because despite your continued sadness, you never surrendered to weakness or defeat. You were never ready to give up. Until, I fear, this very afternoon when your despair was significantly compounded by a recent and unexpected event." He stood. "If you wish, I will call the mayor and ask that he and his wife join us. They would be entirely delighted with your company."

Hesitation vs. Desire. Mistrust vs. Need. She scrunched her face. "Yeah, right. You know the mayor. Good one."

He nodded. "I do. However anything else about me must wait for dinner."

Shit! She hadn't once in her life had a friend; she couldn't remember ever being hugged by someone who loved her, or could have loved her, Brandon long ago fading into an uncertain memory. Now this guy was inviting her for dinner with something very good or very bad on his mind. She didn't know.

Everything about him screamed money and success. He was tall, six-one, six-two, whatever, lean with a chiselled face, a tanned complexion and dark brown hair that was cut short. He was good-looking, but not full of himself. He was confident and definitely accustomed to being in control. Yeah, but he wore a wedding ring that he hadn't thought to mention.

"My name is Jodie…and you're married."

"Indeed I am. Her name is Louise. We've been married seventeen years. I loved her, once upon a time, though she never actually loved me. She's been cheating on me for as many years and more and she has nothing whatsoever to do with what I am about to propose, if in fact we ever make our way to the restaurant."

Shit! She hesitated, staring past the yellow tape at Parker's blood on the street, staring at her feet, feeling absolutely alone.

Then she looked at Castle. "Okay, mister. You can carry my stools. And let's get something straight, I'm going home alone."

Chapter Thirty-Three

Castle & Deacon Enterprises took up the entire sixteenth floor of the Royal Street Tower. He and Jodie were there ostensibly to call for reservations because James Castle never waited in line and he refused to burden himself with a cellphone. The things were invasive and disruptive, that's what he told Jodie. More importantly he wanted to lend credibility to their evening, to what he would propose. His company's revenues each year exceeded 100 million with one billion in assets and 300 employees in fifty locations across the South.

He needed her making that connection and she did. She was as duly impressed by what she was seeing as by his reserved nonchalance. She viewed her corner and Earnie Lebeau's lounge through his scope, quietly shocked, masking her unease with a smirk, asking if he ever spied into bedrooms. He did not, thanking her for the suggestion. Then she saw a photograph of Castle and the mayor shaking hands and when she asked who the other guy was, he replied "The governor."

When the tour was over he placed her stools and supplies into his Infiniti because Fridays through Mondays was his chauffeur's private time. Everyone deserved a private life, he told her. And what she told him was that she was going home on the bus. He didn't respond, opening her door.

The reservation was at Antoine's for 7:30, the luxury ride to the restaurant's valet parking quiet and pensive, separate minds questioning what might be right and what might be wrong. James pondering what he was doing and why, Jodie pondering what he was doing and why.

The ambiance was subdued, the dining room dimly lit, widely spaced tables were draped in white linen, flickering with candlelight, conversations spoken in murmurs between elegantly dressed couples holding hands.

No one had pulled out her seat since Brandon, or placed a linen serviette across her lap. She thanked the waiter for his attention, though she was staring all the while at Castle with a telling expression he could not ignore. For which reason he asked the waiter for a moment.

"Indeed, Jodie. I agree. The setting is somewhat intimate, which I assure you is not my objective. We are here for the quiet and what I hope is a meaningful conversation. Nothing more."

"All of a sudden I'm not sure about this, or about you. This place is really fancy."

"And considerably more appropriate to the matter at hand than a burger place or clamorous jazz bar. So please allay your suspicions."

"Okay, I'm allayed. Happy? Now what is this matter at hand?"

"First, if I may for a moment be indelicate. How old are you, Jodie? In order that I might assure our waiter he won't put himself in contravention of a strict house rule."

"I'm twenty-two and I would like a vodka and soda, Ultimat if possible. I also prefer medium reds from the Bordeaux region. And no, I will not embarrass you, dad."

He let that one go with a grin, signalling the waiter. He was adept at hiding his surprise, discreetly assuring the waiter that his companion was legal. A moment later the tuxedoed server returned with the lady's preferred taste and a double Johnnie Walker Blue with a splash for the gentleman.

"I believe we owe this evening to the stranger who brought us together, Jodie."

"His name was Parker."

Castle raised his old-fashioned in a polite gesture, touching the rim to Jodie's. "To whatever peace Parker may have discovered. A cruel ending indeed." He sipped his scotch. "Now to you, Miss Why. In the first place, I find the notion that I might be anyone's dad exceedingly disturbing, never viewing the idea of becoming one as particularly inviting or rewarding."

"You don't like kids?"

He smiled. "Not unless they're attractive beyond the norm and twenty-two. By which I mean to say, I like you."

She didn't smile. "And I'm lovely. So what is this all about, Mr. Castle? You know, if we're not sitting here holding hands."

"This is about you, all about you. Despite your very rare talent, Jodie, you are clearly not succeeding in life."

"I'm doing fine."

"No, you are not doing fine. What I saw in your eyes through that scope, Jodie, wasn't merely disbelief and horror. I perceived unmistakable envy. Albeit for the briefest instant, a flash in time, you envied Parker laying dead in the street."

Jodie sipped her cocktail. "Gee, thanks. Most guys picture me naked. I know that, girls know that. Except you see me dead in the street."

"On the contrary, I see you as young, particularly attractive, and exceptionally talented. Unfortunately you are not succeeding because you are dealing with the mindless masses who increasingly do not hear, see or care. They simply amble along in a dismal fog ignoring the best life has to offer, faithfully opting to pay less and get less. A peculiar quantity versus quality mentality that has made me very wealthy. They come into my stores and buy whatever for under five dollars in order that I might buy whatever for many thousands. Which makes you very much an anomaly. You and your exquisite work are incredibly undervalued at your current fee structure, for which reason they, the masses, see you seated on your stool looking forlorn and discouraged, if not entirely dejected, and equate your low price with equally poor quality. I mean, how can anyone be certain your self-portrait was actually created by you? Do you see my point?"

She wanted to reach across and smack his smug face. "Yeah, I do. You're saying I'm pathetic, that I should smile when no one notices me, that I look ridiculous sitting on my stool. Well for your information, Mr. Castle, sir, I did hike my fees, once, and that week I wasn't just sitting there unnoticed, I was absolutely invisible."

Time out. He signalled the waiter, ignoring the menus. "Jodie, may I suggest the extraordinary crawfish bisque as the appetizer? The peppercorn swordfish is melt-in-your-mouth delicious and for desert their blueberry bread pudding is the most heavenly delight."

She shrugged. "Yeah, sure."

The waiter recommended baked potatoes and broccoli with a cheese dip to complement the fish and a drizzle of lemon sauce to complete the desert. Jodie nodded, Castle ordered a twelve-year Bordeaux, an exclusive Paulliac Grand Cru Classé, and waited until he was gone.

"Where were we?"

"You know where, I'm pathetic."

"If you were you wouldn't be here. I see no merit whatsoever in self-pity, as opposed to requisite self-praise when possessed of an uncommon talent such as yours. If you do not recognize yourself as the finest, why should anyone else? That is my point and please stop calling me Mr. Castle."

"Where is this going…James?"

"People, strangers, are constantly asking me for donations to their various causes. Some I support, others I do not. Yet you, a virtual street urchin in dire need, tell me you're doing fine when you are not doing fine at all." He paused for the waiter, approving the wine, waiting for the man to fill their crystal stemware. "I want you to succeed. I want to do that for you. Not as charity, but to give each of us a purpose. Because

I'm wealthy and successful doesn't mean I have any real purpose. Now I believe I do, in you. I want to subsidize you. What I don't want is to see you under a bus, metaphorically or otherwise."

"I'm not getting this. You're giving me what, money, supplies, space in your lobby? What?"

"What I've noticed over our very one-sided time together is how nicely you dress each day. I particularly like the French look with the tights and the beret. Very classic indeed. Personally I would happily pay for the pleasure of sitting with you and looking at you, which in your case is oddly problematic. I presume your living space is somewhat modest, that most of your meagre income is directed toward maintaining your public appearance and therein lies your dilemma. You are exquisite, Jodie. A truism which I suspect you are entirely in agreement with. But to successfully exude true beauty you must also feel truly beautiful, which you do not because everything you ever dreamed about is failing."

"Meagre, modest, dilemma and failing." She sipped her wine. "Very nice. You're telling me I'm a loser."

"I'm saying you deserve better, that you cannot feel good about yourself when there is no bright light in your life. I assume you live alone since you called no one to explain this evening, because you have no family or boyfriend who would rightfully be upset by your being here with me."

"You assume right. And, yeah, I live in a shithole."

"Indeed, and not a pleasant image, though I daresay not much longer. Let me get to the crux of all this. I will subsidize you for the next two years. I will put you in a home of your choosing, I'm thinking the Garden District, and give you the funds to tastefully furnish the place. I will lease you a vehicle for that time and give you a twelve-month allowance upfront in keeping with your taste for exclusive vodka and apparent knowledge of fine wine. Then together we will find you a suitable studio with a display window where you can explore beyond your current theme, where anyone strolling by can peer in and see your work hung in proper fashion. And, most importantly, walk through your doors."

She gulped her wine, on the verge hysterical laughter. "Oh, this is absolutely too good. You'll do all that…for me, so that I can feel, yeah, that's right, truly beautiful. Right? And exactly how wide do I spread my legs for all this, Jimmy?"

"I suppose wide enough to slip into your shiny BMW or whatever suits you. And Jimmy definitely does not work for me." He reached into the space between them, refilling her wine. "That is the half of my proposal. The other half developed as we drove here in silence, which has no bearing on what I have just put forth. No bearing whatsoever."

Shit! He was serious. "I'm not getting this, James. Why, because Parker scared the shit out of me?"

"As I told you. We each deserve purpose in our life. Furthermore, as an interface between the two halves, I suggest that you stay this evening at the Sheraton where you can decide in comfort and with another Ultimat and soda what vehicle you would look best in and either yea or nay on the second proposal. You, Jodie. Not me."

She was losing her mind, going absolutely insane. "So this second part, I'm guessing it's what you want out of this instead of getting laid by a virgin. That's right, I'm a virgin with no friends and my parents are dead. So what is it you want, exactly?"

James Castle filled his lungs with air, pausing, letting the pressure build before expelling a warm breath, seemingly defeated. He leaned forward planting his elbows on the tabletop. She was right, he did have an ulterior motive.

"Yes, Jodie you are quite correct. I do want something from you."

No shit. She studied her wine, then him, creating an image of his smug face and thousand-dollar suit dripping with the rich colour. He was full of shit, and what was with the meek and mild act? Asshole.

"This is where I thank you for a nice evening and," she leaned forward, lowering her voice, "tell you to go fuck yourself. I am not interested being some desperate guy's love toy. Goodbye, mister."

His hand shot out like an arrow. "No, please. Clearly I am a miserable thespian displaying inexcusably bad timing. And for that I most sincerely apologize. But please hear me out. Believe me, this is a good thing and I am not interested in sleeping with you." He paused. "Not that you are not completely desirable or that the experience wouldn't be entirely pleasurable. However I have never once in my life mixed business with pleasure. Nor will I now."

She relaxed, still leaning forward, his hand over hers. "Then stop fucking with my brain and tell me what you want."

"I want to discover more about you, your past, your present and future. I want to understand how a struggling street urchin is familiar with fine wines and top-shelf spirits. To that end, Jodie, I'm leaving on a much needed ten-day vacation this time next week and would be delighted if you would accompany me."

Stunned silence. "Excuse me?"

"Separate suites, of course. On the Maya Riviera or the Côte d'Azur unless you have a preferred destination."

"Ten days, is that all? Is that some sort of austerity thing, James? And how exactly do you do that in a week?" She gurgled a laugh. "Let me guess, a private jet."

"Yes. Of course, a private jet. I have a distinct dislike of public transport. And yes, two weeks is an excellent suggestion."

What? No way. "You're actually serious about all this." She took back her hand. "All that other stuff, this vacation thing?"

He nodded. "As for the Sheraton, spend the entire week while you're home hunting and selecting a studio in your brand new whatever. However, nothing in life is free. At the end of the term I will expect a ten percent commission on all monies earned." He sipped his wine, studying her face, her eyes. "Do we have an agreement, Jodie? Not about the vacation, about the first proposal."

Her mind was a whirlwind of emotions she was in no way prepared for, not the least of which was hope tainted with fear. She wanted desperately to believe him because wherever she was going on her own was not where she ever thought she would be. What was the absolute worst that could happen? How could he possibly make her life worse? More importantly, how would she?

That was the ultimate fear plaguing her body and her soul. Despite burying Vermont in the darkest recesses of her mind, she was never completely free of the dread that one day her present would confront her past. Now saying yes to everything he was promising could make her vulnerable and put her in prison.

"This can't be real."

"I assure you, it's very real."

She clasped her hands together in her lap, bowing her head. She needed time. "My passport and driver's permit are expired," she tried.

"Neither situation is an issue. As previously mentioned, I enjoy the friendship of certain high-ranking individuals. You shall have both deficiencies corrected by midweek."

Shit! Why was he so composed, waiting? What was he doing reaching into his jacket? Why wasn't he talking, saying something that made real sense, something that would make her say no and walk out?

James Castle reached across the table, framing the cheque at the edge of her place setting. "I believe this will provide you with a reasonable degree of comfort for the coming twelve months, Jodie. The vehicle and your accommodations apart. And the vacation, of course, should you decide you would like to accompany me."

Her eyes opened wide. "Are you freaking serious, twenty-four thousand?"

He nodded.

She cupped her flushed face in her hands, surprised by the heat emanating from her soft skin. She stared at him, her throat suddenly dry, not trusting her hands to reach for the slim crystal stem. Shit! For what seemed like an eternity she had felt lost and lone. Now, from nowhere, he was giving her a chance to make her life better, worth living, as though she was at last being reborn. Why! She wanted to scream. Then she sat straight. "Okay, alright. Then it's twenty."

Castle creased brow, curving his mouth in a smirk. "Okay, alright, twenty what?"

"Twenty percent, that's what I'll give you. And I would like Cabo San Lucas if that isn't too far away for your private jet."

He was good with that. "Twenty and Cabo. Agreed."

She didn't completely believe him. "Really? Cabo?"

"Yes, Cabo. Really."

"Then I want one more thing."

"Which is?"

"Cake. I want cake for my desert…with a candle. Can they do that?"

He didn't bother asking, her glistening eyes were telling him. "A simple enough request, I'm sure. And what would a cake and candle be without the finest champagne on such an auspicious occasion. Happy birthday, Jodie."

*

Jodie got her cake and, true to his word, she spent the night and the week that followed in a top floor luxury suite that she scarcely had time to appreciate.

Saturday she asked whether a Miata was in his budget, which he believed he could manage. However the bright green roadster wouldn't be hers to drive until Monday when she would receive her Louisiana permit.

Sunday they cruised the streets of the Garden District, Jodie asking that he stop the moment she recognized where she would live. He did, and she was right. She adored the place that would be hers by the coming Friday, the owner assured her.

Monday she went alone to the bank, depositing all but a grand of the twenty-four K. She went to the licence bureau for the permit, for her passport photo, to the dealership for her car and a jewellery store for a diamond ring that would forever remind her of her best birthday ever. She ended her day at her flat, paying the three-month penalty and leaving with her clothes.

Tuesday they met for breakfast at the Sheraton. The day was all about location, location, location and by mid-afternoon, with James' help, she found the perfect studio where, he cautioned her, she would receive clients not customers. And, he added, discriminating clients that would demand the very best from her. Not the least of whom, he presumed, would be her lawyer where they would end their day.

Wednesday, April 05th, Castle flew into Dallas. Jodie treated herself to a spa and pool day where, until the sun began its downward journey, she lay in a dreamy haze floating in seventh heaven between wonderment and ecstasy, disbelief and, she didn't know what, hope.

Thursday he called from Texas; her official travel document was ready. After which she went shopping for home essentials on her credit cards and something special with money that was earned on her stool, not his that she could not yet believe.

Friday she left the hotel and moved into her home that was empty until the appliances arrived with her bed, dining room and living room sets. That was her morning, whatever else she needed or wanted could wait. In the afternoon she did some requisite drawing and later drove to the home of Samantha Danson wearing boots and tights, a belted sweater that barely covered her bum and dark glasses. She was making a statement for Parker.

Ringing the door bell precisely at 4:59, she wasn't at all surprised. The woman standing at the door was mid-thirties and smiling, the man standing beside her was not, Jodie not the least surprised by his male hormonal once-over.

"How may I help you?"

"Actually it's more like how I can help you, Sammy. I'm Jodie Carter. I have a gift for you, from your husband. I sat with Parker for an hour before he was killed at five PM Friday. He wanted you to know that, to remember that. He knew you were cheating on him with this asshole. What I didn't know was that he lost his job that afternoon. The strange thing is, he was pleasant and serene, except that his eyes were terribly sad. He was not a happy man. You did that to him."

The woman crossed her arms, leaning forward. "And you are...?"

"I'm an artist. I drew his portrait, that's your gift. He asked me to come here. Then I saw him die, very badly. He was a nice guy. You, not at all. You are the one reason he's dead. He wanted you to know that too."

Jodie unrolled the artwork. The portrait of a man she had created seven days earlier as dashing and cavalier was now hideous with anguish. The once slightly curved lips were twisted in torment; the eyes she once drew as bright with hope were dark and wide-open with fright.

The Danson woman shrieked, jerking into the man, clamping a hand against her mouth, her other hand instinctively grabbing at the portrait Jodie pressed against her chest.

"Yeah, that's right. Five PM Friday for Sammy. Delivered on time the way I believe Parker would have wanted." She turned and strode away, glancing backward, absolutely pleased with herself. "You two killers have a good time with that...bitch."

Chapter Thirty-Four

Late Friday afternoon James Castle landed at a private airfield, home to his personal Learjet 60SE that was not the property of C & D, a rare gift to himself. He shook hands with the pilot and was driven to his office in the corporate limo.

He met with Cedric Deacon explaining that he would be absent for two weeks. He would be in Cabo San Lucas for discussions regarding personal investment opportunities. In the event of any emergency his secretary would have complete contact information. Otherwise he was out-of-office. Then he left the building, driving the Infinity to a stately carriage home, not quite certain whether he should laugh or curse at the conversation about to take place.

Louise Castle would not meet him at the door, would not greet him with any degree of warmth or affection. She hadn't for years. They were old together before their time, wasting their lives. Yet divorcing her would cost him everything he had worked tirelessly to achieve: the luxury of his plane, the limo and fifty percent of his business. In that regard Deacon wasn't a factor. The shared annual bonus was a magnanimous gift from employer to employee in his view, as clearly stated in the original work agreement that Deacon never viewed as a formal partnership. Nevertheless he was stuck for a lifetime between a multimillionaire's rock and a hard place because that would never happen.

Conversely, were she ever to divorce him in favour of Deacon she wouldn't get a dime and Deacon would simply be unemployed with the usual employee severance and one hundred million if he had either the courtesy or the decency to resign. Which wouldn't likely happen since she would never surrender the good life. She hadn't seen the inside of an airport in ten years, didn't have a dress that didn't come with four figures on the tag, and she adored her luxury Vantage. None of which she could support on her own eighty K.

In his wardrobe room he left one suitcase on the sofa, taking another from a storage closet. He didn't see her standing in the doorway because he had stopped looking for her long ago, not seeing her, not caring whether she was near or far.

"You're leaving again? Really?"

"Good evening, Louise. Yes, in fact I'm am, for two weeks this time. Interesting negotiations are taking place in Mexico that require my involvement."

"What negotiations? You haven't once mentioned Mexico. Is this about Texas?"

"It's about me, an unexpected opportunity that I expect will put me several years back in time when I actually enjoyed what I do for a living."

Her burst of laughter was sardonic. "You cannot be serious. You live a pampered life, what's not to enjoy? And two weeks? Why am I not going with you?"

"Working eighty-hour weeks is no sane person's interpretation of living a pampered life. That would be your life, Louise. And you are not accompanying me simply because this is not a vacation. I do expect, however, that the end result of said negotiations will prove extremely rewarding."

"Meaning I'm stuck here alone and you get what, a good time?"

Not as good a time as you'll enjoy with Deacon. "A gratifying time, I daresay meaningful. An element of daily business sadly missing these past years."

"What's meaningful is what you're packing. What, Mexicans don't wear suits? What exactly is this opportunity?"

He laid a neatly folded stack of casual shirts into the suitcase, facing her. "Art, which I see as a worthwhile investment financially and in its allure. Both the subject matter and its venue informal by their very nature."

"Should I have Sally prepare dinner, or are you in such a great hurry to leave me again?"

He thought for a moment. "Leaving you again has given you all that you see around you, not your casual self-employment as a draftsman, including Sally who is employed by me not you as a surrogate housewife while you play with your pencils," when you're not out fucking my VP of Finance. "This trip is as much for me, for what I want, as for the continuance of the extravagances and liberties you enjoy and take for granted."

"You're a miserable bastard."

And you're an aberrant whore. "Indeed. Thank you. Now please tell the girl I'm leaving shortly and that I will drive her home on my way to the airfield."

She disappeared into the bedroom, reiterating that he was a bastard, leaving him to finish packing. A half-hour later Castle left with the young housekeeper, his display of love and devotion matching his wife's who soon after left home with a suitcase packed for her own two-week getaway with Cedric Deacon.

*

Not that Castle wouldn't have stayed the night to get one in before Deacon; he was simply eager to see Jodie once more, to hear about her week. He was taking her for dinner that was not a date, meeting her at her home because that's what she wanted.

She buzzed him in, greeting him at door in a short ruffled shift dress and sandals, a simple gold pendant enhancing her tanned neckline that had more to do with her breasts than her neck. She invited him in, excited, giving him a tour of her kitchen, the matching sofas, a bed strewn with her vacation wardrobe that he approved, and several bare walls.

He believed her diamond ring was an appropriate token, visibly shocked when she brought a Johnnie Walker Blue with a splash to the sofa he would sit into many more times. He admonished her, of course, telling her the money would have been better spent on side tables, admonished in return not to spoil her day. She told him about Parker's wife and how she transformed the portrait, which he believed was brilliantly apropos. Then she gave him a small box wrapped in silver foil and red ribbon that he accepted with considerable reservation, placing his twenty-dollar cocktail on the floor and pausing.

Before he could tug at the ribbon she put a hand over his. "I bought this with my own money, not yours."

"That money is yours, enough said." The ribbon came undone, the foil neatly unfolded. The blue velvet box was the renowned jeweller's signature that he recognized at once. "Jodie, I expect this gift will prove somewhat extravagant." Slowly opening the lid he sat staring at the trio of glistening deep ruby links and tie pin. "Extravagant indeed. Thank you, Jodie. They shall be part of my very next business day." He put a fingertip to each jewel. "And consider yourself duly reprimanded once more, Miss Carter."

She did, at the same time telling him where she had made reservations.

Dinner was an all-dressed with a carafe of house Merlot at Papa's, casual dining at its finest. He couldn't remember the last time he had eaten pizza, or sat at a table draped with a chequered cloth or, for that matter, breaking a fifty for the meal, tip and tax.

Then with an evening too pleasant not to enjoy, a prelude to an exotic evasion of current realities, they strolled the streets of the Quarter stopping at the storefront she would soon transform into *Jodie's Art*.

"Thank you, James. All this is absolutely beyond incredible. Thank you."

"You may thank me in two years, when I get my twenty

percent. This is business, Jodie, and I expect an enviable return."

"I will succeed, James. I promise I will become someone. But an enviable return? Yeah, good luck with that."

He was learning to laugh again. He drove her home, waiting until she waved from her front balcony before returning downtown and booking himself into the Sheraton.

Saturday morning he arrived for her at 8:00, arriving at the airfield on the half-hour where he introduced her to the pilot who acquainted her with the onboard amenities and let her sit in the captain's seat while he discussed the flightpath, weather patterns and their ETA with the boss.

There was no need for James to explain the young lady. The pilot had flown Castle hundreds of times over their ten years together, many of them with Louise to vacation destinations, often with Deacon when exploring possible business opportunities. They enjoyed a mutual respect.

Whatever the boss was doing, he had good reason and not long after boarding they were taxing into position, Jodie leaning sidesaddle in Italian leather comfort with her nose pressed against a port-side window, straightening when she heard the pilot's voice over the intercom. He was reminding them, as Castle expected, that seatbelts were preferable to broken necks or spinal injuries. Please buckle up, Miss Carter.

Minutes later the landing gears retracted and Jodie's nose was again smudging the window, soaring smoothly to flight level four-three-zero. ETA: Three hours, five minutes.

The flight was uneventful. The bar was stocked with their preferred premiums, although James served coffee, and the in-flight entertainment was Fred Astaire and Ginger Rogers whose dancing was interrupted occasionally to update flightpath information on the screen that went black moments before the bright white foam lining the emerald Sea of Cortés came into view.

They were veering onto their final approach, at that

moment Jodie's lifelong dream seeming more real, angry with herself for the way she treated him that first night, for not believing him, for even thinking he would hurt or abuse her. He was a gentleman; he was educated, worldly and charming. And the wife was a complete bitch like that horrible Danson woman.

The touchdown was smooth, the reverse thrust barely noticeable. When the jet came to a stop, when the pilot opened the door, the interior flooded at once with a muggy 31° C. Stepping into the rippling air and glaring midday sun, stepping onto the tarmac, Jodie was absolutely impressed when they were escorted past long serpentine lines of weary and frustrated damp travellers to an immigration officer separated from the masses by a thick red velvet cordon.

The limousine and driver were waiting far away from the confusion of those others crowding into tour buses, vans, and overpriced taxis. The private retreat of villas promising seclusion and opulence, the finest amenities for one's leisure and the most sumptuous experience in fine dining, was a fifty kilometre drive along the scenic shoreline. The lush property was a veritable Eden exuding the splendour of wealth, their own two-storey personal and private villa situated a mere few metres from the dazzling turquoise sea and the sound of endless crashing waves.

Their adjoining bedrooms opened onto an expansive private patio where they came together and would for fourteen days wake to a magnificent sunrise, ending each fleeting day gazing at a glittering sea bathed in moonlight. A bottle of champagne and fruit basket were in the salon, the bathroom was a private spa more than a functional space and James made very clear that the sole purpose of the kitchen was the corkscrew at which they would take turns.

She agreed.

"The champagne can wait, Jodie. Let's get ourselves into that seventy degree water."

She agreed with that also. Then abruptly she panicked,

blurting a murmured "Shit!" before she could block its escape. Of infinitely greater concern than a corkscrew was that with her hectic week she hadn't given a moment's thought to the beach. How would she possibly explain the eye-patch thongs she hadn't worn since her final days in Florida, when he believed she was a street urchin subsisting in a self-described shithole? She couldn't, not without a major confession she absolutely wanted to avoid.

"What, now?"

She hadn't known the man for as long as they would be together, now she'd be putting on a girlie show she could never justify. Not after that first night, the virgin thing, the spread her legs thing. This wasn't good, not good at all.

"I am fast becoming familiar with your vast repertoire of expressions, Jodie. What could possibly be amiss amidst such splendour?"

"Me. I'm the amiss. I sort of only have thongs because I was never with anyone. I didn't care about strangers and haven't worn them for years. It's a long story, kind of complicated."

"My goodness, thongs." He leaned against the stucco wall, pensive, giving the matter due consideration. "Well that is indeed a grave concern." He chuckled. "For which I see two possible remedies in light of our being here platonically as recently acquainted good friends and business partners. The first would be throwing caution to the wind, since most young ladies here, the more appealing ones at least, and hopefully so, will be similarly clad and appropriately adored for being superlative examples of their species; the second would be visiting the lobby boutique for a more modest fashion that would allay your misgivings." A pause, and a smirk. "Personally, as a gentleman of discriminating tastes and appreciation of all things exquisite, I would naturally prefer the former. However, as that friend and partner, I would certainly conceal my disappointment should you prefer the latter."

"You're laughing at me."

"I would never. I am, however, enjoying your dilemma. Though let me say as a timely FYI that I don't wear cargos or anything remotely and curiously unnecessary or cumbersome. The things are dangerous in the water and revolting on land. I prefer the European fashion of square-cut microfibres. I must also confess that despite not being familiar with your various contours does not mean that I will not, as an appreciative representative of my species, create an appropriate mental facsimile of said delightful contours."

"Shit, James. This is not funny."

"Nothing ever is when we appear vulnerable, Jodie, and what makes anyone more vulnerable than when we are without our cloaks? Do whatever makes you comfortable and I will meet you at the beach. Our time here will evaporate quickly enough. Let's not waste a single moment."

Jodie stayed as she was, scrunching her face. "Gee, thanks for all your help."

He was already at his patio doors. "Anytime. See you later."

She went into her room, throwing open her suitcase, her stomach churning with butterflies, trying to rationalize. A bum was a bum, no big deal. Thousands of strangers had seen her that way and how many had tried their best at a one-nighter? She was beautiful and what was wrong with being admired? Nothing. And he would be a gentleman. Of course he would.

Screw it! She would! She kicked off her sandals, wiggled from her shorts and her panties, her blouse and her bra, rummaging for the SPF. She stood by the mirror, coating her body, bending and stretching, turning and twisting, searching for imaginary flaws. Yeah, she was drop-dead gorgeous. And yeah, he was right one week earlier. She knew it. Yet not perfect enough for the beach or for James, not until the marks from her travel ensemble faded. An hour he could spend wondering, which he would unless he was a eunuch in tailor-made suits.

She chose a red patch with side-ties she would knot for

safety and let dangle. She wasn't much into bows, but the triangles she once believed nicely enhanced her breasts now seemed really small. She hadn't once felt timid or uncertain about herself—until that very moment, standing naked in the mirror dotted with tiny red body parts.

She pursed her lips, furrowing her brow. She felt dismal, apprehensive about what he would think. She put on dark glasses, a wide-brimmed sunhat, wrapped a sheer sarong at her waist, wished herself luck and left.

He was at the water's edge, Jodie humming approval when she called his name. He was lean and muscular; he actually had abs. Okay, alright. What wasn't alright was that he was hidden behind sunglasses. She couldn't read his eyes.

"There is no woman more ravishing on the entire beach, Jodie. You are a divine and living sculpture." He took her hands and twirled her. "I'll be the envy of all men."

"I can't tell you how weird this feels, me and you like this. Anyway, let's get this over with." She gulped air, untying the coverup, doing a three-sixty with her arms outstretched. "This is me, James...pretty much all of me, in fact."

"As delightful as I would have created in my mind, Jodie, had I been reduced to such improper images. And, yes, somewhat weird."

She scanned the beach, frowning. Lovers were strolling hand in hand, others laying side by side on canopy beds under billowy white drapes; women were sauntering along the shoreline as naked as she was, others discreetly sunning topless on chaises longues. And her, openly admired by every passerby, man or woman, standing beside a guy who looked great, who she couldn't touch or hold hands with, wondering what now? She would be the only girl at the resort without the guy she was with.

James understood the issue. "We're becoming friends, Jodie. We shouldn't let weird get in the way of a pleasant time together. In fact, to that end...," he took her hat and her wrap, striding to their reserved lounge chairs that he deemed more appropriate than a bed. A moment later, without a word, he swept her into his arms, splashing his way into the sea, in waist-deep water launching her as high as he could into the air. The scene was incredible, James believing he would most certainly repeat the manoeuvre several times more.

When she surfaced, sputtering and coughing, her arms flailing, her entire head encased in a sleek blonde skullcap, she was scowling, brushing apart the curtain while he was beaming a row of white teeth against a rich tan, standing there feeling quite pleased with himself.

"That was not funny, James. I did not like that."

He shrugged. "This is definitely a Kodak moment, Jodie. Right there, right now, you are the most marvellous sea creature." He waded toward her, stopping at a safe distance. "However I will accept any reasonable punishment you see fit to administer."

"Good. Because from now on I'm ignoring you. Deal with that, smart guy." She swam away, her shoulders and alluring curves glistening, stopping several strokes away, twirling to face him. "James, I can't very well ignore you if you're not with me, can I?"

*

Ignoring him meant dips in the ocean without him. She was no longer shy about her body, that ended the second she crashed indignantly into the sea. She could tell he adored every inch of her, that he was proud being with her.

Ignoring him meant laying stretched out on their lounge chairs with tropical cocktails, when he couldn't ignore her, as her reveries commuted from one private world into another, from her past into her present to her future, to their approaching evening together and the uncertain hours between dusk and dawn.

Later at the villa the lady had priority bathroom privileges while the gentleman attended to chilling the champagne, padding to her bedroom in a fleecy guest robe, deciding that she would. She absolutely would. The place was way too fancy for a tee and shorts. Besides the air was stifling and she was absolutely positive, she hoped, that he had already imagined the most intimate parts of her that she had scarcely concealed anyway. He must have.

When she stepped out onto the second-floor patio in loose-fitting silk tap pants and matching camisole, he displayed due appreciation. He poured the lady's champagne, touched his fluted glass to hers, sipped the effervescent wine and left her to gaze at the mountains and across the sea.

When he stepped out not long after, since his preparations for the evening were less complex than hers, he was in linen beach pants and open linen shirt.

"You're very handsome, James." She sipped her wine "And in quite good shape for a man your age."

He reached for his glass. "Thank you, Miss Carter. I'll do my utmost to maintain my current condition and your approval."

"The day couldn't be more fabulous, James. The jet, the ocean, the villa, everything."

"Everything?"

"Okay, I officially forgive you."

"And I must say, because you will most certainly and justifiably despise me if I don't, you were stunning." He sipped his wine, correcting himself. "Are stunning. Might I dare to wish for more of the same tomorrow?"

She nodded. "Yeah, I can definitely see that happening."

He nodded, smiling, holding out his glass. "Then to fourteen more stunning days."

Days. Yeah, that was the problem.

Dinner that first evening was as promised: Sumptuous. James went in white dress pants, white canvas shoes and a white button-down that he wore unbuttoned over a fitted white tee. Jodie went in a black lace crop top and matching very mini skirt that framed a bare midriff and enhanced her breasts glittering with silver dust, her satin sandals and flounced hem drawing requisite attention to her tanned legs.

When the meal was over they strolled under a moonlit sky along private pathways and along the shore, James carrying their shoes with his pants rolled up. While others were holding hands, or linking their arms, they were not. Because they were suddenly new friends and partners and James knew exactly how easy enticing the girl into his arms and into his bed would be. He also knew that such misconduct would indelibly mar their relationship.

On their patio in the dark, with an old-fashioned of JW Blue on one side of the small table and one filled with Ultimat and soda on the other, changed into their pre-dinner slacks and lingerie, with their feet sharing an ottoman, they sat making plans for the week and by11:00, barely able to keep her eyes open, Jodie was ready for bed.

She stood, feeling awkward. She didn't know what to say or do to a guy who had seen her practically naked all day and in her lingerie most of the evening. She wanted to hug him or kiss his cheek or do something that felt right because not doing anything seemed, she didn't know, not right. But he hadn't moved, sitting looking up at her.

"James, today was the best ever. All this, the moon, the stars. It's surreal, like I'm someone else somewhere else far away."

"You are someone else in that place far away, very clearly someone else and that must never change."

"I'll see you in the morning."

"Jodie," he stood, "I suppose after all you and I have shared this week, the good and the bad, not to mention giving up our cloaks that from my perspective was entirely delightful, we could end our day with a friendly embrace."

"I would like that, James."

They came together and hugged, James thinking his wife

hadn't once squeezed him as tightly or had ever smelled as intoxicating; Jodie lamenting she was in the gentle and warm embrace of a caring and wonderful man who would never ever be hers.

*

Jodie slipped into bed in her darkened room as she was, drifting into a dreamy world with her curtains and doors open, listening to the rolling waves and staring for as long as she could at the good-looking and debonair man on the patio who was her saviour. While James, somewhat more conditioned to the pleasures of fine spirits, lingered on the patio with another JW Blue nightcap.

Sunday morning she padded to the bathroom, showered and rinsed out her lingerie; she tied herself into a green version of the previous afternoon's red and called down for a large carafe of coffee, juice, and a selection of morning goodies. Then she waited by the door in her fleecy robe, pondering the proper etiquette because she had long ago forgotten such protocols. Though when the in-room service did arrive minutes later, the ten was humbly accepted with the brightest white eyes and happiest pink smile she had ever seen framing the biggest and whitest teeth she had ever seen.

When James finally did stroll out onto the patio in his robe, yawning behind a tight fist, he practically stumbled forward expecting a tidy mess from the night before. What he got was a discreet line of ladies's delicates, his breakfast laid out, and Jodie Carter delightfully clad in a tan and three tiny and bright green patches while lounging on a chaise longue.

"I thought I would get an early start on my tan, since I've been here alone such a long time."

"A pleasant commonality in our thinking. I was hoping I would wake to see you this way."

"I figured I can't have the guy I'm with more interested in other girls. What would that say about me? And I want to spend the day here at the pools. I've decided. We can do the whale thing tomorrow. Are you good with that?"

He was. "I want whatever you want, Jodie. This is your renaissance, your time." He smirked, pouring a coffee. "However, if I must perforce see you this way, I insist that you pose for me."

"Deal."

She eased onto her front. She felt good being with him, enjoying him; whereas James, whose breakfast was a welcomed distraction, sat wondering how he would ever survive fourteen exotic and torturous days, wondering how she would look framed on his office desk. Exotic.

*

And to his real astonishment, he did survive.

That Sunday they spent at the pools, floating on mattresses and lounging with cocktails. She posed for him a hundred different ways, with happy smiles and pouty frowns; Jodie capturing James in her Nikon at the four o'clock pool volleyball.

Throughout their vacation they went whale watching and swam with dolphins; he introduced her to scuba diving that she absolutely enjoyed, and golf that she absolutely did not. They went yachting each week, anchoring and swimming in secluded lagoons, strolling along secluded and sandy beaches; they went deep sea fishing, when she was more appetizing than anyone's catch of the day, and horseback riding.

By day she went through a rainbow of tiny thongs and triangles, ending their evenings on the patio under the stars, often after they first went dancing, Jodie nonchalantly bringing each evening of their second week to a close, combatting warmer temps and muggier nights, with several thong teddies. Anything else would seem, she didn't know, childishly silly. Until their last evening. Particularly since James was the quintessential gentleman. Absolutely quintessential. Really.

For dinner that evening she wore a captivating shift dress in midnight blue that fell delightfully to her mid-thighs and swayed as she sauntered by his side, silently, inviting appreciative glances and envious stares with its deep V front and plunging bare back creating an irresistible allure. Sensuous and daring and bought that afternoon with heels that elevated her to a stunning 6'3".

No one cared about James' evening wear, that he was elegant in pleated dress pants, Italian-crafted loafers and the impulsive light-weight raglan sweater that set him back half a grand. Neither did he. What he cared about was being a survivor, that he hadn't slept with her or tempted fate with even the lightest and most brotherly kiss.

Gazing at her, though, mesmerized by her incredible good looks and killer curves, he couldn't help pondering whether she would have loved him or loathed him had he foolishly acted upon his true feelings. Either way, he chose the higher road. She was seventeen years younger and did not need him clouding her future, which didn't mean the difficult road travelled was so high that each night they weren't entwined in rapture until his fantasies became fanciful dreams.

Studying the deep Burgundy colour of her '99 Chambolle-Musigny, inhaling its rich aroma, tasting its delicious textures and flavours, was pretence. Bullshit. The pleasant curve of her lips and the gleam in her piercing green eyes were pretence. More bullshit. She was sad, and she was peeved. In fact she was absolutely and taciturnly pissed with him and she had been throughout the day.

Throughout the entire two weeks they hadn't once held hands, when even friends can do that; he hadn't once kissed her cheek or put his arms endearingly around her shoulders. Hadn't once swayed her in his arms around the pools, hadn't once massaged lotion onto her back, like he had either transmuted into that eunuch or she was unclean and untouchable. When, in fact, she was immensely touchable and very clean. She wanted his hands touching her, to once in her life feel warm and tender hands on her. Yeah, loving hands. As though she couldn't tell.

Because he was blind and stupid didn't mean she was. So what if she was younger? He wasn't any fifty or sixty. Idiot!

No once in her entire life had anyone kissed her. How pathetic and sad was that? What's worse, no one had ever once said they love her.

She knew about the wife, that she was fucking around on a really nice guy with someone who was cheating on his own wife or whatever. What was up with that? Two weeks and not a single glimmer in his eyes or a telling sigh on his breath that he was even remotely interested in taking her to bed. Just teasing her in the sea and the pools, forever the gentleman, teasing her at night in linen pants that told their own story before sending her off to bed like a child with brotherly hugs after she could not have put herself out there any farther without stripping away her teddies and—yeah, throwing herself at him. Asshole.

"Hey, what is that?"

She came back to him, in a daze. "Excuse me? What do you mean, what is that?"

"Your arresting green eyes, Jodie. For an instant you seemed like a wide-eyed fawn staring into oncoming high beams."

She wanted to smack him. She really did. Beautiful eyes, that was bullshit too. Beautiful this and lovely that, all undiluted bullshit. Say what you mean, what you're thinking, that you want me in your bed, that you just want me. Asshole.

"Oh, I'm sorry. I was thinking we should end our evening on our patio. No more walking, no more talking. The patio, the quiet and the darkness. Would you mind, James?"

That's what she wanted. The next morning they would return to their respective realities and then what? He hadn't said what because there was nothing to say. There was no what. He was returning to a complete bitch he despised as though the thousand photos in his and her memory cards had never happened. That was bullshit. She wanted to scream. She wanted to scream and smack his head into consciousness. But she wouldn't. No way. She was better than that; she was a woman, young and desirable.

"I could not think of a more memorable conclusion of our time together."

That's right, Mr. Castle. But I can. "Neither can I. In fact, let's skip desert and the cognacs. I may even stay dressed. It's not like I'm wearing anything under this flimsy thing, Mr. Castle. Do you mind if I don't change? I mean you've probably seen enough of me au naturel anyway. You know, practically naked?"

He leaned forward onto his elbows, whispering. "Excuse me, you are not wearing lingerie?"

She leaned forward onto her elbows, whispering with that female tone that put intelligent men instantly into defence mode. "No, James, I'm not. And the word is panties. I am not wearing panties. Do you have a problem with that, Mr. Castle? I mean, do you?"

Apparently and wisely, he did not, attributing her quiet mood and somewhat direct manner of speech to the unfortunate malaise of the female condition. But then...

Later at the villa James took a few moments, changing into his linen beach pants while Jodie fixed his JW Blue with a splash and her Ultimat with soda. When he came out she was sitting in her cushioned seat waiting, peering out over the vast black and glittering sea.

She pointed to his nightcap without seeing him and when she heard his first breath she pressed a fingertip to her lips with a sensual and drawn out "Ssshhh." She wanted quiet; hers was the only voice she wanted to hear on their final night together: The starlit beauty and the eunuch.

She absolutely wanted revenge. She wanted him to feel as though this was not a memorable ending, that he had fucked-up big-time when they might have held hands and kissed from morning till night like all the other young couples sharing romance. She wanted him to realize that being friends did not mean she needed a brother or that she wanted to be his sister or that she expected more than being friends and partners.

She sipped her drink, ignoring him, setting down the old-fashioned by her seat, thinking that crashing it against his empty head would be a waste of fine crystal. And she was better than that.   She was also nervous and she was eager, half-believing her heart would stop, half-hoping that she would die if she failed.

"It's incredible, unbelievable really." She put a fingertip once more to her lips, her other hand freeing the buttons at the side of her dress closest to him, exposing her leg to the bare curve of her waist. "At twenty-two I have never been kissed, not by anyone. Never loved by anyone, not once in my life." She slowly and delicately freed the other side of her dress with both slender hands, exposing her leg and more of her tanned and enticingly bare waist. Shifting slightly in her seat, she liberated what little material was trapped under her weight, making what little fabric lay rumpled atop her smooth and inviting thighs a delicate apron that she rustled unabashedly as though cooling the heated flesh between them.

She reached for her glass, sipping her drink, intently caressing the length of one bare thigh, then the other with equal pleasure, inhaling a deep and sensual breath. "So soft and smooth. So warm, yet I never once had a boyfriend or lover who would know or remember. Never had anyone who wanted to touch me this way." She sipped her drink, wiping the cool crystal across her moist brow, placing the crystal on the table, unhooking one of the four buttons keeping what was left of her dress together with a twitch of her forefinger and thumb, slipping her other hand inside, cupping a firm and soft breast. "I don't understand, I truly do not."

She parted her legs, leaning forward, standing, commanding her heart and her breathing, James fixated on precisely what she wanted him fixated on, obsessed with. If not then, when? Never.

She kicked off one sandal, then the other, ignoring him, tugging downward at the back of her dress, leaning against the patio's railing, her moist skin shimmering in the moonlight, releasing the lowest of three remaining buttons. "I cannot imagine ever having a lover, ever being loved or loving. Or how wonderful that would feel." She stared into his unblinking eyes. "Never feeling the heat of passion, James, never sharing the heat of my passion." The second to last button went at her waist, making her dress a useless drape, exposing her perfect breasts. "Or the heat of my lover's lips pressed to mine, to my soft and warm breasts." Her fingers went steadily to the button below her waist, Jodie letting her dress fall away. "His warm hands caressing me, exploring me, wanting all of me. Will I ever know that, James, do you think? Will I ever feel true love?"

She inhaled a mournful breath, studying the crumpled silk heap at her feet, standing inches from him naked and vulnerable, the living sculpture that she knew in her heart, hoped with all her heart he dreamed of caressing and loving each day and night. And that he absolutely would because she was absolutely certain that she absolutely loved him.

Her deep breath made her breasts fuller, enhancing her flawless contours. "Goodnight, James. I do hope we can both sleep well."

Chapter Thirty-Five

James Castle sat breathless, staring at the dress. His throat and his eyes were dry; though his skin was damp, wiping beads of sweat from his brow and truly believing his heart was pounding in his chest on the verge of rupture. Because if he was not having an end of life experience, he was certainly having a panic attack. Why didn't she simply drive a knife through his heart and call him an asshole? She called everyone else assholes, so why not him? Because he was one, a big one, the worst kind in fact: a blind one.

But the "Goodnight, James." What did that mean, exactly? And, "I hope we can both sleep well." Really, do you think? What exactly did that mean? Jesus H! She really could be a little vague at times, not saying what she truly intended or felt. He leaned forward, peering into her open room, an invasion into her privacy he would never have permitted himself, rubbing a hand roughly over his moist mouth and jaw. He had never seen anything so completely worthy of an artist's brush.

Easing to his feet, reaching for his glass, he swallowed the double JW in a single gulp. Jodie was laying with her head resting on folded arms, naked on the duvet, staring directly into his eyes. He could see her tears sparkling on her moonlit cheeks from where he stood feeling like the absolute asshole that he was. Albeit a genteel asshole, he argued, a considerate asshole whose foremost concern was her, his friend, never wanting to harm or hurt her. Or burden her with emotional baggage since she would indeed, one day sooner or later, as young women are wont to do, discard him for whatever reason suited her.

He smiled at her, warmly, belying the chill coursing through his body despite the heavy night air. He took a step closer, then another, uncertain what she was murmuring, all but leaping into her arms the moment she propped her weight onto her elbows calling his name in a tremulous voice.

*

The early morning sun was a dazzling gem on the horizon, the fresh morning air prefacing a plague of dense and moist oppressive heat that would reach its peak by midday.

The jet that hadn't yet departed New Orleans would land in seven hours with a two-hour refuelling stopover, giving the newly discovered lovers nine debilitating and depleting hours together.

"Good morning."

"Yeah, good morning."

A shroud of silence. Smiles and grins, a passionate kiss in lieu of words previously whispered throughout the entire night and into the early hours. Her slender fingertips and tender touching; his warm caresses, a strong hand guiding her leg over his, kneading her moist flesh, green eyes peering into brown.

"I was unforgivably stupid, for all the right reasons. Surely you must appreciate my quandary. Please tell me that you do."

"Yeah, you were pretty stupid."

"Touché. Laying here now by the side of a divine angel in some heavenly parallel world after having died a glorious death." He kissed her, stroking her cheek. "I do in some way feel critically wounded. Thankfully not mortally."

She giggled softly. "Not yet, anyway. The day isn't over and you absolutely deserve pain and suffering for making me do that, being in a restaurant without my panties. What if I had tripped?"

"I would hope that several concerned and willing first responders would have rushed to assist you. As would I, naturally." He chuckled. "I have never in my life sat through more spellbinding and exotic theatre. You stole my breath, Jodie. Perhaps you have discovered your true calling."

"Maybe not, but thank you. I'm curious though, how did you get through these two weeks without your seeing eye dog?"

"Point taken. In light of which I assume this is cause for some discussion throughout our final morning and the flight home? That perhaps now we should be holding hands?"

"No conversation, not a word about anything. Do not spoil this for me with silly questions." She clambered over him. "What we're doing is getting me seriously laid once more before breakfast, that is if you're up to it. Then we're doing the morning at the pool where we are absolutely holding hands." She paused, furrowing her brow. "Hey, since we're flying pretty much First-Class, happen to know anything about this mile-high thing? Should I be wearing panties, or what?"

He didn't believe that information was anywhere in the pilot's manual and, yes, perhaps panties would be appropriate.

*

The jet landed smoothly at its airfield on time at 6:15 PM and Jodie was indeed wearing panties that she kept on throughout the flight, although wearing a short skirt and heels without stockings she did occasionally and delightfully taunt and torment him. A punishment he willingly accepted and suffered through.

Not talking about it, about them, throughout the flight was impossible considering Jodie's newly acquired theatrical flair. The common consensus was that she had found a lover, each one agreeing not to use the word as an empty verb during future frantic and sweaty encounters unless and until the word carried clear meaning; and he had taken a mistress, a word he immediately understood would never be used again. Even though, he explained, the practice was very much the norm in certain civilized countries.

She didn't care and, on a related matter, neither did he.

They would have dinners together in public and in private and would spend as many evenings and nights together as possible. He would also find himself wandering occasionally into a certain art boutique on Royal Street with coffee and beignets to make his days more tolerable. He didn't care about being seen with her and, when she asked him why, his eyes went cold answering in a flat voice that erased her smile that he would tell her when he deemed the timing propitious.

Staying with her for dinner or even a cocktail would have been anticlimactic to the vacation, in particular their final evening, James leaving her at the door with a drawn out kiss pressed against warm lips, his gentle hands cupping her face. He would see her very soon.

*

Going home, to a place and existence he wouldn't tolerate much longer, to Louise who he no longer wanted in his life, was the actual and far worse anticlimax. Despite her good-looks which he could not deny, he would forego further punitive sexual encounters with her despite the perverse pleasure he derived from punishing her with each meaningful thrust while musing with an invisible smirk that at least he wasn't stabbing her in the back.

He decided he wouldn't from then on, not that she would ever ask why because she wouldn't care. Nor did she care that he was home, scarcely acknowledging him when he passed by her office door, James pondering with a chuckle whether she had arrived home shortly before him or whether she waited as long as she dared before sending Deacon away. Though once inside he didn't bother asking.

Neither did she did bother; she didn't need his bullshit. He hadn't gone on any business trip.

Wherever he went he was cheating on her. He hadn't once in his life been that deeply tanned, hadn't once since she could remember seemed as relaxed or content. And she loathed him for what she knew was the truth as much as she hated herself and Cedric for yelling at each other the night before, ruining two exquisite and carefree weeks together over a man she deeply despised.

Chapter Thirty-Six

Friday, April 07th, Louise Castle was already aware before James stepped foot into the house. She was elated, beside herself with glee and, when James left his home without the slightest fondness in his farewell, she skipped to her room where she packed for fourteen days and fourteen nights before driving into the open arms of her lover.

She remained in Cedric Deacon's arms and his bed for an entire week of loving, the theatre and dining out, their illicit time together made even more special with a full week of leisure and gambling at a Biloxi casino hotel. She didn't bother with lingerie for their seductive evenings and intimate moments, that wardrobe was already a permanent fixture behind a door in Deacon's bedroom.

Throughout those two weeks they were husband and wife in every possible way, living an idyllic marriage, Cedric coming home to her from his day at the office, doing dinner at home, doing the dishes, lounging on the deck or in the cinema room sipping cocktails and nightcaps before drifting into blissful slumber scented with each other's sweat. Then living their lives together in public at the exclusive resort. Until the Friday they returned to James Castle's home, a day blanketed with black clouds bursting with rain, damp with the kind of suffocating humidity that comes with oppressive heat and incessant downpours. Until their last evening together when the storm invaded the elegant mansion.

"No, Deac. We should tell him…tell him together. We

haven't once had this much time together like a real couple. Tell me this wasn't special, that you wouldn't want this every day."

"How would I face James confessing to an affair lasting years longer than our partnership and your marriage? Even if I did, if I could ever be that callous, hearing those words would kill him and devastate the firm."

"So now I'm callous? Really? Me, not him for all his bullshit?"

"We've kept the secret alive all this time, Louise. It's what you wanted: each of us for different reasons. Something much better than awesome, that's what you said. A definite red flag we were too young and careless to recognize."

"Things change, people change. I have to tell him; I want him out of my life. What choice do I have? He's different, Deac; he's mean and spiteful. And the sex, it's like he's hurting me. He's never there with me. He doesn't even look at me, he hasn't for the longest time. He just does me and goes to sleep or to his office, like I stop existing when he's finished with me. I can't do that anymore. I want this, I want you. I want these past two weeks forever. I want something real with you."

"Louise, that is impossible. We started something we should have ended long before your wedding because you couldn't decide between us."

"Because you weren't interested in committing. You didn't want a wife."

"No. Because you wanted the Castle name, never thinking we would be insanely successful and wealthy. No one did. Now you've got his name and his success while I share that success and his wife. That's the status quo."

"That, what you just said, is cruel. Like I'm what, a weekly dividend?"

"Your interpretation, which didn't bother you for a moment in school or the night before you married the wrong man."

The "fuck you" came from her mouth in a scathing hiss.

He ignored the expletive the way she was ignoring sound reasoning. "If we had done what was right, those first years in school would be a pleasant memory, a treasured secret. But we didn't, we chose each other over decency."

"That is unbelievably hurtful. We are not indecent."

"Tell him that."

"I would. I mean really, Deac, you've never had a jealous moment? You don't think of me being here with him?"

"No. Especially not after all these years. It's natural, if not entirely obscene. It's morally wrong and in business very unethical, but it's natural. We waited too long, Louise. You should have divorced him years ago. He would have gotten over you, even accepted us with time. Not now."

"Then I'll make him divorce me. How can he not realize this marriage has gone to shit, that I don't love him? He fucks me like I'm a rubber blowup while completely ignoring me. And when he's not, I ignore him. I never talk with him and, pretending I'm happy...that's just impossible. I can't do it. I never call him by name, I don't call him at the office, and I never call him when he travels. I couldn't be more obvious and I can't remember the last time he called me for whatever reason."

"So what?" He wanted out. He wanted his own safe sanctuary and a few malted scotch. "I do not see your point, Louise, the way you're confusing reality with fiction. Divorce is not an option. That will not happen, not ever. You divorce him, you don't get squat. He divorces you, you get a good portion of his personal portfolio. That's all, not a cent from his corporate assets. So let's get real here. James Castle will never let you win out over him. It's how we got where we are. He wins, they lose. Me? I've always been the quintessential the office boy, nothing more."

"I could give a shit about the money." She was livid, seriously pissed with him. "You don't think we could get by on a hundred million. You don't?"

"That's not the point. The point is that in twenty years, if not sooner, those assets will double. So not a hundred mil, a billion each as in a shitload more luxury. And, in the meantime, another five million a year in bonuses."

"Really? And who do you think wears a thong at sixty?"

He shrugged. "Anyone who's as vain as you are, Louise. Anyone with a personal trainer and one day each week at the spa. That's who."

That was the first time in their affair that she slapped him, so hard that she squealed from the stinging pain. He simply put a palm to his cheek and gave her space. He went to the bedroom, collected his clothes, made certain nothing remained, and went downstairs where she stood waiting at the door in tears.

She loved him, they had one last night together, and she didn't want him leaving after an argument.

He loved her as much, touching her cheek. Soon James would be in Charleston for a few days, when they would talk. They needed time apart for her to fully comprehend and come to terms with their present and future realities. Divorcing James would mean divorcing him as well.

She had to understand that, deal with that. They were irreparably in the wrong on so many levels, not James.

Chapter Thirty-Seven

Jodie spent her first night at home loading her computer with vacation photos. Sunday she woke late and spent the afternoon making to-do and shopping lists that would complete her apartment and begin work on her art studio.

The entire week was taken up with putting her Shangri-La in order and meetings with contractors, although she did make time for a luncheon with James on the Wednesday and Friday when he kept his promise and held her hands completely at ease. She missed him, anxious for Saturday when he was invited for dinner, when she would show off her new everything, when he could place his JW Blue on her recently bought end tables. And when Saturday did finally arrive, and James for dinner carrying a dozen yellow carnations, he was suitably impressed despite a visibly dark mood.

Though she knew not to ask. Instead she took charge; she made him relax with dancing and soft music between courses, loving him ardently in her bed and waking Sunday to a day of strolling through the nearby park and a romantic lunch in an intimate garden setting of lovers and murmurs that was all she could wish for.

Her weekend could not have been more perfect, until the moment James stood at the door when his dark mood resurfaced, out of the blue proposing a September vacation somewhere very far away and very exotic.

*

Jodie had pretty much forgotten her fear of travel, of making herself seen, her fear that with a driver's permit and passport someone somewhere would take notice that one Jodie Carter was alive and well and living in New Orleans after murdering and burying her aunt and her rapist. No cops had yet smashed open her door screaming "Get down! Get down!" No task force had yet parked outside her address in a dark van to spy and eavesdrop on her, which didn't mean they wouldn't. Or weren't.

Through to the end of May, a Thursday afternoon impossibly drenched with the deep South's daily deluge of copious rains, she worked at designing her boutique that would open on Saturday without fanfare. She didn't want fanfare, she told them, in case no one came, both Earnie Lebeau and James Castle, men from far distant worlds and equally proud of her, scolding her for being foolish. People would flock in and they would be the first through the doors.

The evening was no less miserable. She showered and changed into jean shorts and a loose-fitting tee. She made a light salad for dinner, sitting on the cool floor with her plate and a glass of Chardonnay musing on what she should draw, anxious for the phone to ring, eager to hear her lover's charming Louisiana accent.

Instead she heard the intercom, jerking and splashing wine across her bare legs. No one had come to her door since moving in, no one except James, and she scurried to the windows peering through the blinds. At seeing the black sedan the inner scream strained her throat, bringing a flush to her face; her stomach churned and she stopped breathing. She wanted James, she needed James.

The intercom's buzzer sounded again, somehow louder and longer, a clear and threatening message that they were not going away. She gasped a sudden breath, resigned, combing her hair with her palms, padding to the door in bare feet, her pounding heart nearing the point of catastrophic failure and with a single and delicate fingertip she surrendered.

"Hello?"

"Good evening. I'm looking for Miss Jodie Carter, formerly of Burlington Vermont. Are you that person?"

"Who are you?"

"My name is Jack Lord. I'm a Georgia attorney. I'm here with my associate, Ms. Abigail Evans."

"What about? I've never been to Georgia."

"If you are in fact Jodie Carter, yes you have."

"I am Jodie Carter and I did live in Vermont, but never in Georgia."

"Then may we come in, Miss Carter? The evening air is quite inhospitable."

She was afraid, but they knew her and where she lived. Shit! "Yes."

She buzzed them in.

Lord and Evans were storefront mannequins, a Southern six-foot Ken and 5'6" Barbie without a wrinkle or a smudge of sweat on their flawless faces. She was white-on-white, save her full lips freshly glossed with prune and her lustrous dark red hair. Jodie had never seen clearer skin or a warmer and brighter smile. Her skirt and blouse were white, her sandals, leather handbag and briefcase were white and, like most every Southern belle, she was wearing stockings even on the worst of humid and wet days.

He was the extreme opposite with caramel skin and no hair. Everything else was in shades of blue from his tie to his tasselled loafers and satchel.

Abigail Evans stepped in first, Jack Lord followed extending his hand. Evans scanned the apartment, commenting on Jodie's obvious good taste; Jack Lord did not.

"What is it you want. Like I said, I have never been to Georgia."

"You did live in Georgia, Miss Carter, where you were adopted by Amy and Will Carter."

"What?"

He noticed the plate and glass on the floor. "May we sit,

Miss Carter. We have a good deal to tell you that I am afraid will quickly cause you to lose your appetite."

"You already have." She pointed at the opposite sofa, clearing the floor and sitting on the other. "I was adopted?"

He nodded. "You were."

Jodie reached for her glass, moistening her mouth. "I never knew them, I was never told about them."

"Well I assure you that will change very shortly. They were Georgia farmers. Very successful until they were killed in a car accident days before your second birthday."

"Okay, so I was adopted. I still don't understand what you're doing here?"

Abigail Evans answered. "We work for The Southern Colonial Bank in Savannah. Your mother's maiden name was Maters. Her mother, Jessica Maters, your grandmother, was our client before she passed away some years ago closely following the death of her husband Albert."

"I never knew them."

"Actually you did, until your sixth birthday when you were living in Vermont with your father's sister, Karen Carter."

"I haven't seen her for a long time. I ran away years ago."

"We don't care about her," Lord cut in. "We're here about you and your grandmother, acting as her executors. In her will she left explicit instructions that Karen Carter and a Mark Hampton were never for any reason to benefit from your inheritance which took affect on the day after your twenty-first birthday. We've been looking for you since that day, the abandoned home in Vermont being the first of many dead-ends. Apparently, Miss Carter, until your passport and permit were recently issued days apart, you did not exist. Or you chose not to."

"You said abandoned."

"Very abandoned."

Jodie shrugged. "Whatever. Like I said, I ran away. They

weren't nice people."

Abigail nodded, as if she might possibly understand. "They don't factor into this beyond our finding you. They are a non-issue."

"You said inheritance. What inheritance?"

On that note Lord stood, excusing himself. He needed something from the car, returning moments later with a large moving box in his arms.

The man was right when he said Jodie would lose her appetite, Jodie not at all certain she shouldn't still be terrified.

"That's it, my inheritance?"

"In part," he answered. "Your grandmother did not like or trust your aunt or Hampton to keep these effects sacred for you. The box contains your family history in albums and DVDs from before your adoption to your sixth birthday in Vermont with Jessica and Albert, sealed letters from her to you and several heirlooms."

"I don't remember them. My aunt never spoke about about them or my parents," she shrugged, "so I stopped asking."

Abigail Evans recognized the subtle signs that no man would. "Everything is dated, Jodie. From your parents first days as children to their wedding to you. And your grandmother bequeathed something else to you, ensuring you would live a good life, never taken advantage of or cheated by your aunt or Hampton." She took an envelope from her briefcase. "This is what she most wished you to have."

"A letter?"

"Yes, a letter suggesting that you allow us, The Southern Colonial, to continue acting as the investment counsellors of your sixteen-million-dollar inheritance. Which is your decision, of course."

Jodie's mouth opened on cue. "What! Sixteen million?"

"And some serious change." The woman smiled. "Since Jessica's passing you have accrued a little interest."

"Sixteen million dollars?"

"And change. Yes."

"Holy shit! Do you guys want a drink? Wine, vodka, scotch. Because I am definitely having a drink."

Abigail Evans thanked her graciously, declining as Jodie was on her way into her dining room calling out, "Johnnie Walker Blue, Mr. Lord. The really good stuff."

He turned to his associate. "In the name of good client relations, Miss Carter, I don't see that a celebratory cocktail would be improper. Do you Miss Abigail?"

She nodded, suggesting that perhaps a glass of Chardonnay would be very appropriate to the occasion.

*

Jodie had no reason not to keep her money with Southern Colonial, Lord and Evans agreeing they would meet her in the morning to make transferring the funds to their local branch somewhat less complicated.

When they left Evans hugged her the way women do when something good has happened to one of their own, Lord shook her hand, wishing her a pleasant evening which was somewhat of an understatement, thanking her for sharing her friend's very exquisite scotch.

Jodie didn't waste time when they were gone, delving into the box as though Christmas had come months early. Another understatement.

James didn't phone her every night, feeling he would impose, finding that having a younger girlfriend was indeed somewhat of a lifestyle adjustment. And until she could convince him to carry a phone, that she wouldn't call him every minute of every day, she had to wait for him which didn't happen until the next night when he was expected for dinner.

By morning she had gone through every photo album and her grandmother's private letters. The DVDs she would leave until Saturday, when she would watch them with James after her first day of business.

By the time she was dressed, easing into her Miata, she

was exhausted and if James wanted anything but pizza for dinner he could cook the meal himself.

*

"Pizza here with you will be a delightful change from a week of rich gastronomy and noisy restaurants, Jodie." Though despite being her friend, partner and lover for such a short time he sensed immediately that something was avalanching his way. "What can possibly have you effervescing with such frenzied excitement, Jodie, given that Wednesday you were fraught with worry over your Saturday debut as the city's premier artiste?"

"I have something for you, James, something absolutely special." She handed him a cheque and a JW Blue, absolutely giddy. "This is for the car, the studio, this place, and the twenty-four K you gave me. Of course we'll be renegotiating your twenty percent, meaning you're not getting it."

James Castle was not given to spontaneity, always allowing his mind sufficient time to sort and analyze. "I beg to differ, Miss Carter. In the first place a gentleman does not ever retract a gift. Such an act is unthinkable and reprehensible. In the second, and considerably more germane to this most astonishing revelation, what fortuitous windfall would allow such a reversal?"

"I'm wealthy, James. I mean I am absolutely fucking rich. You would not believe." She practically leaped onto him from her corner of the sofa, straddling his legs and kissing his face. "Okay, I'm sorry. Blah, blah, blah. What I meant was, I am very, very rich." She shook her head. "Okay, not James Castle rich, but really rich. This morning I deposited sixteen million into my account. I'm wealthy, James. Thank you, lover. Thank you. I love you, I do. I absolutely do and not for all the things you're doing for me. I don't need your money now. I need and I want you." She kissed him long and hard. "Now you can be sure, absolutely freaking sure."

"Sure regarding what exactly, my darling Jodie?"

"Sure that I love you, asshole, and not your money."

He chuckled, shaking his head. "Nicknames apart, our deal stands. I will destroy this cheque forthwith and your twenty percent remains in effect. You may not need my money, and that's all well and good. As I most certainly do not need yours. That said, a contract is a contract, verbal or otherwise, and binding."

He was stunned, of course, although he hadn't marvelled at his tens of millions in years.

She put her hands to his shoulders. "Okay, what?"

"Not wishing to burst your proverbial bubble, Jodie. However, as one wealthy person to another, may I be privy to the source and the reason behind this exceptional benefaction? Such large sums do not simply fall from the sky."

"My inheritance, from my grandmother."

"Your grandmother?"

"Maternal."

"So you did have one. Because you have been particularly guarded about your lineage other than your parents passing on prematurely, though never saying when. And of your past, which I suspect you would have me believe began here four years ago."

She remained as she was, resting her hands over his on her thighs. "The lawyers yesterday told me I was adopted, something I didn't know. They died in a bad accident when I was two, when my aunt took me to Vermont, and the rest is a very long story, James. Very long and not very good. In fact, nothing about my past is good. Are you ready for that?"

Men of his calibre were never blinded by the best news, nor were they ever deterred by the worst. "I'm sorry for you, Jodie. And, most definitely, I want to hear every detail."

*

Shit! She took a deep breath. This would not turn out well. She told him about the box of memories, that she once lived in Georgia and knew nothing about her adoptive parents beyond what she was beginning to glean from the box, telling him about the lawyers' visit and her meeting at the bank earlier in the day and everything in between.

"I didn't know my grandmother either, not until last night, or my real parents. She told me in a letter that my adoption was a private transaction when I was practically a newborn. She also wrote that I should never trust my aunt or her boyfriend."

"Years too late. Your parents naturally naming your aunt as your legal guardian, to their deserved credit, trusting her with your best interests going forward from whenever such a terrible tragedy as that fatal day might occur."

"Yeah, well, if that's what they wanted, they fucked-up royally. All they did was make her wealthy with money that was legally mine. She was never very nice and the guy with her was the worst. Mark Hampton was vile, an absolute dirt bag. They both were, I mean absolutely fucking sick. She was a travel agent for anyone wanting to get laid on vacation, including them, and when she went to those places on her own she left me at home with him while he did his thing in local pick-up joints."

He nodded, taking her hands in his. "Did he ever touch you indelicately, Jodie?"

She snorted. "Yeah, I guess he did. When I was a kid we always did this movie night thing when she was somewhere at some resort getting laid. Then I got older and this one time they bought me lingerie, which was pretty sick. I know that, but she said it was okay. She said I should start acting like a woman. That's when they started taking me to these freaked-out resorts that were way beyond casual, when he started with the tighter hugs and putting his hands where they didn't belong. Then one night I heard them giggling and laughing in bed, like they wanted me to hear, and sometime later I discovered why. They were spying on me, James, taking videos of me in my bedroom and bathroom and at the pool the times they were gone when I was sun bathing topless or skinny dipping. They were getting off watching me naked and they wanted me to hear."

He leaned into her, wrapping her in his arms. "Degenerates, Jodie, deserving of the worst punishment. Aberrant and appalling degenerates."

She kissed him. "I'm not finished. Things get worse, a lot worse. And I really don't want to go there because I will lose you. I know I will."

"I assure you that will not happen. Now share this overwhelming burden with me. Nothing you say will scare me away."

She hesitated, uncertain and searching for words. "First you must believe that when I told you I was a virgin, I was. You were my first, James. You must believe that because I do. I always will.'

"I do. Of course, I do."

"The last video, all of them dated, was of him in the cinema room after the movie, undressing me and fondling me after he drugged me when she wasn't there. That, before he raped me twice." Warm tears tricked from her eyes onto their hands. "I couldn't finish watching because seeing him touch me that way made me violently ill."

James was stoic, for her, but she could feel his hands tensing against her flesh. "Jodie…"

She put a fingertip to his lips. "I had one glass of wine, that is all. I swear. And when he was finished he put me in my bed and in the morning told me that he helped me to my room where I undressed myself, which I didn't believe because I was a virgin and nothing felt the same. Then the night she came home they couldn't have jumped into bed any faster, getting off watching everything he did to me. That's when I ran, when I found the cameras and the movies. I didn't wait; I ran fast and I ran far. I stole twenty thousand from her safe, I emptied my savings and I ran. I couldn't risk either of them doing that to me again. I was eighteen and I was smart about it, James. I took all the DVDs. They're in a Vermont bank in case I would ever need proof against them. You know, for the twenty grand because she must have called the police. Then I destroyed my cards, my permit and passport. I wanted to hide, to get as far away as possible, and lived in six cities before coming here when I should have been leaving for the U of T in Tampa." Her body slumped slightly. "Not the biggest deal, I suppose, now that I'm rich. Anyway, that's it. Now you know."

"I presume no unfortunate ramification came as a result of that very savage attack."

She shook her head, her expression woeful. "No."

This time he kissed her, tenderly, taking her hands. "Twenty thousand. Good for you, Jodie. Score one for our side…and I presume that's how the lawyers tracked you, your passport and permit?"

"Yeah. But not only was I convinced he would drug and rape me again one day, I discovered that my aunt stole a lot more from me than I did from her. Eleven million more. When I ran I also took my father's will and some of my aunt's banking documents, like her portfolio. He left me four of eight million that is now twenty-two million, or was four years ago, and she never told me. She never intended to. Hampton was a peddler, a real loser she kept around because they were into the same kinky shit. Her agency was nothing but a convenient front for getting herself laid by strangers. She didn't have very many clients and no way did she need the money."

"Their obvious compulsion with you was unspeakably fiendish, Jodie, but your rightful millions and, above all, the despicable rape…these foul creatures can still be prosecuted. And they must."

She shrugged. "I got over it. "

"You believe you did, which is not at all the same." He eased her gently from his lap. "Jodie, I will not be staying with you this evening. And since no one is yet aware of your gallery opening or that you will soon become the finest on Royal Street, please call your friend Earnie Lebeau and delay his presence for a week. We're flying to Vermont tomorrow to resolve these heinous crimes."

Shit! "James, I..."

He put up a hand, shifting her to one side and standing, asking for her phone. He called his pilot, apologizing deeply for imposing on the man's weekend, assuring him the matter was of utmost importance and that he would make amends in the near future. Then he called his lawyer, instructing him to arrive at the airfield by 10:00 AM sharp.

Reaching for her hand he helped Jodie from the sofa, kissing her, adding with a warm and gentle palm against her cheek, "By the way, regarding your earlier uncertainty, I am very sure indeed. That said, regarding the U of T, not pursuing that commendable ambition is not an option for whatever reason. Once we commit we must follow through. Or how does that speak of our character, my darling Jodie? "

He savoured the last few drops of scotch, his eyes telling her the subject was not closed.

With that and the sparkle in her green eyes, he left wondering how much theatrical bullshit would hit the domestic fan this time.

Chapter Thirty-Eight

Sally the housekeeper was in the kitchen preparing dinner for Mrs. Castle since her husband wasn't expected home until sometime Saturday. The girl smiled at him, surprised and happy to see him. She liked him and not because he paid her double the going rate for her temporary skillset, a practice his wife believed was preposterous.

He was a firm believer in dressing for the job you want. Hoping for success as a VIP anything was idle musing at best and without merit, whereas dressing and comporting oneself, studying and preparing oneself in accordance with one's higher expectations of self was commendable and no less crucial. He also believed in helping those who deserved, the way his father once helped him, and Sally clearly deserved.

She possessed a myriad of positive traits with an outstanding academic record because when she wasn't cooking meals or washing dishes or vacuuming their home, she was buried in books. And that she was undeniably cute, impeccably dressed for her age and delightfully created with a warm Latina hue, could not be discounted.

They exchanged waves and greetings. Her command of English was excellent, his Spanish somewhat of a comedy that she sometimes corrected and sometimes did not. He pointed toward the doors leading onto the patio and pool, screwing up his face. Sally nodded, gritting her teeth together and grimacing: a silent and lovely black-eyed portrait screaming a thousand words. His devoted and loving wife would, of course, be pissed because he was home a day early without having the courtesy of calling. However that bullshit would play out.

He paused at the doors, glancing at his watch, telling the girl to stop whatever she was doing and go home, go somewhere. She and the evening were too young and far too lovely not to be out with friends, and with that he retraced his steps and gave her a crisp hundred.

Ignoring the effusive gratitude, some of which was beyond his linguistic pay-grade, he left her with a wide smile and stepped out into the swirling periphery of the shitstorm.

Louise was clearly a woman waging a fierce battle against the passage of time. The one thing she had not yet pampered herself with was tightening her skin with surgical seams, which James believed was merely a matter of time. She was vain and self-absorbed, accustomed to the good life, his good life, and mysteriously still bitching about the time-consuming hard work that made all her luxuries possible when the curious reality was that she should be bitching that he wasn't travelling more frequently.

Strangely, he didn't feel remotely as though he was cheating on her with Jodie. Even stranger was that he hadn't given the impropriety much thought whatsoever.

"Good evening, Louise."

She scarcely acknowledged him from under the wide brim of her sunhat. "Nice of you to drop by. You might have called me. You're becoming more inconsiderate and despicable each day."

"It's even worse than that, Louise. I sent the girl home."

"What!" She swung her legs over the lounger as though stung by a bee. "Why would you do that? She owes me two hours. What were you thinking?"

He eased into a high-backed wicker chair, snorting disgust through his nose. "She doesn't owe you a damn thing, Louise. I pay the girl, not you. And whenever I decide to give her a very well-deserved break from you, I will. I'm sure you'll manage perfectly without her. And let's not have this conversation again."

"You're becoming impossible, James. And quite frankly I cannot believe for a moment that all these business trips of yours require such lengthy absences."

"Most do, some do not. Occasionally, Louise, I simply enjoy being away from you."

She practically tore away her glasses. "You bastard. I cannot believe you said such a horrible thing."

"That would be miserable bastard, if I recall. And horrible befits horrible. That would be you, Louise."

The "Fuck you" was scathing.

"Indeed. However the truth is, Louise, that as I become increasingly inconsiderate in your mind, you are becoming increasingly unpleasant in mine. Quite distasteful, truth be told. In fact the real truth is that you reached the pinnacle of my loathing quite some time ago. The cruel misfortune is that we are condemned to endure each other's existence till death do we part."

Her eyes could not have been more glaring. "Then do something about it."

"That will never happen. Not until one of us is dead, preferably you, which in your case is irrelevant because you're already very dead to me. To which end I have recently had you removed as a beneficiary of my estate, including this house which is wholly mine."

"What! No way. I'll fight that in court."

"You can't. The case would bankrupt you." He reached out, taking a glass and a bottle of chilled white wine from a trolley. "The very sad reality, Louise, is that you should have married Deacon"

"What?"

"Deacon. You should have married your not very secret lover instead of my family name and my billfold."

"You're disgusting. Deac is our dearest friend. I would

never."

James sipped his wine, staring into her eyes without the least emotion. "What you mean to say is, you would always. You always would and you always did, Louise. I daresay you always will."

"You're vile, and you're delusional."

"One thing I am not is delusional. And about Sally, I find your indignation entirely laughable. I recall extremely vividly one particular Friday nine months ago when you shortened her workday by several hours, the day I arrived home early thinking I might surprise you with dinner. When to my very unexpected surprise I witnessed you and your lover fucking heatedly in my pool. And, I must say, Louise, with such urgency, with such intense passion, for as long as I stood there I could not decide whether I should laugh or cry. When in fact I did neither. I left and engaged the services of a private investigator. I had you followed for quite some time. I also had the bedroom, guest and dining room bugged, which made for several evenings of entertaining listening generously peppered with your high-pitched yelps."

"You are the worst fucking bastard."

"No, that would be Deacon from any decent person's perspective." He sipped his wine, relishing the exchange that was long overdue. He enjoyed superior advantage, enjoyed being on top. He chuckled, or he once did.

"What? What's so amusing?"

"You are. You see for these many months I've known about your escapades with Deacon throughout high school and college. And, of course, the highlight of your long-ago and forgotten bachelorette party. I'm surprised you didn't invite him on our honeymoon. Or did you perhaps conceal him somewhere to wildly fuck while I was golfing? Twenty-three years, Louise. You definitely married the wrong man. Too bad for you that Deacon doesn't feel likewise, which I presume crushed your boundless ego years ago. I mean, truthfully, fucking the man these many years and neither of you with sufficient courage to face me."

"Where is all this going? Will you tell him, or does he already know?"

"Neither. Though I suppose you will in time. If you're the least bit decent." He put the rim of the glass to his lips, smirking. "Naturally, the longer you wait the more he'll despise you for making him the village idiot in my eyes. In the meantime I'll find solace, my dear Louise, in knowing that your dirty secret shared with him is ironically now ours."

Louise Castle buried her flushed face in cupped hands. "You're right, I should have married Cedric. I love him. I always have, more than I could ever love you. But I was fond of you in the beginning, and now you're punishing me."

"I am indeed and more than you think, Louise, for all those years of mocking me, laughing at me and, above all, your dishonesty." He paused, thinking of Jodie and grinning. "I daresay you are absolutely fucked."

"You're cruel."

He shook his head, pursing his lips. "Appropriately vindictive, never cruel. Cruel was seeing you in my pool, now let me bring this delightful heart-to-heart to an abrupt conclusion. From this day forward you will sleep in my guest room and as for our recent abstinence from pleasures of the flesh…you are done because I will never again force my mind or by body into that sullied place."

She lurched forward, crashing an open hand against his cheek. "You're disgusting."

"Yes, indeed. Well, as I was saying, the weekends going forward are yours to enjoy. That is the final gift I shall ever give you. We will no longer vacation together and you will no longer set foot in the Lear or the limo. There will be no more hypocritical dinners with Deacon, social evenings or festive mockeries. In addition to which your allowance is henceforth reduced from a foolishly generous 100 thousand each year to nothing. Regrettably, as much as I will abhor living my weekdays with a whore, I will not maintain or dress one. All I insist upon is that you have him gone before noon on Saturday. I'll tolerate one night, but I will not turn my home into a bordello."

"Then divorce me. Have the decency to do that at least."

"Louise Laplante espousing decency. Good one." He stood, his laughter loud and derisive. "No. And if you divorce me you would never survive on your meagre earnings. You're spoiled beyond description. You have not the slightest idea about limitations. Nor would Deacon come running for more than a plunge into your metaphoric pool. He is not merely a confirmed bachelor; despite your enviable features and inexhaustible proclivities, he has a morbid dread of the ball and chain. He would also forsake a considerable fortune in addition to now being excluded from my will. And on that final note, please remove your wardrobe from my room this very evening and remake my bed to a sanitary state or I will terminate Sally with a generous settlement that will see her comfortably through school and leave you to relearn the most basic of domestic skills."

"You're serious."

"Extremely. I will also be away a few days attending to personal business in Vermont. Though not to worry, make good use of your room and your bed to the fullest extent. I will not hear a word of your torrid ecstasy. That stopped sometime ago when the scripts became predictably monotonous."

*

Without another word he strode into the house and into his study, putting her and Deacon from his mind. He spent the evening preparing for Vermont, forgoing dinner in favour of the world's best scotch, sufficiently familiar with corporate law to believe Jodie's recent good fortune would very soon double. He also believed that criminal law would ensure prison terms for the perverse aunt and, he hoped with all his heart, once incarcerated, a more poetic justice for the predator boyfriend.

Louise remained on the deck a good while, fuming, devastated and feeling humiliated. She remembered that Friday afternoon with Cedric clearly, horrified that her husband had stood watching them, that he was intruding on her most intimate moments and conversations with the man she profoundly loved, making that cherished love dirty.

She despised him beyond words and, despite never once loving him beyond friendship, she thought for a fleeting moment that she could actually kill the heartless bastard for callously and abruptly destroying her life and very likely her future with Cedric.

He was right though. The longer she waited the worse Cedric's reaction would be. She could not imagine the men facing each other, let alone working together once Cedric became aware. Nor could she imagine telling him or the look on his face.

She pushed her weight from the cushy lounger, trudging her way into the house and the bedroom where she would never again sleep. She went countless times from one room to the other, disheartened, and by James' usual midnight bedtime her wardrobe, jewellery and toiletries were arranged in the guest room where she sat curled into her récamier swirling a deep red Pinot Noir and staring helplessly at her phone.

Chapter Thirty-Nine

Saturday was a typical spring day in the sweaty Swamp. By 10:00 AM the air was heated with a blinding sun and high humidity that dampened clothing and surreptitiously stole innocent breaths.

He was thankful Louise remained in her room while he began his day and packed for the trip. He had nothing to say, nothing he wanted to hear; in fact he harboured no doubt whatsoever that he ever would, pondering that complexity until his delightful and captivating Jodie invaded his mind giving him pause and courage. Her life was so much more real and street-level than his.

He coughed a laugh. So, yeah. She would without question resolve the issue with a requisite "absolutely" or "asshole".

With that thought brightening his mood he left home, kissing her at her door half an hour later. Then promptly at 10:00 she was hugging the pilot and shaking hands with her first-ever legal counsel, throughout the flight recounting her life story and showing him the grandmother's will and letter.

Landing in Burlington they went to lunch before arriving at Jodie's bank where they were offered a private office for the short time the lawyer spent examining Jodie's preponderance of evidence against her aunt and Hampton. What he did not see, did not want to see, were the videos. That was strictly a police matter that would happen within a very few minutes.

At police headquarters the lawyer gave the receptionist his card, asking to meet with the highest ranking female detective regarding a matter of molestation of a minor and pornography. Moments later they were sitting with Lieutenant Sandra Dobbs and, again, Jodie Carter recounted her life up to the evening she told James Castle to go fuck himself, omitting that she had taken twenty thousand from the safe, killed them, and had left the house abandoned.

When she finished Dobbs took less than an hour alone with her, skimming through the first set of DVDs and viewing the first several minutes of Mark Hampton drugging and violating her. Then before examining her parents' will and her aunt's financial portfolio, sealing the evidence for the courts, she metamorphosed from cop to woman giving Jodie a tight and commiserating hug.

"So what happens now?"

"You'll make a formal statement, I'll call the state attorney who will freeze their assets, we'll arrest them and they won't go home anytime soon. He'll get twenty or more for aggravated sexual assault because he made you physically helpless with drugs and another ten for producing child porn. She'll get about the same for aiding and abetting the crime and the child porn and probably an extra five for defrauding you. They'll also be put on the sex offender registry and have a very bad time in prison, him especially."

"When?"

"Once we arrest them. They won't get bail, they're a flight risk. Whatever they're doing now they won't again for a very long time."

"Good."

Sandra Dobbs nodded, reaching for her phone. When she finished with the state attorney, she reunited Jodie with James and the lawyer. They were not invited to the party. That said, if they were inclined to stick around, wanting or needing to see Carter and Hampton brought in, she did not have a problem with that.

She left minutes later with uniformed officers, thanking Jodie for the offer, however she wouldn't be needing a key. That wasn't quite how things got done, until she called her precinct shortly after requesting that Jodie and the men meet her at the Carter residence. Apparently Dobbs did need the key and when they arrived they understood why. The place was in a state of incredible disrepair and abandoned, Jodie stepping from the car in absolute disbelief.

The immediate property surrounding the once three-story luxury home was unrecognizable. The gravel driveway leading to the garage was gone, fully covered over with tall swaying grass and wild flowers. The concrete walkway leading from a once tiered and colourful garden to the front steps was uneven and cracked with grass growing through, now leading from a pile of mud jumbled with weeds and crabgrass. The steps were warped and split; the banister and porch dried out and spotted with flecks of faded paint; the windows, coated with years of dust and dirt, impossible to see through. Trees in the distance felled by severe winter winds and heavy summer downpours lay uprooted and crisscrossed.

Inside, the lieutenant leading the way, the uniforms trailing behind, not a single stick of furniture or piece or clothing was left.

Jodie gave them the grand tour. She took them to her room, showing them the damage caused when Hampton smashed at the vent to remove the lens, and a similar mess in her bathroom. She took them to the master suite where they saw a damaged control box and mount with the copper tips of mangled wires hanging bare.

Looking down over the railing, the once crystal clear pool was a shallow bowl of discoloured and fetid rainwater filled with rotting leaves and brush; the concrete was bleached by the sun and cracked, the stainless steel ladders shifted from their footings.

She took them to the cinema room where the rape occurred and into an empty garage. The question was, why empty a house worth a few mil and not sell it? Where did they go and when? Jodie suggesting maybe somewhere that needed a brothel, which didn't quite satisfy the cops or amuse the men standing with her.

No one cleared out a house that size without a paper trail, six of them with the same puzzled expressions standing in a circle until Sandra Dobbs returned the key to Jodie and the lawyer suggested that Karen Carter's Burlington Bank branch would very well be the source of several answers.

What they discovered was that the only transactions over the past four years were pre-authorized payments and any further information would require a warrant which was phoned in by Dobbs and faxed to the manager's private line within the half-hour.

The twenty-two million had risen by an impressive ten percent and monthly statements reflected no activity whatsoever over those years, three notable transactions preceding the inactivity being the cartage company, the purchase of a boat, and a few thousand more for a Houston storage company. Nothing else, not for food, or lodging, gas or booze when the Carter woman would never demean herself by drinking anything costing less than a hundred.

Reading the will, hearing about the abandoned property and a modified version of Jodie's ill treatment, the manager agreed that Jodie likely was owed those funds. However he would have to confer with the bank's legal team and receive authorization from the head office before disbursing monies from the account. And that would not happen until Monday, earliest.

With that disappointment they agreed they should meet Tuesday morning and, leaving Sandra Dobbs to her investigation, flew home.

*

At the airfield the lawyer went home, the pilot stayed behind to file requisite paperwork and James went home with Jodie, stopping first at his preferred wine and spirit store for a '98 Château Petit Village Pomerol, that Jodie thought was a tad over the top for an all-dressed on her floor. He ignored her, adding a JW Blue and Ultimat to the cart.

At home they showered away the long day, changing into casuals, and Jodie ordered a pizza while James attended their cocktails.

"Your lawyer's a pretty cool guy for his age."

"I'm sure he'll be very pleased with your appraisal. He's also the very best. You'll have the twelve million and change by Wednesday and eventually the full sale price of that property whose adverse possession we'll put into effect on Monday. You're a close relative, the taxes are not in arrears, and we have irrefutable proof that the woman did in fact abandon the building and its lands." He raised his glass in a toast. "Congratulations, Jodie. You now have a country estate, albeit somewhat in need of a paint brush."

"No, I don't. I'll demolish the thing and sell the land."

"A wholly understandable stance. However a strategy more damaging to the horrid woman's ego would be you selling both for a dollar. You don't need the money nor the expense and I daresay you would create a very high level of interest amongst the locals."

"Then that's what I'll do."

"We'll get them, Jodie. No one leaves that kind of money untouched, not for any extended period. One day they'll wake feeling overconfident that the statute of limitation has expired, which is not the case. There is no limitation for what they did. We will get them, Jodie."

She giggled. "Yeah."

The intercom's buzzer ended the conversation that would have no further meaning until Tuesday at police headquarters with Lieutenant Dobbs and the Carter woman's bank manager already perplexed by the prospect of losing the many millions, James answering the door since Jodie could not unless she was the quintessential tip.

Pizza was always best when served on the floor with delicious French wine. Particularly, James discovered while eating on any floor for the first time, while his hostess and lover was sitting inches away cross-legged and all-dressed in flimsy silk tap pants and a camisole. Indeed.

"Jodie, may I stay the evening with you?"

"Excuse me?" She shook her head, rolling her eyes, pretending exasperation. "James, please do not become an absolute...," she stopped herself, "idiot after all we've shared. Yes, you're staying."

He snorted, gazing blindly into the reflections on the polished floor. "I apologize, Jodie. After all these many years with one woman, rehabilitating oneself is difficult. I fear you'll have to bear with me a while longer."

"After all you've done for me, are you serious? I will definitely do that for you. I meant what I said, James. I love you. Weird, lover. Big time weird, but I do."

"As I do you, Jodie." He chuckled. "And yes, very weird. Yet I do love you as well and I suppose in the shorter term I should create a special name for you that expresses how I feel."

She bit into her pizza, her green eyes sparkling, her face imbued with an alluring soft shade of pink. She was laughing without a sound. The rigid titanium stick up his tight Southern ass was absolutely beginning to soften and, in that instant, she felt deeply sorry for him.

"James, all those months you were looking at me through that little spy glass of yours, why? I mean, why would you do that?"

"You know why."

"I know what you told me, which wasn't much. Now tell me the real why because now you know everything about me, almost, and I don't know anything about James Castle except that you're freaking rich, good-looking, good in bed, or at least I assume you are, and too civilized for the real world. You are also very unhappy. So what is really up with you," she sipped her wine, "and how do I fit in to this messed-up life of yours? Because as fantastic as this is, you and me, I believe somebody's done something really bad, really pissing you off, and you have to act on that."

"An excellent conclusion, if not somewhat understated."

"Don't you think I should know why since, when we're done here, we'll be getting all hot and sweaty in my bed?"

She had a point and by the time the pizza was finished, and the wine bottle stood empty, Jodie had heard a concise version of James Castle's life.

"No shit."

"Actually I would suggest very much the inverse."

"That's since before I was even born."

"Yes. And I thank you for that very disturbing qualification."

"I don't see the problem. Dump her and get on with life. Shit happens. The guy must have a clue unless she's an absolute bitch. She'll get what she deserves, which is nothing; he'll get her when he needs some nookie, because that's what he loves most about her, and you'll have me all the time because you love me for more than," she leaned into him, wrapping her arms around his neck, kissing him, "you know, my incredibly desirable body."

"Indeed, except for a particular personality deficiency one might regard as male pride."

"You mean male ego. Sort of like that pissing contest you guys do."

He creased his brow. "Sort of like no such thing. Nor have I ever participated in that particular sport. The fact is, that despite our binding contract, the original investment was wholly mine. Without me C & D would not exist. Deacon put nothing into the company upfront and that, my sweet Jodie, would constitute a major slap in the face. As well, whatever incriminating evidence I currently possess against her is now most likely nullified by you and me. Which, to me, is exceedingly more important and pleasing than her."

"So what's the plan, lover? This whole thing is absolutely twisted and nothing's changed except he's probably not bagging her in your home." She shrugged. "So tell the guy yourself; I would just to see the stunned look on his face."

"All things work out in time, Jodie. The life you are now living is a prime example. For starters, she's in the guest room along with her worldly goods and I've cut her allowance. This for a woman who cannot tolerate being ignored. Believe me, this is the best way and she is by far her worst enemy. She can fornicate with him as often as she pleases while in my home, continuing the ruse when I'm elsewhere, or explain to him why she is not. And that would drastically alter their dynamic because he will not take her in, nor will he ever, leaving her completely on her own to continue as his on-demand corporeal companion, a woman who's forgotten how to boil water. So yes, she will leave me one day soon and will not receive a dime. As for Deacon, I would never ruin myself or the company with pouty foolishness. We're stuck with each other as he continues in blissful ignorance or until he sacrifices a vast sum of money. And, as for us, which is far more important, I foresee a somewhat less pretentious home devoid of haunting memories sometime in the not very distant future."

Chapter Forty

Sunday morning Louise Castle woke late, trapped between two realities and making the worst decision of her life that would soon make the first seem fanciful.

She loved Cedric too much to leave the man she loathed. Losing the hundred thousand was devastating enough, but divorce would practically put her on the street. She would lose face and her social circles would collapse; she would risk losing Cedric who would never choose her over the company, never ask her to move in let alone marry her. They had been lovers in love too many years to pretend anything else, despite feeling all those years that she was cheating on Cedric with James.

*

Sunday James and Jodie spent the morning at home being lovers and their afternoon in the park acting like lovers, not letting Vermont, Louise or Deacon spoil their day or invade their evening when Jodie had absolutely no difficulty staying awake until midnight.

Monday James made the first of his usual three out-of-office calls to his secretary, staying current without speaking with Deacon. Then he flew to Burlington with Jodie and the lawyer where they initiated proceedings for the adverse possession of the Carter property. That's when the call came through from Sandra Dobbs asking that they come by police headquarters "because nothing about Mark Hampton or Karen Carter is making sense. They simply disappeared, vaporized into thin air."

"How is that even possible?" Jodie asked. "They had cars. They bought a boat and were headed for Houston."

"His ex-employer confirmed Houston and the camping trip, happy to see him go. Apparently Hampton wasn't very good at what he did, yet out of the blue he was making a mega leap into big-time management. A job that never existed. Nor was there ever a Mark Hampton or Karen Carter anywhere in Texas. Just everything they owned for a short while including a Lexus."

"Possibly an accident, Lieutenant." James Castle offered. "They were on a road trip after all."

"Nope. No dead bodies, no hospital records, and the Houston storage people sold everything at auction after a two-year no show, including the luxury ride. The cartage people here did recall that she was more than a little full of herself, the marine guys saying pretty much the same, that she was worth looking at twice, buying a boat for a boyfriend who was lucky for more reasons than getting a boat. Which explained the boat in part, but not Karen Carter: Miss Sophistication with millions in the bank who ran a travel agency cum swap club sleeping on the ground in a tent and cruising with her chin on her knees in something the size of a rowboat." She turned to Jodie. "Wherever they are now, they're getting from A to Z by bus and taxi because no permit or registration renewal exists in any state for either one of them."

"They must be somewhere, Detective," James tried, "perhaps surviving on menial labour until they feel sufficiently safe to surface once again."

Jodie cut in. "James, we're talking about Karen Carter here, someone who despised doing dishes and her own laundry. And he wasn't any better. They were absolutely full of themselves."

"Then they had cash in the safe," Sandra Dobbs replied, "initially anyway. We're talking about four years here. That's a long time to survive off pocket money. The storage thing was meant to confuse us hounds. That's a given, and I have to assume the Hummer got them from campground to campground or state parks on back roads, dumping it and the boat the more nervous they got or before the tags expired, keeping a low profile without realizing you didn't come to us when you should have." She leaned back, waving a finger at Jodie. "And let's be clear, missy, that was a lecture. Now, for all we know, they might have cruised down the Mississippi into New Orleans."

"A grievous thought at best, Lieutenant, if not for Louisiana laws regarding such vile creatures being somewhat more stringent than your own."

"Then I'm stuck, because who drags a boat behind a big yellow truck with bright green out-of-state tags to run and hide? Who does that?"

"It's creepy thinking they're somewhere walking around, doing whatever," Jodie mused out loud.

"Until they mess up, because they all do."

Yeah, which wasn't very likely, Jodie kept to herself.

*

They left Sandra Dobbs late in the day with assurances of periodic updates.

Ending their day at the hotel in separate suites for the sake of Jodie's reputation, James Castle placed his third call to his secretary. He was to call his wife that evening, something he hadn't done nor wanted to do in nearly a year. First, though, she transferred him to Deacon's office on a pretext that came readily to mind, a brief conversation that immediately made him seethe. Not for what Deacon said, but more precisely his tone. The man was as cool, calm and as collected as always. Not the slightest trace of a tremor affected his voice, meaning the duplicitous shrew had not yet told him.

Though never one for delaying the delivery of unwelcome news, he called her; he asked a single question, got the curt answer he was expecting and disconnected. Stalemate. Then, crossing the hall, he knocked first and stepped into

Jodie's suite.

"I believe that in the short-term at least, I misinterpreted the situation and misread the woman. She's retaliating against my amendments to her lavish lifestyle, depriving her of future 500-dollar handbags and thousand-dollar dresses. Taking me down with her, as it were."

"She won't tell him?"

"Foolishly she will not, which of course will eventually lead to the loss of house, home and Deacon. She's made a very critical error, Jodie, which for the duration places me in somewhat of a peculiar situation."

"What will you do?"

"Make her life significantly less pleasant by terminating the young housekeeper and, worse, ignoring her. She won't last very long when faced with daily drudgery and isolation."

Jodie's lips curled into a wide grin.

"Now what might be flourishing in that artistic mind of yours, inspiring your apparent glee?"

She giggled. "I can boil water, lover."

"Indeed."

With that James left her, changing for dinner and a pleasant summer evening of holding hands and strolling through art galleries and boutiques before nightcaps in his suite and ardent loving in hers.

Tuesday morning they went separately to the lobby, meeting the lawyer for breakfast and arriving at the bank promptly at nine. By ten o'clock Jodie Carter's fortune had practically doubled to twenty-nine million, leaving the Burlington Bank manager disappointed and his Southern Colonial counterpart elated.

Then she paid for lunch, which she insisted upon, before flying home where James stayed with her through to the following Monday when he travelled to Sacramento for the week.

The next day, however, he went to Sally's campus

apartment sadly dismissing the girl with a believable explanation of a pending divorce, a two-year severance, and a cheque that would cover her entire college education with a suggestion that he should be amongst the first to receive her curriculum vitae. Thursday and Friday, except for a quick end of the week meeting with Deacon that left him completely mystified by the man, they enjoyed their time together at *Jodie's Art*.

Saturday she woke early for the first day in her life as a businesswoman, as CEO, CFO, manager, sales clerk, maintenance woman and in-house artiste renommée of *Jodie's Art*. She made coffee, then breakfast and more coffee. She showered while he stood appreciating every naked inch of her and chuckling. She ignored him, dressing, then undressing, dressing again in long then short, tight then loose, until she got things right.

Kissing him at the door she hurried to her car muttering something about cheap assholes never coming into her boutique. He had nothing to add, shrugging and closing the door, fairly certain she wasn't talking about him.

*

Jodie opened the doors of her boutique at 10:00, still mumbling until her first client sauntered in five minutes later in the person of one James Castle. He was a man who drew attention to himself no matter the room he was in, a man who exuded wealth and success no matter the clothes on his back, which on that auspicious day were oxblood loafers and navy blue slacks, a white button-down open at the collar and pale blue blazer sporting a pinkish silk pocket hanky.

Her second client ambled in on the half-hour equally enthusiastic, greeting her with a warm embrace that lifted her feet from the floor.

Earnie Lebeau was an impressive character at six-foot-six and a solid 380 pounds of black do not fuck with me dressed entirely in white from his hand-crafted shoes to the silk pocket hanky adorning his three-piece tailored suit, his Cajon drawl and casual manner belying his true nature. He was an astute and educated businessman and not someone to make unnecessarily unhappy.

Castle and Lebeau had never met, though they recognized each other by Jodie's respective descriptions of them, clasping each other's hand before wandering through her gallery critiquing and praising her work while she stood alone by the cash with her arms crossed, shaking her head, thinking they were idiots. Nice guys, but idiots who didn't know shit from sugar about art and, at that moment in time, seeing them together, she had an epiphany.

Lebeau purchased two pieces for his wife, commissioning six more for his lounge on the condition they appeal to his sophisticated patrons. James did likewise for his home office and another six for the lobby and his office at C & D, not to be outdone, Jodie asking if they were coming back on Sunday because it was already 11:00 and no one else had come in. However no sooner had she said that than someone did. An older woman very fashionably dressed who betrayed no indication whatsoever that she might know James Castle, although she would later surprise him by not putting the charge on her corporate expenses.

However the men left before the woman made her selections, neither was accustomed to idle moments in their days, James agreeing that he would drop into Earnie Lebeau's lounge with Jodie later that evening and hopefully with good news.

By noon she wasn't anywhere near being excited, one person strolling in near 1:00 and a few more by 2:00, from which point the door didn't stop opening. In fact she was so busy, if not a little flustered, she had no time to think of James, let alone calling him, and by closing at six o'clock her receipts totalled over five grand that did not include the commissioned work she would begin the next day.

Needing a few moments to breathe and decompress before going home, she locked the doors; she hung a *thank-you* on her display window, went into the back, and sobbed.

Seeing her arrive home shortly after with reddened eyes, James naturally assumed the worst. Disappointed for her and fully prepared to pamper her with kindness, he wasn't the least prepared when she leaped into his arms, testing her very short skirt with her legs wrapped around his waist, and screamed "five thousand, lover" into his ear that he was certain would ring for several hours.

In spite of which their dinner was a sumptuous and romantic celebration with champagne, soft music and dancing in a quaint courtyard setting. James was elegantly dressed in a black tailored suit and crisp white shirt minus his tie; she was dressed in a short sequinned dress, three-inch pumps and, he mused, not much else. Though when he enquired she patted his cheek and told him he would have to wait until he brought her home. Then, when that should have happened, thanking him for another lovely evening, believing he was taking her home for urgent discovery, she wondered why not when for some reason he parked a block from the corner she would forever remember.

Lebeau had their table ready. His lounge wasn't exactly a gentlemen's club, however not doing one's best at impersonating one would generally end badly and not for Earnie. The waitresses were all young and attractive university students whose boyfriends could never afford Lebeau's cocktails or wine.

The place was a class act with some girls wearing teddies and heels, others meandering between tables in babydoll sets, others in panties and bras, some backless and some not, others in mesh or vinyl bodysuits. Though he never told the girls what they should wear, each of them sharing half the purchase price of whatever garment they chose to model for the evening, James chortling when hearing that Earnie Lebeau's was as much a lingerie boutique as a very popular watering hole for sophisticated gents and their companions.

For Lebeau's part, when hearing the day's best news, his best champagne was on the house and, by the time they left, Jodie owned several new pieces of lingerie and James was adamant he would become a regular patron.

Chapter Forty-One

Sunday Jodie began her day a little more energized and positive, sitting at her easel creating affordable miniatures until practically falling from her stool when the lawyer and pilot walked in together with their wives whose portraits they were commissioning for their respective offices. Both men assuring her they were in no way part of a James Castle conspiracy to boost her morale.

They were her first clients of the day, though not the last, James wisely adopting a more guarded stance when she arrived home exhausted but with her green eyes dry and bright.

Monday the chauffeur came for him when the morning sun was barely a glow, an hour later he was in the air soaring toward San Antonio. Meanwhile Jodie lay in bed with a good deal on her mind, deciding she needed help on a couple of fronts. She had quickly discovered that managing everything required of her at the gallery was a daunting expectation, impossible, preventing her from focusing on what she did best, without which she would have no gallery. And James fully agreed the previous evening, given her meteoric rise to fame, suggesting that she figure things out sooner than later. And she did. She would hire a small sales team to share the seventy-hour workweek and a cleaning service to maintain the place.

Her other issue was more complex, extremely delicate, and she wasn't at all sure how to approach Earnie Lebeau. Or how he would react when she did. The man was charming and urbane, but he also knew things. He knew how to get things done and he had connections. Not everyone who went into his lingerie lounge was a refined and worldly billionaire who she loved.

She decided she would call him. She would meet him at the lounge or invite him for a late dinner; she had something important to discuss because what she desperately needed was something she could not figure out on her own.

*

At *Jodie's Art* she first created *Experienced Help Wanted* signs for each of her display windows, she called a maintenance service she'd seen in adjacent stores, hiring them on a trial basis before calling Lebeau and leaving a message saying, you know, whenever. He returned the call midday suggesting that she drop in for a drink after she closed.

And that's what she did, more nervous with each passing hour until she locked her doors and within a couple of minutes walked through his, each of his girls remembering her with friendly smiles and waves as his thirty-something hostess guided her to his office that totally surprised her. Where she had created in her mind an illusion of something dark and ominous, a gun or two and a pit bull or Doberman poised on its haunches in the corner, she stepped into a large space that was bright and welcoming; the walls were lined with all manner of books and a world map dotted with red pins and thread tracing his travels.

What most caught her attention, what creased her face with concern, was his neatly arranged desk bordered with a row of brass and chrome framed photos of the family—Jodie realizing this would not be easy. That said, she had come to him for help with single-minded purpose and determination.

He waved his arm in a theatrical arc, gesturing for her to sit. "How was your day, Jodie?"

"Fabulous, really great."

"Well you do not look like you have had a fabulous and really great day, more like something serious is going on with you. What is it, chérie?"

"I have a problem and I think you can help me. I hope you can help me."

Lebeau leaned over his desk, planting one huge arm over the other. "Is someone causing you grief, chérie?"

"In a way, I suppose. It's sort of complicated, Earnie. The thing is, I'm actually here about James."

He beamed a big and bright toothy smile. "I like the man, a disappearing breed even down here. I cannot imagine a man of that stature having difficulties he cannot navigate on his own. What is this about?"

"It's a long and absolutely weird story, Earnie."

"Then we should have that drink and moisten our throats." A moment later a waitress came in wearing stockings, garters, panties and a bustier, carrying an Ultimat and soda and his Bowmore single malt, neat. When she was gone, "Now what is this weird thing, chérie?"

She told him about Louise Castle and Deacon in as much detail as she could, about the day she first met James Castle and how, Lebeau recalling his own vivid memories of that terrible day. She explained Louise Castle's refusal to divorce him and what James stood to lose if he acted first.

Earnie Lebeau reached across the desk for a chrome and brass frame, sharing the photograph with Jodie. "I have been with the lady thirty years. I met her in college and started this place with her on a shoestring. I did the bar, she did the tables. Things were not very easy until one evening one year later, when walking home we passed a lingerie store and the rest is history. The idea was entirely hers, one I did not much like at first. The next night we had maybe a dozen men come in, the second night we had several dozen men and their ladies. We hired a girl on the spot to help us that evening, a customer we sent shopping the next day and by the end of that month we had six girls." He chuckled. "Then came the kids one, two and three that we still cannot get rid of and here I am. Long story short, chérie, with all the dozens of beauties I have had out there working their way through college in those skimpy little outfits," he paused, "not one time." He replaced the photograph. "This Deacon fellow, and the wife," he shook his head, "I cannot pretend to imagine what went through James' mind that day. What I can tell you is that he was not thinking anything good. Righteous perhaps, and very justifiable. But nothing good."

"The problem is, Earnie, C & D is rightfully his company. He simply made a huge mistake making Deacon his equal."

"It would seem he has made several: the best friend, the best man, the girlfriend then wife. And all those years." He swirled his scotch. "I am truly sitting here wondering why Deacon is not already the late Mr. Deacon."

"Because that would put James on death row, he would lose the company and his wife would be the take-all winner. That's sort of counterproductive."

"So what is it you want, Jodie? What exactly do you believe I can do for you, chérie?"

"I want James to myself, Earnie. I want him to feel free, not trapped. And I want them hurting the way they hurt him, and a whole lot more for all those years. Not that I want them dead; not that I wouldn't do that for James. Because I would." She sipped her vodka, managing a normal heartbeat. "They've been laughing at him all these years while all he's done is make Deacon super wealthy and give his wife the world. He's a nice guy, Earnie. He doesn't deserve what they did or what they're doing. That guy, the one who killed himself on the corner weeks ago, his name was Parker Danson. He was a nice guy also. Now he's dead because of a cheating wife who didn't care at all that he killed himself, happy and smiling and still screwing some other guy before Parker was even buried." She saw the question in Lebeau's eyes. "Yeah, I did his portrait. Just not the one I gave her that she won't ever forget. I made very certain of that. That's what I want for James, that Louise Castle and Cedric

Deacon never forget how despicable they are. I want them holding hands and taking a lover's leap off some bridge. That's what they deserve. The question is, how do I accomplish that? Like getting Deacon to shun her so James can finally dump the bitch and not get burned. James losing a mansion is peanuts and he's got the money to bury her in court. There is no prenup, because back in the day they had no crystal ball. She went freelance and he went with Deacon. But he does have proof against her, against both of them." She thought for a moment, staring at the glass in her lap, shaking her head. "You know what, forget the bridge idea, Earnie. Way too romantic and way too fast. I want tragedy, not romance."

"This thing you want may be good for James, Jodie. How good will all this be for you? We are talking serious business here. You must be prepared for that, chérie?"

"Very sure. And because I'll have James, very good for me. And I'm not talking about his millions either. I don't need them. Since meeting him, and because of him, my fortunes have changed." She sipped her vodka. "What I mean is, I have one, a fortune, and can pay any price for whatever you can help me do. Any price, Earnie. No limit."

"Well that is good to hear because most things dark and dirty cost good money, chérie. Be aware of that."

She pointed at the photograph of Lebeau's wife. "James never cheated on her, not once, like you. But could you ever imagine coming home...?"

Lebeau raised an open palm, grinning. "Chérie in that very whimsical scenario there is a dead man floating in my pool."

"Yeah, because you would kill him."

He didn't answer quickly, studying her, bringing his clenched fists together at his chin "No, I would not. He would happily and willingly kill himself, Jodie, without the slightest hesitation. Meaning that you do not wait for them to jump from any bridge, or push them and get your lovely little self in prison.

Instead you ask them politely and calmly to jump…et voila, chérie. They jump, like they are leaping into nirvana."

What! She put her glass aside, letting out an exasperated breath, wondering why all of a sudden he was talking bullshit. "Yeah, right. And how exactly does that work? I'm being serious here, Earnie."

He nodded, grimly. "I am very aware of that. I am talking about scopolamine, chérie, what the street calls Devil's Breath. Extremely scary shit that will block their free will and make them into zombie-like children in a blink. You will literally control their minds and their bodies and they will have zero recollection of whatever it is you would like them to do. Zero. So yes, we are both being very serious here."

"I'm sorry. But how do I get this thing?"

"You do not, I do at two grand a gram. Enough for them to fly like fairies off whatever bridge you choose. That said, if you do this, you will listen up and you will do everything I say the way I say it. This will not be a walk in the park. And Jodie, once you have it, I was never involved with you. Understand that."

"I'll bring the money tomorrow after I close. Now how do I use this Devil's Breath?"

"The first thing is you take responsibility, you learn on your own what exactly it can do and how. Now go home and do that. Come up with the best feasible plan, something simple and doable. Getting fancy will only get you seriously hurt and into serious trouble and let us not talk anymore about killing anyone." He pushed his bulk from his desk. "Tomorrow, once I hear your plan, I will tell you what you do not know with a crash course on how you will not mess-up."

With that he stood, hugging her before escorting her through the lounge to the entrance where they wished each other a pleasant evening.

*

Sleeping was impossible and drawing would of necessity wait

until she was in her boutique the next day. Her mind was supercharged with a maelstrom of fanciful images and revived emotions she hadn't felt since first fleeing Vermont.

Instead she lay in bed with her laptop and a glass of Bordeaux, reading, more stirred with each site she visited. Scopolamine was everything Earnie had promised, and more. All she had to do was determine the absolute best way of making them willing and forgetful zombies who would do whatever she wished.

She remembered what Earnie said about the imaginary dead guy in his pool, and that's what she wanted. She didn't need them dead; she needed them hurting each other in a meaningful way that would free James of the bitch and get him full control of his own company. That's what she wanted; that's what she would make happen and she had the solution, which made the next day painfully long.

*

Earnie Lebeau was larger than life behind his desk with an untouched Bowmore neat within easy reach. Jodie Carter's Ultimat and soda was waiting for her on a table by the soft leather chair she had warmed the evening before.

When she came in he stood. Jodie, still delightfully fascinated by Southern gentility that for generations was outdated in the north, placed a thin envelope on the desk before sitting.

"Two thousand in hundreds. Is that okay?"

"That is okay. More importantly, how are you? I presume that with this you intend proceeding as previously discussed?"

"Yes. And I believe I have a very simple and doable plan, as previously discussed."

He reached for his drink, slouching slightly into his seat. "I am listening, chérie."

She didn't hesitate. "James is home with me every Friday night; this Friday I'm telling him I had a small problem with my car, a recall or something. Then Saturday I'll borrow his car because I'm missing something in the pantry for making him a special breakfast or whatever and when I'm gone I'll have his house key copied."

"And when exactly do you sneak in, Jodie, with your cloak and your dagger? And what will you do once you are inside?"

"On a Friday, when he's gone. I hired an assistant today and should have a second body in place sometime next week. So not this week or the next, the week after when James is far away on business. You know, giving him an alibi completely absolving him of any complicity and giving myself two full weeks to get things right. Friday because that's when Deacon is always with her at the house, which couldn't be more perfect. Sort of like a double whammy."

Lebeau sipped his single malt. "Which also could not be more peculiar that Deacon has not yet figured out that James is virtually opening the door those nights. I am hoping this gets better, chérie. Much better, in fact."

"It does get better because Deacon never leaves the office early, but she does. Friday is when she would always do her groceries for weekends and entertaining with James. Now she goes out shopping for something that will make her play night at home with Deacon something special. That's my plan, without a cloak or dagger, Earnie. In broad daylight Friday afternoon wearing trendy boots, designer blue jeans and a chic sweater that are not from my closet, that will make me fit in, that I'll get rid of when I'm finished along with leather gloves, an absolutely cool hat, glasses and, once I get inside, a surgical mask." She giggled. "Besides being cautious a young lady must also appear fashionable, especially in that snooty neighbourhood." She returned his smile, then got serious. "Yeah, I did my homework. Scopolamine is everything you said, absolutely bad shit and before you ask, Earnie...no cameras. There is a code because James is a cautious man, the same code he uses for everything else. Anyway," she reached for her vodka and soda, sipping, "that's where I'll get her, from behind whatever door she comes in through with her hands full of goodies. This Devil stuff works in an instant, Earnie She won't have time to drop her bags before she invites me in for a glass of wine."

"Good, you are inside. Now how does this story end?" was the logical next question, Lebeau becoming guardedly impressed. "Tell me something I do not know."

"The actual ending is a work in progress, Earnie. I'm thinking a surprise ending, a real holy shit! ending. Something that will make James jump up and down and sing 'Alright!'. First, though, we ladies will have a civilized one-on-one. I'll tell her that she's destroying James for no reason, that he's a good man. She will admit never loving him and having a sordid lifelong affair with Deacon; she will divorce him as soon as possible and without any settlement whatsoever. Deacon is the one she will hurt, making things right because everything is his fault for never marrying her. She'll start a heated argument with him the moment he arrives Friday evening expecting hugs and kisses, insisting that he should marry her immediately after the divorce, that he should man-up and do what he should have done years ago. And if he refuses, which he will, she will hurt him for using her as a whore. Hurt him in a way neither one will ever forget, the way James will never forget or forgive what they've done, the way Samantha Danson will never forget the terrible fright I drew into Parker's eyes."

He was impressed, he just didn't tell her. "In a way you will not be there to witness. This is not about gloating. This is all about getting even. The glory of it comes from succeeding and them not knowing they have been played. And you are still not done, chérie."

Yeah, somehow she didn't think so. "Okay, what?"

At that he chuckled. "You will book a room somewhere you can change into those fancy clothes and leave your handbag, where you will take a long shower wearing those fancy clothes and boots when you are finished with her. You do not want any trace of that stuff on you. Then you will bag those wet clothes and boots and lose them somewhere on the street. James not having cameras does not mean his neighbours will not. And for the same reason, going in or coming out, you will keep your head down and make good use of this city's fine taxis anywhere except the front of that house." He sipped his scotch. "Then you are done. You will go home and have dinner with James who will never hear about this from you. Be content that one day soon he will tell you about them."

"Thanks, Earnie. Thank you for helping me, for helping James."

"De rien, chérie." He slid a small brown envelope across his desk. "There is a capsule inside. Do not open this or touch that capsule until you are wearing those gloves inside the home when all you need do is empty it into your palm, throw the powder in her face and step quickly back. Because she will drop her bags and for a very short while she may be a little unpleasant before joyfully inviting you to sit for that drink."

Chapter Forty-Two

Jodie's experienced hire began the next day, giving her the freedom she needed. She had never seen James Castle's home; the thought hadn't once crossed her mind. However the first Friday after her clandestine meeting with Lebeau, she did.

The jet was one thing, yeah, and the limo, but the white two-story carriage house accented with glossy black doors and shutters and the half-moon driveway trimming a manicured lawn decorated with fountains and trees was stately. Even more magnificent was his wife leaving home at 3:00 and not returning until five.

James came home to her that evening and stayed through the weekend, insisting Saturday morning that he did not require a special breakfast, giving in when she was more insistent that, yeah, he did and that she needed the car keys. Though sometime later when the first morsel exploded flavours and richness into his mouth he graciously and at once conceded that she was absolutely right. Her chocolate pancakes studded with chocolate chips that she drizzled with ruby-red raspberry sauce and dusted with confectioner's sugar were a heavenly delight. Too exquisite to spoil, too delicious not to savour.

Nor was he disappointed with her romantic dinner and dancing that evening, or their fabulous Sunday together until he left her feeling exhausted, spending his evenings at his home the following week trapped in his own bedroom and office because he simply trusted Louise about as much as he desired her company.

Throughout the week nothing at C & D was different, except for James dropping his wife's framed photograph into his trashcan Monday and telling his secretary that's where it would stay. She'd been sitting there mocking him far too long and now she was defiling Jodie's excellent work.

Deacon was as smooth as ever and James used most of his week discussing a new franchise location in Wilmington that would enhance their already successful presence in North Carolina where he would fly into the week after. And once again he spent his weekend from Thursday evening through Sunday with Jodie without once thinking that Cedric Deacon was in his guest room inoculating his wife.

On the Friday, though, before greeting him at the door wearing a loosely belted silk robe and coquettish grin, Jodie had discovered that Louise Castle was a vile creature of habit.

*

Her second hire began Monday morning about the same time James was skipping down the steps of his Lear, missing her and ready for a week of continued and positive negotiations.

Jodie focused her days on drawing, spending her evenings on planning every step of her fast approaching Friday encounter, practicing what she would say and wondering how Louise Castle would react.

Thursday she left the boutique early, checking-in to the nearby Sheraton. After an early dinner and a cocktail in the bar, solidifying her strategy in her mind, she went shopping for her next day ensemble, keeping things simple yet sophisticated because James did not reside on a street where the less fortunate would go unnoticed. Rich folks held neighbourhood watch in very high regard.

Back in her suite she called down for a vodka and soda, spending what remained of her evening tearing off tags, modelling and performing in front of the mirror, repeatedly throwing imaginary powder at her shocked and wide-eyed reflection while perfecting her side of a conversation she believed would be absolutely delightful. Then when she went to bed she slept like a baby, waking to an early summer's day that she could see from her window was dense with moist and sticky air.

The stickier the better, she murmured, the faint image staring back at her smirking devilishly. Oh yeah.

She was dressed and sitting in the dining room by nine. At 10:00 she sauntered into the boutique where she stayed until noon enjoying the women's company, talking with clients about her work they were buying, and drawing.

She went to Earnie Lebeau's lounge where she left six pencil art drawings of shapely and alluring young women whose seductive contours she made all the more enticing with flowing veils of coloured silk and passion in their eyes. She left them with the hostess, with a note for Earnie hoping his day would turn out as well as hers. Then she went for a quick lunch she would eat without wine at the Sheraton before going to her room feeling not the least bit uneasy.

She showered, taking her time, dressing without jewellery for her afternoon with the wannabe Mrs. Deacon, leaving at 2:15 with her glasses, gloves and hat in a bag through the dank and dimly lit inside parking and onto Canal Street because no one working the Front Desk ever took notice of the black and white monitors.

One block farther on she discarded the bag, completing her look and hailing a cab she exited one block from James Castle's home, expecting she would see the woman leaving the house within the next ten minutes.

The day was sweltering, Jodie blending well with the street's social stratum in her boots and jeans, her cotton V-neck sweater that was already damp and the mesh cowgirl hat shadowing her face.

She walked the length of one sidewalk before crossing to the other side. Doing what Earnie said, not being noticed by pampered housewives or their housekeepers except for being an attractive young woman out for a stroll on a muggy New Orleans day. Until like clockwork, precisely on the hour, Louise Castle drove onto the street as Jodie stepped onto the sidewalk.

She continued on, slowing her pace, watching the Vantage disappear around a corner a few blocks down, turning casually onto the property and into the house as though she might have been the owners' lovely young daughter.

Inside she went first to the security panel, punching in the code and holding her breath several seconds. Nothing. She was good to go, which she did with a purpose. She went through each of the main floor rooms peering through windows and checking for doors. She climbed the spiral stairs, running her hand along the polished black banister, walking into his office and bedroom, peering through those windows, deciding the main floor living room windows is where she would stand and wait.

She walked out not yielding to temptation, ignoring the wife's bedroom and office that would look out over the backyard and pool, forgoing the lower level where she would find the theatre, game room and wine cellar that James would show her the day he would make his home his own. Or not. Perhaps selling the place for a single dollar the way she had days earlier to a struggling Vermont family who could never afford a nice home, but who could certainly afford the taxes on hers that was worth millions.

Standing in the living room, leaning against a wall by the windows, she glanced at her watch. 3:31 and counting down with much of what she earlier believed was firmly ingrained in her mind completely gone or buried so deep she couldn't retrieve a single thought, telling herself that despite her resolve and even heartbeat she might somehow be nervous. Instead, for the minutes remaining, she focused on her revised business plan, one she had not yet discussed with James.

She wanted more than selling her artwork rolled and tied with a ribbon. She wanted the stores adjoining hers on either side, one for a framing shop that would complement her art, the other as an atelier where she and other artists would work in private studios without the interruption of well-meaning clients. She would also come clean and tell James about her year at Tulane and that she was going back, already accepted for the upcoming fall semester, because that's who she was. She was Jodie Carter.

4:27 with ongoing memory loss, believing she would simply greet the bitch with a simple yet sincere "Hello."

James' home wasn't anything she had imagined. The entire house was minimalist and contemporary except for the designer kitchen, very elegant and very exclusive. All that was missing was love, the art on his walls abstract and cold. Nothing held meaning, Jodie pondering whether she would ever see her work that was now hanging on his office walls. Of course she would one day, as Jodie Castle.

4:50. Jodie took off her hat, protecting her nose and mouth with the surgical mask. She took the brown envelope from her jeans, tearing it in half and staring at the tiny capsule with a whispered "Shit!" Earnie couldn't be serious. There was scarcely enough to put in her glove let alone throw at the bitch. Shit!

4:58. Her moment of truth. The bitch was home. Now do something good for James or fuck things up big-time. She was determined, something good, leaning closer to the windows.

Louise Castle was reaching into the Aston Martin's trunk for the grocery bags and trudging toward the front door without closing the lid.

However many seconds later she came through the door, cursing the heat and oppressive humidity, her face flushed and moist with sweat. Placing the bags on the floor, she turned to close the door, gasping, the scream stuck in her throat. Excellent. At that instant Jodie stepped in hurling a tiny cloud of the dark powder, slamming the door shut with her foot and stepping back.

She was expecting something like "What the...!" or "Who the...! Though neither happened, Louise Castle for a fleeting moment standing facing her and visibly bewildered, her deep pink complexion spotted with powder.

"Hey, Louise." She tugged the mask to her chin. "I dropped in for a little chat with you about James and Deacon. You got a moment?"

"Yes, I do. But who are you? Should I know you?"

"Call me Marlee. I want to be your friend, Louise, but first I want you to feel happy. Can you do that for me? Can you feel happy, as though you don't have a care in the world?"

"Of course, Marlee. And I do feel happy, happy that you're here with me."

They went into the living room, sitting across from each other, Jodie following another of Earnie's precautions.

"I'm not expecting James this evening, Marlee. However Deacon should be here in an hour for dinner."

"That's very good, Louise, because I need you to do something for me. You know, as a very good friend."

"I will, of course. Anything for you, Marlee."

"Well here's the thing. You're hurting James deeply, making him miserable for absolutely no reason. He's a good man, Louise; he understands how much you love Deacon and he wants that to work for you. He forgives you and Deacon, but you're hurting him badly and that must stop at once. Today."

"He is a nice man, Marlee. He always was. But I do love Deacon, when he's not being difficult with me."

"Of course you do. That's why I'm here, for you and for Deacon. Because what you must do, Louise, is admit to James in writing that you never loved him, that you could never stop your sordid affair with Deacon. Can you do that for me, Louise, and leave the letter on his desk?"

The woman smiled warmly. "I will, of course. I will this very evening."

"Good. Thank you. And Monday morning you must

begin divorce proceedings without any desire on your part for any settlement whatsoever. That part is very important, Louise, and James will not contest. His only wish is for you and Deacon to find happiness together."

Louise Castle nodded, as though agreeing to bake a cake. "I understand. I will certainly do what you're asking for James. He's such a nice man."

"In fact, Louise, Deacon is the one you must hurt because all that you've done, your cheating, is his fault for never being man enough to face James and marry the woman he supposedly loves. He should have married you years ago, but he didn't because he rightfully believed you would never stop loving him, that you would always be there for him whenever he needs the company of a beautiful woman, the warmth and passion of a beautiful and willing woman."

"He is a very good lover, Marlee. But he leaves me. He always leaves me." She sighed. "I hurt so much when he leaves me."

"And now you know why. When he comes here this evening, Louise, I want you to right away start an intense argument with him. Do not hesitate and do not falter. This is your last chance for the life you deserve with him. You will insist that you marry as soon as the divorce is settled, that he should be a real man and do what he should have done years ago. And this part, Louise, is the most important. If he refuses, if he laughs at you or wants to leave you again, to get away from you again, you must hurt him very badly for treating you all these years as his personal whore. You do not deserve being his whore. You must hurt him badly in a way that neither you nor he will ever forget. Treat him as cruelly as he has always treated you, in a way that will make James feel good. Can you do that for me, Louise, and finally be happy? Can you hurt Deacon that cruelly?"

"I will the moment he arrives, Marlee. I will because right now I don't like him very much. I never believed I was his whore, but I see now that I was wrong. I am his whore. Thank you, Marlee. I will make him marry me or I will hurt him cruelly the way you want."

"Good. That's very good, Louise." Jodie stood. "Because he absolutely deserves suffering in the worst possible way. Now I really should go and you should get yourself ready for him. Wear something very sexy and sultry, something that will absolutely make him desire you like never before. Dress to kill the guy, Louise. Do that for me and for James."

"I will, Marlee. I will."

Jodie went to the windows, stooping for the torn envelope and capsule, then to the door. "Goodbye, Louise, I truly hope that you and Deacon each finally get what you deserve."

Without another word she was gone, the way she had promised Earnie Lebeau, and passing by the Vantage she slammed the lid shut.

Chapter Forty-Three

Louise Castle went to her bedroom the moment Marlee left her. She didn't quite understand why, but she liked the younger woman believing they would soon become best friends.

She undressed and showered, sitting at her vanity drying and styling her hair, pondering what she would wear for Cedric that would leave him speechless and aroused, finally deciding he would never survive the sheer white babydoll and G-string she would make even sultrier with clear stiletto slippers when she would frame her body in the glossy black trim of the main entrance. Something she would never have worn or done for James.

Admiring herself in the mirror she was fabulous, mere weeks away from forty and would pass in anyone's mind for late twenties. Desirable? Yes, definitely. She was flawless, every part of her tight and smooth, working with a trainer at the gym each morning maintaining perfection, enhancing her body even more with weekly treatments at the spa. How Cedric was able for all those years to love her so ardently and leave her so heartlessly each time was beyond belief and slipping into her lingerie, seeing herself that much more delectable, made her in that moment utterly despise him.

Going into her office she sat at her desk, determined, writing the letter for James because Marlee was right. She should divorce him and make Cedric do what was right. Because if not that very day, when?

Then no sooner had she signed her contrite confession than Cedric's voice permeated the house through the intercom, which piqued her even more with the sudden awareness that they had never exchanged keys to their homes.

Crossing the hall she centred the document on James' desk and went down the stairs to the door, no longer excited that she was for all intents and purposes, her intent and her purpose, naked; instead she was increasingly annoyed with him for spoiling her exotic moment intended to stupefy him. In spite of which, when she did swing open the door, the flimsy ensemble instantly produced the desired effect.

"Whoa! Louise, you are ravishing this evening."

"Thank you, Cedric."

Ravishing, yes, and getting royally pissed. Something else that irked her. Not once since he had taken her virginity in her parent's home had they ever called each other by cutesy names, not once when laying naked and depleted by heated passion, or draped in his arms dancing, or sitting curled into each other by her fireplace or his sipping wine. Because he was afraid that one day one of them would slip with a darling or sweetheart or whatever at dinner with James when not touching each other was difficult enough.

He stepped in, closing the door, digging a deeper grave with a catcall she did not appreciate as she strode into the living room feeling like a whore and wishing she hadn't dressed like one.

He went straight into the dining room bar for her bourbon and James' scotch while she stood where she was on the verge of loathing him. Still, she would not falter, she would not disappoint Marlee.

"Divine, Louise." He passed her an old-fashioned chilled with a single cube, eyeing her from head to toe, making things worse by putting a hand to her bare waist and squeezing, too blinded by beauty to see she was fuming. "Very, very nice. Dinner is definitely on hold. Let's get you out of this thing and onto the bed."

This thing? "Do you love me?"

"I do, very much. You know I do."

"Do you want me? I mean truly want me."

"I can't think of anything I want more. Like I said…"

"Good, because I'm divorcing James."

For an instant the words engulfed him like a toxic cloud, twisting his face into a betraying grimace. Then, too late, he caught himself, coughing a laugh that instantly set the tone for the evening. "Good one, Louise. In the meantime let's get me cleaned-up and us onto those cool silk sheets."

She pushed away his hand. "I'm serious, Cedric. I'm divorcing him Monday morning, first thing."

He stumbled backward, the stunned expression frozen on his face. "No, you are not. Why would you even think of doing such a stupid thing?"

"Yes, I am. Because you love me and want me and we should be together, always and forever. Not just when you feel like fucking someone."

He gulped his scotch. "First off, Louise, we don't fuck. We make love. And I don't recall being included in this decision."

"You said yourself, it's immoral and unethical."

"I also told you it's too late. Are you kidding me?"

"We're hurting him, badly."

"No one's being hurt. But what you're thinking is crazy. Look around you. You honestly want to lose all this?"

"I'm not losing anything because I'll have this and more with you."

"You know that won't happen. Not Monday, not ever. We are what we are, Louise. And even if you did divorce him, how would I out of the blue tell him about us? How would I possibly work with the guy? So let's get real here."

She snorted. "You work with him already, Cedric."

"I do, and I've got no problem with that. This, you and

me, when I'm with him it's like he knows and doesn't care. Like I said, it's natural. And we are not having this ridiculous conversation."

"We are having this conversation, Cedric, because you're exactly right. He knows."

"What?" He drained the scotch in a gulp. "What does that mean, he knows?"

"He saw us fucking in the pool and, FYI, that was definitely fucking. It's what we do, so let's not pretend otherwise. In fact he knows everything, and I do mean everything, which should be a great relief to you."

His face went purple. "Shit!" He strode to the bar, filling his glass halfway. "Are you fucking serious…the pool?"

She nodded calmly, secretly relishing his panic. "For Christ's sake, Cedric, for once be a man about this. He knows about us, I'm divorcing him, and I am marrying you."

"No, you are not." He gulped more scotch, spraying much of it across the room and gasping for air, wiping the back of his hand hard across his mouth. "Holy fuck! I cannot believe this shit. What the fuck am I supposed to do Monday?"

"Not Monday, Sunday. Because you are not leaving here until he walks through that door. We will tell him together that we love each other, that we always have, and that this is no longer my home. I'm going home with you and that's where I'm staying, the way we should be. He's ready to forgive us and I've written him a letter explaining how sorry I am for hurting him."

What was left in his glass disappeared down his throat, provoking a raspy and wet cough. "You are fucking insane, Louise. I mean certifiably and fucking insane. Where is this load of shit coming from? You are not moving into my home and I am not marrying you, never. And what was in that deluded mind of yours wearing that thing when you had this shitstorm waiting for me?"

"I wanted you to want me, the way I've always wanted you."

"I always did want you, Louise, but all this bullshit stops right here right now. Facing him Monday will be difficult enough and this, me with you tonight, will make things dramatically worse." He put down his glass. "We're done. I'm done."

Louise Castle put down her glass. "I thought we might be, Cedric. And I'm good with that. First though, give me a moment. I want to change and have one last drink with you because we will never see each other again. Please do that for me."

He blew a stream of hot air between his lips. He wanted out; he did not want to be there. "One drink, Louise, then I am gone. And you're right, we will never see each other again."

She climbed the stairway to her room hoping she would see him gazing up at her nude perfection, wanting her, hoping she would see a glimmer of hope in his eyes, shrugging off her disappointment at seeing him in the dining room. He was pouring expensive booze that wasn't his into expensive crystal glasses, for what? What would they talk about now that he made clear what she was to him? Marlee was so right: His personal whore. But no more. Never again

When she came down the stairs in bare feet dressed in a skirt and sweater he was sitting on the arm of a sofa as though ready to spring toward the door. He was agitated, his face damp with sweat, not exactly the polished and debonair lover who came through her doorway moments earlier marvelling at her beauty.

Her bourbon was sitting on the coffee table, the single cube already melted. "Thank you, Cedric, for not running out while I was upstairs. I want our affair ending the way you deserve, the way I deserve for you hurting me, for making me a whore."

"Meaning what, Louise? A last kiss, a last hug?" He shook his head. "That doesn't work for me. We're done and this is all on you."

She shrugged, reaching for her drink, sipping then smiling, thinking again of Marlee who would soon become a good friend. "Not a kiss, not a hug. Something more meaningful, Cedric something much more deserving," her hand went to the back of her skirt, her cold eyes piercing his, her outstretched arm closing the space between them, "for making me a whore."

The first of two rounds from the chrome-plated .410 derringer ruined his suit, blasting a hole in his chest and jerking him backward onto the sofa with terror etched on his face, a ghastly wail escaping his twisted mouth; the second round killed him and she went upstairs to bed, dropping the skirt and sweater onto the floor, content that she had done something wonderful for Marlee and finally something nice for James.

*

By the time Deacon had whistled his way into James Castle's home, naturally assuming he was minutes away from doing likewise with his partner's wife, Jodie had discarded the mask and capsule in its envelope while sauntering along Canal Street.

Once in her room at the Sheraton she wasted no time stuffing her hat and boots with her glasses into a plastic laundry bag with her gloves on and stepping into the shower fully dressed, feeling weird but following Earnie's instructions. She was humming, absolutely pleased with herself, elated by her seamless and flawless day, hoping with all her heart that Louise's evening would play out well, hoping for the worst possible outcome for Deacon and the best possible for James and for her.

The drug would wear off by morning, which was comical because Louise Castle would not remember a thing and Deacon would, definitely making his life considerably worse. And for the same reason Louise would not petition for divorce on the Monday, which didn't matter at all because James would have the letter admitting to years of cheating and, she expected, something even better that would come from the evening if everything Earnie had told her was true.

After several minutes of musing and humming, feeling giddily exuberant, she stripped away her sweater and bra, her jeans and her socks, her gloves and her thong. She shampooed her hair, stepped out and towelled herself dry; she scrunched her damp tresses into impish curls with mousse, scrunching her face and sighing at seeing the sopping mess she left in the tub that soon after was a heap in her pristine suitcase.

She slipped into fresh panties and bra, a minidress and low-heeled pumps. She glossed her lips a deep red, completing the look with a ruby pendant and earrings before thoroughly checking the room and leaving, losing the bag and suitcase in a dumpster at a construction site abandoned for the weekend.

Arriving home she called her hair salon for a last-minute appointment before relaxing with an Ultimat and soda, waiting for James after another hectic day at *Jodie's Art*. No way would she wait until Sunday for his exuberant "Alright!" that she knew would more likely be a refined "Indeed."

Chapter Forty-Four

Saturday morning Louise Castle woke to a grey, wet day and the relentless drumming of huge raindrops splattering against her windows blurring her view.

Turning her head she propped her weight onto an elbow, confused. He wasn't with her. He wasn't there, his clothes weren't strewn across the armchair and she was wearing a babydoll she would never think to sleep in.

She sat, looking toward the door, calling his name. Nothing. She called his name again, curious because Saturdays were special times for them when they could wake together, make love and do breakfast together like a real couple until he would once again leave her.

She threw back the duvet, swinging her feet to the floor wide apart and checking herself, puzzled by the sweater and skirt combo laying there. Nothing, when she would always wake coated with his scent and her vagina pleasantly throbbing.

She went to her closet for a robe, feeling a chill despite the midsummer heat and humidity. She padded to her bathroom, peed and combed her hair, splashing water onto her face, wondering at the night before that she could not remember for the life of her.

She plodded down the stairs, feeling moody and despondent. She would phone him and ask why he would stay away on the most special night of her week without calling. She would invite herself over; she would spend the day and the night with him since she no longer cared at all about James, more convinced each day that she would soon do what Cedric would never. She would bring the men together.

Stepping onto the main floor, she turned toward the kitchen thinking she would brew a coffee and plan her weekend wardrobe when she noticed the scotch and bourbon bottles on the dining room table, when she never drank alone and certainly would never put scotch to her lips, which meant Cedric was with her the night before.

She ambled toward the bottles, puzzled why she hadn't put them away, glancing into the living room and screaming, lurching forward and crashing into the table, the shrill sound echoing throughout the house.

Cedric Deacon lay sprawled on the sofa, his pale blue suit coated with dark red blood, his legs twisted, his eyes and mouth gaping with fright. She couldn't breathe or move, her body and her mind frozen with fear and confusion. Until she saw the gun, her gun, and the shattered glass, gulping in air, clutching her stomach and her throat, groaning a long and plaintive "No," blinding tears streaming from her eyes in unstoppable rivulets.

Time stood still. What did she do? What did he say or do that would make her do such a dreadful and horrific thing? She couldn't think, couldn't make sense of what she was seeing. She loved and adored him; she would never do anything as unthinkable. Then she saw the clock on the kitchen wall: 8:56. She'd been standing in a daze staring at him for an hour.

She made her way around the table, gripped by mounting fear and grief, pouring a generous bourbon, emptying and refilling the glass, telling herself aloud to rationalize and begin thinking clearly. She had bought the gun for protection, like every smart-thinking woman in New Orleans, never believing she would ever shoot someone, never imagining she would kill the man she couldn't live without in her living room.

People were murdered every week in the Big Easy for

any number of reasons and Cedric was dead. She couldn't hurt him more than she did. He was also wealthy; he looked the part and would be a perfect victim. That's what everyone would believe, that's what she would forever believe in her heart.

She drained the glass, calming her nerves. She would take his wallet and jewellery, wait until dark and somehow get him into his car because James wouldn't be home until late Sunday. She would drive somewhere she wouldn't be seen, leave him and find her way home. Then, whenever she would hear the terrible and tragic news, she would be a convincing grief-stricken lover and unrepentant wife.

She would bury Cedric and at long last be free of James.

*

Jodie woke Saturday morning bright-eyed and eager for the day.

James arrived at her home near 7:30 the previous night, exhausted from a week of successful negotiations, although quickly revitalized with a long and cool shower and longer still between cool satin sheets with a heated and vibrant young woman making up for years lost. Then, not quite finished with him, when she was grudgingly pulled into a another requisite shower, he believed she might at any moment convert the cool water into steam. Which he didn't mind at all.

Dressed for another muggy summer evening, dinner was a green salad, crawfish pie and a crisp Pinot Grigio. And later on her balcony, staring at the stars and holding hands, she laid out her strategy for expanding the boutique that he eagerly endorsed and she would begin making happen on Monday; Jodie deciding that, yeah, she would tell him in the morning when she could scarcely disguise her high spirits despite the thunderous dark sky and pelting rains.

She rolled onto her side, tapping his shoulder with a fingertip until he had no choice.

"What?"

"You know what."

"Again?"

"Yes, again." She straddled him, leaning forward, bracing her arms by his shoulders and kissing him. "You're very good, mister."

"Thank you." He craned his neck, sighing defeat, bringing his hands from her bare hips to her waist to her breasts. As difficult as she was to refuse when she was fully dressed, when entirely naked the mere thought was impossible. So he didn't. He pulled her in closer. "However, miss, I must insist that you do the work as I further recover from my week and from you."

"No problem." Moving her hands onto his shoulders the one-woman rodeo reached its intense crescendo thirty minutes later when she shrieked and jerked and shuddered and sat anchored in place with her arms crossed and staring at him. "Are you serious? You can do that, lie there like that with all this squirming and bouncing on you? Seriously?"

"It's a business technique, my love. The less interest one shows exponentially increases the interest of others at the table. You did very well for a beginner. Bravo."

She smacked him, pulling away, stretching for her phone. The calendar was flashing. "Shit."

"The popular expletive meaning what, exactly?"

"That I forgot. I'm having my hair done at noon. Looks like you're on your own for a few hours."

"Disappointing, my love, though timely. I accumulated a massive workload throughout the week. A few hours alone today would greatly lighten next week's schedule," he chuckled, "and assist my body in its rehabilitation."

"You mean temporary repair. Just be here with me for dinner and in a good mood. Do not get yourself all heated up because of her. That's my job, lover."

"Indeed. Dinner in the Quarter." He reached out, smacking her bum. "Please make a suitable reservation in my name."

After yet another shower they made breakfast together and left together, James not bothering to forewarn his wife. The more he was intimate with Jodie, the more he loved her; the more he despised the thought of Louise and being anywhere near her was many times more distasteful than he ever believed possible. Facing a life sentence with her was a punishment he would never accept or endure for being their victim. What's worse, he was his own victim for playing games with her and not confronting Deacon for the sheer pleasure of seeing his distorted face and laughing at the babble that would surely sputter from his mouth. Something he should have done months ago before thoughts of one day losing Jodie became uppermost in his mind

He could cope with Deacon for the sake of the company and his employees, though not her for much longer when he would put her on the street, sell the house and build a home for him and Jodie that would never be tainted with soiled memories.

*

Louise emptied the bottle into her glass, filled with dread. She hadn't once touched a dead person and the fact that she killed him or had loved him brought her no comfort whatsoever.

She put on rubber gloves she had recently bought for washing her dishes, first pulling his school ring from his finger, his Rolex and gold bracelet from his wrists. His neck chain, though, was another matter. His jacket was stuck to his shirt that was glued to his chest with blood and leaving part of the reason someone had killed him was not an option.

Clenching the links in a tight fist she put a palm against his forehead and tugged hard, twice, believing she would vomit or lose her mind. Instead she reached for her glass, swallowed a mouthful and stood for a moment before taking off his shoes and belt, reinforcing what everyone would believe happened.

Next she pulled gently at his jacket with one hand, pressing her fingertips against his shirt, gagging at the sound and feel of one fabric peeling away from the other, reaching inside for his wallet. Doing the same on the other side with less care she took his titanium pens before digging into his pants pocket for his money clip.

That was the easy part, getting him into the garage through the kitchen would not be.

She put everything into his shoes and put them in a corner, taking a moment, studying the body. Most of the blood was on him with minimal splatter on the sofa cushions and arm that she could easily wash clean after dragging him through the house on a blanket that would make the task easier and keep her floors free of potential blood that had coagulated and turned brown. The glass she would clean up later when disassembling the derringer she would hurl far into the muddy Mississippi the next morning after scattering in several public places what she had taken from him.

First, though, she needed to sit and rest, refrain from panicking, realizing with a deep breath and long sigh that she was no longer frantic, that she was actually calm. With several hours ahead of her before the storm and darkness would give her complete cover she would take her time and avoid making life-threatening mistakes.

Dropping onto the sofa facing Deacon she drained the glass, wondering why she hadn't closed his eyes or his mouth, wondering how he felt being killed and probing her mind for what he could have said or done that was so terrible he would leave her that way.

*

By noon the storm's fury that was wicked even for The Swamp had worsened, showing no sign of letting up anytime soon. Day was night with abandoned sidewalks and blurred high-beams streaking past him from behind the wipers hectically thrashing water from his windshield where James sat shaking his head and mumbling for very good reasons.

They were fools, of course, the thoughtless ones

blinding him, believing the brighter lights wouldn't turn heavy enough raindrops into liquid cannon balls; and for Jodie insisting she would maintain her appointment on such a foul and dangerous day.

He would also arrive at the house precariously close to the hour and, if presented with the opportune moment, he would insist that Deacon shit or get off the proverbial pot, take the whore home and keep her there or put her into the hands of someone who would. She was well acquainted with the rule, his rule for his home. He had also made abundantly clear that he would never spend another Saturday night in her duplicitous company so that when he turned into his driveway and the blue Bentley gleamed in the beams of his halogens he was neither astonished nor angry. In fact he felt nothing, except that he would relish the moment. She was what she was, as was Cedric Deacon. Each one deserving of the other.

However what he found peculiar was that no light shone from the windows on a day that was ominously dark, lending a menacing air to the usually elegant setting of colourful flora under a canopy of decades-old live oaks that was now washed over in shades of glittering black.

Stepping from the Infiniti, eager for the fray he was entering into, the hellacious winds instantly tore at the tails of his trench coat, wetting his face and stinging his eyes, whipping his neatly combed hair into a wet and dishevelled mess.

He never ran, running wasn't part of his makeup, and this evening in particular was solely about composure, about maintaining one's dignity before thoroughly abasing them from his rightful place on the moral high ground.

Turning his key in the barrel was titillating, giving him a sense of intrigue, part of him wishing he would find them somewhere awkward and humiliating like finding Deacon trapped between her legs on the staircase or pounding her in the Roman bath.

Stepping over the threshold the interior was as dark as

he expected, and quiet. He stood listening, assuming they were in bed luxuriating in peaceful slumber after mocking him for the last time. Until stepping a few feet farther he abruptly stopped, nodding his head and screwing up his face in a caustic smirk, hardly believing what he was seeing, at once fascinated and delighted that his fervent wish had come true.

She was slouched on a sofa with her legs wide apart wearing a scanty G-string and babydoll opened from her waist to her breasts, her belly rising and falling with each laboured breath. Her face was smudged with makeup, framed with damp copper-coloured hair; her chin was pressed to her chest, her arms laying limp by her side. She was drunk, completely anesthetized, an empty old-fashioned laying on its side by her feet. In every way the portrait of a whore past her prime.

He stepped in closer, elated, ready for the ultimate moment, expecting he would find Deacon in the same condition, instead he stumbled backward into the wall, his loud and anguished shriek startling Louise into semi-consciousness.

He went to the body, staring down. "Louise, what have you done?"

"What?"

He faced her, pointing down. "That! How the hell did that happen?"

She raised her head, straining her eyes. "I don't know," she answered, slurring. "I found him like that. I don't know."

He turned a full circle, seeing the gun and the shoes placed in the corner, the bare wrists and finger, the money clip on the coffee table with Deacon's wallet. "When did this happen?"

She shrugged. "I don't know. Last night maybe. I found him here this morning. I don't remember."

He took a deep breath, realizing he was trembling. "This is not good, Louise. Not good at all. You are in the deepest possible shit." He rubbed his face hard. "Though clearly better Deacon than me."

She snorted. "No, James. Not better."

He went to the bar, pouring a double JW Blue, downing every drop. "Go upstairs, Louise, and dress into something a whore wouldn't wear. And quickly, I'm calling the police. Unless you prefer being seen in this despicable condition."

She bolted forward, reaching out. "Please don't, James. I can fix this. I have a good plan."

"Most regrettably, Louise, you do not. You will not make this go away. You killed the man and, quite frankly, I feel neither sympathy nor compassion for either of you. Now go upstairs. I don't expect your freedom will exceed a mere few minutes once I place the call."

She tried standing, swaying and toppling backward. "Please don't. Just leave me. I can take care of this. No one will ever know and I promise I'll divorce you, James. I will, I promise."

"You did that last night, Louise, extremely effectively, for which I am immensely grateful. However I will not implicate my law firm in a murder trial which will presumably conclude badly for you from what I see here and substantially deplete your resources."

"Then I can't tell you how much I now regret not reloading my gun, James. Because you did this, you made all this happen."

Despite being in the company of a dead man and harbouring no doubt that she would joyfully end his existence, he chortled, shaking his head at the thinly veiled threat. Although he did reach into his pocket for a pen that he slipped through the derringer's trigger guard before walking into the kitchen where he called 9-1-1 to report a murder.

Regardless of his assurances that the situation was under control, that he was in possession of the weapon, and that the perpetrator was somewhat incapacitated, no cop anywhere would give up the glory of being first on the scene with lights flashing, of putting on the cuffs and leading the guilty into deserved justice.

When the cops arrived the entrance into the house was wide open and brightly lit. He had replaced the gun and was sitting stretched out across the spiral stairway leaning against the wall, looking and pointing at his wife who hadn't moved. If he felt anything, he felt numb disbelief that he was finally free of them at such a great and needless cost. But free all the same.

When she was led away in handcuffs, rain boots and tears, cloaked in a rain cape, she went into the storm without looking at him. Cedric Deacon, who was never a friend and no longer a partner, followed soon after zippered into a black bag and strapped onto a gurney.

When the detectives in charge of the case remained behind with more questions, taking photos and collecting more evidence, James enquired as to the likely outcome of the trial.

Guilty by her own admission, facing the death penalty in a state favouring the punishment was a reasonable expectation with the remotest possibility of life in prison without parole for twenty-five years, because the state would prove intent and providing that her own legal counsel was the very best. Which somehow he doubted.

When they left he poured another JW Blue two-fingers deep, returning to the stairway where he sat pondering his immediate and distant futures. He would not attend the trial unless given no choice. He would sell the house as soon as possible and more immediately fill a mission truck with all that was once his wife's to cherish and adore more than she ever did him. He would assume full control of C & D, changing the name without delay to Castle Enterprises. And, when all was said and done, when Louise was incarcerated for life or awaiting the grim day her life would legally and duly end, he would build that home for them and take Jodie on a world-wide vacation.

He snorted, recalling the day they met, raising his glass in a heartfelt toast to Parker Danson whose tragic and horrible death had brought them together.

Pushing his weight from the steps, he went into the kitchen with no urgent reason to convey the terrible, and terribly wonderful news. He simply wanted to hear her voice, to tell her what he truly felt.

When Jodie Carter answered, expecting the call and with such youthful exhilaration in her voice, he said, "They arrested Louise for yesterday murdering Cedric Deacon and I do love you very much. I'll be home with you very soon, my love." What else could he say?

When he disconnected Jodie stood by her bed stunned and elated, scarcely believing the incredible good news, her smile widening by the second. She could practically feel the sparkle in her green eyes, jumping up and down and clapping her hands together, skipping and hopping around the room, thinking she would absolutely kiss Earnie Lebeau, jumping high into the air with her arms and legs spread wide and screeching a gleeful "Alright!"

Other Mystery – Suspense - Thriller Novels
By Doug Booth:

Split Verdict

The 4th Man

The Madam

Family Lies

Mother of Pearl

From Inside Her Bedroom

The Feast of Tombola

Deferred Prejudice

The Hunt for Gilligan Rose

The Fatal Diners' Club

Silent Conviction

A Christmas Killer, Comfort and Joy

Pariah In the Mirror

Girl on the Corner

***

No One to Tell (Creative Non-fiction)